NORTHWAY

A NOVEL BY

ERIC C TRENT

WESTWIND PUBLISHING

KEMP, TX USA

Original Publication and Printing

December 2025 by Westwind Publishing Company

* * *

* * *

* * *

ISBN
979-8-9985889-0-7 (paperback)
979-8-9985889-1-4 (hardcover)
979-8-9985889-2-1 (ebook)

Library of Congress Control Number: 2025906976

Westwind Books is a division of Westwind Publishing Company
Kemp, Texas USA

www.westwindpublishing.com

For Kelli Celestia

Consciousness is not an act, not an idea, not even a quality—it is the very basis of creation.

—*Sadhguru*

Reality includes both the past and the future, but existence includes only the present and is totally dependent on the reality of past and future universes. Without them, there is no existence now.

—*Dr. Fred Alan Wolf*

Man is ruled by Earth
Earth is ruled by Heaven
Heaven is ruled by Tao
Tao is ruled by itself

—*Tao Te Ching – Verse 25*

PALINGENESIS
(CHAPTER TEN)

Stratus clouds were moving inland. They covered the sky above the marsh flats and raced northward over the Valley. The day was darkening. As the clouds advanced, they began to descend toward the earth, bumping against the mountains at the head of the Valley.

They mutated, becoming nimbostratus, grayish and without form. A chilling breeze whispered through the cottonwood trees, claiming yellow victims that spiraled to the ground and lay dead in the soaking muskeg. Birds had long disappeared. The air was dense, nearly saturated with vapor.

Mark was in the woods, hiking along a well-worn trail. He was dressed in blue jeans, a bone-colored sweatshirt, and brown rubber boots. He wore neither a jacket or rain hat. He did have a two-foot stick in his left hand, but he carried it only for the simple reason that he wanted to feel the wet wood against his fingers. The Hidden Observer secretly watched the boy move along the path, crane his neck to look at possible movement in a nearby tree, mumble something incoherent, and continue on, the alder stick waving about as though clearing the path of unseen impurities. Mark was so intent on his immediate surroundings that he failed to notice the approaching weather front. Here in the woods, it was always darker. Darker, and rather dank, in the early autumn coolness. The tall spruce leaked resin freely, and this added a sweet, watery scent to the air.

Moss covered much of the ground, laced through with runners of trailing raspberry. Ancient stumps, also covered in moss, sported profusions of small flowering dogwoods, though the blossoms were long gone, and late-season bunchberries had taken their place on the tiny stems. Mark stepped to the right of the path, then to the left, so that he could bend down and examine the little red fruit. On the path itself, he cared not where his feet landed, so long as he avoided the many puddles of rainwater that collected in low places between the rotted stumps. Ahead of him, the trees thinned out, and the meadow offered easier walking despite the slippery grass and sedge. He tramped on, heading toward his favorite part of the glen, near the banks of Jordan Creek.

He hadn't been there for several weeks, not since the sunny days of August. He approached the edge of the creek and just stood, looking at the slowly moving water. Jordan Creek was a rather muddy slough at this time of year, and the creatures who made their home in its water, on its banks, or in the nearby meadow, were inactive today. Beaver, otter, and muskrat claimed this ecosystem as their own, but they seemed fewer in number with each passing year. The creek, forming a natural boundary between the meadow and Thunder Mountain, had a few deep pools created by dams made of spruce, alder, and willow. The beaver community—what remained of it—had performed very little maintenance of late, yet these structures offered easy passage to the other side. Beyond the far bank, the ground tilted slightly upward and then became lost in the shadow of large evergreens. This was Mark's destination.

He followed the bank for a short distance. Here and there it was undercut, the dirt being quite soft, and in a few places, there was even some loose clay. His favorite beaver dam came into view, a tremendous structure nearly fifty feet in length, supporting a deep reservoir that flooded the banks in times of heavy rainfall. Beavers were intelligent in their construction practice; the branches were placed with the thick end upstream, and the smaller twigs meshed at the bottom, forming a tight bond. The entire structure was packed with mud, and it could support Mark's weight dozens of times over.

Now he crossed to the other side, and at the far end was a small, rushing channel, where water found its only escape from the huge pool. He jumped out and over the torrent, landing hard. His boots sank into gray mud. And then he hiked into the trees, looking ahead and seeing the ground sweep up in front of him. It was fascinating! He knelt, and letting go of the alder stick, put his finger on the exact point where the angle steepened. And he wondered, how many people had ever done this? The mountain soared upward at a forty-five-degree angle, he figured, and there was *no gradual steepening at all*. He peered up, his view all but blocked by the spruce, which, as he well knew, was replaced by hemlock trees as the altitude increased.

There was the trail that Mark himself had created, and it bore up the slope, connecting to the older, more established trail nearly a thousand feet above the creek. One could then follow the older trail up to treeline and beyond. Mark had his usual urge to climb on, to go explore the upper meadows. He had hiked to the summit of Thunder Mountain on several occasions, including that first memorable adventure when he was only seven. And he had been told not to go alone, but he wondered what it would be like, to leave Dad and Stephen behind at sea level, and travel solo to the deer lettuce and the snow patches. He had indeed never gone alone. But yes, the heights beckoned!

Mark walked back down to the dam, to recross the creek. This was when the breeze picked up. The birds had disappeared, he noticed. His nose began registering wetness; the air becoming saturated with vapor. The adventure was over with; he stepped out onto the mud bank, preparing to fly across the narrow channel, to the alder branches and the safety of the dam.

The sprinkle began, growing quickly into a steady drizzle. It stung the surface of the beaver pond and made splattering sounds on the huge leaves of devil's club. The breeze continued; colder it became. The clouds, all but touching the ground, moved slowly along, unaware, it would seem, of the wetness they left behind. Mark was soaked before he made his jump.

And as he leaped, he had the sudden vision of a black bear rearing up on its hind legs, at this exact spot. Airborne, his body passed right through the holographic display. Instantly, the vision was gone, and Mark realized two things. First, his left hand no longer carried the stick—it was on the ground at the base of Thunder Mountain—and second, that it was absolutely ridiculous to have the first realization come to him at a time like this. He slipped, and unable to control his movements, plunged into the rushing channel.

Half-submerged in the cold water, he jerked his head right, then left, trying to get his bearings. He felt the current swing his legs around in a quarter circle, felt his mouth fill with muddy water, and then saw nothing but wood as his forehead made contact with a large branch—the edge of the dam, a voice inside him was saying—and his right hand scraped across a branch as well. The channel was trying to drag Mark downstream, and he thrashed about, trying to secure his other hand.

Suddenly, and for just a millisecond, everything went dark, and when that millisecond had passed, he existed once more.

What had just happened? He slowly pulled himself out of the water, up onto the pile of alder and spruce, and wiped the water from his eyes.

He was shaking with cold as he ripped off his boots and poured out the water. He was shaking even more as he removed his sweatshirt, wrung it out as best he could, and put it on again. He was shaking as he stuck his boots on, stood up, and walked slowly across the dam, to the undercut banks of clay, and onward toward the meadow.

Mark's breathing returned to normal as he made his way across the glen and homeward. His sweatshirt was covered with dark, rotting wood fragments, and his boots made loud sucking noises. His mind replayed the accident a number of times as he walked the path between the ancient stumps. The rain continued, but he scarcely noticed. His jeans now felt like a skintight wetsuit, but he didn't care about that either. He thought only of what might have been, if he hadn't been able to grab something and pull himself to safety. If he'd had that stick in his hand, would he have been unable to …?

Perhaps he had just died, back there in the creek, when everything had gone black. Then an instant reincarnation, and he had been deposited back into this body. Perhaps that happened thousands of times in a person's life. No, an *infinite* number of times; could that be it? Mark's head swam with possibilities, thoughts that he could never share with Stephen or anyone else. Not even Jerry, but then again, that problem had already taken care of itself.

Thrashing around in that beaver pond, arms flailing uselessly … but Mark carried no thoughts of amusement in his mind, only quiet contemplation as he walked across the narrow clearing that marked the National Forest boundary. Something strange had happened, and a voice that came from nowhere in particular told him the strangeness was going to happen again; was in fact happening every moment of his life, because every moment was now this moment. He tried to answer this voice, but it faded and was gone.

Did he hear a dog bark?

He came out of the woods, within sight of his home, and walked alongside the backyard fence. He was still cold, in his wet things, and he shivered aloud as he jumped onto the porch. Sheka was not there waiting for him, though he was sure it was her bark he'd heard. He opened the back door and went inside. Warmth! He kicked off his boots, left them in the furnace room, and went on past the den. Mom was preparing something, a green salad, Mark thought. She gave him a curt glance but said nothing, only shook her head and went on with her lettuce and cucumbers. He continued on to his room, where he changed clothes. He stuffed his wet pants and shirt in the hamper, noted the stupidity of this action, but did nothing about it.

Then he went to the living room, sat on the couch, and stared out the big front window. Sheka was curled up near the fireplace; Mom had probably let her inside. His pet was fast asleep, and through the corner of his eye, Mark watched her feet run. Rain splattered against the glass in front of him. Dad was not yet home, and Mark had no idea where Stephen was. He kept his attention on the window, looking out at the world he felt was truly his.

It was five o'clock on a Friday afternoon in September … but in a manner that could not be explained, Mark knew it wasn't. It was every time, and it was every place.

§

Mark finished his homework over the weekend. On Monday, after lunch hour, he was in the seventh-grade biology lab, his head bent over a 40X microscope. His eyes were on a number of gliding little shapes, paramecium, and his ears were in tune to the drone of the teacher's lecture. It was a common thing in this class—lecture alongside lab time. One learned twice as much in a given period. Well, theoretically. The fact remained that one listened to what paramecium were supposedly like, which was fine and dandy, and one watched what they were actually like, and then a comparison was made ….

§

He rode home on the school bus, arriving at his stop late in the three o'clock hour. He walked across a large undeveloped area, full of gravel, sand, and rounded cobbles that were once glacial erratics. Above his head, the sky was clear. Ravens soared about, making grotesque noises. A fresh breeze sprang up, and Mark was startled at how cold it felt, even with his pile jacket zipped tight. He stopped, looked up at the summit of Thunder Mountain, and listened to the wind sigh, up there in the heights. And then, whirling around, he looked up the Valley, his eyes becoming fixed on the white, tumbling mass that bore down from the icefield beyond. It looked so cold!

Winter was coming, and it was coming soon. Snow would cover the ground, and there would be lots of sledding, lots of snowballs, and lots of shoveling. It was going to be a good, cold winter, the temperature below freezing for weeks on end, he hoped. When the wind howled, the chill factor would harden the marrow of his bones.

Mark turned around and continued home. He thought that he would like to be up there, on top of Thunder Mountain, when the first snow touched its crown, while the world below continued to suffer raindrops. Ho! He would be the first, the very first, to witness the falling flakes, those intricate designs which, as anyone should know, held a mathematical key to understanding both the physical and non-physical universes.

He breathed slowly as he thought about the latter universe. Was that the one reaching for him, where everything was truly alive? The one that spoke to him whenever he sat upon his beloved granite boulder and stared into the glassy waters of his pond ... was that the voice of the real reality?

§

He sat on the floor in front of his locker. He and Jeff ate their lunch and studied the assignment for their geography class. It had gotten to the point where they never used the cafeteria—too crowded. The school's open policy concerning lunch hour made life easy, Mark reasoned, so long as there were no eighth vs. seventh confrontations, which, after the month of September had passed, became less frequent. Jeff often pointed out the lingering danger, though he didn't actually use that particular adjective. Most twelve-year-old students didn't.

Mark did. And now, a couple of eighth-grader bullies were passing by. They kicked at the outstretched legs. Mark remained silent and pulled his legs inward, but Jeff glared as the pair moved on, whispered an obscenity, and pretended to heave his notebook.

Mark watched them go, wondering about feeling superior to the seventh-graders the following school year. He didn't think he would. In a sense, they would be the same age as himself. Something told him that time wasn't moving. Students were moving in time.

§

And with October came frosty nights. All the leaves had fallen and were rotting away, covering the ground with a cold, slimy loam. The bunchberry dogwoods had dried up completely. The migrating geese were already far to the south. Jordan Creek would freeze and thaw, over and over, in the coming weeks, the first subtle warning of the white season.

The loop road began its seven-mile swing through the Valley only a short distance from Mark's home, and along its shoulder Mark was traveling. He wore his pile jacket this day, green in color but quite faded with age. The tall spruce trees moved slowly past as he walked, and he was feeling *free*.

He was talking to himself, and he was drunk on the fresh air.

His lips moved, and he carried on a conversation with a second Mark. The second Mark would answer back, Mark would speak again, and Mark 2 would respond. The Hidden Observer could see interesting vapor signals rise above the solo figure that trudged along the glacial subsoil, nine inches from the pavement's edge.

The sky was gray; the temperature must have been somewhere around thirty-five degrees. It was afternoon on a Sunday, and the day smelled of snow. It hadn't snowed yet this season, but the clock was ticking. Last night had been clear, starry, with a biting cold that froze the puddles and the swamp ponds behind Mark's house. Looking at the clouds today, one could see the change. They were dull, composed of crystals instead of liquid water. Running into cold, humid air, these crystals would attract supercooled droplets and form the magic flakes.

His conversation was taking a turn, as was the loop road itself. Mark 2 vanished and was replaced by Mom. Now the talk was of no light nature; he began to have one of his arguments. He was sick and tired of her attitude concerning house chores. If she wanted to write up a damn schedule and agree with the boys on who did what, well fine! Just stick to it, and no changes made without consent of all parties. Sounded reasonable. What twelve-year-old consented to abrupt changes in the pattern, anyway? "You are not cooperating in this" wasn't how you (parent) talk to me (child), because such a comment was a premature conclusion and judgment.

The vapor signals grew in strength.

And was he really an exception, a standout, someone who should be happy to do hours of chores each day when the other kids in the neighborhood did not? Why, was it because he was her son, and the other kids were not? Hotly, Mark accused Mom of being too mommy-like, too orderly, too scheduled, too much of a … a something; Mark couldn't find a word for it. That was it! Ha, ha! No word for it.

When disembodied Mom answered, it was with his own carefully chosen words and carefully chosen sentences, opinions, facts(?), easily destroyed, shot down, torn to pieces by Mark's next onslaught of criticism. There was no way to lose in this make-believe setting, the feelings of anger and frustration made only of steam. He had never, and perhaps would never, actually talk to her like this. For *the* mountain's sake.

§

He lay on his bed, daydreaming about the previous summer, when he was playing his last year of Little League baseball. He remembered having been chosen to the All-Star team at season's end. On that fateful day, while still in shock after a horrible loss that wasn't associated with the sport, it was his suffering of two additional losses that seemed to change who he was, or more accurately, bring him back near to what he had once been.

There was the regional tournament, which his team won, and then there was the state tournament, which became a complete nightmare. It was here that he stopped daydreaming. Instead, he began to think that he had never done anything of the sort, had never played baseball, had never been cheered on or applauded, but rather was creating the past in the present moment.

He had a sudden vision. He was holding a paintbrush, and when he swooped left-to-right on the easel, he created a future, and when he swooped right-to-left, a possible past came to life. And then he watched as he swooped the brush up and down instead of side-to-side, and his eyes widened as he witnessed the creation of a possible existence in the present. The pasts and the futures seened lost, and all he could see was an existence he didn't understand. It was compressed, dense and very dark. At that same instant, his arm began to ache, and he dropped the brush.

The vision was gone. He got a little scared, rolled over onto his stomach, and napped.

§

Through the winter haze, the sun was a pale orb, contributing little heat to the day at hand. Rather, the light seemed to come from the land itself. It was dead quiet, cold and dry, the world held in an icy grip, yet the gripper was unseen and therefore unidentified. The snow lay a foot deep, a fine powder. The evergreens looked dark and gaunt, burdened under their own blankets of white, as though sleeping, quietly awaiting the warmth of April, which was far away.

The air was still; no birds were in flight. The ravens were unseen, perched hidden in the tops of the spruce. Occasionally, one of them would break the silence with a single-tone *oh-wah*, as if trying to inject a spark of energy into the seemingly dead forest scene. And here in the woods, the stumps were covered; white mounds stood between the widely spaced trees. The puddles, hemmed in by green and yellow muskeg in September, were no longer there. Along with the trailing raspberry, they were lost and forgotten under the white powder.

Life went through a metamorphosis in startling fashion. Mark slipped on an icy root that lay hidden under the white death blanket. He fell, cried out, and then swore as the dry snow met his face. A quarter-mile away, a western hemlock shuddered ever so slightly from the shock, and letting go its white coat, became enveloped in a stinging mist.

The ravens, high in the trees and invisible, took turns with their *oh-wah* sounds, and now the silence was truly broken.

Mark stood up, whacking snow off his clothes. His face was red, his ears felt like cubes of ice, and the snot in his nose was completely frozen, leaving him only his mouth through which to breathe. He was wearing his pile jacket, and underneath was one of the ragged sweatshirts he loved, but he was still cold. He had on his red rubber boots today, over a single pair of gray wool socks. On his head was a wool cap, and on his hands were fiberfill mittens. He hadn't really planned on being outside for very long, but once in the woods, he could not, as usual, count on himself for anything.

When he'd left the house, it was seven degrees below zero.

He'd been thinking to himself, just before his face-first, about how much he loved to be outdoors, more than anything else in the world, even on a day like this, where the cold air tried its best to squeeze the very life from him. Or was it really trying to do so? His feet were numbed within minutes of entering the forest, but he hadn't really noticed this at first, as he tramped through the snow-covered underbrush, his mind far away from what he sometimes thought of as reality.

He was pretty far from the house. Following an ermine track, he had traveled along an old ditch, cut long ago by a giant bulldozer in an attempt to drain water from behind his backyard. He had been determined to see just where these weasel tracks led. The previous winter, Stephen and some of his friends had set a couple of traps in the area, and they had gathered quite a collection of little white pelts to show off at school. Mark had never trapped ermine, or anything else. He had once decided to try his hand at snares, as he imagined living off the land, and assuming, of course, that the rabbits he caught would understand they were a food source. He even designed a large figure-4 on paper, for the purpose of catching a deer. It was to be a huge log, supported by a cross of alder limbs, with a mushy salt ball for bait. He imagined the look on Mom's and Dad's faces when they saw him hauling his prize up the yard and onto the back porch.

But after a time, the idea grew old, and Mark found himself wondering why he would want to do something like that. Finally, the big trap collapsed by itself, in his mind, and he never considered it again.

The ermine track had ended in the usual fashion, disappearing under one of the giant, snow-covered stumps. After this discovery, he had decided to cut to the left and hit the meadow near Jordan Creek, eventually returning home via his favorite trail. Fighting through a stand of thin willows, he'd begun to loosen snow from the higher twigs, and the fine powder got into his eyes, down his neck, and in between his boots and socks. When at long last he'd arrived at the meadow, his ears were pale white, and he was breathing hard through his mouth. It was so dark in the meadow! The sun—it could not be found. It lay quite low on the southwest horizon, obscured by the trees that hemmed in the large glen.

Closer to the mountain. It was then twelve degrees below zero. Mark had staggered on, through the deeper snow of the meadow. Beneath the white blanket was the trail, which he had started himself, connecting to the path up on the ridge. He had come back here last summer and marked it, every hundred feet or so, with red ribbons, to make it look official. Now, the ribbons hung, faded and torn, their purpose unclear to any other hiker but himself. Of that, he was sure. Just maybe he would replace the ribbons with brighter ones, so that people would someday follow *his* trail to the very top! After all, his way was the correct way.

Stumbling away from the creek, he had suddenly located, by accident, a small frozen puddle. Slipping across it, his boot had struck an icy root, and he had sprawled in the chilling white powder. And the hemlock had shuddered. And the ravens had watched.

Now Mark stood up, and after brushing the snow from his clothes, his thoughts about loving the outdoors on a day like this vanished. Instead, all he could think about was how cold he felt. Good Mountain, it was freezing! He couldn't feel his fingers, his toes, or his nose, and every intake of breath felt raw in his throat. He didn't know exactly how long he had been outside, but he knew that if he was smart, he'd better head for home immediately. His pants were tight against his legs, and a cold rash was setting in on his thighs. His teeth suffered from the chill air, with every intake of breath. He looked around him, at the snow, and for just a moment, hated the white stuff for being there; kicked it with his numb feet.

His hands! He made fists out of them, inside his little fiber mittens, and began to wring his arms about, in a frantic gesture to warm them. Suddenly his eyes seemed to shut themselves tight, and for an instant that stopped his heart, Mark thought the lids had frozen to his cheeks. He was in deep trouble; he just knew it. Whirling around, he streaked for home. He was losing control of his mind, and Cold was sitting back, rubbing palms together and chuckling, anticipating a victim.

The day fading; it was now sixteen degrees below zero.

Mark galloped along on frozen poles that were his legs. He yelped when the limbs of the willows slapped his icy face. His ears began to pound, a drumbeat of doom. His arms were now flailing themselves, without his command. Looking at them as he ran, he gave a choked-off cry of panic. Home, home! Looking ahead, he saw no welcome lights. On further, he told himself, the clearing must be on a little further, but nearing, hopefully. On and on he ran, ears drumming, hands gone, feet gone, nose gone, mind on the edge. Home ahead, it must be near!

Then he felt it beginning once again. His mind connected with the voiceless voices, and his brain commenced the processing of information. He answered this unseen entity without the workings of his throat, and suddenly, things weren't quite as bad as they appeared, on the surface ....

This is it, Mark, the grand finale! Oh, there have been all those others, but this is the big one. Ah, lie down in the soft snow and die, thirty feet from your fenceposts. A strange way to go, say the members of society, shaking their collective heads and turning away, but what do they know? This young man, this Nature Boy, is true to the end. Look what he stands up against, and to make it this far is absolutely incredible.

Oh, what a fitting ending, a beautiful climax, to succumb at last in the great outdoors, a moving, natural funeral the ravens will oversee. The mountains will cry approval and shed snow, and the Northern Lights will fire away, uncontrolled, across the night sky. Oh, Mom and Dad, why be upset? It will be easy to get over, after a time, and besides, there is another son and a daughter to look after. Mark isn't yours, he is Nature's child, born to die in the woods … what's that? God, you say!

Yes, religious angle. Mustn't leave that out. The world around, all of it, is the God, and oh, Mark is the fierce and devoted follower, blending with Nature from his head right down to his toenails! Proud to lay down and inhale his last, blow out the candle, and let his flesh crumble and mix with the snow, then to melt down into the acid soil. Food for next year's weeds. Fantastic. And the mind survives ….

And friends? Oh, come on, seriously? To think all those friends matter for anything? Friends? All those acquaintances wouldn't care. Mark and I did have a good time, and he had a rather strange influence on me (they would all say), but doggonnit! It just doesn't make that much difference now, I mean, I'm not exactly crying my guts out for the boy ….

That's for Nature to control. Because it understands.

Cares.

Loves, and offers the true forgiveness.

And then it began to drain off, creeping into celestial shadows. Mark looked up, saw the clearing, the backyard fence, and the kitchen lights. He plowed his way to the gate, swung it open, and without shutting it, ran up the path that Dad had shoveled the day before. He fumbled with the doorknob and stepped inside the furnace room, which was ninety degrees warmer than the air in the woods.

He fought with his boots, finally yanking them off and slinging them into a corner. His face began to feel hot, seemingly on fire, and the snot, rapidly thawing, obeyed the law of gravity and salted his lips. He stood up straight, with his socks on, and removed his jacket. Then he stumbled out toward the kitchen, nearly losing his balance, as the bottom of his feet were swollen and rounded, as though extra fat had accumulated.

Franck's *Symphony in D Minor* was coming from the living room, indicating that Dad was in there, probably wishing not to be disturbed. Dinner was in the oven, Mark could tell. Amy was in her room; Mark could hear her as he walked down the hall. He pushed open the door of his bedroom and entered. Stephen was lying down, engrossed in a Mechanix Illustrated. Mark ignored him, left the door slightly ajar, and sat on his own bed.

His mind began to slow, the racing thoughts dwindling away. His head felt lazy, and he found it extremely difficult to remember precisely what he had said to himself, the past few minutes, in his outburst, his Appeal. And, as before, he found it even more difficult to understand why he couldn't control it. It was as though he knew who was speaking to him, and he knew who he was speaking to, but he couldn't give this unseen entity a name. It came from the trees, the wind, and the stars. Could it be a form of consciousness that actually created the world around him?

He would figure it out, he had to. Something was depending on him to do so.

Then the door creaked, and Mom entered the room, asking where he had been, and telling him not to go out again, as it was much too cold. Besides, it was almost time for dinner, so he needed to wash up and get ready. Pork roast, cornbread, blackeye peas, okra and tomatoes. Special dinner for a special occasion. Turning a new leaf. Time to make resolutions, and then do one's best to make those resolutions come to fruition.

It was New Year's Day.

§

In the center of the playground, Mark stopped and knelt, and his knees made contact with the covering of hardpack snow. He set down the large box he was carrying and began to unload its contents. He produced a large D-cell battery assembly, a plastic tripod mount, launch rod, firing system, and igniters. And then, very slowly and very carefully, he lifted out MN323, the *Ganymede*.

He set it down onto the snow and went to work on the tripod, fitting the legs into the hexagonal centerpiece. He shoved the long metal rod, complete with its steel blast plate, through the mounting clasp. Standing up, he wet his finger and checked the wind conditions; decided that a vertical trajectory was feasible.

It was a flawlessly clear afternoon in March, with the sun resting on the treetops and burning away at the remaining winter snowpack. The snow was now in granular form, old and gray. It was a late spring, the cold season hanging on longer than usual. In the end, the sun would be the victor, rising higher with each passing day, following the invisible ecliptic wave. Today, the temperature had risen to a high of forty-six degrees, and Mark had shed his pile jacket in favor of one of his ragged sweatshirts. All around, the world was dripping, drying out, and there was a definite sense of rebirth and renewal.

Mark had completed the *Ganymede* nearly a week ago, but inclement weather had forced a delay and subsequent rescheduling of the launch date. Stephen had shown interest in being present when the big moment came, but today he was at a Boy Scout function, and Mark was determined to take advantage of the blue skies forecast that had—amazingly it would seem—held true. The launch time was now at hand. T-minus seven minutes, and all was in go posture.

He strung out the firing assembly along the snow, then planted the tripod firmly and made sure of the launch rod's vertical position. He opened a cardboard tube and let a C6-5 engine slide into his hand. Turning, he picked up his model and inserted the cartridge up inside the tail, fastening the metal holder that firmly secured the engine. And then he just held his rocket up close and admired it for a moment. It was a beautiful model. Eighteen inches tall, with a set of three giant fins, alternating with a trio of smooth ailerons. It was painted orange and white.

Inside the fuselage was an eighteen-inch parachute, linked to the streamlined nose cone by a short twine. The nose cone was secured to the main body with a strong rubber band. Mark held his model and gazed at it. He ran a finger along the leading edge of a fin. The fins were the one problem. He had performed only a so-so job of fine sanding, and he could feel a slight roughness, even below the coat of paint. Still, he figured it would fly all right, and besides, this was only his second complete project, and he had learned so much about the building of these sensitive rockets.

Turning again, he fed the launch rod through the guide tube on the outside of the fuselage. Gingerly, he slid the *Ganymede* down until it rested on the blast plate, the enormous fins trailing off the edge on all sides. Reaching for the plastic package that lay in the snow, he fished out an igniter and bent it in half. It was a thin wire, about three inches long, and its center was coated. Mark formed a small toe at the bend he had just made, then slowly pushed the igniter up the engine's nozzle. Next, he splayed the two ends of wire, and to each he fastened a terminal clip of the firing system.

Walking back to the other end of the electrical assembly, Mark saw, out of the corner of his eye, two younger girls leaning against a neighbor's fence and watching the proceedings. He smiled, bent down, and attached a pair of alligator clips to the battery pack. *Hang on a moment, kids!*

Indoors, he had prepared the ejection equipment by inserting a roll of wadding between the engine and the parachute. Now all that remained was the final countdown. He picked up the firing mechanism, took a few deep breaths, and checked his watch again.

T-minus thirty seconds. Mark inserted the arming key. The yellow light came on, indicating a go for launch. Mark put his finger on the firing button; kept an eye on his watch. He was getting nervous. This rocket just had to work, it just had to! For a moment he thought about all the sick possibilities, such as the igniter burning to a cinder and falling apart before it could react with the solid fuel. Or perhaps, during the flight, one of those enormous fins being stripped away by the air friction, sending the rocket into a horizontal flight, ending in a dramatic explosion on the ground, hundreds of feet away. Good Mountain, what a rotten thought!

The final countdown seemed to take a year and a day. Mark shut his eyes as he whispered the tale of shrinking digits. Four. Three. Two. One. Zero ... FIRE. He mashed the button with his left thumb and opened his eyes.

With a loud *ssssSSSST!!* that seemed to deafen the earth itself, *Ganymede* ripped upward into the blue sky. It shot higher and higher, climbing straight up out of Mark's view. He strained his eyes, and with his heart pumping madly, he sought a glimpse of his orange and white beauty. Then, after a five-second lifetime, he saw it—a long trail of black smoke, incredibly high. It was the tracking charge, which served as a means of spotting the rocket, and without any propellant of its own. And then, with a dark puff, the ejection charge blew off the nose cone, and out came the big parachute, followed by the wadding. The rocket stopped, curved over, and then began its slow, tantalizing descent to earth.

Mark's neck began to quiver, but he hardly noticed; he was staring in complete awe. Never had he seen a single-stage rocket go so high. After a moment, he came to a conservative estimate of thirteen hundred feet as the model's highest point of altitude. Now he watched it fall to earth, as presumably did the two girls across the way. He began to walk along the playground, still looking upward, never taking his eyes off the *Ganymede*, which was nearing the granular snowpack from where its flight had begun. He ran up as it came near, caught it carefully in his hands, and looked at it. He brought it close and kissed it on the fins, one after another, the first three kisses he had given in a time too long to remember.

§

It was dark, and the tide was coming in fast. Mark stood there on the beach, frowning as he thought about it. Actually, the tide didn't come in, it rose, and although he constantly reminded himself and others of the distinction, he continued to make the mistake. He was on a weekend camping trip to Portland Island, and Dad was back there in the trees, repacking the Coleman stove. Mark was ten feet from the saltwater. Off to his right, he could see the dark form of their boat, a thirteen-foot fiberglass Gamefisher, secured by ropes which stretched up the beach to the line of trees near camp. It had been a wild ride across the bay, the swells being pretty rough the entire trip, and it had taken them some time to find the one suitable campsite, here on the southeastern corner of the linear island.

It was a Saturday evening, and tomorrow was Easter. Earlier, in the twilight, he and Dad were in a meadow that ran along the edge of the beach, gathering flat supporting rocks for the Coleman, and had come across an old, whitened stump, tall and thin, standing in the center of the clearing. It perfectly resembled an Easter rabbit, sitting on its haunches and peering across the water, ears perked, as though watching for intruders as it prepared its millions of eggs for the children.

Dad had found a pole, a length of gray driftwood, which made for a beautiful walking stick. It was curled over at the top end, forming a wonderful, knotted handle. He had left it stuck in the yellow sand, far above the rising tide, and Mark looked at it now, only a few yards from the hissing foam. The angle of the beach steepened, however, and he doubted whether the water would get up to the stick, or to the boat. It was nearly ten o'clock, and high tide, occurring about four hours later, would be moderate.

He sat down, then leaned backward. It wasn't really that cold out, perhaps fifty degrees or so. He let his head drop onto the sand, and he looked up at the clear, starry sky. The waning gibbous moon blotted out just a few of the thousands of pinprick lights that filled the black void through which the earth moved. At Mark's feet was the southern horizon. He watched the stars for a while, watched them travel slowly from left to right. For a moment, they all looked alike, but then he began to study them, putting them in their place.

Directly in front of him, just above the horizon, was Sirius, the brightest star in the night sky. Mark watched as the Dog Star displayed its rhythmic blue-to-white-to-red characteristic. He made out the great triangle created by Sirius, Procyon, and Betelgeuse, the latter a red giant in the shoulder of Orion. To the west, Venus and Mars were low in the sky and would soon drop below the horizon. The constellation of Leo was rising in the east, and high above, over his head, was the yellow twinkle of Capella, his favorite star of all. He fastened his eyes on it and became transfixed on the bright amber dot. And he let a new thought drift from his mind to his physical brain. He remembered yesterday, at school.

Jeff and Allen had lately been giving him a hard time concerning one of the girls in their geography class. Mark didn't like her at all, because she was a loudmouth, and as far as he was concerned, a complete airhead. Still, she was very popular with boys, and Mark would have found it extremely uncomfortable to be the object of her attention. The class had broken up into groups for the entire week to play a simulation World Power struggle, a study into the political aspect of the geography curriculum. Each "country" had a turn at declaring war, remaining neutral, or calling for a World Conference. And there was ample time for discussion between countries; treaties could be drawn up, pacts made, forces joined, and troops readied on paper for combat.

On Friday, Mark was the acting ambassador for his country—he was already the president—and was visiting a war-torn nation of girls that had been brought under control of Mark's country the previous day. At the moment, he was discussing his next plan of action with the foreign ambassador, none other than sexy Miss Airhead.

The plan, Mark said, was to attack one of his former allies, which he believed to be an easy victory, but he needed some backup support, and he didn't want this girl nation to become stubborn and hostile in its position as captive; rather, he wanted what little forces its "population" could give him. There was a clause in the rules pertaining to points allocated or not allocated when a country succumbed to an attacker. These came in the form of wheat, potatoes, vegetables, oil resources, timber, etc., and Mark explained that there were plenty of points to spare, and besides, when this particular phase was over, there would be only five countries left, and two of them would be subdued and under his command. Assuming he won. But the dice were not in his hand alone, seeing that a third, independent country had a turn for action before Mark did, and he was leery of what it might do, for it had no treaty with Mark ....

And then it happened. Even in this, the uppermost echelon of bargaining powers, one is still pretty much an organism of Earth, and Mark was suddenly gripped by the possibility that perhaps, if he was very careful, he might obtain an unobstructed view down the canyon. And if she noticed, well ... so what? Embarrassment would give way to girlish nervousness, and from that could spawn results to be cheerfully considered. She would never bother *him*, knowing all too well the story that would be spread!

But as it turned out, the canyon was not grand, something he had never quite ascertained from a normal, high-altitude position. Simultaneous to this fact becoming clear, the foreign ambassador looked up, witnessed the exploration, grabbed at the unbuttoned top of her blouse, and let out a string of negatives that brought the warring world around them to a standstill.

Mark backed off, red as a tomato. He went slinking away to his own country, where Jeff and Allen were snickering. The trip had been for naught; he had failed to gain support (as had, in a sense, the foreign ambassador), and he felt dozens of eyes boring in on him. He dared not look in *that* direction again for the rest of the period, even when his country had signed a treaty with the two remaining powers, thus ending the game.

He heard footsteps behind him. Dad had come down from the campsite, looking for his new walking stick. Mark pointed off to the right, while still gazing at Capella. The steps moved off, and Mark began to weave his head, as he felt a crick in his neck. As his eyes turned east, he saw an enormous meteor sweep the sky and explode into red sparks. He jumped to his feet, pointed and yelled, and then realized the uselessness of this action. Dad came back over, without his stick, and told Mark that it was still a yard or so above the water. The two of them walked along the beach for a while, looking across the expanse of liquid.

From behind Douglas Island, a string of bright yellow and white became visible, moving slowly northward. It was a ferry, on its way to

Haines. Mark watched it slide up the canal, imagining for a moment that he was aboard, looking through the darkness at Portland Island, and wondering, could there possibly be a soul or two standing on that dark, lonely beach, straining their eyes at the ship and wondering, could there possibly be anyone on the outside deck of the vessel, staring intently at the long, thin island, and wondering ....

Dad said that he would just go and hit the sack, that he was tired. They walked back to the boat, and Mark realized that the water was really getting pretty high. The stick was nowhere to be seen. It was gone; the ocean water having claimed it for its own. Dad was angry as he walked up the slope to the trees. Mark just stood for a bit, looked at Capella one last time, and then went and joined him.

After a few hours, Mark woke up and heard the water below him. He got out of his sleeping bag and noticed that Dad's was already empty. His boots were on in a flash, and then he was running down to the sand. Dad was out there somewhere. Mark raced over to the boat; in the darkness he saw that it was in the water, parallel to the shore. He struggled up the slope, where he saw Dad untying the lines. They pulled the boat up, far above the water, and secured the lines once again.

Back in his sleeping bag, Mark congratulated himself at length on what he had done, helping to save the boat and their transportation back home. Good grief, they might have been stranded here on this little island for a long time ... without a radio, there would be no help from the Coast Guard, not unless they managed to attract attention with fires.

All this time, Mom would worry, but she wouldn't remember where they had planned their campout and could therefore offer no help to the authorities. Could that really happen? Might they have had to live off the land, catching fish, setting snares, and eating wild cucumber and boiled rockweed? In fact, the more he thought about it, the whole thing sounded like a downright adventure. Rats! Why had they managed to tie up the boat, anyway?

Finally, Mark's eyes closed, but just before he drifted from the present moment to eternal reality, he wordlessly spoke his answer. Yes, he would very much have loved being stranded here.

In the morning, they packed up and prepared to leave. The water was rough; two-foot swells poured onto the beach. Mark was both unsure and excited as he stepped into the Gamefisher. Dad started the small outboard, and the boat raced into the breakers, bucking them and moving on to smoother water. They turned up the shore and made for the northwestern end of the island, and as they passed the small clearing, Mark looked for the rabbit, but it had disappeared somehow; was lost from view on this Easter morning.

§

He would look back, remember, and reflect on those events that were important. These were the events that he knew, deep inside, signaled the beginning of the change, and the inevitable plunge toward Commission. He didn't ask for it to happen, and he didn't want it to happen. He didn't want it *not* to happen. It just happened, and the year he'd just remembered was the balance point. The paintbrush. The pasts, the futures, and the present.

Mark realized his legs were quavering. He was sitting on his bed, and he was trying to think, wanting to remember even more. A warm, gentle voice that made him stiffen, and then relax, told him everything was all right, that a proper script was being followed. He was unsure whether to believe this voice from nowhere.

Before Mark could decide, he heard the other voice, the one that came to him in those weird moments. Unlike all those previous occurrences, however, this was his own voice, emanating from an entirely different corner of spacetime.

… and then something very strange happened. I was not a child, I was not an adult, I was not a human. I was just a soul, a mind, inserted into a piece of stuff in the galaxy, and I didn't know why. No concerns about society, no concerns about fame or fortune, no concerns about family. I just wanted to know why I was asking questions about solid and liquid and fire and the pressure of my feet against the ground, but I was getting no reply from anyone at all. Instead, whispers were coming from the trees, and the wind, and the stars.

The voices spoke to me without words. My responses were likewise inaudible, but my silent tone was sometimes angry and frustrated. I believed the tree, wind, and star voices were trying their best to get through to me, and that I was failing them.

I did not do it then, not in that year when the voices were strongest yet, after I had fallen through the bear and into the cold water … my Birth. No, the Commission was three years later. But that earlier time was the balance point, the year I remembered most of any year of my life. The year that was truly every year, every day, every single moment.

Sitting on his bed, Mark tried to understand why he was hearing his future self talk to him. He wasn't frightened, just puzzled. And then he turned his head; looked over his shoulder.

There was nothing there. In that instant, the whole room disappeared because it occupied no space. Time was taking no time to happen. In that same instant, the room was back, and everything was the same as before.

But not exactly as before. Something had twisted, something had turned ....

And reality had cleared its throat.

CHAPTER ONE

There was a time, when the living and the dead were in constant embrace, the difference between the two impossible to calculate. There was the universal mind, and forever it had permeated all there was. Indeed, all the pasts, the present, and all the futures were together in an almost singular nirvana, and there wasn't any need for thought or sensation. Time took no time to happen.

There was a space, and an endless space it was, yet it occupied no space at all. It could not be measured, for there was no starting point. There was no yardstick, and no raw materials with which to construct one. There were people in a sense, but they were not human; they knew not themselves as individuals or as the whole, for without perception of space, there could be no physical brain and therefore no question to ask.

And there was no pain, no joy, no words to describe this time and this place. There were no wars, no mating urge, and no illegalities. The time frequency must have been zero, and the space frequency, whatever it was, could not have been a rational number, as this fraction had no identifiable value. In the midst of it all, something observed itself and ....

The world shattered; there is almost no trace of any such life on this Earth. A processor was spawned into existence, and it rapidly condensed into a physical entity that recognized its own voice and no others. At great cost, the incredible knowledge of all that was, and all that would ever be, slipped from the grasp of this new machine. It was a calculator, a brain, a self-proclaimed examiner and analyzer of this new time, and this new space. If this brain could have listened to its own programming, the faint echoes of the lost would be heard, however this brain was much too busy creating new definitions for such words as faint, echoes, and lost.

To escape the boundaries of simple existence, which was now understood as such a terrible hindrance, people began to understand how to dream at night, to explore beyond their solid, upright bodies and question the beginning of it all, and the possible ending. A deeply powerful feeling rose to the surface, one of foreboding, as the population grew and movements became increasingly more difficult to predict. There came the first arguments, the first egos, and the first attempts to conquer. The mechanical revolution wrapped itself around the people and protected them like a baby's blanket.

It was now so easy to feel good. Indeed, one could even do so by making someone else feel bad. There were many ways to accomplish this, but the most important thing to remember was to keep focused, create a plan, and then act—let nothing distract from the goal—and when the prize was won, assimilate the experience into one's self, to learn from it, and to grow in confidence as well as in social stature. The human existence required getting the competitive edge and keeping it. It required the old to teach the young about truths regarding survival, the teaching of the physical universe handbook, how to live in prosperity, the real definition of the fittest ....

Time took time to happen. Space had space to exist. There was now time to force understanding upon others, and there was now space between the billions of stars and galaxies. An irresistible force was at work, a most powerful anti-entropy effect, which the people thought they understood. It came in the form of an expanding universe, one that separated the human brain from the hologram of reality. This force was studied in depth, and answers were accepted, answers that were completely incorrect. This force produced machines that roared, machines that flew, and machines that sailed. These machines roared, and they flew, and they sailed directly through the ancient voices, which were now scattered and unfocused, little more than cosmic background noise. These voices were no longer heard, as people now dreamed less during the day and much more at night; their dreams were now purposed only to clear the mind and refresh the body, so that both might carry on the mission, with each new dawn.

§

… machines that sailed.

The Nilsson family was aboard one of these.

It resembled a pocket-sized ocean liner, it was blue and white, and it was running at seventeen knots. To the left and to the right were forested mountains that rose from the saltwater, and beyond them were taller peaks capped with snow. In the channel itself, there were rocky islets upon which seals napped, and bald eagles nested in the trees that lined the narrow beaches. It was a partly cloudy afternoon, and the air was warm even though the water was frigid.

This vessel carried people, and it carried automobiles; the latter, ranging from compacts to conversion vans to freight trailers, were below the superstructure. The passengers, four hundred and fifty of them, were on the two main decks. Some dozed, others read books or magazines, and quite a few were enjoying lunch in the restaurant. Many were outside watching the breathtaking scenery that moved slowly past. Ketchikan was far astern; the ship would arrive in Wrangell before dusk.

The Nilsson family was indoors, passing time in one of the mezzanine deck lounges. Mama and Daddy were both asleep in reclining chairs. Amy was awake, in Mama's lap, and she was wide-eyed and staring as usual. But Mark, and his older brother Stephen, were crouched on the far side of the lounge, engaged in conversation.

They were planning the Big Sneak Away. Rule number one was simple: absolutely no talking until they were completely out of the lounge area. Rule number two was that Stephen would do all of the leading. And rule number three was that they must be back in less than five minutes. Now, Mark pointed out that rule three might be hard to follow, as neither of them had a watch, and besides, it was unclear to him just exactly how long five minutes took. Stephen said he would keep an eye on the ship's clocks, for the Sneak Away to be a success. Mark nodded.

They crawled, on hands and knees, past everyone in the lounge, and at the entrance, Mark whipped his head about, to look at Mama and Daddy. They were still asleep, but Amy was staring right in their direction.

Well! She couldn't tell on them, could she? The two boys crawled right out of the lounge and into the starboard hallway. Here they stood up and breathed a sigh of relief.

"Where are we going to go now?" Mark asked.

"I don't know. We haven't been all over the boat yet. I want to go up to the next deck. I think there are more people up there than down here. Isn't the snack bar up there somewhere? Come on, just follow me and look around, and poke me if you can see Daddy anywhere."

Stephen moved off, down the hallway, and Mark followed. They stole through the tiled passage until they reached the forward stairwell. Up they went, and soon found themselves in a large foyer, near a curios shop. Walking back toward the stern, they passed the snack bar, where people sat and enjoyed sandwiches and soft drinks. They reached the aft doorways, paused for a moment, and then decided to go out on deck for a look around.

"Remember, Daddy said no," Mark told his brother, once they were hugging the rails, watching the gray-green water go by. The bow wave of the ship curled away from them toward land, followed by the smaller stern wakes, and the white foam that gushed from the propellers brought detritus and green rockweed to the surface. Mark stared at the wakes as they ripped the shoreline, where seagulls waited to see if edibles might wash up on the sand beach. Stephen tapped him on the shoulder. Mark turned, and the pair walked up the starboard side of the promenade deck, past a group of tourists who were hoping for a glimpse of porpoise fins rolling in the waves. The wind, created by the ship's forward motion, tugged at their shirts, and it grew worse as they approached the bow. "Let's go back inside!" Stephen yelled.

They did so, and moments later were standing once again in the center of the large foyer. A passageway led forward. "I wonder what's up that way?" Mark pointed. They went to find out, Stephen doing the leading. They entered a very large room, filled with older folks and a few children. It was the main forward lounge, and the entire front was windows, dramatically showing the path of travel.

"This is great!" Stephen said, looking about. "I want to get Mama and Daddy and show them. I think they'll want to come up here for the rest of the day." Mark opened his mouth, but Stephen wagged a finger at him. "Look, I'll go and get them, and you stay here. You can get us a good place to sit. Now don't leave!"

"Okay" Mark answered, then suddenly realized it was the first time he had ever used that word.

Stephen disappeared.

Mark sat in the lounge, quite alone, though the room was filled with people. He knew it had been a long time since they had stolen away, and Daddy was sure to be angry. And Stephen! Now his brother would go back, babble on about a big room upstairs, completely forgetting that it would give away the truth, and then what would happen? Why had Stephen done this, anyway? And Mark took every order his brother gave him; this had to stop! What if Stephen got lost? That must be where he was—lost. And if the both of them didn't get back to Mama and Daddy soon, there was going to be a lot of trouble. A spanking. Or something of theirs taken away.

And so, very slowly, Mark got up and left the forward lounge. He walked back to the stairwell, trying to remember if this was the path to the mezzanine sitting room. Gripping the banister tightly, he descended, and when he reached the lower deck, he started off down the portside hallway, reaching what at first looked familiar—reclining chairs, people napping or reading books. But as he glanced around, he began to panic. The room just didn't look right. He saw no sign of his family. He rushed about the perimeter, straining for a glimpse of Mama and Daddy, then realized it was no use. His family was not there.

He left the sitting room and continued down the port side of the ship. He was getting quite scared now, and was beginning to understand Time at last, because he knew it was *flying by*. He reached a second stairwell and started down it. It was a long way to the bottom. And when he got to the landing, he knew he had made a mistake; he was now on the car deck. He raced back up the stairs, turned right, found the starboard passageway, and now everything became clear. His family was on the starboard side! He ran up the hall until he got to the lounge, then walked over to where his family had been.

They were gone—Mama, Daddy, Stephen, and Amy. They had disappeared.

Now he was really shaking. Alone, on a big boat, with his hopes of getting out of this alive quickly slipping away. Where could he go? Aimlessly, and very much despaired, he walked out into the passageway. He hiked up the stairs to the promenade deck once again. Walking along the corridor, he passed one family after another, heard the clinking of glasses and the rattling of plates as he made his way past the snack bar. He continued forward until he reached the large foyer. If nothing else, he decided, he would return to that wonderful lounge at the front of the ship, and maybe it would make him feel a little better.

He entered the forward sitting area and peered around, looking for an empty seat. He walked up to the windows, across the front, and down the other side.

"Well, there he is! Right there!"

Mark whirled around and faced his parents, his brother, and the staring baby eyes. He walked over to them, his step faltering and his head filled with a mixture of relief and dread. He started to speak, opened his mouth to say something about how nice it was to see them again, and how they were all together at last, in the big forward lounge ....

Mama grabbed him by his collar. "Where have you been?" she rasped. Mark was struck hard by her vicious tone, and he tried to take a backward step, but Daddy was right there to hem the boy in. He tightened up, let his head drop, and stared at his black tennis shoes, studying the laces and the shiny aglets. He started to speak, hesitated, then said "I was ... just lookin' ... for you".

Mama let go of his collar. He listened to her as she continued with her lashing remarks, about how he had caused another uproar, how they suspected that he might have fallen overboard and drowned, and so on, and so on. Somewhere in there, Mark would have welcomed the chance to say a word or two about Stephen having left him all alone, but his mind fumbled, and he had not a chance to defend himself. And Stephen was just standing there, with a silly grin on his stupid face! If only he could find the right words, but he was too young, and he hated it.

Daddy led the troops over to a large vacant area of the lounge, where they could all stretch out and relax, and from where they could obtain a good view out the forward windows. Mark thought to himself that someday, maybe five years from now, he would mention that they could have thanked him for leading them to this room! He slouched into one of the padded, blue vinyl sofas and let his chin drop to his chest. He knew that Mama and Daddy were still angry and disappointed that he had become separated from them, but he decided not to think about the incident anymore. And after a while, the whole thing seemed to die off, and the excitement of the trip welled up in him again. He grew restless, stirred about, and finally got up the nerve to rise from his seat and approach the front windows, where he stood marveling at the scenery ahead of him.

Clarence Strait was narrowing, and the islands seemed to block the passage ahead. The land was covered in evergreens, mostly spruce and hemlock, although Mark did not yet know these names. Off to the east, beyond the first line of ridges, was an imposing wall of snow-covered peaks, incredibly white and brilliant in the mid-afternoon sun. As he watched, the ferry turned in that direction, as though sensing a water path between the islands. And indeed, a narrow channel appeared, which angled back to the north and provided easy passage. A blue shape glided from behind the trees, a couple of miles in front of them. Mark squinted his eyes, trying to figure out this new mystery, then identified the shape as another ferry, coming from the opposite direction.

Soon, many of the passengers were on their feet, coming to the window and pointing to the ship in the distance. It was sailing almost directly toward them, and the two ferries would pass in very close proximity. Mark was joined by the rest of his family, and they waited anxiously for the vessel to come near. The other ship turned and approached to starboard, and as it slowly glided by, Daddy got out his binoculars. He looked through them for a moment, then let Stephen have a turn. Mark heard his brother say something about the vessel's name, which was in big white letters on the bow. "*Malaspina*", Daddy corrected, and Mark repeated the name to himself; thought it was a grand word indeed. He liked the name of this ship as well, though he had no idea the meaning of "*Taku*", or "*Malaspina*". Someday, he would have to find out.

The Nilssons were content to remain in the observation lounge and watch the scenery pass. There were about seventy-five people in the room, some of them asleep, others talking to one another about their vacations and trying to decide which towns to visit, and several families discussing and sometimes disagreeing on information their travel agents had provided them. Mark heard two of them talking about someone named Johnson signing a bill that would get rid of the silver in quarters and dimes.

At about seven in the evening, Daddy went to the snack bar to get a few supplements for the evening meal, which Mama was unpacking from a small travel case. He returned laden with coffee, juice, and cherry pie wedges, and as the family ate, the ferry rounded a sharp point, and the town of Wrangell was before them. It was still miles away, but it looked quite lovely in its mountain setting, with the Coast Range forming a breathtaking, seemingly protective backdrop. The Nilssons feasted and watched the community draw nearer, and suddenly, the ship's horn blew loudly, announcing the arrival and waking the many passengers who were taking evening naps in the lounge.

The ship glided to the Wrangell terminal and was soon tied securely to the dock. As had been the case in Ketchikan, Mark and his brother were allowed to go outside to watch the line of cars drive off the boat and disappear into the streets beyond. And then the loading procedure began, the autos being guided down the ramp and into the vessel's car deck. And lastly, the bridge was raised, as if to salute the ship itself, which let go a long, single blast on the horn, signaling that departure was forthcoming.

As they drew away from the Wrangell terminal, it was still light outside, and still warm. The time was half past eight, but the sun had not yet dropped behind the island hills to the west. Mark, Daddy and Stephen were at the stern, where the foam built as the ferry rapidly gained speed. They watched as the barnacled and creosote-coated pilings shrank in size, finally dropping away below the horizon.

Back in the observation lounge, the family prepared for bedtime. The boys protested loudly, since it was still light outside and they wanted to see the town of Petersburg when they arrived. The ferry was entering Wrangell Narrows, a rock-studded passage filled with buoys and shore markers, and Mama hastened the children, getting them into prone positions and covering them with blankets, as if not wishing them to see this hazardous waterway. Amy was already dozing in a small vinyl sofa of her own. Soon Mark was wrapped up and staring at the ceiling, becoming lost in an exploration of the wires, cables, and pipes that ran above him. The ship's vibrations had a gentling effect on him, and soon his eyes closed.

In his period of unconsciousness, he didn't actually dream, but even so, the entire trip was coming back through his mind, and he relived the past nine days. The first day's journey, passing through a town called Raton. Then northward to Denver and beyond. A late start on the third day, only as far as Cheyenne. And then, through beautiful country, making it as far as Missoula, and a night at a motel, so much better than the plastic air mattresses in the station wagon. On and on, through Idaho, crossing the state in two hours, Mark was told. Spending an evening at Grand Coulee Dam and taking in the wonderful light show. On into Canada that very same night, arriving at a town known as Kamloops just after dawn. A long scenic drive to Prince

George, and then a one-day layover in Vanderhoof. And on the eighth day, the end of the road at Prince Rupert, with the marine voyage to begin the following morning.

And that morning was today. Now he was drifting back even further, to a time before the trip had even begun, when he sat on Grandmother's lap and told her that he was going to be moving to Alaska. And Grandmother whispering in his ear—no, no, he was not going to be moving to Alaska. It was too dangerous, too cold, many big ice holes to fall into. And Mama and Daddy looking on, their faces taking a turn for the worse, strained and uncomfortable their expressions were, and Mark feeling the wetness in his eyes because he knew that he was right, and that Grandmother was wrong. He *was* going to move to Alaska, and the tears began to roll, because Grandmother would not accept the truth.

He sat up on the sofa, his blanket falling to the floor. It was pitch black in the lounge, but lights were moving past the ship. It was Petersburg, and his lips parted as he spoke the name to himself. Mama came over to him. "Can't you sleep?" she asked softly. Before Mark could answer, the ship's horn blew, and as before, at Wrangell, the lounge was soon full of upright passengers, only this time they were wrapped in sheets and scarves, moving ghostlike to the windows. They stood and watched the lights of the harbor slip past, with the multi-colored lights of the terminal just beyond. Mark wondered why he and his family, and all the others around him, didn't get to stay in those fancy staterooms, where there were bunks and private toilets.

It was an eerie scene. The boat swung toward land, came to the dock, and stopped moving, the vibrations decreasing and then dying away altogether. Mark didn't know it, but the time was twelve midnight. He yawned, but he also felt wide awake. He searched with his eyes for a long time, taking in the darkness and extreme quiet of the lounge. Instead of lightening its passenger load since leaving Prince Rupert, the *Taku* seemed to have gained a tremendous lot, and perhaps the number would increase again here in Petersburg. The staterooms must be full, he decided; that's why he was sleeping on a sofa. He looked up at the ceiling again, and he saw something that took his mind off the town, the people in the lounge, and the trip itself.

It was a large red bell, directly above him. Something about it made him very uncomfortable. He motioned to Daddy and then pointed. "What is that?" he whispered. "Is that something makes people get real scared?"

"Just an alarm bell," Daddy answered. "If anything went wrong on the boat, that bell would ring, and we would know about it. But it won't go off. Now, go back to sleep, all right?"

That bell going off? Mark went rigid. He was lying right underneath it and would hear it louder than anyone. Something would happen. They would hit an iceberg, or there would be a fire. In the midst of his tranquil sleep, that frightening red bell would clang, and he would bolt up, screaming for help. Daddy moved off to join Mama at the windows, and Mark jerked around to look at Amy and Stephen. They were both asleep, Amy drooling and Stephen making humming sounds through his nose. Mark lay back and just stared at the bell, expecting it to sound off at any moment, but it did not, and once again he lapsed into deep sleep, where time and space frequencies were much different for him.

Perhaps he dreamed about the bell; he couldn't remember. When he woke, the first thing he saw was the awful red shape above him. Funny he hadn't noticed it until Petersburg, but now it dominated the entire lounge. And then ....

For just a moment, something felt wrong with his left hand. He shivered, and without looking at his palm, he sensed that it was covered with red stain. He forced the strange thought from him.

Then his mind was filled with another thought; it was light inside and out, as morning had come. He looked around and saw that he was the last to wake. Mama, Daddy, and Stephen were pointing to the forward windows, and Amy was crying for breakfast, or just attention perhaps, but she wasn't getting either one. Something very interesting must be just ahead, Mark decided, and then it hit him. They were coming to their new home at last; the *Taku* was arriving in Juneau.

He got up from the sofa and joined the others. Staring out of the windows, he got his first view of the town. It was still miles away, up a narrow channel, but it was obviously larger than any of the places they had docked, and it was, Mark decided, certainly more impressive. A large, round-topped peak rose directly behind the city. Indeed, the mountains had taken on a more dramatic look since the previous day. Mark had a fleeting remembrance of something Daddy explained to them when the trip began. Juneau was the only mainland town along their route, and the mountains on the mainland were bigger and higher than those on the islands.

Suddenly, Mark felt a miniscule shock, as if a low-voltage current had passed through his body. Now he was looking up through a great, natural keyhole in the world itself, and he was about to be carried right through that keyhole, up near the top of that rounded mountain peak … where he was already standing and looking back toward the ship. It was a premonition that the boy could not understand, could not comprehend, and then another sudden, invisible wave passed through him, leaving him dizzy for a moment. He was entering a secluded place, cut off from the rest of the world. It was a new, raw beginning for his mind and body. He shivered, and then the strange idea left him as suddenly as it had presented itself. Now, all he saw was a town with low buildings, the only exception being a tall white structure that dominated the "skyline".

Daddy pointed to it and said it was the Federal Office Building, and that nearby was the State Highways building, where he would be working.

Stephen came over to where Mark stood. He said, "It's the Federal Office Building, and nearby is the Highways building, where Daddy will be working". Mark could have laughed, but he let Stephen have his say. He noticed that Mama was now holding Amy while talking to a stranger. He watched her intently. She was making conversation with what appeared to be a husband and wife, while a boy several years older than Stephen looked on. Mark had seen the boy earlier on the trip, but they had never communicated. There was quite the chatter between the adults, and Daddy soon joined in.

Mark listened. He heard the words "contractor", and "elementary school", and something called "Mendenhall", but otherwise made nothing of the conversation. But then Daddy motioned the boys to come over, and the family gathered on the sofas.

"He says the house we asked about isn't ready, and he wants us to look at another one nearby. If we want it, we might be able to move into one of his duplexes by Tuesday and pay one month. He mentioned a couple of good motels we might try, just for the first night or two. What do you think?"

Mark and Stephen turned their heads.

Mama answered, "She says they have a camper behind their own place that we could stay in, if we wanted to. I think it's lucky we got to talking with them." She turned to the boys. "It looks like we have a place to live without having to search at all."

Mark had never thought about where they might live, or for that matter, just what they would do once they had driven the station wagon off the boat and into the town. All he knew was that Daddy had been offered a job here, and that had been the reason for their abrupt departure from the only place he had ever called home.

And now Juneau was upon them. The horn blew, the purser began to announce disembarking procedures on the loudspeakers, and the lounge began to empty. It did indeed look as though most of the passengers were going ashore here. The Nilssons picked up their things and started down to the car deck. They quickly found the station wagon and sat inside it, waiting for the ferry to tie up. Soon, the car ahead of them was moving forward, and Daddy started the engine, announcing as he did so, that their new friends drove a white Fairlane, and it would lead them a few miles down the highway.

Whatever that meant, Mark thought to himself. And then they were out of the vessel, rolling up the transfer bridge and into the town. Immediately, Mama pointed out the Fairlane. The people inside, the same husband-wife-son combination, were waving for the Nilssons to follow. Daddy drove close behind, and the pair of cars swung through the crowded parking lot, up a narrow street, and through a couple of inter-sections. Then they traveled along a wide, bumpy avenue to the far end of town. Mark saw residential areas tucked into small valleys alongside the badly paved, two-lane highway. After a time, they turned off into a park-ing lot, and there was a motel. Daddy got out of the car and went over to the Fairlane, talked with the strange man for a bit, and came back.

"This is a good place, and tomorrow we'll go and see the duplex. I have the directions here."

Mark got out of the station wagon and grabbed his personal suitcase. And ten minutes later, he and Stephen were unpacking their things, and then they were quarreling about who would get which side of the double bed. Mama got out the last of the food, Daddy came from the motel office, and as the family ate, they talked about how good it was to be in their new town, and about how nice that Fairlane family was. Then Mama and Daddy sat down and began to discuss the plan for the next few days. Mark and his brother were left to themselves, and Amy was once again asleep in a nest of blankets.

It wasn't long before Mark grew restless, and finally he asked to go outside. Mama looked up and nodded. "Want to go with me?" he asked Stephen as he started for the door. Stephen shook his head and began to search for something in his suitcase. Mark shrugged and went out into the cool afternoon.

It had become cloudy over the past few hours, and Mark shivered as he walked about. The parking lot was unpaved, and he looked curiously at the rocks. They were speckled. He had a sudden remembrance of the time, two days earlier, when they had stopped at a roadside lot to rest, between Vanderhoof and Prince Rupert. There was a small brook, almost hidden in the trees, and a worn path had led up from the turnoff and into the woods. Mark and Daddy had followed the path for about one hundred feet until it began a steep grade. As they had turned to go back to the others, Mark had noticed a large rock in the middle of the path. It was speckled, the first of its type he had ever seen, and he had told Daddy that he wanted to take it with him. He was denied permission, and now he realized that it didn't matter; from where he now stood, he could see hundreds of the strangely spotted rocks. He kicked them about for a while, then turned to look at the mountain which soared upward, directly behind the little motel.

Maybe he could just sneak up there and climb it! Mark had never stood so close to a mountain in his life, and he had little perception of heights, but he started for the woods anyway. He didn't get very far. As he moved to the edge of the foliage behind the motel, his feet sank into black mud, and he was afraid to go any further. Might he sink deeper, and finally disappear into the earth completely, just like the man in that movie he'd watched, a couple weeks ago? He stepped back, and after making a poor effort at scraping his shoes, he decided, with a heavy heart, that he would have to wait and climb this mountain another day.

But he couldn't take his eyes from the flora. The trees were big and green, with a clean, wet smell. Plants the likes of which he had never seen were within reach, if he dared cross the muddy zone. Some had tiny thorns, others snaked their way across the ground, which was covered with a thick blanket of moss, and some of the plants were so tiny their leaf shapes could not be discerned. Mark wanted to run over there and let his hands dig into that thick moss. The greenness of it all had him drunk—it was like a jungle, but not like a jungle at all. It was raw and wild, rough and tumbled, this immense wilderness in front of the little boy with muddy shoes. Mark felt a greatness around him, and the breath escaped his lungs in a rippling way that made him feel all the more enchanted, somehow attached to the natural splendor around him. It was like a movie theater, with a screen that kept getting larger and larger while moving closer and closer to him, and he alone was watching the film. It was an epic unfolding before him, and by viewing it, he was receiving a special preview of an otherwise unexplored world ....

"I decided to come out after all. You been back here very long?"

Startled, Mark whirled and looked at Stephen. He raised his arms, then let them flop back to his sides. "I got stuck in the mud," he said, in a voice not quite his own.

§

On Tuesday afternoon, the Nilssons moved into the duplex, situated at the edge of a rural subdivision. It was brand new, the floor tiles having just barely set, and the smell of overcoat and enamel was quite strong in every room. Mark, excited by the big empty residence, found that he, along with Stephen, would be once again spending the nights on those clumsy air mattresses and sharing a room on a permanent basis. The family's stock of furniture and household goods, sent by freight line, had not yet arrived. Several boxes containing toiletries, washcloths, clothing, and fragiles were scattered about the otherwise bare living room.

Daddy was always gone, it seemed, driving the station wagon to some place unknown to Mark, who spent much of that first day poking about the back yard, which was surfaced with glacial subsoil. There was no grass, not even a weed. Nearby, several houses were under construction, and an elementary school and large playground was just a block away.

But directly behind the property was the forest, and an impressive stand of spruce, alder, and cottonwood hemmed in the neighborhood. A perfectly natural urge for tree climbing swept through Mark, and Stephen as well, but they dared not venture far from the house because, as Mama told them, a hungry bear might well make a meal of them.

Mark didn't believe a bear would do that, but he obeyed Mama just the same.

On the second night, the brothers were sitting on their plastic beds, talking. It was dark, and they didn't hear their parents moving about, so it was a good time for a pow-wow.

"Why is Daddy gone so much?" Mark asked.

"He's looking for a way to get food".

"What do you mean?" Mark watched Stephen's eyes drop, and he heard the quaver in his brother's reply.

"I heard them talking about the job. He doesn't start until Monday, and he doesn't get paid for a long time. I think he's gone to make some friends and find some food. That bread we ate tonight was from a church, I think."

"We don't have much food, do we?"

"I don't know," Stephen answered. "I just heard Mama say that everything would be okay in a week. And then Daddy said he knew how to make things work."

Mark covered himself in a heavy blanket and closed his eyes. He heard the rain pelting the window of their bedroom, although he was unaware that a frontal system was moving past and that tomorrow would be cloudy and cool. He did know, however, just as his brain shifted into sleep mode, that the fish he and Stephen had eaten for dinner was a trout, because his parents said it was. He also knew that Daddy had shot it with his .22 rifle, in a creek somewhere nearby. He knew this because Stephen had told him; his brother had overheard those whispers as well.

§

It remained cloudy for two days, but on Saturday the weather cleared. Mark had slept late, and when he woke, he heard strange voices from out in the den. He got up, and still in his pajamas, went out to see what was happening. His eyes fell upon the strange man who had provided the Nilssons with their temporary home. Mark had learned his name the day before—Hendricks. He, his wife, and their nine-year-old son Brian lived a few houses down the road, and they had come over for an early visit.

Mark heard something about how the two had to go into town for some shopping, and would Daddy like to take Brian squirrel hunting, as he had promised during the ferry trip? Of course, Stephen could go, and Mark as well. Daddy replied that yes, he would be glad to, and then the Hendrickses departed, Brian very excited and yelling to Stephen about the .22 rifle his parents had just given him. Mark watched as Daddy reached into the front closet for his own .22 caliber, which had been zipped tightly in a leather case and packed in the trunk of the station wagon, all the way to Alaska. It had killed the trout. Stephen, who had been sitting at the makeshift dining room table, jumped up and went to put on his boots, and Mark, still yawning, followed to get dressed.

It was already past noon, the sun high in the sky and the air surprisingly warm, when the four started out. They walked through the backyard, then came upon an old dirt road that entered the woods behind the subdivision, and they followed it for quite a distance to the west. Behind them, a tall, steep ridge lifted upward to the sky, and Mark turned around for a moment to look at it. Daddy had told him it was called Thunder Mountain, and Mark loved the sound of the name.

Stephen asked about the road, and Daddy explained that it had been plowed during World War II, when American troops had been summoned to the area to set up temporary encampments in case of a Japanese attack on Alaska. All of this was way over Mark's head, but he listened intently just the same, catching the words "soldier" and "war", and it sounded odd to him, especially seeing that they were now walking down the road themselves and carrying rifles. "Almost no one lived here in the valley before the war," Daddy informed the others.

Mark stopped in his tracks for a moment. Now he knew where he lived. It was the "Valley". He loved the sound of this name as well.

Brian was ahead of them; he was an ambitious youngster who never kept the safety on his gun and looked ready to fire a shot at the first thing that moved. Daddy kept calling him back, telling him to keep his finger away from the trigger unless he was really set to shoot. Mark had fired a gun but once, when he was three, Daddy having let him shoot at a small wand behind their home. He had bullseyed the target, but since it had been a one-time affair, Mark had no way of knowing if it was pure luck or genuine talent.

Soon they came upon a peninsula that separated two large ponds. A couple of sandpipers cried out and zoomed away, but Daddy warned Brian not to raise his weapon. And just as he spoke, there was a loud noise from the woods in front of them. It sounded like an extremely fast tongue-clucking, then after a moment, the sound changed to a squeaky chattering, smacking noise. Daddy called the team to a halt, then nodded to the three youngsters. "Red squirrel," he said in a low voice.

Mark had never seen a red squirrel, only a few gray ones at city parks. He was almost frothing in anxiety, straining his eyes in his search for the animal in the trees. The hunters began to walk slowly to the wooded section of the peninsula. Daddy and Brian took the lead and separated, fanning out to right and left of where the squirrel was. Mark and Stephen watched, fascinated. After a moment, the two who carried rifles disappeared and were calling the brothers to follow. Mark walked stealthily into the thicket of trees. Daddy and Brian were underneath a large hemlock, and now Mark could see movement in the branches as the creature danced upon a soft, needled limb, then leaped to another one.

Stephen came up and stood with the others, shading his eyes to watch the rodent. Daddy said to them, "They're very little, even the grown-ups. Can you see it all right? It's a reddish-brown color. Look at it playing on the top of that tree! When I was little, I used to watch squirrels for hours, and only once did I ever see one fall from a tree. I remember when two of them were playing follow-the-leader, and they were jumping from one tree to another. One of them slipped and fell all the way to the ground. The little things are show-offs, and they never seem afraid of anyone, not even a hunter with a gun."

Mark thought he noticed a change in Daddy's voice, but he wasn't sure. Brian was given a nod, and the boy aimed carefully at the squirrel. The animal paused its movement at the end of a drooping limb, preparing to jump to another.

And that was when Brian fired.

The shot rang out, a high-pitched *crack*, and the squirrel let out a series of hurried squeaks and bolted for the tree trunk. Brian lowered his gun and let the butt drop to the forest floor. "I missed," he said to nobody in particular. And he frowned at the space in front of him.

At that moment, a strange *groak* noise filled the thicket, and a large bird, nearly jet black in color, zoomed overhead and vanished. Everyone jumped, and Stephen asked, "What was that?"

"A raven," Daddy answered. "Legends around here speak of them as being very wise, sometimes playing tricks on humans and other animals. They're also said to deliver mysterious messages to the minds of other creatures." Mark felt himself shivering, and he didn't know why.

He looked for the squirrel, but it was hiding itself on the opposite side of the tree. Stephen ran around the base of the giant hemlock, trying to spook the animal, and after a moment, this strategy was effective; the squirrel darted from cover and jumped to another, smaller tree that had a cluster of many leaves and broken twigs near its top. The animal was nearly invisible. Daddy raised his rifle and looked through the scope, while the barrel of the gun moved in a peculiar, circular pattern. Suddenly the motion stopped, and Daddy said, in a dry voice, "I've got him".

He pulled the trigger, and there was a second *crack*. The small furry shape tumbled out of the tree, performed a couple of somersaults, and landed with a soft thud on the forest litter. Brian rushed up and bent over the squirrel. Daddy and Stephen came up next, and Mark, suddenly gripped by a feeling of queasiness, crept forward to stand behind the other three.

The little squirrel was dead, of course. Daddy picked it up by its red tail and held it out for the boys to see. "I just want to tell you something," he said, in that same dry tone. As he spoke, a thin line of blood ran from the animal's nose and stained the ground. "I shot it in the back, and I really didn't want to. But I think it's important for all of you to see this—a small wild animal that has been shot. I don't ever want to see any of you going around killing for pleasure or for the sake of being able to kill."

The little squirrel was twirling around slowly, and now its back was facing Mark. A neat red hole showed plainly where the bullet had entered. Daddy laid the rodent face down on the forest floor. And he announced that it was time to go on home.

They started off, but after a few steps, Mark, stopped, turned around, and walked back to where the squirrel lay. He looked over his shoulder to see if the others were watching, and they were not. He reached out with his left hand, and as his index finger made contact with the warm little body, his throat worked.

I know you won't ever move again. And I feel bad leaving you here like this. But it's all right. The World will take care of you now.

Goodbye, little squirrel.

Hustling, he caught up with the others, who were still crossing the peninsula.

CHAPTER TWO

In the morning clear, the mountain peaks were a radiant pink. Cold air settled in from the heights, and the world hushed. The spruce, murmuring among themselves the evening past, were in silence this day. The earth sought warmth from the sun, and the sun tried to deliver, but it was low in the sky, behind the treetops, succeeding only in pushing waves through the plane of the atmosphere. They were lovely hues indeed, but seemingly absent of heat.

Dogs were curled in the snow, insulating their produced energy as best they could. Birds had remained nested long after daybreak and were now huddled en masse on the trees now exposed to the yellow ball of hydrogen. The streets were vacant, the cars locked away in garages or left alone in driveways, their metal bitingly cold. Footprints of all sizes, the only evidence of human activity, were old and deformed; the surface of the snow was a hard crust. On this, a Saturday in January, existence barely idled.

The Nilsson home was especially quiet. The little modular house, into which the family had moved several weeks ago, sat on its huge lot, a property with no trees, hedges, or even one small bush. Frost patterns, wild conglomerations resembling dense, tangled foliage, turned from silvery white to blinding ochre as the sun hit the back windows. Above the roof, space itself seemed to waver about as the heat from within escaped and was lost forever to the dominating chill.

In his room, Mark finished dressing, then walked softly out to the hall, went into the bathroom, closed the door, opened it again seventy seconds later, and shuffled to the living room. The air in the house was cool, and he shivered as he approached the huge front window, which faced north and was entirely free of the confusing ice paintings. He stood and looked upon the upper end of the Valley.

Across the dirt road was the playground, and beyond that was the elementary school. Further in the distance was another line of suburban homes which, like his own, were newly built. A tall stand of evergreens formed a natural boundary to his neighborhood, but further still, on what seemed like the edge of the world, towered the white peaks, so close to the boy, and yet so far away. And the centerpiece of all this, the glacier, lay at the very head of the Valley. Frozen solid it was, but also appearing as a white torrent, sweeping down from the huge icefield. Down here in the Valley, everything was green and white; up there, beyond that first row of imposing mountains, all was white and black, the granite nunataks biting through the ice in a setting almost unreal.

Mark felt lightheaded as he stood and looked upon the winter scene. He wanted to go out there and become a part of that wild paradise. He knew that he was forbidden to wander far from the house, although he had, more than once, drifted off to the woods and missed dinner. He blinked his eyes as he remembered a recent episode, when he had returned to find his meal cold, and Daddy angrily ordering him to eat it anyway and learn his lesson.

He shivered again, turned and walked silently about the rest of the house. He heard the oil furnace come to life, out in the utility room, and then hot air began to blow through the many ducts on the floor, creating a wind effect and stirring the rest of the family from their sleep.

Soon Mama came to the kitchen and began to prepare breakfast. Stephen appeared, dressed sloppily in faded corduroy jeans and a mottled sweatshirt that was on backwards. Not a word was spoken. Mark watched the proceedings, a carbon copy of last Saturday, and the one before that. The rattling of pots and pans, the breakfast dishes brought out and set upon the maple dining table, and the sound of margarine beginning to sizzle. The baby was now awake, and her mufflings could be heard in the master bedroom. Mama rushed about, getting the silverware, going to see about Amy, and starting the eggs, never asking for help from the boys, who looked on as stone statues. The rushing of water from the small bathroom made it clear that Daddy was up now as well, preparing to join the others.

Mark glanced at the clock on the kitchen stove, and his eyes widened as he realized the time. He had finally learned the hand positions and what they meant. It was late in the morning, and his day was nearly a quarter over with. He sniffed the eggs, the toast, and the bacon, wondering just what he would do once he was finished eating. He could stay inside and read the books once more. He had brought them from school yesterday, had read them to Mama and Daddy, and he had to take them back on Monday. He could go out and try once again to build an igloo. The snow was much harder now, and Daddy had said that it could be cut into square blocks. But he frowned on these two ideas. He wanted to go outside, not just by the house, but to *travel*, not remain stuck in the yard, the snow there already marked to the furthest corner by his footprints.

Now it was breakfast time. Daddy came in, and they all sat at the big table. Amy was in her spruce highchair, which Daddy had completed a month ago. They ate and talked about the beautiful day outside—what a deep blue sky, too bad it wasn't summer and warm enough for a picnic! Mark chewed his bacon, noting that it wasn't the hickory-smoked kind that he liked so much, but stayed out of the conversation. He was usually quiet at the table, concentrating on the food in front of him, answering only when he was spoken to.

Of course, his thoughts were quite expansive, as he sat there, but they were also very much private. He looked down at his plate. On it was two remaining strips of bacon, a heap of scrambled eggs, and two triangles of toast, both of which were partially eaten. The fork was in his left hand, where it belonged, but it was no longer conveying food to his mouth. He reached down with it and began to poke at the eggs. Piled high on the right side of his plate, they became a mountain, with prominent ridges and a steep face dropping away toward his bacon. And now another metamorphosis, as the two strips of meat were pushed together, then slid along until they bumped the yellow mountain. The fork separated the strips at one end to form a V-shape.

The mountain was on the sea, and he had just created a narrow inlet, a fjord, a safe harbor. The toast became two islands out there in the ocean, as if to hide the bay from all but the most inquisitive. And the fork, traveling along the plate on its tines, was a ship, guided by a captain who knew something exciting must lay beyond the low islands. The ship zigzagged through them, discovered the fjord at last, and sailed right up the inlet to the base of the steep mountain, anchoring near the beach as the sun began to set far to the west, over near where Stephen was, and ....

"Mark!!"

He looked up and saw Mama glaring at him. And he was angry; whispering a goodbye to the little world in front of him, he shoved his fork into the mountain and began to eat it. The fjord was next, and finally the islands were gone. He finished his meal in silence, then stood up and announced that he wanted to go out for a walk.

"And I won't go far," he added. "I want to go all the way around the school, and see how long it takes me."

"Okay, but put your coat on, all right? I don't want you out very long, Mark. It's really cold out there today." And Mama gave him a look which told him he had better not forget the last time he was late coming home. He turned away, to prevent her from seeing his lips form the reply.

In the furnace room, he put on the green rubber boots he had received for Christmas, then reached for his heaviest jacket. After snapping it closed around him and drawing the hood, he put on his wool gloves. Just as he reached for the back door knob, Mama called out to him, reminding him to stay within the neighborhood.

The knob was cold, even through his gloves. He took a long breath, opened the door, and stepped onto the porch. It was coated with a sheet of ice, but Daddy had thrown sand on the wooden steps to make the footing more secure. Mark crunched to the front gate and into the driveway, walked past the station wagon, and stood in the middle of the road. The drive was unpaved and full of chuckholes, which looked like tiny craters under the packed snow. Mark turned right and followed the lane in a half-circle around his school. The frost bit at him, and his breath came out in a steam which rose upward, dissipating in the blue void above. He slipped often, in his rubber boots, and before long, his feet began to tingle with the cold.

On one side of the road was the ballpark, and on the other side was the woods. Its border was a frozen swamp, full of dead trunks which rose like skeletons out of the dark ice. The ice resembled frozen root beer, the water being irony to begin with, and the ground below, a rich humus, contributed to the brown color as well. Mark walked on by, coming at last to the point where the road made a sharp bend to the left and ran along the far side of the school building. The woods, and Thunder Mountain, were at his back, and he faced the western side of the Valley, where only a line of shrugging hills separated this glacial flatland from the saltwater.

He came to the front of the school, his mind having been almost a total blank to this point. He had no idea how long he had been walking, only that he had been very conscious of the cold air and the beauty of the winter scenery around him. As he came to the next bend in the road, however, he saw some tracks leading through a break in the woods. They ran along a narrow clearing, where a line of power poles marched off toward the loop road.

Mark stopped and peered at the little pathway through the forest. He hadn't noticed it before, and was immediately overcome with an urge to explore and discover. It couldn't possibly take more than a couple of minutes to follow that path to its obvious end, and he hadn't been gone that long, had he? He started off, over the pile of graded snow at the shoulder of the road, and onto the hardpack trail. Within moments, he was alone in the woods, cut off from the school, the houses, and the streets, with only the power poles and the footprints as evidence of any human activity. It seemed colder and very quiet, there among the hemlocks, and he stepped carefully along the frozen path, coming closer to the loop road, which he was not allowed to cross.

He was halfway there, with only a couple hundred feet to go, when a figure appeared at the far end, heading in his direction. Mark's first thought was that the forest seemed to shrink back and take on secondary importance to the newcomer, who now commanded center stage. And then a wave of fright passed through him as he watched the figure approach. It was a stranger, and there was no one nearby to help him, should the stranger turn out to be hostile. But as the distance between the two lessened, so did the size of the oncoming human, and Mark soon realized the figure was that of a boy, a boy no larger than himself. When they were ten feet apart, they both slowed their pace, then stopped and sort of studied each other.

"Hi! It's really cold out, isn't it?"

Mark looked at the boy's face. It was red, except for the nose, which was a pale white. He shrugged and put his weight on one foot, then the other. Finally he said, in a small voice, "I know. But I like to come out anyway. I live over there, by the school." He waved his mittened hand.

"Yeah? I go there and I'm in the first grade. My teacher is Mrs. Harrigan."

"My class is right across the hall from yours. I've never seen you on the playground."

"I'm just out here, walking around. I don't even have mittens on. It's really cold, isn't it? My mom said I would be cold. We just moved here last month, from California."

The boys continued to study each other, and Mark noticed, for the first time, that the footprints he had been following were small, all of them probably made by the boy he was now having a conversation with.

"What's your name?" the kid from California asked.

"It's Mark. What's yours?"

"My name is … Jerry. Well, really it's James. My dad's name is James, but everyone calls him Jerry, and me too, so that's what you'll have to call me."

Mark wasn't listening very closely. He was desperately trying to think of a way to get some control of this, but he didn't know how to begin. His own sentences were coming in short, direct fashion, and he didn't want to talk to Jerry this way.

"What do you like to do?"

Jerry said, "I like to play baseball and basketball, and I like to make kites with my dad, and to ride my bike. In the summer, I mean. But I really like mountains, more than anything. I love to look at the mountains around here. Don't you? What do you like to do, anyway?"

Mark looked into Jerry's eyes. He answered, in a quavering voice that he could not control, "I like mountains, too. No one else has ever told me that they like mountains before. I thought I was the only one who did."

Jerry became excited, and said, "You know which one I like the best, of all the mountains here? Come on, I'll show you. Come on, to the road!" And he whirled and stumbled off, yelling back over his shoulder for Mark to follow. And Mark, wildly intrigued with the mystery of which mountain it would be, ran after him.

They came to the loop road, and the trees fell back. As the towering white peaks burst into view, Jerry stopped and pointed. Mark looked in the direction of the outstretched arm, and as he did, Jerry said, in a proud voice, "That one! That's the one I like. My dad showed it to me right after we moved here, and I think it's the best mountain in the whole world!"

Off to Mark's right, the long ridge of Thunder Mountain ran north, straight into the base of another, taller peak situated near the front of the glacier. But beyond them, several other peaks could be seen, peaks that were not visible from Mark's house. From this angle, they flared upward, a savage meeting of rock and sky, and it was toward the very highest one that Jerry pointed.

Mark felt a shudder, as he too stared at the peak. He thought he had seen it before, but had never heard it being pronounced such a monumental sight. As he continued to gaze at the sharply rising, black and white behemoth, he felt a certain chill which was totally unassociated with the air around him. He saw the mountain, truly saw it, for the first time. And finally, after the long moment of gazing, he tore his eyes away and looked at Jerry, who seemed to be in a hypnotic trance as he gazed upon the distant summit.

"Jerry. Do you want to climb it some day?"

The boy looked at him. "Climb it? I've never been on a mountain before. I want to climb it, but I never could. Look at it, up there! It's so far away, and it's so hard to climb up. No way could we get up there."

And suddenly Mark knew he should get home, and quickly. "I have to go, or I'm going to be in trouble. I'll see you on the playground before school, all right?"

"All right. Bye, Mark". Jerry turned and began to walk along the shoulder of the loop road. Mark watched him get smaller with the distance, until he could no longer see him. He turned and started back through the woods, looking up at *the* mountain until it was hidden behind the tops of tall, silent evergreens. He thought about Jerry, and about what the two had said to each other. At first it had been like any meeting of boys, but then the talk of the favorite peak had entered in, and this had fascinated him. He relived the whole thing as he headed home, and decided he would look for Jerry on the playground before school on Monday.

He reached the ballpark and looked back up the Valley for another possible view, but the entire line of peaks was now gone, hidden behind the imposing wall of Thunder Mountain, also one of Mark's favorites; he lived in its very shadow and had longed to walk upon its summit. Daddy had hiked up to the top a few weeks after they had arrived in town, bringing home a fantastic adventure story as well as a multitude of aches and bruises. Climbing mountains must be fun, Mark decided, right then and there. Someday, he decided, if Mama let him, he would climb up Thunder Mountain, and then, when he was old enough, he would take on that mammoth pinnacle of rock and ice that was lurking beyond.

His home was in front of him, and he swung open the gate; it squeaked in the dry cold. He jumped up to the back porch, turned, and looked at the snow-covered neighborhood one last time. Then he stepped inside the house, feeling the warmth rush at him. Mama was there in the furnace room, doing laundry, and she turned away from the washing machine as he entered.

"Have a good walk?" she asked him. Mark nodded, then stopped and turned to her.

"I saw a boy, and we talked. He's in another class at the school. His name is Jerry. You know what we told each other? We said that we liked mountains more than anything, and that we wished we could climb the one that ... well, you can't see it from here. You have to go up to the loop road, and then you can." He stopped himself, for he had just made a blunder. He looked at Mama's eyes for a sign of disappointment.

"Oh. You went that far, huh?" she drawled out. "You didn't cross, I hope. Well, you weren't gone that long, I guess. But your ears certainly look red enough! One of these days, they're going to freeze up and fall off from being so cold."

Mark got up the nerve to grin, and Mama spoke again. "You want to climb a mountain, do you? What will you think of next, anyway? Do you know how to climb a mountain? I didn't think so. You better watch out what you get into your head, or you're going to find yourself in a jam someday where no one will be able to get you back alive."

She was teasing, he told himself, as he removed his outdoor things. But then Daddy's voice came from the dining room, and Mark headed in that direction.

"Heck, Mark knows how to climb, don't you now, Mark?" Daddy was at the table, a pile of bills and canceled checks in front of him. He looked at Mark through his thick-rimmed bifocals. "I told you we'd go climb up Thunder sometime. I suppose we will this summer, if you really want to. Sound exciting?"

Mark's expression was one of total agreement. His mind was spinning in a pleasurable way, as he pictured himself and his new friend undertaking what until now would seem the impossible. He *would* climb up that big peak someday, he knew he would. He felt a destiny of sorts, one he could not explain in words or thought. The great adventure had been set in motion; was already beginning.

§

For the next few weeks, the weather remained clear and cold. Bone-chilling winds tore through the Valley, and school recess was often held indoors, something the first-graders loved. Mark and Jerry met and visited whenever possible, though it was not easy to carry on an interclass friendship except during those few outdoor play periods.

In his own class, Mark had numerous friends, most of whom were intrigued by his learning ability. He received the highest marks in spelling, arithmetic, and language arts, although his "conduct" grade was questionable. He knew that he interrupted the teacher too much. He knew that he sometimes gave other students the impression that he was smarter than they were.

He and his classmates had been advised on the grading system shown on their report cards. The letter "E" was for excellent, "S" was satisfactory, and "U" was of course unsatisfactory. Mark did not like the sound of the word that began with "U". He had heard whispers that several of these meant that a student would "flunk", and would have to take first grade all over again. Could that really happen to him—flunk—just for sometimes talking out of turn?

The school year continued on, slowly it seemed to Mark, who began to watch the hands on the big clock more and more every day. He had quickly learned how to tell the time instantly by looking at their relative positions, the angle they formed, rather than searching out the numerals that stood out boldly around the perimeter of the circle. He began to close his ears to Mrs. Carpenter when he felt he already knew the answers needed to "pass". He figured he was intelligent, but no more so than he thought the other children should be.

Stephen was in the second grade, but Mark and his older brother never saw each other during the school day; the scheduling arrangement for lunch, recess, and P.E. kept them apart completely. They did, however, return home at the same hour, telling each other how their day had gone, and repeating their stories to Mama, who smiled and tended to Amy. One day, Stephen had arrived home a few minutes after Mark, with his coat torn, announcing that he had just been in a big fight with two others in his class. There had been quite a rhubarb about that when Daddy got home, and a subsequent phone call, which the boys, in their room, were not allowed to hear. Mark had thought to himself that Stephen was about to get a "U". Soon, however, the incident was forgotten, and neither of the boys had any trouble of that sort thereafter.

Winter melted into spring, and as the ice and snow disappeared, Daddy became increasingly busy with his work. He explained that lots of new road construction meant spending much time in the field, and he was frequently missing meals and sometimes entire weekends. The family would sit on the front porch during the cool evenings of April, watching and listening for snowslides to come sweeping down the almost vertical west face of Thunder Mountain, which sounded just like its name when one of the awesome, blistering white torrents poured from the heights. Mark would gaze at them through Daddy's binoculars for what seemed like hours, feeling the power as the strong vibrations rumbled through his body, waves that seemed to shake the entire Valley.

One night, Mark was awakened rudely, as light filled the bedroom and Daddy entered. Stephen sat up, wiping his eyes as Daddy said, in a loud whisper, "Come and see this, and be real quiet".

Wordlessly, the boys followed him through the darkened hallway, past the kitchen, and into the furnace room. Mama stood at the back window, and the curtains were pulled away just enough to show a small section of the yard. Mark was ahead of Stephen; he was the first to peer out into the night, and the glow from the neighbor's back porch lamp was enough for him to make out the shape of a black bear cub, struggling to push over the Nilsson's garbage barrel, which was full of half-burned refuse.

Mark's eyes opened wide, as he had never seen a wild bear, and it looked to him as if it weighed a thousand pounds. He told Daddy so, and Daddy just grinned and said, "More like seventy. It's probably a year old."

Stephen pushed Mark aside and had a long look. "Can we go outside and see it better?" he asked. Mama looked about to faint, and Daddy said no, that it would scare the cub away, and besides, its mother was probably watching from the edge of the woods. The family continued to take turns at the window as the little bear pushed and shoved at the barrel, which was an old fifty-five-gallon drum, likely twice the weight of the cub. Finally Daddy said the show was over, and he rattled the back door knob. Instantly the cub whirled around and began to lope toward the forest cover. Within seconds, it had disappeared into the night shadows.

What a thrill that was, Mark decided. He had something great for Show and Tell this time! He went back to his bed, but he was too excited to sleep. He and Stephen whispered about what they had seen, and they decided to get up in the middle of tomorrow night, to see if the cub was there once again.

The next morning, Mark stood in front of his class and told the wonderful tale to the spellbound audience. Indeed, he painted quite a picture, until Mrs. Carpenter finally raised a hand and stopped him. All through the day, the other children looked at him and continued to ask him questions about what had happened. Did it have huge claws and sharp fangs? Was it really a monster? Did it roar like the one on the Walt Disney movie? Mark felt good about his adventure, and he told them, "Just wait. I'll see it again tonight."

He and Stephen made their plans, agreeing that Stephen, who was always getting up in the middle of the night anyway, should wake his younger brother. Mark had slept for several hours, without dream, when Stephen shook him.

They got up and crept through the house, as they had the previous night, only this time it was so much more an adventure because they were alone. They reached the furnace room and just stood waiting for a moment. Then Stephen took a step forward and reached for the white, silky curtain that covered the back window. "I'll bet it's there," he said in a shaky tone. Mark thought he would ask his brother later about where he'd learned the word "bet"; right now, he felt his throat closing, and he stood on tiptoes, anxious for the first possible view. Stephen's fingers touched the curtain, and as he began to draw it aside, an explosive *WHACK!!* ripped through the night air and shuddered the window. Stephen yanked back his hand, and Mark jumped off the tile floor. They looked at each other, and simultaneously, they screamed.

Lights illuminated the hallway, and the boys heard Mama and Daddy talking to each other. And then their parents came rushing toward them, flipping every switch within reach and setting the house ablaze with photons. "What was *that*?" Daddy asked nobody in particular as he threw open the back door and stepped onto the porch. Mama, her face ashen, was right behind him, paying no attention to the frightened boys, hardly noticing that Mark and his brother were even there. She moved to join Daddy on the porch; both wore only their night robes. Mark was frozen solid, even though the indoor temperature was just right.

"It was a shot, I know it was!" Daddy yelled out. Mama gasped. And Stephen, his face shaped to fear and disbelief, started to bawl.

"They ... shot the bear cub ... didn't they?" he managed to wheeze.

Daddy turned and looked at Stephen, as if seeing him for the first time. And his eyes traveled to Mark, who stood very stiff, lips unable to move, mind racing. The boy saw pictures of a lifeless black hulk on the ground, somewhere in the yard. His eyes were wide, and he felt a lead ball in his stomach.

Now they could hear other voices, coming from behind the house next door. One voice in particular could be heard above all the others, a man's voice, and his words came as a frenzied rattling.

"Where ... can't see ... and hurry up, will you ... I think ... yes, I got it all right ... and just look ...."

Off to the right, beyond the Nilsson's yard, moved the ghostly beams of flashlights and gas lanterns. Mark, forcing his legs to respond, peeped out the window, stared at the many lights, and saw a troop of men walking quickly toward the garbage barrel.

"First shot! And I'll tell you, if you hadn't, then our good Lord would not have saved a single child ...."

Daddy whirled around, his face a mask of complete frustration. "Both of you get to bed right now, and I mean it!" he shot at the two frightened boys, who immediately took off for their room. Mark jumped into his bed, covered himself well, and curled into a tight ball. He lay in the dark, listening to Stephen's whimpering, and caught the faintest of conversation from the back porch. After a moment, he heard Mama raise her voice in anger, then the door slammed, and the lights in the hallway were turned off. And although he was wide awake, he managed to close his eyes, and before he knew it, he was asleep.

The fact didn't really set into him until the morning. As he was pulling himself out of bed, he remembered the entire incident, and after dressing quickly, he walked out to the kitchen to see if Mama and Daddy were talking about it. When he saw them, he slowed his step, moving silently to his chair at the dining table. His parents looked sullen and very tired. Mark began to feel his initial reaction to the rifle shot coming back to him. His heart sped up, and his head was like a hot air balloon. Stephen came to the table and joined the others. No one spoke, and Mark ate his corn flakes, which tasted today like sawdust. Mama got up, mumbled something about Amy, and headed down the hall.

He had to go out to the furnace room, to get his things on for school. Walking past the window, with its white, silky curtain, he wondered, in a nightmarish sort of way, what he would see if the shades were pulled back.

And then he stopped and went rigid. He heard a voice that wasn't exactly a voice. It was as though an entire series of thought communications filled his head, and he was being asked to listen, very closely.

His lips moved, as he silently answered this unseen entity.

I know, I couldn't keep this terrible thing from happening. You say everything is all right, and you say I will learn from this.

But I don't know who you are.

The paralysis was over. He got on his boots, his sweater, and his cap, and then moved back to the kitchen to get his lunch box. He was joined by his older brother, and without a word, the two left the house through the front door and started for the playground. It was filling rapidly, the children screaming and laughing, rushing about and playing, waiting for the first bell to ring. Mark walked through the crowd, looking for Jerry, but couldn't find him.

And at Show and Tell, someone remembered, asking him if he had seen the bear last night. Mark was about to answer, then changed his mind and stopped for a moment. Finally his mouth opened, and he whispered, "No."

That little squirrel, the past summer. Mark remembered it well. There was a lesson there, although Mark still wasn't sure what it was. But this was something else entirely, it had to be. He asked himself, why was it so different? Well, because someone had shot the cub for a reason that was absolutely crazy. As if it would have eaten some child! Mark could have run it off with a wave of his hand, Daddy had proven that.

He thought of the mother bear, who must have watched the entire thing from the cover of the forest, unable to come charging, certain to meet a bullet herself. He would go into the woods, find her someday, and apologize for what had happened. He promised himself that he would, certain that the strange, voiceless voice had suggested he do so. And with that thought in mind, he settled down and focused on the big clock above the classroom door.

In the evening, he was watching television, and he could see perfectly through the huge front window. It was a cloudless night, and the black shapes of the mountains rose up in the distance. He was concentrating on the program but also glancing up now and then, as if expecting a change in the distance. And presently, as if by magic, he was rewarded. A thin line of silver, brilliant and shimmering, took form over the glacier. It began to weave back and forth, and as it did so, changed to green and yellow. Soon, other curtains of light appeared and joined the first, in a kind of cosmic dance; the entire northern sky was suddenly ablaze with the vertical, wavering planes of fire. Mark rose and walked to the window, hypnotized. He put his nose on the glass and stared, wide-eyed, at the scene in front of him.

It was beautiful. Daddy had told him about the Northern Lights, and now he was seeing them for himself. He watched the drifting towers of luminosity fade in and out, blend and mix, in a quiet symphony of absolute splendor. Mama came into the room, and Mark gestured; she saw the Lights too, and called for Daddy and Stephen to come. Soon, four of them were watching the silent display, and Mark felt bad that Amy was asleep, and anyway too young to understand.

After the auroras faded and disappeared, Mark turned off the television. He walked to his room, and suddenly tired, got on his bed. He let out a long breath, then took off his clothes and dropped them onto the plain brown carpet. He lay down, pulled up the sheet and blanket, and closed his eyes, the Northern Lights fresh in his mind, the multi-colored waves playing and replaying. Sleep came easily that night, and he did not think about the bear cub again for a long, long time.

CHAPTER THREE

The shadow of Thunder Mountain spread over the eastern half of the Valley. Day had dawned, but the sun was still rising behind the long, towering ridge, and a thin layer of fog hovered over the quiet, sheltered neighborhoods. Every so often, the silence was broken for just a moment, as tree swallows emitted high-pitched tweets during their swooping maneuvers.

At this hour of the morning, the natural odor of summer growth and greenery could not be detected. In some ways, it seemed as though the living earth was still pondering whether to expend energy or hit the snooze button. The air was cool and damp, and when Daddy opened the back door and stepped onto the porch, he slipped, then jumped to the ground to avoid falling.

Mark and Stephen were right behind him. Cautiously, they stepped down to the gravel, and without words, they started along the path to the back fence. They were dressed in rough outdoor wear, and Daddy had a small rucksack on his back. He also had his .22 rifle, while the boys carried nothing but light heads. They were hiking up Thunder Mountain today, in the middle of the boys' summer vacation.

Making a circle around the sloppy, undeveloped clearing behind the yard, they started down a narrow, overgrown roadway that curved to the west and intersected another, upon which they had traveled the previous year, on the squirrel hunt. Mark thought about that as he walked. Brian would have loved going with them, he was certain, but the Hendricks family had moved to Sitka during the winter, to set up a new construction business. Mark wished that Jerry could be along on the adventure too, but Mrs. Floyd had put her foot down immediately when the boys appealed.

Too bad, he decided, hustling to catch up with Stephen and Daddy. Nothing could lessen the intensity of the great day at hand, and his mind was once again racing, as he thought about the climb that was forthcoming, of the snow and the rocks, and the steep places where one had to use a rope. Of course, Daddy was not carrying any rope, so maybe it wasn't really going to be that way at all. But, from where their house sat, the very top of the mountain could not be seen, and who could know what kind of obstacles lay between them and the rocky summit? He walked along, abreast of Daddy and Stephen, his tongue exploring the gap where he'd lost a tooth the previous week, and he told himself that whatever lay in store for him, he was ready for it.

Daddy had brought a few of those rocks back with him when he had hiked up the ridge solo, and in touching them, Mark had felt a surface that seemed almost outworldly. He couldn't wait to get up there and touch them again, in their natural element, to lay on the ground with them, so high up there in the sky! It was going to be a long day, a very long day indeed, following a trail up through the forest and beyond, to a place from where he would be able to see the islands and inlets, the peaks of the icefield, and the houses in the Valley, which Daddy said would look like tiny matchboxes.

After a time, the gravel road opened up into a field, and to their right and left, a collection of rundown shacks and shanties sat on rotted wood foundations. Just beyond, an old logging road jutted off, and Daddy explained that this was where the hike would truly start; the trail began at the end of this logging roadway. They had already walked a mile and a half, following Thunder Mountain toward its lower, forested end, which stuck out into the marsh flats near the airport and the highway to downtown. Now, Daddy said, they would cut back, following the trail from the logging road up the rising humps and hummocks to treeline, and from there, hike up the grassy slopes all the way to the top.

Mark knew nothing of forested humps and hummocks, nor of any grassy slopes beyond. What came to mind, as the three started up the logging road, was a windswept height and icy rock. After all, he had seen pictures of mountain peaks in a book at school, with flags sticking up and the people dressed in heavy outfits, their arms raised in triumph. And look how *he* was dressed! A sweatshirt, jeans, and small hiking boots. No gloves, no hat, and no pack. A bit disappointing, perhaps, that it wasn't going to be like the pictures, but to hear Daddy tell it … and besides, Daddy had climbed to the top last year dressed in a similar manner, and had come down with enough stories to last a lifetime, so there had to be something grand to look forward to.

"I ate snow for water", Daddy had said to them, long before. "It was cloudy, and I was up there in the mist, unable to see thirty feet in front of me. At one point, up there in the meadows, I slipped and before I knew it, I slid all the way down a grassy hill into a small hump at the bottom. Almost broke my tailbone. What a day!"

He had gone on to describe the trail itself, and how it was marked by red ribbons, to show the way. He explained that a simple red band around a tree trunk, or a single tassel hanging from a branch, meant that the trail kept on straight, whereas a double loop and tassel was a signal to change course and head in the direction of the tassel. "There's even a blue mitten hanging on a small tree up there, to help mark the path," Daddy had chuckled, and Mark thought it was very funny, now hoping to see it when they passed.

They crossed over a slow-moving stream, on a wooden bridge that was worm-eaten and full of holes. Daddy said it was called Jordan Creek, and that it ran along the base of the mountain as far north as the woods behind their house. Up ahead was a clearing, and a sign on a tree announced, according to Daddy, the National Forest boundary. Many logs were strewn about, some of them absolutely enormous in size, with new green shoots growing straight up from their moss-covered surfaces. Mark figured that, in a hundred years or so, there would be a line of trees standing there, and just as that idea settled in, he saw that very thing in the distance—an incredibly straight line of trees. He pointed this out to Daddy and Stephen, and they all agreed that the trees had grown from an ancient, fallen trunk. He wondered why he hadn't noticed such a phenomenal thing before, seeing that these lines of trees were now just about everywhere they looked. And Daddy said that during the war, trees were cut here, at this old logging site, even though it was already part of a protected forest area.

It seemed now that the lower end of the ridge was directly before them. Quite suddenly, a path appeared and led off to the right, with a faded pink ribbon hanging limp from the branch of a small willow. Mark felt his excitement growing, and he imagined that someone, long ago, had placed these trail markers just for him. It was an invitation to follow the old, worn trail upward into the soaring heights. Daddy led the way, and the three of them started up the gently graded path. More ribbons could be seen in the distance, but most of them were unnecessary, as the trail could not possibly have been lost. The trail continued upward, straight as an arrow for a time, then bore off to the left and intersected a small creek. There it ended, and now it was obvious that the only way to go was up the steep, rushing brook. A number of boards had been laid across the creek bed, and they served as a staircase that carried the hikers ever higher. Mark had a sudden, very funny idea that they were climbing a water mountain, with a heavenly spring at the top. He wasn't about to tell this to Daddy and Stephen.

"There's a surprise up ahead!" Daddy shouted, above the noise of the falling water. "See if you can guess what it might be."

"A big waterfall!" Stephen yelled back with confidence. "With a cave behind it!"

Mark didn't see Daddy grin, but he knew that it wasn't a waterfall, there would be no cave, and that Daddy was smiling. Just as he was forming his own idea about what lay ahead, the staircase rivulet leveled out into a pool, and Mark saw two other things at the same time. The sudden uprising of the mountain, directly in front of them, and also the cause of the round, glassy pool. It was a wooden dam, some fifty feet long and ten feet in height, with a great collection of dead branches stuck in its upper spillways. It was old and rotted, like the Jordan Creek bridge down below, but it was a fascinating sight, here in the woods, at the base of Thunder Mountain.

They spent several minutes picking about the structure. Daddy said the dam must have been built to run a generator for the logging camp down below, and perhaps even supplied electricity for a sawmill. Now, sand had clogged the spillways, and the water trickled between the weathered planks without a sound. Indeed, the entire scene was one of eerie silence, the sounds of the rushing brook having faded in the lower distance. Mark felt a shiver passed through him, and he momentarily forgot that there was still a mountain to climb, as he stood there and viewed the old dam.

But then Daddy adjusted the strap on his rifle, slung it over his shoulder, and signaled the way forward once more. At the left corner of the dam, in shadow, was a ribbon, and the path once more became evident. It led straight up, over a moss-covered knoll, and into stands of tall, thin Sitka spruce. Markers could once again be seen in the distance, and they were generously placed. At every right and left twist in the rising trail, at every little bottleneck between stumps or fallen logs, and sometimes, in places of absolutely no significance whatsoever, the red ribbons appeared. Daddy remarked that the person who had hung the plastic strips had certainly been determined to have all those who followed remain comfortable in not becoming lost, as he had never seen such an established trail before. Mark thought about that. It was an "established" trail, he told himself. He liked big words, and would never forget this one.

It was dark here, on the mountainside. Still early in the morning, the air was cool, and there was no breeze at all. As he walked behind his brother, Mark began once more to look at his surroundings, with a growing interest in the natural construction job that was sliding past on either side of him. The spruce here were thin, without flaring stumps, and the bark on the hemlocks had become a dark brown, the texture much more flattened in contrast to the ribbed bark of the western variety, down there in the Valley. The ground was covered by thick, golden moss, itself a myriad of tiny plants, some with green, triple leaflets, and others with yellow stalks as thin as a strand of hair. The blueberry bushes were small and mostly without fruit, as the lighting was poor on this, the steep west side of the mountain. At every small ravine, cut through by a tumbling brook, there was a stand of devil's club, the spines of which covered the trunks, the stalks, and the undersides of the huge leaves, the latter resembling, Daddy said, those of bigleaf maples. Fallen logs were everywhere, covered with the moss, and Mark remembered a term Daddy had used before, in describing a scene such as this.

"A devil's playground," he had called it. "Large sandy areas in the desert are often called devil's playgrounds, and so are places in the woods, where everything appears so old. Everywhere you look, fallen logs, some of them a yard across, and every one of them covered by a blanket of thick moss, and the ground also buried in muskeg. All around the edge of these places, there are stands of devil's club, which is exactly what you'd expect, I guess! You could run through such an area, jump around, fall, and never get hurt—until you struck a sharp rock underneath the velvety green floor. They say it's where the devil plays at night, when no one is watching. A devil's playground."

Mark had wondered just why on earth the devil would want to play. Today, something told him that was indeed possible, if the setting was just right … yes, where sin had yet to be committed.

The trail carried them along the side of the ridge, in a forest so dense that a view out over the Valley was impossible. Every so often, the terrain would open up into one of the "devil's playgrounds", where the fallen logs dominated, and the trail ran through, over, and sometimes under the rotting giants. It was a rainforest, a northern, almost boreal type of jungle, and Mark was quite caught up in the wet luxury of it all. As the hikers came to a fallen log that was actually part of the trail, spanning a shallow ravine, Mark's eyes were not looking where they should have been. He disliked crossing logs, especially thin ones with the bark fallen away, exposing the slippery pith. But here he was watching the hemlocks, with their lazy, turned-over tops that made wild designs and patterns against the filmy gray sky. The fog over the Valley was thinning out, and soon the natural ceiling would be a deep blue ….

Suddenly, his foot hit a spot of loose bark, his knees buckled, and he let out a screech that came more as a loud hiccup. He halfway fell, halfway jumped from the log, then landed on his side in the small ravine. A spiny leaf of devil's club slapped him in the face, and he yelped.

Daddy and Stephen whipped around and stared into the little ravine. Mark, his face covered with dirt and tingling from the needling touch of the leaf, stared back, and Daddy, instead of rushing down to see if he was all right, began to laugh.

"Better watch where you're going next time, or you might just find yourself down there in Jordan Creek!"

Slowly, carefully, Mark picked himself up from the bed of moss and climbed back to the trail. Scowling quietly at the slimy log, he fell in once more behind the others, and the hike continued.

The trail inclined more steeply. And now it was a most uninteresting path that Mark followed. He was upset about what had just happened, and he looked at nothing more than the heels of Stephen's boots. To their right, the mountain continued to sweep upward, as though telling the hikers that however high they walked, the earth would rise higher still. A break in the forest cover appeared in front of them, and they stopped to rest and to get their first view out over the Valley and beyond.

A few buildings were visible from this altitude, and they looked ever so tiny. Stephen asked Daddy how far up they had climbed, and Daddy said, after thinking for a moment, that they had probably hiked upward about one thousand feet. They could see Lynn Canal on the western horizon, the saltwater looking silver and flat as it made a sharp border with the greenness of the mainland. Sitting down, they gazed out upon the lowlands and drank water from the canteen Daddy had produced from his rucksack. Mark imagined that he was no longer on Thunder Mountain, but instead on the big mountain he loved, the one Jerry had shown him on that day in January. He was climbing it, Jerry was with him, and they were taking a flag to the very summit, for all the world to see. He knew that he would be getting a good view of the big peaks today, and he hoped that when they got to the top, he would attain a marvelous head-on look at the snowy wonder that rose into space, a few miles from where he now sat.

His anger at falling off the log was soon gone, and so was the fixation on his brother's gray boots. After resting, the boys rose to their feet, anxious to continue, and Mark found himself in front, the result of a sweeping gesture on Daddy's part. He accepted the post eagerly, proud to be the new leader of this great adventure. Again he was drifting away; he was in charge of a multitude of pioneers who searched for a way through the mountains in hopes of reaching a land fit for settling. Here in the wild, it was dangerous, with all sorts of big animals and poisonous plants, and the size and steepness of the mountain ranges through which they were passing—it all added greatly to the hardships the band of travelers must endure. But, he would get them through, just as Daniel Boone had done. Late in the school year, Mrs. Carpenter had read them the story of the famous pioneer who led a party of migrants through something called Cumberland Gap, and now Mark was living it himself, in his sweatshirt and his little hiking boots.

There was a particularly treacherous area coming up! A steep gorge, with a two-inch wide path on which to walk. Below, a raging river, and from above, rocks flying past, whistling overhead and falling to the water, over a mile straight down! Actually, the trail was now passing some bushes which forced Mark toward the outer slope of the ridge, but his mind was making wonders of the situation. Halfway through the "obstacle", there was a rustling from behind a nearby bush, then something exploded out from it with a *swisssh!*

Mark jumped back, the river gorge and the falling rocks instantly gone, to the furthest corner of his mind, to another place and time. "What is it?" he asked Daddy in a trembling whisper. Daddy pushed ahead and took the rifle in his hands. "Grouse" he answered in a whisper of his own.

Mark had no idea what a grouse was. "Is it scared?"

Stephen looked at him, excited. "It's a bird," he informed his brother, trying to imitate Daddy's voice.

And it *was* a bird. It had kicked a hole through a pile of forest litter that was apparently its nest, startling the daydreaming boy. A female ruffed grouse came strutting out into the open, and as Mark watched it, Daddy took careful aim and shot the creature. Immediately after the loud report died away, there was a second rustling, and two younger grouse came flapping out through the hole in the nest and went airborne, out of sight among the trees.

"Rats," Daddy said, as he bent over the dead mother. "I didn't realize it had young ones. But they're old enough to fly, so I guess it's all right. She must have laid her eggs early in the season for them to be so grown up."

He took a plastic bag from his rucksack and put the grouse into it, announcing to the boys that Mom would cook it when they got home, and that it tasted rather like peppery, spicy chicken. Mark was unable to decide whether to be excited or uneasy. He thought to himself … okay, that's why Daddy had killed it. He hadn't killed for pleasure, or for the sake of being able to kill. Mark remembered the words.

Now the climb was turning into a hunting trip, Stephen pointed out. They were living off the land. Mark hated it when his brother looked at him while making profound statements. He could never figure out why Stephen had to make such a show of "pointing things out", as if he, Mark Nilsson, had no mind of his own.

Maybe, he decided, there were enough grouse on this trail to fill Daddy's pack, and when they got home, it would be a wild feast, just like Daniel Boone had enjoyed. Except, of course, Daniel Boone probably never did much eating at a dinner table.

The trail twisted and turned, finally angling off to the right, following the maze of red ribbons. Daddy pointed down the slope and said something about how one could walk through the woods behind their house and climb up to this point, intersecting the path right about here. Mark filed the information, thinking it might be useful someday. A new trail, perhaps. Maybe he would blaze it himself.

Something blue caught his eye, and at the same time, Daddy sang out, "There's our mitten!" It was stuck on a small hemlock, and appeared to be waving at them as they passed. They were on level ground now, but before them were more hills, the ridge creeping ever upward, toward the inevitable treeline. After a few short rises, however, the land began to slope away on both sides, and Mark knew they had gained the crest of the ridge. They were finally walking along the backbone of the mountain.

Another set of zigzags, and then something rather interesting lay before them. It was a small meadow, tilted at a sharp angle, through which the narrow path led. Daddy said, from behind Mark, that the first time he passed through, he had almost stepped on a field mouse while crossing the open stretch, and that he had been amazed that the creatures lived in this high meadow. Mark listened and kept his eyes on the ground, fearful he might squash one of the tiny animals. In a moment, they were at the upper end of the meadow, and a large, white patch of snow became visible, in the bottom of a long, narrow depression. They were getting up into the heights at last, Mark thought to himself.

He jumped down into the marshy trough, expecting to hit a surface of packed snow. Instead, his legs disappeared into a seemingly bottomless white slop, and before he could let out a squeak, the entire patch of snow began to slide down the trough, carrying the boy with it. Mark grabbed onto the weeds that stuck out of the soft, moist earth, and he climbed out of the snow, which began to slow its downward motion, coming to a halt several yards above the steep drop-off to the left.

His pants were soaked, and he shook them to dislodge the many balls of slush that were caught inside the hems. Daddy and Stephen picked their way across the depression, and Mark took the rear once again, walking clumsily and feeling totally disoriented. At the top of the next hill, Daddy turned and spoke.

"Now don't you think that was a pretty sorry move you made back there?"

Mark hung his head and studied the tiny clover plants that rimmed the edge of the knoll. After a moment, he looked up and declared that he was sure that the snow was firm, and that it wouldn't have slid.

"Well, if you're going to do much hiking, you better learn to watch out for such things," Daddy answered. "Remember, Nature doesn't act the same way here as it does in your backyard. Understand what I mean?" Mark stared at him, then turned his head.

If only Daddy knew. *If only he knew how much I know. I wish I had let that snow carry me right off the edge, right out of their sight. I would have slid down into a ravine and come to a stop somewhere on the face of the mountain, probably when I hit a log. And then I would be alone, and although they would look for me, I might stay lost for a long time—long enough to belong to the mountain, and no longer to Mama and Daddy. I would live down there forever, in that ravine.*

Perhaps another child's face would have puffed out. There wasn't the slightest hint of anger in Mark's expression, and he looked up at Stephen and Daddy. And then he said, in a low voice, "I'll stay away from the steep snow".

He knew his surroundings had spoken to him. And he was convinced of the credibility of his silent response. He couldn't understand why, but that didn't seem to matter.

Daddy nodded, then turned and led the way up into a new stand of trees. They were small, stunted, and looked as though they had seen years of wind gusts and heavy snowstorms. The ridge was narrowing, and the sun, rising high in the southeast, now began to shower its rays upon the ground, which in turn began to warm the air around the climbers. That signaled the rise of mosquitoes, by the millions, from the ground to the air. They moved in clouds, all around the heads of the three hot and dirty humans. They got into Mark's eyes, nose, and mouth. Daddy swore as they walked into an especially thick swarm, at the edge of a marshy thicket. He dropped the rucksack to the ground, yanked open the main compartment, and pulled out a can of insect repellent.

"About time we put on a little of this stuff," he said as he waved the can around in an effort to spread the hovering mass. For the next few moments, the sound of hissing spray filled the air, as the hikers covered themselves with the awful-smelling contents, Stephen soaking his blond head with the white mist. Daddy took back the repellent, began to replace the cap, and then straightened and fired a salvo at the cloud of insects above them, a tactic that didn't work, of course, but which sent the two boys reeling with laughter. Daddy, also beginning to snicker at this act, tossed the can into his pack, and they were ready to go again.

Ahead, the trees were thinning out. Mark's legs were beginning to feel the strain of climbing, but he felt a new, second wind coming to him as he got his first glimpse of the high meadows. All during the early morning trip through the dark forest, the world had seemed small and dense, the very air itself pressing in on him. Now, with things beginning to open up, he felt himself almost lifting right off the ground, and his eyes grew wide as the incredible spaces and immeasurable distances registered in his mind. A last remnant of trees, and then there were no more; they were falling away below, and the amber hills, spotted with snow and a few green shoots, were in front of them.

Stephen began to wander off to one side, and as Daddy called him back, the boy stopped and pointed at a small patch of snow. "Look at this", he called over to the others. Mark followed Daddy to where Stephen was, and they looked at the patch of white. A line of tracks ran through the middle, and Daddy bent to examine them.

"Deer," he announced at length. "See the two curved lines, like crescent moons? And the little round marks behind them? Those are the dewclaws. I was hoping we'd see them. I didn't know if there were deer on this mountain, but I suppose that answers the question. Deer tracks".

They continued on, and now they chose their own heading, with no trail cut in the ground, and no ribbons. They slanted off to the right, following the contour of the slope, which now rose more steeply, especially to the west. After a time, they began to diagonal up the hill, slipping often on the new green stalks that had pushed up from the dry, yellow grass. Daddy said that, before autumn, these shoots would be higher than their heads; that they grew like bamboo. They certainly resembled nothing Mark had ever seen down in the Valley. He felt as though he was in a different world, and he couldn't wait to get to the very top of the hill, to get a view of the other great peaks, and also the lowlands.

The sun burned down on their heads, and the mosquitoes continued to whine around them, following them as they ascended. The air was calm except for a few hollow gusts of wind that seemed to come from nowhere, and then cease just as quickly. They moved slowly up the rising hill, for a hundred feet, then another hundred. Mark was getting impatient, and he fervently hoped that when the line of grass and sky was finally attained, there would be nothing left to climb.

Still further to the right, the ridge sagged, but then it flared upward, higher than Mark would have believed. At once, however, the answer came to him; Thunder Mountain split into two separate ridges, and there was a great basin between them. From the floor of the Valley, the point to which they were now hiking could be seen, but from the next valley to the east, an entirely different peak was observed. And at that moment, Gastineau

Channel burst into view, far below, and Mark could see the highway that led downtown, and the whole of Douglas Island. They stopped for just a moment to take in the sights, then they continued on, reaching the crest of the ridge moments later. A small, gentle rise took them up and to the left, and Mark could already see in his mind what came next. The peaks of the icefield would come into view, including, of course, *the* mountain. He couldn't wait another minute!

Without speaking, the hikers continued up the final slope. Daddy was in front, and as he came to level ground, some twenty yards in front of Mark, he spread his arms and sighed. Stephen was next, and then Mark fairly ran up the last stretch, using his hands on the ground in front of him. He reached the others and gasped for breath, then raised himself to full height. He looked to the left, to the right, and straight ahead.

A cool wind came whistling up from the basin, and as it struck Mark in the face, he almost lost his balance. His eyes took in the sight, and his heart continued to pump at double speed. To the far left and right, the display was just what he had imagined, but he hardly noticed the fact. His mind was not on the periphery. Instead, his focus was on the surging white tide directly in front of him. The great peaks rose in silent wonder, cold and still. A line of them seemed to march out of the icefield itself, and for a moment that seemed too long, Mark could not even recognize the one that he called his, but at last the moment was over; his lip curled, and he smiled as all doubt vanished.

The very highest of the mountain group stood in the center of the range, and as Mark looked at it, he felt himself start forward, almost walking off the edge and into the basin. He felt an urge to lift his arm out, to try and touch the soaring giant. A short ridge dropped from its summit, which was doubled into two separate peaks. Then the south face plummeted thousands of feet to a distant valley, north of the mountain on which he now stood. To the east, another ridge, short, steep, and full of spiny towers, climbed to the broad shoulder, then disappeared in an intriguing way. And to the west, a third ridge, partially covered with snow, angled downward behind another, smaller mountain.

He felt as though a twine of some sort was connecting him to *the* mountain, much like a string connected a kite to the one flying it. For a moment, he could have sworn he was in a grassy field, kite string in hand, and someone nearby was trying to distract him from his one-on-one pleasure.

Mark looked at the towering peak for what seemed to him an eternity, then he heard fading voices. The strange vision was gone. He turned and saw that Daddy and Stephen were heading to the left, to the very top of Thunder Mountain, which rose another fifty feet to a flat plateau. He hurried after them, his feet having stiffened up while he'd stood motionless on the ridge. After a moment, he made up the distance, and the three walked up to the very highest point, which was barren of grass. A few rocks stuck out of the ground at oblique angles, and Mark saw that they were exactly like the ones Daddy had brought home last year. And then he looked out, and there was the Valley.

He could see all the way to the islands and beyond. The Valley itself looked as though it were directly beneath them. Daddy pointed out the loop road, then some of the neighborhoods, and Mark realized that his own house was not visible. He would have to walk down the slope a bit, toward the great drop-off, in order to see it. At the head of the Valley, the glacier swooped down from the icefield, and it looked awesome, its tributary rivers of ice visible as they rounded the nunataks and added their lateral moraines to the main mass.

But he couldn't take his eyes off *the* mountain for very long. So perfect, so natural in its existence, so necessary to complete the inspiring panorama. The saltwater inlets, and the island peaks with their own white summits, drifted forever to the horizon, but Mark concentrated instead on the view inland, his eyes inexorably drawn to the tower of snow and rock Jerry had pointed out to him, from way down there in the Valley. Goodness, look how far up he was now! Daddy had said they were about three thousand feet above sea level, but when Mark looked at the great mountain, he appeared to be only on a line with its very base. Could he go up there some day? He shivered, and remembered what Jerry had said, that he could not possibly make it to the top.

Daddy saw him looking at the awesome peak and shook his head. "Really a pretty one, isn't it? I looked at it myself for such a long time, when I was up here last August."

Daddy leaned back against a small hump of bare ground and began to take the lunch goods from his rucksack. And as he unpacked, he continued to speak. Mark listened intently to the talk of mountains, especially of *the* mountain.

"I used to think that I would be a mountain climber someday. I grew up in mountains, there in the Appalachians, and when I began to travel around, I noticed for the first time that much of the land on earth is flat! It really made me feel funny inside, whenever I found myself away from the hills. Well, when I first came up here to Alaska, many years ago, and when I saw what mountains are really made of, it made my head spin. But, I suppose, there was always something more important to do than climb a mountain. I don't know where the years have gone. I'd still like to tackle something like that", he nodded in the direction of the snowy mammoth, "but I just don't think I could make it anymore. I've let too many years slip past." And Daddy sighed as he began to pass out the meal he had carried with him to the top of Thunder Mountain.

Soon, Mark had let *the* mountain drift from his eyes and from his thoughts. He and Stephen were eating greedily; the lunch consisted of bread, cheese, raisins, and juicy apples. The bread was home-baked. It was what Mama called "house bread", shaped like a flat football and sliced thin. Daddy had brought about twenty of the elliptical pieces, but they were disappearing fast, as Mark and his older brother were stuffing them into their mouths as fast as they could pick them up. And raisins had never tasted so good.

Afterward, Daddy led the boys on a tour of the summit ridge. They walked along, gazing out toward the Valley, and picking up any rock that looked interesting enough to take home. They saw many bird nests, built right on the ground, and one even had some eggs left in it. Daddy found it odd that they had never hatched, and said that the parents might have been grabbed by a sparrow hawk. He pointed up, and Mark saw a bird with sharp, thin wings hovering about two hundred feet above them.

Occasionally a raven would soar by, making a sound of *groak*, as though telling the humans they were trespassing, and would they kindly go back home? Mark saw a bald eagle, perched on a high rock ledge across the basin. It was a thrilling time for the boy, up there on the summit of the long, sharp ridge. The sun was warm, although a thick line of belted clouds was moving in from the west, obscuring the peaks of the Chilkat Range. Daddy had sat down to rest and to tighten the laces on his boots, and the two boys moved off to be by themselves for a short while.

They crept to the very edge of the ridge and peeked over the rim to see the tumbling west face of the mountain, down from which the avalanches had roared, only two short months ago. Stephen pointed out the Nilsson's house, now visible, and tiny as it looked, Mark could make out its light blue color.

"Did you hear what Daddy told me?" Stephen asked. "He said that bears can climb up a mountain face as steep as this, just like a goat. Do you think we might see one, if we look hard enough?"

Stephen really did have some strange thoughts, Mark often believed. He frowned, but continued to gaze down the slope as far as he could, which wasn't very far, as the angle increased some two hundred feet below. And Stephen grinned, put his hand in his sweater pocket, and pulled out something. It was a brown, mushy-looking apple core, the remnants of his dessert.

"Throw it off the edge," Mark suggested. "Maybe you can hit our house, if you throw it out far enough."

"No! I can't throw it that far," Stephen answered. But he cranked up his arm, and the apple core sailed off into space, fell downward, and passed from sight. The boys strained for a view, but it was gone. As they looked, there was a flash of black, and another eagle soared past, carried by an updraft. It drifted right over Mark's head, saw them waving, and with a shrill whistle, took off for the eastern summit of the mountain.

The boys were jumping up and down, elated, and then they were running back to where Daddy sat checking the bullet load in his rifle. He nodded and said that he'd seen the eagle as well, and he figured that a pair of them were spending the day up here to hunt small animals. "Their nest is probably down by the beach somewhere, but sometimes they spend time in the highlands, so they can eat something besides fish. I'd kind of like to go and see where they are, but it's a ways off. Besides, I think we should be heading down, because those clouds are moving in pretty quick. I don't want to get caught in them again. Are you boys about ready to get started?"

The brothers nodded glumly, and with that, the party began to descend. They walked to the point where they had gained the ridgetop, and Mark looked back over his shoulder at *the* mountain. It stood cold and proud, he thought, as though it were waiting for the clouds to come and try to blanket its icy mantle. For a moment, he felt an odd form of anxiety, but he turned and followed the other two as they dropped over the edge and begin to diagonal back the way they had come, through the green shoots and the deer lettuce.

Several ptarmigan scooted across the ground in front of them, and Stephen asked Daddy to shoot, but Daddy said no, the grouse was enough for them. They eased down the slope to the treeline, sometimes walking directly through the patches of stale snow, never stopping to rest. Mark found it quite fascinating to see the trees getting closer and closer.

The clouds, which had crept up on them ever so quietly, were now covering a great deal of the sky, and soon they were puffing overhead, hiding the sun. The light dimmed, and it seemed to Mark that all was quiet, the birds and the insects gone. Ahead of him, he could see the lowland marsh flats, and some of the clouds were now dropping to the ground, becoming grayish and without form.

Daddy began to throw strained glances at the darkening sky, then at the boys. The air began to feel cold, and there was a low-keyed rustling in the distance, which Mark did not recognize as the wind blowing through the forest below them. Daddy hurried the group along, down to the snow patch where the deer tracks ran, and by that time, it seemed nearly dark, though it was the middle of the afternoon.

A drop of rain hit Mark's eyelash, and he told Daddy. "Well, then come on, both of you, let's get down off this blasted mountain before the sky falls!"

Daddy's tone was harsh, and Mark was taken back, as was Stephen, and the two boys threw each other a quick glance of worry. Mark walked along the trail, hoping the sky would not open up and really let them have it. So far, his mind told him, you've been lucky. It's been a great, warm sunny day. You've seen the big mountain peaks, there have been no major obstacles and no ice towers to climb, and you've enjoyed a terrific lunch. Now look what's happened. Daddy's starting to get angry, all because the clouds have covered the whole sky!

It began to sprinkle as they started down through the woods, and as they looked ahead in amazement, the grayish clouds pushed through the trees directly in front of them. The misty fog swept over the hikers, and instantly Mark's outer clothing was saturated with millions of tiny droplets. Down they climbed, Daddy looking back over his shoulder and telling the boys to hurry up unless they wanted to spend the night here on the ridge. Mark wanted to shout back, to tell him to shut up, that he was doing the best he could, when the party came to an abrupt halt.

Daddy had lost the trail.

After a short hesitation, he started off, down and to the right, and the boys followed him. The going was rough, through blueberry bushes, up and over logs, and across micro ponds that sucked at their boots as they passed. After a while, the mist became thicker, but the rain diminished and nearly stopped altogether. When someone spoke, which wasn't often, there was no echo; the voices came out flat and somewhat squelched, the cloud mist absorbing most of the sound. The plants against which they brushed were coated in moisture, and soon Mark was soaked through to the skin. But he kept on, behind the others, and after a long, almost endless plunge downward, they came to a wide, steep ravine, with a small creek rushing along its bottom. Mark hadn't seen a red ribbon for over four hours, not since they had left the trees behind on their way up.

"I think this is the one, but I'm not sure," Daddy told them. "Wait here, and I'll go down first. Watch what I do, and if I should slip, then don't do what I did. Now look, it won't be long until we get to the bottom, so let's all be patient, okay?"

Stephen asked mildly, "Are we past the blue mitten?"

Daddy threw him a stony look. "Don't worry about the damn mitten, okay? I'm trying to get you two off of this mountain, all right? Just be quiet, and hold on a second!"

He started down into the ravine, and Mark watched him go, hardly believing that this was really happening. A while ago, nothing could be better, but now … Daddy slipped, but went on down to the brook, and after a moment, called for them to follow. The brothers dropped down to where Daddy stood in a small thicket by the stream's edge.

"I think we can follow this most of the way down," he said in an impatient voice. "Come on, and stay close behind."

They wound their way down, following the little creek, which looked about the same size as the one that ran through the dam they had passed, much earlier that day. Mark hoped that it *was* the same, but the creek began to turn and lead off to the right, plunging more steeply down the slope in a series of waterfalls. Daddy hopped up onto a fallen log and started over to the far side of the ravine, and Stephen followed. Mark took a step, but then drew back. He began to shake, and he looked for something to hold on to, a tree branch, anything, but there was only devil's club, to the left and to the right.

Daddy looked back at him. "Come on! That log's a foot wide. We just walked across," he nodded at Stephen, "and so can you. Come on, boy!"

Mark took a step, then fell to his hands and knees. His fingers dug into the log's covering of thick moss, and he began to shake again. His voice came out as a quaver. "I don't know … if I can," he said in a soft, cracking tone.

Daddy exhaled loudly. "Oh, for evermore!" he shouted through the mist.

Mark crept further out onto the log. He hated it, and he hated the devil's club, he even hated the joyful sound of the little brook that laughed its way along, below the log. He hated the rain, he hated the two who watched him, and he hated ... he hated everything. The whole world. "Just when I need you," his lips moved. And he scrunched his way across, ever so slowly, and as he reached the other side, he was shaking so much that he slipped off the side of the log and fell, as he had done earlier in the day. He crashed against the moss-covered slope of the ravine, and his head smacked an old stump. Tears came to his eyes, and for a moment that seemed an eternity, his face was pressed up to the soaking, orange-colored rot. "Jerry," he said to the ground, "I'm glad you couldn't come."

He heard Daddy nearby, felt himself being yanked upward, and then hauled over to where Stephen was. Daddy said nothing more, just led the two boys over into the next ravine, and the next, and finally downward once again. A few minutes later, they were off the mountain, standing at the edge of a clearing, with the end of the logging road in plain sight.

They were below the clouds, but the mist had once again developed into a steady drizzle. They slogged along the dirt road, pausing once to take shelter underneath a large spruce as the rain increased. As they stood there, Daddy finally spoke again, and this time his voice was soft and controlled.

"Well, looks like we made it down just in time," he said. "I think this rain is going to continue for the rest of the day and into the night. Guess we better be getting on home, because your Mama will begin to wonder if we're ever going to come back."

It was indeed late. As they started off down the road, Mark felt as though he had been awake for several days, and he found it hard to remember exactly how this morning had started. They passed over Jordan Creek, on the worm-eaten bridge, and it seemed like years ago that he'd first seen this structure. He was dead tired as he clomped along, through the long forest shadows. They were walking abreast of one another, for the first time since they had sighted the red ribbons, in the early hours now far in the past. Mark thought about those ribbons. One could not possibly have gotten lost, but somehow they had, and he never wanted to forget what Daddy had told him, about the manner in which Nature could act. He looked at Daddy through the corner of his eye. No longer was he angry at him, and he even felt a bit ashamed for having fallen off the log. Someday, he would go up there, and alone, he would walk that log, from one end to the other, to prove that he could do it.

The shadows deepened, and the drizzle continued. Mark was cold, and when the lights of the house finally became visible to the three worn-out hikers, it was almost totally dark. Daddy opened the back gate and let the boys slip through ahead of him. And then they all hurried up to the back porch where, seemingly years ago, Daddy had lost his own footing and slipped. It was the longest day Mark had ever lived.

They went inside, and Mama was waiting for them in the furnace room. "Look at you," she sighed. "And I was about to give up. Thought a bear might have attacked you." And she told the boys to hurry and get out of their wet things.

As Mark went down the hall, he could hear Mama as she continued to talk. She had watched the mountain all day, watched as the clouds had covered the top, and she'd hoped they wouldn't get caught in them. Well, her wish hadn't come true, Mark thought. He heard the beginning of Daddy answering, but he followed Stephen into the bedroom, closed the door behind him, and along with his brother, changed out of the soaking wet clothes.

Soon, the family was sitting around the dinner table. They talked about how the hike had gone, as they waited for the heating of the dinner Mama had prepared for them. Daddy had put the grouse in the refrigerator, and he promised the boys they could have it for dinner the next day. "If," he said with a grin, "your Mama knows how to fix one." And he winked at Mama, who shrugged and said that she would bake it in the oven, unless Daddy had a better suggestion. And Daddy replied that no, he had no better suggestion, and that his mouth was already watering in anticipation. "And just now," he declared, "anything sounds good enough, right boys?"

Mama served them the scalloped potato casserole that she had made, watching it disappear along with the remains of the house bread. She left the kitchen to go see about Amy, who was supposed to be asleep for the night. And Stephen immediately spoke up.

"Do you think she'll ever let us go again?"

Daddy almost choked, as the words must have sounded very funny to him. Mark decided, in his own mind, that somehow, he would hike up Thunder Mountain any time he wanted, when he got bigger. He'd find a way to go up that mountain where there were no ravines, no logs to cross, and no creeks to slosh through. He'd mark it with his own red tape, to make it look official!

But now he was tired, and he was bruised from his head to his feet, so with a yawn, he pushed his plate from him and was on his way to bed. Stephen came after him, and in less than ten minutes, both boys were snoring in their room. Mark slept without dream, or at least without the remembrance of one, but in the dark, his eyes reopened. He sat up in bed, as though awakened by a mysterious force.

He didn't feel sleepy, nor did he feel wide awake. Through the door, Mark heard voices. He stood, walked softly across the room, and drew the door ajar. He listened intently, as Mama and Daddy talked.

"—didn't mean to make it such a long day, but even so, they looked very tired to me. Did you think it would be that hard on them?"

"Hard on them? Sure, it was their first big hike, and they were a little clumsy, falling over roots and things, but what do you expect? Mark comes up to about … here on me. He's more liable to trip over things." A pause. "They don't look at it that way. It was an adventure, something they'll never forget, and just watch, in a few days, they're going to be asking to go again. Ha, ha! I might be asking again myself. I tell you, it's fun up there."

There was another pause, then a metallic sluicing noise traveled down the hall. Daddy was cleaning his rifle.

"But you think they acted pretty well?"

"Pretty well, yes. Sometimes I had to get them going when things got rough, particularly on the way down."

"I always did wonder, just what they would be like growing up here, in this part of the country. We've been here for a year, and I ask myself, are they already different than they would have been? Do you ever have doubts about it?"

"Uh, uh. You know what I think. Here they can be as free as they want. I hope they're sixteen before they ever have to read a word about Viet Nam, things like that, the stuff we've been going through. All those flower children running around … I wouldn't want my kids growing up like that. You can bet they have the best chance to grow up straight, right where they are."

Mama was walking toward the kitchen, Mark could tell. He tightened his grip on the knob, ready to close the door quickly and hop into bed, lest she start down the hall.

"Which do you think is the more different of the two?" The sound of a plate being scraped. "Huh? You hear?"

And now there was a much longer pause. Daddy finally spoke, his voice quite soft and funny-sounding. The words of his reply would ring clearly in Mark's ears; they would stay in his mind for many years to come.

"I'd rather not say. Because if I do, and my answer is Mark, or if I do, and my answer is Stephen, and if I tell you why, we're going to end up arguing about it, and we don't want that, do we?"

Mark closed the door, backed away, and slipped under the covers once more. He closed his eyes and drifted off to sleep, a sleep that was again without dream.

§

In the morning, the clouds had risen, and from the back porch, Mark looked at Thunder Mountain. It looked back at him, and Mark thought he saw it smile.

CHAPTER FOUR

Came a new spring. Gone were the snowdrifts of winter, and the living world had received the signal to reach skyward. The skunk cabbages, with tightly rolled leaves and thick, healthy stalks, were rising from the mucks. In the shadow of western hemlocks, spreading wood ferns began to unroll their sticky fiddleheads, while out on the fringe of the meadows, the blueberry bushes grew leafy coats and opened countless purple buds.

The sky became full of barn swallows that dove helter-skelter at the mosquitoes now rising by the millions from the swampy, backwater sloughs. The sun felt warm to the world.

On a Saturday afternoon, Mark wheeled his bicycle from the storage van, swung onto the hard vinyl seat, and took off down the dirt road, away from his house. He swerved to the right and left, avoiding chuck holes and the small, speckled granites that lay packed into the glacial subsoil. He wore light clothing, and the wind, created by his forward motion, sent a chill through him, as though the sun had been eclipsed. He pedaled along the drive, turned in front of his school, and continued on to the loop road. When he arrived, he paused a moment to check the traffic. Then he was off again, along the pavement, heading northward.

To the right, Thunder Mountain was sliding by, its shadow projecting obliquely toward Mendenhall Glacier, which cascaded from the icefield in a white surge that seemed to pour straight to the boy on the bike. He was going all the way to the end of the road, to the edge of the lake, to see the glacier up close. He had never traveled there alone, and he hadn't been there with his family in quite some time, since that evening they had gone to see a presentation at the glassed-in visitor center. As the land began to change in front of him, his excitement built. Passing the loop turn-off that led to Auke Bay, he kept on until he reached the terminal moraine line.

Here, the glacier had advanced until melting had begun to increase faster than the downhill flow of ice. A series of small hillocks, long and thin, spread across the Valley, marking the forwardmost progress of the ice, some two hundred years in the past. Mark paused his riding a second time, looking at the peaks and feeling the glacier closing in on him. The air began to have a coolness about it, a direct influence of the glacier itself. Bullard Mountain, a steeply rising bulk directly to the right of the glacier's snout, completely hid the line of towering slopes that Mark had now worshiped for the past two years. He put his feet to the pedals once again.

The road straightened, and Mark sped down the centerline, as traffic had diminished to nothing. The trees thinned and were gone; now, huge granites, some of them as large as Mark's bedroom, lay on either side of the pavement. A big, gentle turn to the left, and the front of the glacier appeared suddenly, with the crystal clear waters of its lake spanning the entire face. Mark wheeled to the edge of the parking lot, propped up his bike, and walked along to the visitor center, his eyes never leaving the cold, surging mass of ice. Open fissures and mammoth crevasses, colored deep blue by the sun's rays, backed by the powerful sight of dark rock and incredibly high snowfields, which sighed as their cold sweat was lost forever to the sky ... it was amazing.

He climbed the concrete steps to the observatory and went inside. After browsing for a while in the lobby, he went to the main room and looked at the scenery through one of the spotting scopes. He picked out a couple of mountain goats on a steep meadow, and gazed for a while at the tunnel that had been cut through the right edge of the glacier by a huge meltwater stream from another, smaller glacier that hung in a valley near *the* mountain.

He walked out the rear door of the visitor center and began to hike along the sandy trail that skirted the base of a large, gently sloping hill. The hill was barren of moss, and quartz veins ran up its side. From the top, the hill sloped off quite sharply. Years ago, when the glacier had advanced down the Valley, it had moved over this very hill, and the weight of the ice had split the rock, causing the southern end to stand at a steepened angle. This stoss-and-lee pattern was visible on every hill in the vicinity, though fast-growing alders were beginning to hide the surface of the rock, and with it, evidence of the glacier's movement.

Mark continued to follow the sandy trail, and after a moment, he came to a point where the rocky hill stood directly to his side. In the smooth, gray biotite, there was an engraving. It read: Ice Limit 1936. Mark leaned over, put his hand on the cold rock face, and let his fingers slide over the indentations. Just over 30 years ago, the point where he now stood had been covered by ice! He could hardly believe it—the glacier was nearly a half-mile away, and the area around him was covered by willow shrubs and Sitka alder.

Walking on, he came to one of the big quartz veins that ran up the face of the hill. He leaped onto the rock and carefully hiked up the side, following the squiggly white band in front of him. As he approached the top, he saw a tiny stream running down the vein and disappearing into the ground. Intrigued, he ran up the gently sloping rock to the point where it leveled off, and when he arrived, he stopped and pulled back.

There was a pond in front of him. It was thirty feet long, half that distance in width, and it was so dark and glassy, an effect caused by the rocks themselves, that Mark could not see to the bottom. The alders rimmed either side of the pool, and a large boulder, fixed into the earth, rose on the opposite bank. Beyond, the hill dropped off and fell away to the lowlands, and Mark could see the silver-gray line of the roadway.

What a place! He crept to the water's edge and knelt down. Sticking his finger into the motionless surface of the pond, he judged it to be no warmer than forty degrees. A set of concentric rings spread quietly toward the opposite bank and far corners of the tiny lake. Mark stood up and sighed. It was unreal. He had never before seen a lovelier piece of natural splendor, and as he gazed upon it, his mind went to work.

The tiny pond was a lake, moderate in size, perhaps ten miles in length, and four miles to the opposite shore. A mountain rose up in the distance, and the one rock that stuck above the surface was an island, covered with small evergreens and looking beautiful in the midst of the clear, highly reflective water. A peninsula jutted out from the base of the mountain, and it was wide, flat, a perfect site for a small town. Way off to the left, a narrow inlet speared into the woods, where once again the snow-covered mountains took over and marched off into the distance, to eternity.

Mark ran all the way around the pond and climbed up onto the rock. He sat and looked out over his new little domain. He looked at the water; it was so clear and yet so dark, seemingly bottomless! And from where he sat, he could see the glacier, and further away, the peaks that rose beyond. He could twist around and see Thunder Mountain, the Valley, and the marsh flats. He could see all the way to Admiralty Island, and here in the center of it all was the little pond, which had quickly become his own. He sat on his mountain, looked over his lake, and studied the "shoreline", deciding that a community like no other in the universe could exist here. He looked down upon the "town" he had just created, and he imagined a ferryboat carrying people from one side of the lake to the other, people quite different than the ones he had known up until now. Mark looked at the far side of the pond, where the hill dropped off and the real(?) world began once more.

There was a breeze at his back, but he didn't notice. The rock was jagged and uncomfortable, but he didn't notice that either. The clouds were pushing across Lynn Canal and heading for the mainland, but all the boy cared about was his little earth within the earth. For an hour, he daydreamed about the pond, and soon he had created quite a setting, a new world right before him. This pool of water—this lake—was where he could come and dream. He felt strangely at home on top of the rock formation, able to view all the world, yet be completely alone and to himself.

Now the daydreaming was coming to an end. The breeze was picking up, and he shivered in his thin t-shirt. He began to wonder about the lateness of the hour. The sun's position was of no help; it was now hidden behind the advancing cloud front. He had left home at a little past one in the afternoon, and Mom had said they would be having dinner at the usual time. Soon he would have to leave this wonderful place he had discovered and head on back to the house. But he would return to the lake soon, that was sure, and maybe he would even let Jerry see it.

He felt something in his pocket, and pulled out the letter from Grandmother, which he had received the day before. He unfolded the manila paper and read it once more, his lips moving. Occasionally a sound came from him. Everything was fine here, she had written. How was he? It had rained. The grass needed to be cut in a day or two. Would he play baseball next summer? Hoped to hear from him soon.

Stephen had received a letter also, and of course, there had been a much longer one for Mom. Mark had asked to read it, as he always did, but Mom had only shook her head and said that he would not understand it. And Mark had gotten angry, saying that yes, he certainly could understand it, and that someday, he would sit down and write a letter, or a book, or something, so full of big words *she* would never understand it, and what did she think of that? And then, after a very brief staring contest between the two of them, he had announced that he was going to ride up to the glacier, but again Mom had shook her head and said no. It was nearly dinnertime, and maybe he could go tomorrow instead. And Mark had been so full of defiant anger that he had stomped to his room and slammed the door, only to have Mom follow him, open the door, and yell at him for making a scene. And the next afternoon, which was today, he had indeed gotten on his big red bicycle and ridden to the glacier. What an awful mother she could be.

He screeched out through his teeth, to help accent the thought, and brought a quickly closed fist down onto the sharp granite boulder where he sat. A flash of pain made him dizzy, and his screech became a muted groan. He lifted his left hand and looked at the outer edge of his little finger.

There was blood. He touched the wound with the fingers of his other hand, which were dry and dirty. This only made the cuts hurt even more. He brought the injury to his mouth and sucked at it, groaning again as the pain became a dull throbbing. Then he drew back his hand, watching as the finger reddened once more. He reached for the letter he'd been reading, then quickly put it down and looked wildly about him. Hopping off the rock, he bent over and put his hand into the icy waters of the pond.

The pounding became fainter, and soon the pain was gone. He continued to lift his hand out of the pool and dunk it in, bathing the cuts until the blood stopped. Then he straightened up and blew softly on the wound, to gently dry it. Walking over to where the alders grew thick at the far, narrow end of the pond, he pinched off one of the bigger leaves and pushed it against the cuts. Holding it there with his right hand, he made his way back to the boulder, climbed up with difficulty, and sat once more on its tilted summit.

He looked down at the place he had struck, moments before. The granite sparkled back at him, as though proud of its existence. He smiled and shook his head at it. He gazed out over the pool, which was flattening once more to the glassy surface it had been, before the accident. Again he smiled. As the breeze swept over the hillock and rustled through the alders, he turned his head, watched the bobbing branches, and felt the smooth leaf against his finger. He drew in a very deep breath. Hurt? Pain? He felt nothing but a sense of goodness, and even more so, reverence for the pond, the boulder, and the alder. They had spoken to him, and he had listened. This place was *his*.

The clouds now covered most of the sky, but Mark was not concerned. He decided it was time to leave, however, so he threw a last look all around, at his new world, and then jumped off the rock. The leaf flew out of his grasp and fluttered down in soft rocking movements, settling at last on the pond's surface, ever so gently. No concentric rings. Mark watched, his breath having momentarily stopped, as the alder leaf rested on the surface of the tiny lake, which totally escaped the influence of the fresh breeze.

He whispered goodbye to the pond, galloped down the slope, and a few moments later was in the parking lot, where his bike stood as he had left it, without a safety chain, yet unmolested. He got on and spread his left hand out to the handlebar, feeling no pain. And then he was off, bucking the wind that now rushed up the Valley to meet the glacier in a head-on collision of cool air and cold ice.

As he pedaled home, he thought about what had happened back there, at the glacier. What an afternoon! Finding that wonderful place up there in the rocks, where he could now go whenever he needed to be alone. And that mess he'd got into with his hand—well, that was all right. The letter! He knew he'd forgotten something. The letter was spread out on the side of the boulder, unless, of course, the wind had picked it up by now and carried it high in the air, over the glacier and up onto the icefield, dropping it into a big crevasse where it would never be found. In a way, he hoped that was exactly what had happened. If he could never read it again, then it was probably best that no one else should happen upon it. He could turn back and look for it, but no … it was too far, and besides, it wouldn't be right to go back there to the pond again, after telling it goodbye.

Thunder Mountain was sliding by again, this time on his left. As he zoomed along the centerline of the road, the top came into view, and also the sharp drop-off where, nearly two years ago, Stephen had thrown his apple core. He began to silently chuckle at the thought of someone driving down the road toward the glacier and have the mushy thing hit smack dab in the middle of the windshield. Looking up again, he figured, from the math he was learning, that the horizontal distance from the ridgetop to the road was at least fifty times as far as his brother could possibly have hurled an apple core, a rock, or anything else. Then he laughed so hard he nearly lost control of his bike.

A while later, he turned into his driveway, swung open the gate, and walked his bicycle to the storage van. After shutting it inside the big wood-framed structure, he jumped onto the back porch and entered the house.

In the furnace room, he gave his wounded finger a quick going over, to see if the cuts were really that visible. Deciding in the negative, he walked through the den and out into the living room. Mom was sitting in the green recliner, looking at a magazine, and Dad was poking through his record collection. And there was Amy, on the floor with her favorite jigsaw puzzle, featuring Popeye and Olive Oyl.

"Well, I'm back." He shuffled over to the couch, dropped into the corner, and sat there hugging a square cushion.

"You are. Well, I can start dinner, I guess. How was the glacier?"

What kind of a question was that? How was the glacier? "I guess it was okay."

"You mean, you didn't ask it," Dad said, turning from the record cabinet. Mom laughed and shook her head. "I guess that didn't come out the way I wanted it to. I'm glad you're back, though. It looks to be getting cloudier all the time."

She left for the kitchen, and Dad nodded after her. "She just got finished with your brother. Stephen came in here to show her how his aircraft carrier was coming along, dripped glue all over the carpet, and she really yelled at him. Made him clean it up. Sent him to you boys' room. Ah! There it is …."

Dad pulled his selection from the cabinet, and Mark dropped to the floor, where Amy was struggling with her puzzle. Popeye's face was missing, and his pipe seemed to hang in midair. The little girl was busy with something else, however; she tried fitting two random pieces that lay off to one side. On the whole, the puzzle was coming along rather shakily, being worked on the tufted brown carpet, rolling like waves, the cracks between the pieces amplified. Mark reached out and tapped Popeye's head with his finger.

"No!" Amy shouted. Mark jerked his hand back and saw Dad looking at them while trying to cue the record.

"What did you do to your hand?"

"Huh?"

"Your finger. Look at it, all cut up. Did you just do that?"

"Oh, that. Scratched it against a rock while I was up there." He motioned out the window. "It doesn't hurt. What happened was, I hiked up to this place, which is really—"

The record began, and there was a pause; both were momentarily caught up with the sound that filled the room. Dad relaxed in his rocker, eyes half shut, as though put into a deep trance. Mark waited for him to come back to life, knowing that it might be in vain; Dad could remain like this until the side was finished playing.

But after a minute or two, his father straightened his posture and looked up once again. He smiled a thin smile and waved to the far right speaker.

"A man named Hanson composed that. Hmmm … listen to it. I guess you've heard it play a hundred times, but just listen to it."

Mark nodded. "This place is up on a hill, and from the top, you can see … you can see a lot of …." He stopped, and let out his breath. *Don't tell him. It's your secret.*

"It moves along so effortlessly, but it carries such power! It makes such good use of all the instruments!" Dad motioned wildly, using an unseen baton, as though conducting the Eastman Rochester Orchestra himself. As the movement settled down into a quieter period, his arms settled with it, finally resting on his lap as before.

"No, I'm sorry, what were you saying about this place you found?"

Mark shook his head. "Oh, nothing. I could never tell you where it is. It would be too hard for you to imagine."

Dad frowned. "Oh, would it now? What makes you think I haven't seen this place already?" He seemed to be joking, but Mark wasn't sure. "And you're going to sit there—no, don't turn away, Amy can do that herself—sit there and tell me what I can imagine and what I can't? You're what, nine years old? Ho, ho! I think you have some catching up to do, if you want to say that you can imagine as much as I can. Yeah, I remember when I was nine years old. Used to discover all kinds of things, out there in the woods where I lived. I'd come home, burst into the house, and be telling my Grandmom what I'd come across. Of course, she would be in the middle of whipping my brother for getting into trouble down the road, so he'd be yelling his fool head off, and all the dogs would be howling along with him, and I'd be trying to get her attention so I could show her the strange mushroom I'd found, or tell her about the wonderful, secret thicket I'd blundered across, or whatnot." The music crescendoed.

Mark couldn't decide whether to laugh or frown, and finally he chose a low giggle that made Amy look up, curiosity written on her small, rounded face. Dad shrugged and continued.

"Oh, anyway, what I meant to say was, that I can pretty well picture just about anything you might describe, because I've probably had a similar thing happen to me, long ago, or perhaps just the other day. You understand? What's hard for you to realize, Mark, is that I've lived a long life already, and you don't know a tenth of it. Why, if I started to tell you my life story right now, we'd both have six-foot beards by the time I was finished. We'd be sitting here, drinking some sort of medicinal tea, and in a creaky old voice I'd be saying, 'Well, I'm finally through, now what's *your* story?' And we might not even be able to remember why we were doing this to begin with. Honestly, we'd look like that old character what's-his-name, Rip van Pumpernickel!"

The phone rang, and simultaneously, the music came to a halt, as the first movement was over. Still amused, Mark heard Mom calling for him to come out to the kitchen. He got up, almost tripped over Amy and her puzzle, then rushed to the telephone, snatching the receiver from Mom's grasp. "Hello?"

"Hi. This is Jerry."

"I know!"

"You sound like you're laughing. What're you doing over there, huh?"

"We're getting ready to eat. Listen, I've got something to tell you. I went to the glacier today, on my bike, and—"

"I got something to tell you, too. Richard said that—"

"No, listen. Mine's more important. I found this place you wouldn't believe. You have to see it."

"Where?"

Mark gritted his teeth. "At the glacier, Jerry! Didn't you hear me?"

"Oh. You went to the glacier?"

Mark almost hung up. "Just forget it. I'll tell you on the playground."

"No, tell me now!" Jerry's own voice became impatient.

"Well, I guess you'll have to see it, like I said. It's a really neat place up on top of a hill, behind the visitor center. We can go next Saturday, if your mom will let you."

"She will. I can't wait to see it."

"I haven't told anyone else about it." Mark lowered his voice to almost a whisper. "I don't want my mom to listen to this. I don't think she can, the stove fan is on, you hear it? And my dad, I think maybe he's already seen it, but that's all right."

"Okay, we'll go on Saturday, unless I have to go to town with my parents. Now, I was saying, that Richard told me, and you gotta hear this, that *he* heard—"

"No. Tell me on the playground. I have to eat. See you later, bye!"

"Well, bye." A soft click.

And Mark headed back to the living room, wondering why he hadn't let Jerry tell him his own bit of news, and just why he had let him in on the secret of the pond, after being reluctant to tell Dad. He sat down once more on the sofa, noticing that Amy had finished her puzzle.

"Look", she pointed to the completed project. Mark nodded and congratulated her on setting a new record time. "Want to try one of Mark's, now that you're so good at them?" he asked her. And then came Mom's voice from the kitchen, reminding him to say "mine", and not "Mark's", that Amy was old enough to be talked to like a child, not a baby.

He sat and listened to the music, and watched as Dad became absorbed once more, in the quieter second movement. It sounded sweet, mellow, and contained a touch of poignant appeal, a yearning that captured the boy's attention. As the piece came to a close, Dad shook his head and sighed.

"Lovely, don't you think? Guess the third movement will have to wait until after dinner, because I'm not about to have clacking dishes going at the same time."

"Let's eat, everybody," Mom sang out. "Stephen!"

"Used to drive your mom crazy, that symphony did," Dad said. "That first movement, which changes key so often. She'd rant and rant about how she used to be a music student, and part of her college band, and about how she knew good and well that what happens in that first movement is against the 'laws' of music, and she was taught that music can't be written that way!" He chuckled and turned off the amplifier.

"But you heard it yourself, and it sounds perfect, doesn't it? Right where Hanson wanted to, he changed the key, and then again, and again, and it *works*. Don't tell me it can't be done!" And he looked at Mark, who stared right back.

"I mean, why follow the rules all the time?" Dad continued. "Sure, it's good to learn them, but when it comes time to make your move, you do it. You go your own direction, and if it looks, feels, or sounds right to *you*, then by heavens, it is right!" He slapped his knee for emphasis. "You understand what I'm saying?"

There was total silence, until Dad got up from the rocker. "Well, let's eat, before it gets cold."

"Yes, I do," Mark answered.

§

Sitting on the back porch, Mark cared nothing for the activities inside the house, nor for the activities going on in all the houses of his neighborhood, the town, the world. He had his own place now, and although he didn't mind showing it to someone else, he knew that its true appearance, its true purpose, would be seen only by him. This was a great thing, a prepared thing, a thing so necessary that no other thing would ever get in the way. He'd make sure of it. He had to. He'd been appointed caretaker. By something ....

§

"And see what a good view there is, down the Valley? I could sit up there on the boulder all day, and look around at the glacier, at the marsh flats, at the pond, and never get tired of it."

Jerry climbed up onto the large boulder that had, the week before, become a mountain. "I do like this place," he replied, standing up and looking all around him, with his arms outstretched for balance. He sat down upon the rock, as a king would sit on his throne.

"I proclaim this area as mine," he said in a deep tone. Mark waved him off.

"Can't do that. I already have. I claimed it last week. But I like the way you said that. Oh, I'll tell you what. You can be a part-owner, as long as you agree that I found it first, and that I have the right to take away your ownership or whatever it's called, if you ever start acting like a dumbo."

"It's called a title, I think. My dad works with those." Jerry slid down off the rock. "Okay, I agree. I bet I could find a neater place of my own, if I looked hard enough."

Mark pointed out toward the saltwater. "Well, go ahead, and we'll compare them. But listen, Jerry. I don't want you to tell anyone else about this place at all. You're the only one that gets in on it, all right? You gotta promise not to tell anyone at all."

"No, I won't tell. Not even my parents."

Mark looked at him for a moment, wondering if he should say anything about his private world he had dreamed up the week before. Up until now, he had shown it to Jerry as it "really" was, and hadn't let on a thing concerning the secret mountain, the lake, or the town, upon which his friend was now standing. He looked down at Jerry's feet. They were crushing buildings and people, thoroughly destroying the little community. Of course, whenever Mark came back here alone, everything would be all right.

The two spent most of the afternoon by the little pond, dropping tiny stones into the glassy waters and watching as the oily swells took off for the furthest corners. There was not the slightest hint as to the pond's depth, although there was a full five-second interval between the pebbles meeting the surface and the rise of bubbles to the top. Jerry decided that it was bottomless, that there was a hole right through the earth, and that there was a similar pool exactly halfway around the globe, where the hole came out.

"That can't be true," Mark told him. I looked at a globe once, to see where the opposite point on the earth was. Mrs. Thornton helped me. It's in the ocean somewhere. Below Africa, I think."

"Oh." Jerry looked at the pond for a moment. "Well, then maybe the water's salty, huh?"

"Come on, Jerry! The water is not salty. Here, let's explore the rest of the hill."

So they left the pond and traveled along the crest of the long, rocky glacial formation, stopping to look down through mysterious cracks in the hard granite, examining the pinkish quartz veins, and veering off to scale a miniature summit and claim it for their own. It was a cloudy afternoon, and a chill wind blew, giving the feeling of approaching winter rather than of a warm, glorious weekend in May. There seemed to be no one else at the recreation area at all.

"Last year," Mark said as they bounded along the low ridge, "was even better than the first time. You should have gone with us. We ran into some mountain goats up there, near the top. Boy, did we scare the daylights out of them. I've never been so close to a wild animal in all my life, not one that big, anyway. And if you can imagine what *the* mountain looks like from up there ... wow! Someday, Jerry, when I get all the stuff I'd need, I'll go climb that thing, and you can come with me. I mean, after a while, your mom won't be able to tell you that you can't. And you said that you'd changed your mind, that you really thought you could make it to the top."

"We took some friends to the airport last week," Jerry answered. "And from out there near the water you can really see it good! I showed my mom and told her that someday I'd want to climb up it, and she told me the day I did something like that, she would throw herself on the floor and have some kind of nervous breakdown."

"Really?" Mark was puzzled. "I don't think my mom has ever had anything like that. I remember, a few days after Amy was born, she told me that she felt faint, and that if she fell down on the floor, I had to run across the street and get the neighbors right quick. I don't think it's the same thing, though."

The ridge began to drop downward, and the boys could hear running water below. They came to a sharp cliff and peered over the edge. It was a small canyon, and a rushing, whitewater stream flowed down and to the right, out beyond their view. The canyon had steep rock walls, some of which were actually being eroded, undercut from the force of the fast-moving creek. A stinging, cold mist rose out of the gorge, and the boys watched, fascinated.

"It must be Steep Creek, the one that falls off Thunder, right up there," Mark pointed. "Look, we can go left and follow the trail around and over the bridge, so we can get out on the rocks above the canyon."

Hurrying to the point where the trail crossed the stream, they crashed through the trees until they emerged directly above the foaming water. They dropped into sprawled positions and moved out on their bellies until their eyes protruded over the ninety-degree cliff.

"This is great! Ha, ha, how much will you give me if I dive over the edge?" Jerry shouted above the turbulent roar.

"Nothing!" Mark shouted back. "You won't be alive, and I'd have to keep the money for myself!"

Jerry stood up. Spreading his arms as before, he said, "This is my kingdom, and I have just claimed it for myself, and no one else." Turning, he addressed Mark. "I told you that I would find my own place, and that it would be better than yours."

Mark shrugged. "Well, go ahead and have it. I still like mine better."

"Are you kidding? Just look at all the power down there! That roaring water. Look at the walls, and the mist. This is the greatest place on earth!"

Mark got to his feet and shrugged again. "Well, go ahead and have it. I still … oh, listen. My place isn't powerful like yours. It's quiet, and there's a little pond. So what? I don't have to shout to hear my own voice when I'm there. I can think, and I can daydream whenever I want." His voice began to falter. He was getting too close, he decided, and just stopped and looked at his friend.

Jerry shook his head and laughed. "You sound crazy. Whenever my mom starts talking weird, my dad always says 'Brain Damage!' in a loud voice, and starts giggling. It makes her pretty mad. Well, I think you have some 'Brain Damage' too!"

Mark glared at him; he knew what was coming next.

"Shall I tell Wendy?" Jerry gloated. "If there's anyone with brain damage, it's her. Well, we all know the truth now! You heard what Richard said. What a pair you make. Why don't you go over to her on the play-ground and tell her about your little hill!"

Jerry was laughing so hard he nearly slipped and fell on the slick, wet rock. Mark almost wished that he would, that he would tumble over into the gorge that he seemed to love so much, and be swept away to the lake, the river, and finally Lynn Canal, and maybe by that time, his laughter would stop.

It was just plain awful. Why *would* Richard tell Jerry, and not him? He had forgotten all about that during today's exciting adventure, but now Jerry had brought it up again, and he couldn't shake the thought. Wendy, of all the girls in the world. Back in first grade, she had thrown her arms around him, right outside the class, and told him that she loved him; tried to kiss him while his friends looked on, smiling. But that was so long ago, and Jerry had never even known about it, thank goodness. Secretly, he thought that Wendy, although not the smartest girl he'd ever known, was sort of pretty, and that just maybe, if she wanted to, they could come up here and see the pond together, if what Richard said was true. No one else could know; they could never be allowed to find out about that!

Of course, Richard did tell stories now and then, and Mark wasn't about to walk over to her on the playground and say hi. She would be right in the middle of a bunch of her friends, and it would look just plain awful.

"Why don't you like my little pond anymore?" Mark asked, as they made their way back to the trail, and the bridge. "You liked it just a little while ago."

"Sure. Until I found this place. Now I can have a kingdom of my own." Jerry pushed ahead, taking confident strides, obviously proud of his new territory.

"Well then, you have your place, and see if I care. I have mine, and we'll make a border between them. Right there." Mark pointed to where a level gully ran below two of the low, bushy summits, on the crest of the ridge. "Anything on the far side of that ditch is mine, and anything on this side is yours. Okay?"

"All right," Jerry nodded. "And we can have wars between our countries, and my powerful kingdom will easily beat your little one with its pond and its boulder!"

"Look here, we're coming to the border," Mark announced. "You have to ask to come into my country. I guess there's no war going on right now, and so we can visit each other. Besides, we left our lunch sacks up there by the pond, and we have to get them. Come on, to the center of my kingdom!"

As they galloped once more to the top of the ridge, where Mark's boulder and miniature lake were, he decided that this was probably the best way to let Jerry in on his secret. Never would he tell him the rest, but if Jerry wanted to play the game of countries and war, then that was fine. They dropped down to the pool's edge, and Mark brushed against the very same alder from which he had pulled the big leaf, seven days in the past.

They stood for a minute, looking at the dark water. "You can see your reflection," Mark breathed. "Even when the sun's not out. It's so clear, so flat, and it lets you see who you really are."

He was staring down at the pond, not watching Jerry. And he was unaware that his friend had lifted a giant, flat rock above his head. As his mind became lost in the glassy surface in front of him, Jerry heaved the granite.

It flew past Mark's shoulder and dropped, plunging into the deep little pond with a heavy *splounch*. Mark was so startled he cried out loud, and he watched in shock as the giant waves rolled outward. Up came the bubbles. The swells hit the little town, riding over the streets, drowning the residents. They swamped the ferry, which was making its way to the far shore. The scene was ruined. His World shattered; there was no trace of any such people left on his Earth. He turned around and faced Jerry, a cold sneer forming on his lips.

"Why did you do that?!"

His voice came out in a scream, and Jerry, who had been smiling in satisfaction of what he'd done, took a step back.

"Huh?"

"I said—!" Mark stopped and looked into Jerry's light blue eyes. "I said," and his voice lowered. "I said, why? It was so quiet, and then you threw in that boulder. It scared me half to death."

"Come on, we've been throwing pebbles into that pool all day long. Whatcha so frightened of, all of a sudden?"

"You're a guest!" Mark yelled at him. "You're in my country, and while you're here, you'll act like a guest! You hear? If I was over there, in your country, I wouldn't go tumbling rocks down into your misty canyon without asking you first. Boy, there's going to be a real war now! You go over there and stand on your rock bank, and I'll stand here on my mount— I mean, my boulder, and we'll throw rocks at each other. Each other! You'll find out how far I can throw."

Jerry turned a circle; he was getting pretty angry himself. "Okay, I will! I can throw further than you anyway."

"No, you can't!"

"Yes, I can!"

"Well, I know one thing you can't do!"

"What? What?"

Mark's brain was processing wildly; he was grasping for something he could do better than his friend. He could think of one thing.

"I can dream better than you."

A silence, and Mark swore he could hear the pond itself. "Yes, I can dream better than you. Not asleep in bed, but when I'm awake, and staring into the water of my pond."

Kicking pebbles of granite with his tennis shoe, he looked down at the flopping laces. He could feel Jerry gazing at him as a stranger from another planet, another place and time. And he thought, *maybe I am* ....

"You are so damn weird."

Mark's head jerked up. Jerry had said *damn*, the first time he ever had, at least the first time in front of his best friend. If Mom had heard that! She'd never let him play with Jerry again. Of course, if she only knew the many times he'd said it himself, when he fell and bruised his knee, or at night when his mouth touched his pillow, after a spanking from Dad.

Jerry lowered his shoulders, then put his hands in his front pockets. "I never said that before." He grinned. "It sounded like an adult, didn't it? Well, I'm sorry I threw the rock. I promise that the next time we go over to my kingdom, you can throw a rock down into the creek, and I won't mind."

"I'm about ready to start home," Mark said. "Here, let's get our lunch bags. That one's yours, with the plastic hanging out of it."

They gathered up their respective trash and began to walk around the pond, which had once again flattened. As they reached the drop-off and the quartz vein, they instinctively turned for a last look.

"Just promise me, Jerry, and I mean really promise, okay? Just promise to be careful with this place. As long as I'm alive, I've got to take care of it. See, it really is mine. I'm part of it. And it's part of me."

Jerry blinked. "What do you mean?" he asked, staring at the pool, then at the boulder.

Should he tell him? *Should I tell him?*

Mark stood rigid, his eyes fixed on the glassy water. And his left little finger began to sting.

"It's got my blood in it," he said in a soft, wavering voice. "And I've got its blood in me."

CHAPTER FIVE

Summer was a year in itself, in sharp contrast to the cool spring and the rainy autumn, and the polar opposite of the white flurries of winter. It was a time for running and jumping, for picnics and beach parties. A time to feel free and easy. Far away, above the Arctic Circle, the greenness that lay atop the permafrost was the setting for a frenzied existence; the foxes, lemmings and pikas lived in fast-forward mode, a whirlwind of activity lasting barely eight weeks, but here in the temperate zone, things were more leisurely paced.

Mark had no favorite season, but he anticipated summer the most, for it was the time to fulfill the plans of spring. When the school year was over, and the bells had rung their last, he was ready for the warm, three-month year. He had mapped out, in his mind, all the things he would do and the places he would go, with Stephen or with his friends. Alone, he would visit his pond, the place he had discovered the spring before last.

The clouds moved across the gulf, shattering his dreams. It was a cold, wet June, the steady drizzle falling for days on end. The ground-level mist blotted out the peaks and completely blanketed the earth with its sheen of moisture, welcomed only by the evergreens that drank heavily, their shallow roots sucking water from the topsoil itself. This year, summer was holding back, hesitant to show itself.

And the clouds moved in yet again, across the marsh flats and into the Valley, rising above the glacier as if searching for a route across the icefield and into Canada. They met resistance and dropped their load in quiet fashion, those horizontally developed belts of white and gray, and the silence of the rain was overpowering.

Mark watched his plans go down to ruin. He spent much of the time indoors, drawing landscape pictures, watching television, or reading books from the downtown library. In the few hours of darkness each night, he was in bed asleep, after thinking about alternatives for the next day. It was not a happy time. On occasion, Jerry would come over to spend the afternoon, and sometimes the urge to go outside and hike around would become unbearable, and so into the rain Mark would go. Tramping through the marshes that lay beyond the road, and slipping about the ferns and the skunk cabbage, he would be soaked through but uncaring; his mind would come to the rescue, the daydreaming would begin, and it would save him. By midsummer, the rain would become his friend.

§

The fishing trip, originally planned for July, got underway at last. Dad said the delay was probably good in the end, because the trout wouldn't be the least interested in salmon eggs before the spawning had begun. As Mark, Jerry, and Doug left the yard via the wooden gate, Mom shouted after them.

"Remember what we said about bears. It's not just blueberries they'll eat!"

The three boys yukked it up, mocking bear growls as they stepped into the forest. Mark was leading the way, confident that if they followed the newly plowed drainage ditch, it would take them straight toward Jordan Creek, though he had never hiked the area before. He didn't let the others know this, rather he made it look as though he were an admiral sailing his home waters.

Doug had a small backpack in addition to the spinning rod in his hand. He was a year older than Mark, in Stephen's class the year before, and had heard of the outing Mark planned. And Stephen, of course, had told his younger brother that he'd better let Doug go along if he wanted to, because his friend was bigger and stronger and could pound fifth-graders into the ground. It didn't frighten Mark at all, but even so, Doug was not someone he would have chosen to spend time with. They'd never talked. Stephen was on his own little excursion today, attending a beach picnic with one of his pals.

Jerry had a spinning rod of his own, and Mark's was of the spin-cast type, given to him by Dad earlier in the summer. It was old and worn, and it looked uncomfortably cheap compared to the others', especially the one Doug carried. It was shorter than the usual six feet, but actually this could be an advantage when fishing narrow streams with clusters of overhanging branches.

Mark had never been on a real fishing trip in his life. Dad had taken the boys to the backwater sloughs of the creek the previous summer, and while Stephen had used the spin-cast rod, Mark had made a little pole from a broomstick, with a bent pin speared through a rubber worm. He had been fascinated with Dad's tackle box. It was full of worms, numerous flies, lures, and tangled leaders with their bright silver swivels. Dad had purchased a spinning rod last year, and more than once had come home with a nice Dolly Varden from the lower end of the creek. Mark had been allowed to accompany him on a few of these trips, but this was his first real adventure with no adults, and so despite the archaic appearance of his equipment, the rod, with its cork handle, felt good and light in his grasp. His new pair of brown rubber boots felt just as good on his feet.

They reached the end of the ditch and passed through a stand of thin willows. Suddenly the world opened up around them, and Thunder Mountain stood directly above the boys. It was a meadow, and a huge one, full of amber weeds, rotted stumps, and alder shrubs. Birds darted from branch to branch among the young trees, and the heat of the sun was felt on the boys' faces.

"What a neat meadow," Doug said in his high, singsong voice. "Do you think the creek is on the other side?"

"Of course it is," Mark answered, but his head was turning wildly to take in the scene. It really was a neat meadow, and so close to home! He wished to explore at length, but the others were moving on, and he hurried to regain his place in the lead. His rod stuck Jerry in the back and bent into a bow shape. Jerry turned around and glared.

"Sorry," Mark said. He moved ahead of the others, and soon the three of them were at the far end of the meadow. And there was Jordan Creek, flowing lazily along. It was a muddy stream, and the bottom was orange, the soil full of iron. It looked to be anything but a suitable fishing hole, from where the boys stood and stared. Mark gazed at the creek, not knowing whether to speak or remain silent.

"What we need to do," Doug said, "is to find a place where the water's running faster and empties into a deep pool. That's where the trout like to gather."

They followed the creek around a bend and past a small beaver dam that was slowly rotting away. Below, the stream became clear, and it rushed quickly past the next bend, emptying into a pool exactly as Doug had described. As they looked at the creek, Mark saw the fin of a pink salmon glide across the stretch of deep water. The fish was ugly. It was a dark red hue, and its upper jaw had taken on a hooked appearance. Its back had become humped, and the flesh seemed about ready to part from the creature's bones. It was a male that had become too weak to jump the small dam above, and it would soon die here, in this pool.

The smell of rotting fish was everywhere, and a few dead and stiffened salmon were scattered along the banks. But according to Doug, this was perfect. Mark crept down the mossy bank and sat on an old stump, to prepare his fishing equipment.

Jerry and Doug sat down too, and for the next few moments, the boys busied themselves with their tackle. Jerry said that the place "looked and smelled like something out of a ghost story", and indeed the trees were old, with whitened trunks, the angel hair moss hanging from the bare limbs. The shadow of the mountain had stretched out beyond them, and the sun, which had beat down upon them in the meadow, could not be found.

"Look what I've got here," Doug announced, as he reached into his daypack. He pulled out another tackle box, a paper sack that presumably contained his lunch, and a small, rolled aluminum package. He tossed it over to Jerry. "Have some of that," he offered. "Dad always takes it on a fishing trip, and I managed to sneak out with it today."

"What is it?" Jerry leaned over. Mark, fiddling with his leader and hook, let his eyes travel to the package.

Jerry unrolled the foil and took a whiff. "Ah! It's chewing tobacco. My dad has some of this too. He has this big copper vase that he spits into. My mom hates it."

Chewing tobacco! And Doug was only eleven years old. Mark pretended to be unconcerned with the entire proceedings, and bent once more over his tackle. A swivel was already secured onto the end of his nylon, eight-pound-test line, but he had to attach the hook, and he struggled, trying to remember how Dad had shown him the clinch knot variation. Out of the corner of his eye, he watched, fascinated, as Jerry took a pinch of the brown material and passed the foil back to Doug. The older boy pulled out an extremely heavy amount and stuffed it into his cheek. He looked like a squirrel, Mark thought, face bulging as though full of nuts.

Jerry followed suit, and asked, out the right side of his mouth, if Mark wanted any.

"In a little while," Mark answered, totally unsure of himself. Jerry was eating the awful-looking junk too! And instantly, he remembered. There *was* a big copper "vase" in the Floyd's living room, without plants. So that's what it was for, he decided. But he could not believe that Jerry was a tobacco chewer. Maybe he was just doing it to look big in front of Doug, who now sat on the bank and tying his line while spitting yellow juice into the creek.

Suddenly Mark felt anxious, as he watched the other two. They seemed to have found a medium along which to communicate with each other, and he was left out of the picture entirely. Well maybe so, he decided, but there was no way they were going to get him to chew any of that tobacco.

At least not right now.

In a moment, the three fishing rods were ready for action. Mark stood up, glad to be on his feet and moving around once more. Sitting there, he had attracted the attention of flies, countless numbers of which swarmed over the fish carrion that lay on either side of the gurgling creek. He pulled the small bottle of red salmon eggs from his front pants pocket and opened the lid.

Doug saw him and came over to where he stood. "Uh, uh," he said, shaking his head. "You don't want to use those. See, I have some in my tackle box. Pink ones too. They don't work, I tell you. I know, I've tried them."

"Why not?" Jerry asked. "That's what I was going to use. We got those," he nodded, "from the sporting goods store."

"Listen. What is it that trout eat? Salmon eggs. And take a look at that jar. Do those look like salmon eggs? I'll tell you what they are. They're probably low-bush cranberries, put in a jar with some fish juice and sold as salmon eggs. That's what my dad told me."

Mark's hand was trembling, and the top layer of red eggs was bouncing around like jumping beans. But he looked up and said, "Well then, what are you going to use?" He felt small next to Doug, who seemed quite an authority on trout fishing.

"Huh! We'll get some *real* eggs. Watch this, and you'll see how."

Doug was wearing hip boots, and with his rod in hand, walked out into the stream. He waited for a moment, his eyes searching the pool in front of him. Jerry and Mark watched from the muddy bank. Doug spat once again and then let fly his hook, which traveled in a flattened arc over the water, splashing in near the far side. He began to reel, the bail clacking shut and the line rising out of the creek, dripping a multitude of tiny droplets. The leader, with its bare hook, slid over the upper back of a female pink salmon. Doug breathed aloud.

"Don't want to get it in the tail! All right now ...." He jerked the rod back and snagged the fish behind the gills. It thrashed about, too weak to put up any real fight. Doug eased backward, up the near bank, carefully so as not to break the thin line. The salmon, which looked to weigh about ten pounds, was soon laying in water only an inch deep, tail rising and falling, in a last attempt to escape the shallows and return to deep water. Doug released the bail, let out extra line, and put his rod down on the bank. He then raised his flannel shirt, pulled a five-inch fishing knife from a previously hidden sheath on his belt, and waded back to where the fish lay, its gills undulating rhythmically, but uselessly.

Mark and Jerry watched, in total amazement, as Doug stabbed the fish through the head, lifted it high out of the water, sloshed his way to the bank, and climbed up to the moss. He dropped the salmon on the ground and fell to his knees beside it. Jerry chewed his small wad furiously, and Mark felt his throat closing as he guessed what Doug would do next.

He and Jerry crowded around, looking on intently, as Doug stuck in the knife once more, this time at the fish's anus. He ripped upward, almost as far as the gills. Immediately, a pink mass flowed out from the salmon's belly, thousands of tiny eggs held together by a slimy, thin jelly. Next came a pale, translucent air sac, which Doug popped with the point of his knife.

"What did you do that for?" Jerry asked, his eyes a foot wide. Mark was beyond words.

Doug giggled softly. "I dunno. For fun, I guess." He scraped all the eggs out of the fish, then held the slit open with his knife. The rest of the innards were visible, and Mark could see the heart, still beating. The glassy eyes looked almost human, and they stared at Mark, as if pleading for help that it knew, deep down, could not come. He felt an immense sorrow for the fish, but Doug's next words were somewhat reassuring.

"The thing is, it would have died here in this pool, without getting far enough upstream to lay its eggs right. It was too weak to finish the trip, I think. My dad says that when a salmon dies before it's supposed to, it lays its eggs quickly, even if its male partner is not around, or already dead, so the eggs probably won't get any milt. The trout and those little minnows would eat most of them anyway, so that's why I snagged this one."

Now the fish was deceased.

Mark felt a little better; he supposed Doug was right, although he had no idea what "milt" was. He started to ask, but Doug and Jerry were already sticking their hooks into the egg mass, then lifting them out with a gob of the little pink spheres attached. Mark followed suit, and then they all walked along the bank, separated themselves by about ten yards or so, and began to fish. Mark was the furthest downstream, at the lower end of the pool, and he cast in his line, then watched as the hook settled near the bottom and bumped along in the slow current.

At once, a swarm of minnows, none of them even two inches long, crowded the bait. They were scarcely as large as the barbed hook, but they ripped and tore at the eggs in a savage manner, looking for all the world as if they hadn't eaten in weeks. Upstream, Jerry and Doug were cursing under their breaths, and Mark knew the same was happening to them. He heard Doug say "Damn" at least a dozen times in the next few minutes, but he himself kept silent, throwing in his line again and again, pulling it from the water to check the bait between casts.

After a while, he began to get a bit daring. There was a submerged log, studded with a couple dozen thin, spiny branches, and it stuck out at a sharp angle from the mud bars below the pool. His line traveled along the bottom of the creek, and when the eggs were a foot from the log, he knew it was time to pull out and cast once again. But he wondered if perhaps a fat trout was waiting underneath the fallen tree. If he could let the line slip down far enough, able to pull straight back upstream in case of an impending entanglement, the trout, if it was truly there, would see the bait.

Preparing to let out an extra two feet, he cast straight to the far corner of the pool. The line sank, and the hook drifted along the bottom, nearly hidden by the swarm of minnows. It disappeared underneath the log, and Mark pulled back, cautiously, to check the position of the hook. Then he relaxed the rod once again, and the eggs moved out of sight.

Jerking the rod in rapid movements, he waited for the strike. As he pulled back quickly, he felt a resistance, and the tip of his rod bent alarmingly. He gasped out loud and yanked back the rod. The hook did not come, and the resistance was steady. He pulled back further, and the rod bent into an even greater arc. He felt a chill go through him. The hook was caught; he had snagged either the log itself or one of the limbs, which impeded his view and prevented him from seeing the end of his fishing line.

For a moment, he thrashed his pole about, muttering to himself. The others saw him but made no move to come and help. Doug was twitching his own pole, at the upper end of the pool, and Jerry was busy putting an extra-large gob of eggs onto his treble hooks. Mark felt a great unease, as if the fishing trip was already at its end, at least for him. He stepped down into the water, his boots sinking into the orange-gray mud, and reeled in his line until it stretched tight. Then he reached out with his pole and hunted around with the tip, trying to find the hook and free it. But the branches! There seemed to be thousands of them, and he swished the tip of the rod, trying to feel a way between them, to push forward in the direction he knew the hook lay. The rushing of the stream below the pool began to annoy him, and he felt the presence of the others, behind his back, fishing and having a good time while he looked like a genuine fool, a greenhorn fisherman, having snared a log within the first ten minutes of the outing.

He lost his temper, gritted his teeth, and snapped back the rod. Instantly, the tension was gone, and for a moment, he thought he had broken his line, and in doing so, lost the only hook he had brought with him. But as he pulled the line from the water, the leader was still attached, and he yelled a cry of success. He reached out, grabbed the hook, and brought it close to examine it. His mighty pull had straightened it a bit, but after a moment of tedious pressing against a nearby tree trunk, the barbed end looked good as new.

"Lucky," he heard Doug call out, from the upper end of the pool. "I watched what you did. I thought your line was a goner!"

"So did I," Mark breathed. He headed toward the newly dead salmon, to their egg supply.

"Have some of that tobacco now," Jerry sang out, making his way back to his own fishing spot. "It's layin' there by Doug's pack."

Mark started to open his mouth, to once again decline the offer, but he stopped and looked at the foil pouch, which gleamed back at him, even in the forest shadow. He dropped his pole and went to inspect the contents at closer quarters.

You are crazy, he told his hand, as it opened the package and reached inside. If Mom and Dad could see you, there would be a talking to, and perhaps a whipping like you never knew.

But he pulled out some of the tobacco, which was sticky and looked like chopped, rotted wood fragments rolled in pine pitch. The smell rose up his nostrils, and it wasn't bad at all. He turned to see if the others were again watching, and they were. "What do you do?" he asked in a small, high voice.

"Stick it in your mouth," Doug answered from the far side of the creek. "Right here," he added, and jabbed a finger inside his cheek, so that a bump formed on the outside, to clarify the position where his own wad lay trapped against his gum. He spat heavily.

Mark opened his mouth. He was nervous, like the first time he had received a shot of Novocaine. He felt the tobacco against his cheek, and he almost pulled it back, but slid the pinch along to where his molars would be in another year or two. Immediately his mouth filled with saliva, and his jaws ached, a feeling similar to that associated with the first gulp of orange juice, early in the morning. He dropped the package to the ground and stood facing the others, his mouth full of spit. The taste was so different than the smell! He coughed out the saliva and held his tongue against the small wad, feeling the sweet burn on his taste buds.

So now he was a big time outdoorsman. Fishing on his own, without Dad, and spitting tobacco juice all over the ground. He rebaited his little hook and once again fished the pool, careful not to let the line drift near the log or get too close to the spawning salmon that appeared from time to time.

A minute later, Jerry's voice came out as a shriek. Mark looked over, and the tip of his friend's spinning rod was jerking about. "I got one here!"

"How big, how big?" Doug reeled in and came splashing over to him. The fish was deep in the water, and hadn't as yet thrashed on the surface.

"I can't tell. I saw it before it ate the hook, but I couldn't tell how big it was. Let me get it to the bank …."

Jerry stepped back and pulled his line after him, without reeling. The fish came up, fighting wildly, and was soon flopping on the mud bar. Jerry snapped the pole back, and the little trout was yanked up onto the moss.

Jerry bent over it. Mark strained to see how big it really was, and Doug, who had started across in their direction, now went back to his position at the head of the pool and resumed his own casting.

"It's not that big after all," Jerry announced, and picked it up. The fish wasn't really a trout, as a close inspection would prove. It was a Dolly Varden, a member of the char family, and the main inhabitant of Jordan Creek. And it was indeed small, perhaps five inches in length. Jerry held it high above his head, proud as could be.

Doug laughed. "That thing's tiny. Throw it back, and we can catch it again next year, when it gets big enough."

But Jerry was stubborn. "I want to keep it. I've never caught a fish before, and I want this one. I can take it home and cook it—fry it in a pan!"

Doug laughed again, but only for a second, because an instant later his own pole was bent. He let out a whoop and began to reel. "Everybody look! I think I've got a big one!"

He stepped backward to the bank, as Jerry had done. Mark could not believe his eyes or his ears. Within a minute there had been two strikes, and all he'd gotten were nibbles from those annoying minnows. Doug slung the fish onto the bank, got out his knife, and while holding the slippery trout in one hand, rapped the knife against the back of its head. Soon, the flopping became a series of soft shudders, and then all motion stopped.

Mark walked along the bank, and soon all three were standing around the trout, which lay still among the weeds and moss. It was a rainbow, about ten inches in length, and the colors shone brightly, especially to the boy who hadn't as yet caught a thing. Mark worked his little wad of tobacco, became full of anxiety, and spit the mush out onto the ground.

To him, the fish was an absolute giant.

Doug decided to take a break and have a bite to eat. Mark and Jerry had brought nothing with them, but they stood near while the older boy began to chew a sandwich. After a couple of bites, Doug looked up, his eyes went from Jerry to Mark, and he said, "Not a bad catch, huh? Maybe you'll get one too." His hand, holding the bread, glistened with trout slime. He swallowed, paused a moment, and then spoke again. "Stevie Boy tells me you don't dream much at all." He looked squarely at Mark's face. "Is that true?"

Mark, staring at the ground, whispered his answer. "Not at night."

"That's strange, really strange," Doug said. Jerry started to say something but stopped himself. Doug continued eating, and Mark went back to where his rod lay. He wondered why his brother had told Doug. Stephen knew because Mark had told him so, many times. Stephen would tell about his dreams at night, and Mom and Dad talked about theirs, and so did Mark's friends. But Mark couldn't share what he so rarely experienced himself. Maybe his parents knew the dreams he described to them were made up, maybe they didn't.

Jerry came with him. "What was that about?" he asked. Mark shook his head. "I don't know," he lied. "Come on, let's get back to fishing."

He was upset, but fishing fever quickly resumed, and he couldn't wait to put his hook in the water. He felt that it was his turn to catch one, and it would be even bigger than Doug's rainbow. He waded into the shallows and let fly his line, this time below the pool, where the small ripples dominated. The eggs became lost in the fast moving water, and once or twice, he was sure the hook had swept across one of the spawning salmon.

The shrubs crowded him on his right, and further in that direction, the creek widened into a reservoir that filtered around an extremely large beaver dam. As he let his line drift with the current, Mark's senses registered two things. The first was a light but definite tug on the fishing rod. His nerves fired as he anticipated the strike. And the second thing was completely different.

His nose picked up a scent, from off toward the enormous dam. He pulled out the line, swung it back, and let it drop for another try, and the smell became stronger still, stronger than that of the fish corpses around him. It was rank, and yet slightly sweet, much like the smell of an abandoned hornet's nest.

The bait was carried downstream, and Mark felt another nibble. As he pulled in his line a second time, he instinctively turned his head in the direction from which the light breeze carried the strange odor.

The black bear was forty feet away, and it sighted Mark as the boy turned. It was on the far edge of the huge beaver dam, near a small channel that rushed past the tangled mass of branches and mud. It reared up, waved its arms, and let out a series of coughing wails. Mark, his eyes wide and mouth open, tried to move, but he was paralyzed from the waist down. He looked at his fishing pole, and the moving water, then snapped his head up again. The bear was still there; it was not an illusion.

Suddenly, he had a flashing vision. His body passed right through the bear and down into the water. Just as suddenly, the vision was gone. He let out a strange moan, and his legs responded at last. They swung him around, and his energy had returned.

He saw Jerry as he splashed upstream, and heard him yelling something about scaring the fish away. Then he saw Jerry's expression change, and he knew that his friend had spotted the creature as well. Jerry opened his mouth and let go a scream for all the world to hear.

Mark shook his head, unable to speak. He thrashed along, and then climbed out of the water. His pole fell to the ground, but he kept on until he reached the level bank. Doug was up and running.

"Where is it?" he asked in a hurried tone. And then he caught sight of the animal, which had come down to the creek to snag its dinner. "Jesus! Get out of here, quick!" he yelled at the others. He picked up his rainbow trout in one hand, his cheese sandwich in the other, and was off toward the meadow.

Jerry came running after. "It's going to attack and kill!" he shouted as he galloped through the weeds. "Mark, hurry, or you'll die!"

Mark was stumbling along in slow motion, his mind a whirlwind of thoughts. A bear was right behind him. His pole was on the bank. The sun was in the sky. The roots were in the path. The stream was moving normally. A tiny char was on the grass. And the bear ....

He stopped in his tracks.

The bear was the mother of the cub, which had been shot, long ago.

He shivered, then looked around. The alders were far off, at the bend in the creek, and the bear was no longer in sight. It wasn't coming after them at all. He turned his head and shouted at Jerry.

And then he began to walk, quite slowly, back the way he had come. To the bend in the creek, and then over to the alder trees. Jerry stood and gaped at him, unbelieving.

"What are you doing?" he yelled from the edge of the meadow.

Mark's voice came out softly, and it was controlled. "Bear. Come here. Please, can you hear me?" He was getting near the creek bend. "Listen. I want to tell you that I'm sorry for what those men did to your cub." His voice began to rise. "Please, tell me that it's all right, that you understand how sorry I am for you." He stopped, then looked into the dense growth. There was no sign of the bear, no movement, nothing. All was silent.

He put his hands in his pockets and lowered his head. He felt the tears drop to his cheeks, and he whispered, to the buttons on his shirt. "I

know you heard me, bear. If you promise not to hurt me, I'll promise that
nothing will ever happen to you, or your cubs, ever again."

He was sobbing, and after wiping his eyes, he turned away from the
creek. He walked, like a drunk man, back to the meadow, where he found
Jerry crouched behind an ancient stump. And he sniffed, swallowing hard,
as Jerry looked up at him with fright in his eyes. Mark shook his head.

"It's gone, Jerry. I went to look for it, but it was gone. I guess we scared
it pretty bad."

Jerry stood up, and he gave Mark a look similar to the one when the
two first met, in the path through the snow. Both boys were trembling.

"Why did you go back there? Did you want to get eaten up alive?"

"I wanted to see the bear up close," Mark lied for the second time in
less than ten minutes. "I've never seen a grown one before. I knew it would
run from us. The only reason I ran myself was because—" he stopped,
looked down at the trailing raspberry, and noticed that the berries tended
to be in groups of two, three or four.

"My pole's back there," Jerry said. "And so is yours. And did you see
Doug? I don't know where *he* ran off to, but he hasn't come back."

"Well, let's go back to the creek. I think the bear's gone for the day."
Mark forced a grin.

Jerry was hesitant, but after a moment, the two were again standing
by the pool where the fish had been caught. Doug's pole and tackle box lay
on the bank, but the older boy was nowhere in sight. His pack was leaning against a small tree, with the roll of tobacco on the ground in front
of it. The boys decided, after a short discussion, that they would take his
equipment back to Mark's house, and Doug could pick it up later, as it was
evident he wouldn't be returning to the creek.

"He was a scaredy-cat, wasn't he?" Jerry forced a nervous laugh. "And
I thought he was the brave kind, or something. But no, he turned out to
be a real chicken!"

"Listen. I want to fish some more. Just for a minute, or maybe two. I
haven't caught anything yet."

"You kidding? You still want to fish!" Jerry seemed quite impatient to
leave, having all but forgotten why they had come to the creek in the first
place.

Mark baited his hook and stood on the bank, this time above the
giant beaver dam. Everything looked the same as upstream, with the
spawning salmon in the water and on the banks. The smell of bear was

gone, replaced by the smell of carrion. Jerry stood near the trees as Mark cast his line, and he watched as the baited hook traveled to the small rushing channel at the edge of the beaver dam, right where the bear had been sighted. He watched as the rod bent double, and watched in awe as Mark proceeded to haul a fourteen-inch Dolly Varden to the bank a moment later.

Mark grabbed a large, flat rock, and pounded it against the fish's head, as he had learned from Doug. He was beaming widely as he stuck his index finger through the Dolly's gills and out through its mouth. Lifting the fish over his head, he laughed in his moment of triumph. Jerry's eyes had a look of shock that just wouldn't go away.

"I can't believe that! One minute longer," he said in a low, scowling mockery.

Sure he can believe it, Mark thought to himself. That fish gave up its own life so that I would be happy again, after such a scare.

But he would never tell Jerry the truth. Jerry would think he was crazy.

They started home, Mark wearing the pack and Jerry loaded down with the tackle boxes and Doug's fishing rod. They came to the meadow, and the sun burned down upon their heads. Mark stepped lively, his brown hair bouncing, and his eyes glittering as he felt the weight of the two Dolly Varden char, held by a stick in his left hand. The birds appeared, chirping and zooming around as the boys crossed the open field and headed for the drainage ditch.

"Where do you think Doug went, anyway?" Mark asked as they fought their way through the stand of willows. "I hope he didn't run straight to my house and tell my mom. You know what? She'll think we're dead and have someone, I guess the Forest Service, come looking for our chewed bodies."

Jerry frowned. "That's sick. But you are right. About the Forest Service, I mean."

They picked up their pace along the ditch, and a moment later the house was in sight. They raced up to the back gate, swung it open, and tramped over to the porch. Mark hopped up to the door and put his hand on the knob.

Someone was turning it from the inside. The door flew open, and Mom stood there, a strange expression on her face. At once, the boys realized their single fear was justified. Doug *had* been there.

Mom talked rapidly, chattering like a little girl. "I was just about to call the police. Doug just left here, for home. He said a bear attacked you in the woods. He said he thinks you're dead, and he was the only one who made it out all right. I called your dad. He's on his way home. And here you are. Here you are."

She had been crying, Mark could tell.

And the sun, high in the sky, was now a black dwarf. Mark seemed to collapse inward, his breath short. What could he say? Mom had not asked a question, but apparently was expecting an answer all the same. He looked to his feet, and then at Jerry, who wore a blank expression. He shrugged, and his voice came.

"Uh ... maybe you should have called the Forest Service—not the police." He looked at Jerry again, and the two began to giggle uncontrollably.

Mom raised herself up to an unbelievable height and stared at Mark in a way he had never seen before. She let out a screech, quite foreign-sounding, and both boys jumped. Mark's spine tingled. And for the next few minutes, there was a scene that was much too ugly, and Jerry was—Mark later thought—unfortunately caught in the middle of it.

§

Late in the evening, things had settled down. Dad and Mark had gone over the events of the day and come to an understanding. Doug's parents had driven over and picked up their son's fishing gear. Doug was not with them. And Stephen had arrived home from his beach party to find that no one was very interested in how it had gone. As quickly as the panic had begun, it was lifted away.

Forty feet from a black bear, and then contaminated with the animal, passing directly through it. Deep inside, he knew there was a message of some sort, something to be deciphered, and it would come to him at the proper time ....

He woke up, startled. It was three weeks later, and the room was pitch black. The glow-in-the-dark hands of the clock on his dresser told him it was just after four in the morning. He looked at Stephen, who was curled into a ball. Sitting up, he glanced at the door, which was ever so slightly ajar. He sat up straighter, the covers falling away, and he was shaking a little. He'd just had a dream, the first he could recall in a very long time, and the ability to remember it scared him. He took a deep breath, and another, and began to relive what his mind had just shown him.

He had been somewhere most odd, moreover a collection of odd places, all fused together. It was a gigantic contraption of metal, glass and plastic. It was a restaurant, an amusement park ride, and a station of some sort, all rolled into one, and it was occupied by hundreds of people. There were enormous windows, and although it was dark outside, he could see what appeared to be alien craft taking off and landing.

He had no idea why he was here, but he did know that he had to leave. So did others. Many people were hurrying to get away from this place, while many more stayed behind, unconcerned. Mark felt an over-powering urge to join those who were departing, and he descended to the bottom of the weird tower of artificial constructs, fighting to catch up with those who now filed quickly toward the strange, dark station. He didn't know why he had to leave this place, but that didn't matter.

In the darkness of night, he could see a train at the station, and the people were climbing aboard. It was a mad rush, the faces of the people strained, full of tension. Mark got on board as well, and he began to recog-nize friends among the crowd. These were not friends he knew from his waking hours, but they were indeed people he'd somehow known forever and for whom he had warm feelings. How he knew them, he couldn't say, but again, it didn't matter.

The train accelerated, and suddenly the journey became obvious. They were heading for a place called North. He, his friends, and all the others on board, moving toward a single destination. What he would do when they arrived, he could not guess, but like most everything else, *it didn't matter.*

The train slowed and came to a stop. Something was wrong. Mark got out of the car, put his hand on the step railing, and yelped. The metal rail was icy. He jumped to the ground and strained his eyes in the darkness. Snow! The air was terribly cold, the train's engines had stalled, and the cars were frozen to the track. The people were pouring from the cars, the children crying, and the adults burdened with the few belongings they had managed to bring with them. Terrifying, dischorded pipe organ music was emanating from the heavens.

Mark looked wildly about, searching for the familiar faces, but they were mingling into the crowd, which was now traveling on foot, away from the frozen rail train. The line of humans stretched on ahead, to the horizon, and Mark attempted to join them. The horrifying, non-harmonic sounds of the pipe organ increased in amplitude, and he became frantic as he stumbled forward, but the deep snow hindered his movements. He looked up and gasped. Out there, on the edge of the world, stood a single mountain, its slopes draped in winter white, in blinding contrast to the blackness of night. To its base the crowd was streaming. And the mountain's identity was unmistakable.

The dream had flickered out; he never caught up with his friends.

He sat there on his bed for a long time. His heart began to resume its normal pace, and his head was clear. But he knew he would sleep no more this night. He glanced over to the window and then, as if hypnotized, he rose from the bed and walked past his brother. He put his hand on the metal slide and pushed the glass open.

It was quite chilly. He looked at the playground and his school; in a matter of hours, he would cross that playground and begin the fifth grade. The tall trees beyond were dark shadows, silent guardians of the night. The mountains were giants that slept with the earth. He poked his head out and looked upward, at the sky.

Thousands of stars blinked at him. He stood on his tiptoes and gazed at them for minutes, then tens of minutes. His eyes were full of crusted sleep, but he did not wipe them; he was glued to the pinpricks of light set against the blackness of eternal space, the most glorious thing he had ever seen.

He looked across the heavens, searching for something; he knew not what. He stared intently at a bright, yellow star in the celestial northeast, high above the ridges that obscured *the* mountain. Mark did not know its name, or if it had one. But at that moment, it became his.

I will learn every one of them. Especially the bright yellow one, shining high above the *mountain, for it is mine. Look at them! Blue, red, yellow and white stars. From here to the end of the universe, and further. Always further.*

Does North lay out there, beyond the end? Is the end also a beginning? A return? And the *mountain. Is that a symbol for North, here on Earth?*

I am going North.

CHAPTER SIX

A thin layer of clouds hung over the Valley, all that remained from yesterday's storm. The rain had settled quickly into the earth, and the puddles were gone. The breeze was cool but faint. And the birds were coming to life, the die-hards that remained in the north country for the winter.

From the playground, the view was tremendous. The mountains rose in splendor above the stands of tall spruce. Their tops met the sheet of frozen vapor, and their upper reaches were dusted with snow; soon the flakes would be falling to the floor of the Valley itself. The peaks were sighing, as cold air rushed off their slopes and settled to the lowlands, and the dim sunlight reflected upward through the clouds.

They were on their way home from school. Mark and his older brother were in deep conversation as they crossed the playground, kicking their way through the speckled granites. Mark felt the earth around him, pressing in on him as he walked, yet he talked in a light tone, as he and Stephen gave each other an account of the day's events.

A vacation was ahead of them, and Mark could almost smell Mom's cooking as they approached the house. She would make the dressing and the cranberry sauce tonight, and she would be up early tomorrow to prepare the turkey. Dad had completed the fireplace only days before, and the flames would surely roar this evening as the boys stayed up into the late hours. Stephen would take control of the television. He watched it more than anyone else, wearing out his eyes on the bright screen. Dad would read one of his favorite novels. Amy would try to help in the kitchen, perhaps be given the task of stirring, or rinsing utensils, while the good smells continued to pour from the stove, reminding all that a great day of feasting was at hand.

Mark would be outside.

When the boys reached the house, Mark raced through the kitchen, down the hall, and into his room. The magazine, in its manila envelope, lay on his bed. He ripped open the envelope, flopped down on the mattress, and began to study the November star charts.

It *must* clear up by nightfall, he muttered to himself as he squinted at the diagrams. This was his second issue, and he had learned so much already from both the magazine and Dad, who filled him in on the finer points of astronomy. The science had taken control of him like nothing before. He thought constantly about the stars and the planets, and he'd finished a report only last week, which he presented in oral fashion to his class at school. He had absorbed the information in an almost desperate manner, as if the sky would fall and be gone forever before he learned what the sky truly was.

Now, he felt like a master of the stars himself. Only one problem remained, and this one couldn't be solved without Nature's help. There hadn't been a clear night for weeks.

The weather had been awful. Overcast skies had more than dominated, they had overpowered the Valley, the mountains, the entire town. The days were gloomy and dark, and the stars had remained hidden for almost a month. The boy, laying on his bed, had gathered his facts and learned the secrets, but unfortunately could not put his new knowledge to use. Nature's timing had gone all weird, and when he was alone, Mark asked Nature why it was making him wait so long.

But the forecast was encouraging. The clouds were to be swept away by this evening, and clear skies were in the picture for the next few days. As he quickly read the pages of the magazine, Mark felt an excitement rising in him; he awaited the moment when he would rush outside, crane his neck, and stare upward at the bright dot known as Capella, his favorite star in all the heavens. Not just a star, but a mysterious symbol, the meaning of which would someday be understand, he was certain.

He heard Stephen enter, but didn't look up as his brother threw his books across the room and onto his own bed. He continued to scan the magazine for a long period of time. Only after an hour did he finally become vertical, and he went out to the living room to check the cloud cover from the big picture window. It was already past twilight, and the thinning clouds had become quite dark in appearance. In the kitchen, Mom was busy with the dressing and the homemade cranberry sauce, tonight's dinner having already been prepared. Mark wrinkled his nose as he stared outside at the slowly moving sheet of water vapor, which now looked as dark as the sky itself. He detected a sweet and sour recipe of some sort, probably meatballs he decided, as he thumped his fingers against the double pane of glass. The window was cold, reminding him again that winter was just around the corner. The breeze, though slight, had carried a chill all through the afternoon, and he'd had to keep moving during recess on the playground, lest he begin shaking like the autumn leaves, many of which, this year in particular, remained on the cottonwoods.

The station wagon turned into the driveway, and he watched as Dad shut off the headlights, got out of the car, and walked up to the front door, carrying his briefcase. The door opened and Dad stood in the foyer, looking at Mark and putting on a mock shivering act.

"Getting cold out there! Guess it's time to pull out the sleds and fix the runners, hey? That is, if you're interesting in sledding at the glacier hills this winter."

"Of course." Mark liked sledding, in fact he liked anything that involved speed and daring, anything except running across big, slimy logs over a ravine. Once, the previous winter, he had taken a bad spill during a hair-raising plunge down a virgin slope. No one else had yet dared test the steeply angled hill, and Mark, feeling like a pioneer at the top, had become a tangled mess of arms, legs, winter clothes, and sled runners at the bottom.

He blinked, remembering. He would try that hill again this winter— if it ever came—and be the first to reach the bottom unscathed.

"November, and still no snow," he complained, still looking out the window. Dad shook his head as he put his coat into the front closet. "Don't worry, it's on the way. These things run in cycles. A few early winters, then a few late ones. Huh! I've never heard of a green Christmas around this town!"

"There's one every year."

"Oh, there is?" Dad gave him a wise look. "Don't tell me. I know what you're going to say. You'll argue that the spruce and hemlock stay green all year, never losing their needles, so there's always a green Christmas. 'Just look out the window' you'll say on Christmas morning. Right?"

Mark shook his head. "No. Wrong."

The wise look was gone. "I see. Calling your old man wrong. Explain, boy!"

"Evergreens don't keep their needles year-round. They're always losing them, but only a few at a time, kind of like the way we lose our hair. The rest, you had correct."

Dad chuckled loudly and got out his comb. "Actually, when you get to be my age, that analogy just doesn't work too well. Anyway, I was only testing you. Wanted to see if you knew that. Look here, if you think you know so much, then tell me, how many moons does Saturn have?"

Mark thought for a moment; he'd been reading about this only weeks before. He knew that Jupiter had the most, and Saturn was next ....

"They discovered Janus a few years ago, and that makes ten. But they think there might be more."

"Correct. In fact, I'll tell you, when they send a craft up close, I bet they discover dozens and dozens more. Let's wait and see! Something about that planet ... always gets to me."

Mark shrugged agreeably, and they drifted into the den, where Mom was setting the table. He slid into his seat and watched out of the corner of his eye as Dad kissed his wife. It was a short kiss, like always, and Mark wondered, were the kisses much longer in the past, before there were children in the house? And his dinner plate, with its desert rose design, became very interesting for the next few moments.

Stephen drifted in. Amy came next, and then the food. It was meatballs. Mark ate and listened as Dad gave the day's report of the goings on at work, much as the two boys had done earlier among themselves.

He thought about what he and his brother had discussed. Stephen was in the sixth grade, and one of his classmates had brought in, to exhibit, a real live turkey. Apparently, it was a gift to the youngster's family, as it sat in a cage decorated with tiny chef hats. Mark's class had made a tape recording of a play, designed by the students themselves. It was about the very first Thanksgiving, when the natives were invited to Plymouth to share in the great celebration. Mark had played the part of one of the visitors. His name was Squanto. He'd brought deer and fish to the "white people", to help with the feast. It was a small part, and all he said was a variety of "ugh" noises and broken sentences. And it had sounded very funny when the tape was played back, and he had turned red as can be.

He realized now just how silly he must have looked, in front of his class, making those sounds. And he realized, too, that if anything, it was unfair to recreate the natives in this manner, but he didn't know how to explain this to anyone.

He ate dinner quickly, and was on the verge of excusing himself, to head for the window and check the clouds again, when Dad motioned to him.

"And this is what you'll want to hear. Frank was telling me this afternoon about the trip his cousin and nephew took, up onto the icefield. They went up there by helicopter and skied around quite a bit, taking lots of pictures, and doing a bit of climbing."

Mark, all ears, sat like a statue.

"Frank must know as much about these mountains as anyone in town. We got into a pretty good conversation later on, and he told me some things about the mountains here, things I never knew. Like that one you seem to have fallen in love with. There's something mighty interesting about that peak. Can you guess what it is?"

Mark was almost beside himself. Something interesting about *the* mountain, he thought to himself. His mouth opened slightly, and he let out a squeaky "What?"

"That thing's unnamed, and has never been climbed. I could hardly believe it myself. Right there, almost in full view, and unclimbed. I asked Frank if we were talking about the same one, and he made it clear that we were."

Mark swallowed hard. The top of his head became prickly, and he bounced slightly, from the motion of his heart. Never climbed! He grinned at Dad to show that he'd heard, and then he stood up and moved slowly out of the den. He went to the front window and peered into the twilight. Out there was *the* mountain, hidden from this angle, but there, nonetheless. Unclimbed!

The sky was clearing somewhat. He saw a few stars beginning to show as the clouds continued to thin, and he turned and went back to his room. He gave his charts a last viewing, then put on his heavy coat and wool cap. And a moment later, as his brother was turning on the television and Dad was reaching for his book-of-the-evening, Mark was stepping onto the back porch. The time was now, the place was now. The stars were his.

He went to the storage van and pulled out one of the army cots. A moment later, he had it set up in the far corner of the Nilsson's lot, near his favorite entrance into the woods. He wanted to be as far as possible from the porch lights. Somewhat methodically, he stretched out on the cot and just gazed up at the sky.

He watched the clouds thin out, and he wondered what the kids at school would think of him, if they saw him stretched out on an army cot in the corner of his backyard. He decided that he didn't really care. He didn't care what they thought at all, not even Jerry. Then he decided that perhaps he might care a bit what Kathy would think, because secretly, he liked her somewhat. But then again, she was just another girl, another human being. He was his own. Another breed. From another place and time. He recognized Nature as his home, his family, and his friend. If only he could tell someone.

He shook his head. What had he just done? Why had he thought like that? He pushed the idea away, felt it sink deep within him, and concentrated on the sky once more.

And there was Capella! It hung in the center of the sky, almost directly above him. Squinting, he could make out the rest of the constellation Auriga. He began to look wildly about, feeling a thrill rush through him as he identified the constellations, and the bright stars, one by one. The Big Dipper and Ursa Major. Polaris, around which the other stars circled. And the tiny foursome which made up Lyra, with its own bright beauty, the gently twinkling Vega.

Setting in the west was Deneb, the brightest star in the constellation Cygnus. To its left was Delphinus, the dolphin. Mark watched the latter for a time, and from this night forward, it was to become one of his favorites.

The Milky Way was a giant arc, and the boy was fascinated at the thought of looking through the plane of the galaxy. Those stars were so very far away, and a powerful thought struck him. Even at the speed of light, it took years for those stars to send their beams across the void of space and into his eyes. He was looking deep into the past, and yet for some reason, it seemed as though the past was with him, enveloping him, at this very moment.

He rose up, stepped away from the cot, and walked absently across the yard until he was at the front gate. He swung it open, his neck still crooked. And then he was wandering off down the road, looking at the sky and feeling as though he belonged to it. He walked around the neighborhood until he reached the turnoff to the loop road. Heading in that direction, he began to feel the strange tremor, and the faint voices, coming to the surface for yet another round.

So much there is to learn. So much to explore, here on this Earth. The people that I live with, and my friends, are there to help, but I don't need much of that.

Ah! Look where I am. Coming to the loop road, and we all know what that means. My mountain will appear in a moment. There it is! See how it rises, up into the night sky, a dark form, but not without a life of its own. How can I look upon something as wonderful as this and not feel the mystery of it all? It tugs at me, asks me to join in the search for the true meaning of this life, and any other that is yet to come. I will do as it asks, for I am a part of it.

It was dark on the road, but Mark sensed a gentle, steady light all around him. He didn't know from whence it came, but he knew that he was close to an explanation. He felt the pressure in his throat, as if a heavy scarf was settling in folds around his neck. And then a fresh breeze whipped around him, stirring him from his reverie.

He stood still and looked about, watched as the trees swayed in the wind, heard the rustling of their green boughs, and felt the gravity at his feet. And he sighed as a car approached, its headlights aimed directly at him. He stepped back as it zoomed past. Hands in pockets, he turned and started back the way he had come.

He always did that—went back the way he had come. Why, he wondered, did he find himself in such patterns of forward and reverse? Perhaps the very walk was the medium along which he carried his inner thoughts, coming to the surface as the glory of Nature slid past his periphery. And when the outward thrust came to a halt, he was brought back to the conscious state of being, and there was nothing left to do but turn, reverse his course, and head home.

Home. That word was powerful, he decided, so powerful that he found himself using it to describe not only the artificial environment in which he ate and slept, but also the world around, the one in which he ran, played, and daydreamed. The mountains and the trees, the pond and the boulder; to him they were the most powerful things he had ever observed, reached out to, and touched. And when he was in their hold, he felt his other home, and the faces he knew, begin to slip away and fade into the more obscure, barely detectable part of reality, almost … not even there.

That cosmic nightmare dream, just a few months ago. It contained his search, but also different faces. Why?

The house was approaching, and the lamps burned yellow through the large front window. He knew that security lay within those walls, but a different kind lay elsewhere. Why?

He looked up as he walked, and the stars, leaving all else behind, were moving with him. They were the most powerful things of all, those stars, and they would never leave him. Was he composed of them? The answer was unclear.

He went to the corner of the yard and refolded the cot. After storing it in the van, he climbed up to the porch and entered the house; felt the warm air and detected the voices of his family. He started for the living room, then stopped and bent down to pick up a few extra logs from the woodbox. The smell of smoke was not yet in evidence, and a crackling sound told him that Dad was just getting the spruce kindling to blaze away. He hefted the logs, felt a splinter jab into one of his fingers, but did not stop to pull it out. It was only wood, he told himself, as he carried the heavy load out through the den.

He dumped the logs into the iron rack, and Dad nodded his thanks. Stephen was glued to the television, and Mom was in the kitchen, still preparing tomorrow's meal.

"Notice your sister," Dad said, poking the kindling with one hand and reaching for heavier wood with the other. "She was the one yelling to have a fire tonight, and now that I've got it started, she's nowhere to be seen. I might have guessed. She has the same, very short attention span you boys did."

"A short what?" Mark asked.

"Means you can't concentrate on anything for very long. When you were as little as Amy, you'd ask Mom or I to read you a story. After about three pages, you'd get tired of it and want to draw a picture. And halfway through your drawing of a tree or a building, or whatever, you'd be ready to play in the backyard, on that squeaky old swing set."

Mark grinned to himself, remembering the swings he and Stephen used to play on, back in New Mexico. When the swinging began to get a little too rough, the supports would leave the ground, and Mom would be looking out from the kitchen window, ready to come running in case the whole thing came apart, which fortunately it never did.

Dad settled back in his easy chair, and Mark left the room. He shuffled into the kitchen and asked Mom what she was preparing.

"Well, nothing much right now," she sighed. "Most of the hard work is over. But I've got to get all my ingredients together for the pie. Listen, which would you rather have to drink tomorrow, milk or tea?"

Mark lifted his eyebrows. "You mean I have a choice?"

"Of course, it's an occasion."

"Then I'll have wine," Mark decided at once. Mom gave him a look of impatience, to which he merely shrugged off, and then he turned and hopped on down the darkened hall toward his room.

Amy was sitting on the hall floor, reading a little book. Mark started to open his mouth and tell her that she was straining her eyes in the dimness, but changed his mind and quietly tiptoed past. He fingered his doorknob, then paused as he heard the radio on the other side. Stephen had forgotten to turn it off.

He stood still and listened. It was a song, and the voice was imploring him to go and tell someone how much he cared. Guess that song just wasn't meant for him, he thought. He supposed that he cared some for those around him, but most of all he cared for the world at large, and it cared for him. Wasn't that enough?

His hand slipped off the doorknob, and he turned his attention to his sister, sitting in the darkness. Her back was to him, so he could not see her face, only her long, thin brown hair. Did he care for *her*? He looked at her and pretended that something had happened to her; tried to think how it would make him feel. And he decided that of course he must care for her, because she was so young and innocent, and she hadn't yet been caught up in the madness of society.

He walked back to where she sat and knelt beside her. Putting his arm around her, he drew her close and read the little book with her. Amy couldn't actually read much of anything, but she'd had the story told many times by Mom and Dad, and Mark was certain she knew every word, and that she fully understood the pictures. The story was about a cat, and the cat didn't know how to meow. When it tried to speak, it made the sounds of other animals instead. It would sound like a pig, or a goat, or a dog. Finally, a parrot in a cage had to demonstrate the correct way to sound like a cat, and all was well. Mark had always figured that if a parrot could sound like a human or another animal, then why not a cat, but he knew this wasn't the author's point.

"Pretty good book, isn't it?" he whispered in his sister's ear.

She nodded. "Want to read it again?"

"No. But listen, Amy. Remember I wrote Grandmother a letter and finished it last night? I'm going to send it to her tomorrow. Oh, that's right, I have to wait until the next day."

"Why?" The little girl looked up at him.

He smiled. Holidays were everyday to her, and that seemed right, Mark thought. "Tomorrow's Thanksgiving. The mailman will be home eating turkey, like the rest of us. But I wanted to tell you, that if you would like, I'll let you write something to Grandmother, at the end of the letter. Your name, or whatever you can write, so she can see it. Okay?"

"Yes!"

He went to his room, shut off the radio, and got out the letter and a pencil. A moment later, the two were busy together in the darkness of the hall, Amy writing her name and a brief salutation, and Mark giving all necessary assistance, while the book served as a tiny desk on the carpet.

Mom had left the kitchen, heading for the living room, when she saw them. "What are you two doing?" she called out.

Amy jerked her head up. "Writing a letter!" she yelled. "And we're busy," she added, as Mark giggled to himself.

"Sorry," Mom excused herself, and backed away to join Dad by the fire. The interruption over; Amy bent once more to her task until finished.

"Can you read it to me?" she asked politely. Mark hesitated, then nodded. "But I'll read it very quietly," he told her.

> Dear Grandmother,
>
> How are you? I am fine. I have not written in a long time, and I am sorry. Thanksgiving is in two days, and we are cooking a big turkey! Next summer I am going to play baseball, I think. This year it won't snow at all. I hope it does soon. When I want to be by myself I go to the glacier and sit on a Rock by a Pond. Can you come up here and see me some day? You will like it here. The mountains are pretty. I went up one twice. Please come up here soon if you can.
>
> I will write again. Please write soon.
>
> Love, Mark
>
> Hi Grand Mother! I can write!
> Love, Amy

He put the letter down and looked at the girl. "Do you like it?" he asked.

"Yeah. When can I write a letter? When I get as big as you?"

"That's right. When you get to be as big as me, you can write a letter, and I won't have to help you because you'll know as much as I do. Well, maybe as much."

"Mark, will you play ball with me?"

"Tomorrow we'll play with your ball. It's too late tonight. You should go to bed. Why don't you go and watch the fire for a bit, before you do?"

She rose, then scampered into the living room, while Mark sat alone, smelling the wood smoke and hearing the crackling of the freshly chopped spruce. He must care about Grandmother too, considering how he'd ended his letter. He wouldn't write that if he didn't mean it, would he?

And then Amy was back, falling into his lap. "I watched the fire. Well, I have to go to bed."

Mark laughed to himself but didn't let it show. "All right. Have pleasant dreams, and I'll see you tomorrow." He mussed her hair, and started to lift the girl from him, but she wound her arms around his neck and kissed him on the cheek. He heard a scraping noise, coming from far, far, far away, millions of miles away. It must have been Dad, breaking up the remains of the fire, as the crackling sounds were now faint, yearning sighs.

"I love you, Mark," Amy whispered.

§

The family slept late, except for Mom, who was up and working on the turkey ahead of the sun. Mark had a light, relaxing breakfast, then joined Amy and Stephen to watch the holiday specials on television. Dad was gone for an hour, taking a few gifts to friends and a supply of goods downtown in support of a dinner for the needy. Soon the house was filled with the aroma of turkey and trimmings, and the table was decorated in fine style.

The Nilssons had begun a tradition of their own, a few years back, and the boys spent part of the early afternoon bringing it to life once again. They set up Stephen's electric train set on the table, in a small oval around the area for the main dishes. The control panel was positioned to the right of where Dad would sit, at the far end. Wires were then hidden beneath a pile of fake shrubbery.

Next, a Union Pacific loco was placed on the rails, and the boys coupled it to a flatbed, onto which would sit the gravy boat. Behind the flatbed, a hopper was attached, and into it, Mark and his brother loaded the cloth napkins. A second hopper contained the salt and pepper shakers.

Dad came in as they were applying the final touches, and he shook his head. "For heaven's sakes! I thought we'd had enough of the dinnertime rail yards." But he grinned all the same, and then helped stuff the longer wires under the table and out of sight.

True, it had little to do with Thanksgiving, Mark thought. Well, it *was* something different, and difference was what he thrived on.

Dinner, for the most part, went smoothly. It was a long, drawn-out affair, unlike most of the meals in this household, which were over in twenty minutes or so. But Thanksgiving was such a big dinner, and was served in such a strange leapfrogging of dishes, that it was nearly an hour from the time the small copper bell was rung to the moment when Dad finally pushed his plate from him.

When Mark heard the dinner bell, he had rushed to his chair to find a pleasant surprise. Wine! He had been kidding the evening before, but there it was, right beside his fork, red and sparkling. Dad saw him staring at it and told him that if he wanted to get plastered, just looking at it wasn't going to help. And Mom had grimaced and told Dad that he was going to make an alcoholic out of their son, and that she knew this had been a bad idea in the first place, and why had she ever gone through with it? Mark thought it very funny that Dad smiled but didn't answer his wife.

Everyone was served, and the train derailed only once during the entire process. Mark reached over to set the affected car back on the track, and as his fingers made contact with it, there was an instant where he could swear the car was freezing … and just as quickly, his skin was back to normal temperature. He let out a short gasp, knowing this was some sort of message, but he couldn't figure out what. He told no one about it, and he could see that no one had noticed.

Mark ate heartily, and he gulped the rosé, feeling the warm glow in his stomach. He and Stephen exchanged cheers often, clinking glasses and proclaiming the day as one of great thanks—thanks that they were allowed to participate in such an adult habit.

Afterward, when the meal had drawn to a close, Dad said "Wait. Don't get up yet. Now we're going to say the blessing."

The others looked around the table in an odd way. A blessing? They never said blessing, for as long as Mark could remember. Besides, the meal was finished.

"Now that you've eaten and can feel your stomach bulging with food, why don't each of you sit very still and try to think of something good, something that will make you joyful for the excellent meal you've just had. The past hour has been fun, and so you remember that, while you're thinking."

Everyone closed their eyes. Mark thought, was this going to be another tradition? Blessing at the end of Thanksgiving dinner? But he relaxed and searched his mind for a good thought.

Where did the food come from? It came from the farm. The farm needed rain, it needed sun, and it need the air that was all around. It needed the Earth and Sky. The farm was a part of the larger world, the true World.

The farmer had grown the food, had slaughtered the turkey, and had depended on them for his own livelihood. Just as he, young Mark, depended on the farmer. But the farmer depended on the Earth as well. Perhaps *he* was giving thanks to the Earth, at this very moment. He better be!

Thanks for the mountain that is mine.

Thanks for the pond, and the boulder.

Thanks for the trees, and the cool wind, and even for the many rainy days. They are so necessary.

Thanks too, I suppose, for Amy. At least I can tell her that I care.

Oh, and thanks for that weird thing that happened during the meal. It was a message of some kind, and I promise to figure it out.

And that was the end of Thanksgiving dinner.

§

Much later in the evening, he went outside to look at the stars again. He carried with him his second helping of the pumpkin pie which, except for the outer crust, was gone before he had made it as far as the road. He looked upward, nodded a greeting to Capella, to Ursa Major, and to Polaris.

Walking along, he noticed the clouds piling in from the southwest, a day ahead of the schedule forecast. They appeared gray and murky, even through the darkness, and they threatened to blot out the thousands of tiny pinpricks, the twinkling dots of light that so hypnotized the boy as he moved slowly down the street.

The constellation of Delphinus was setting, and he was walking toward it, traveling the same route as the previous night. When he reached the loop road, he turned and looked for the dark shadow of *the* mountain. And he repeated his thanks for its existence, for without it, what would he be? He would be a nothing. He would be like many others. This mountain saved him.

The stars did, too. He stretched out his arms, to opposite horizons, both of which were hidden behind the mountains and the trees. He gave thanks for the sky above, even for the fast-approaching clouds which were now racing to cover Aries, Taurus, and the rising twins, Castor and Pollux.

Jerry was his friend, but only that, he decided. He relied on him for good conversation. Of course, it had been Jerry who had pointed out *the* mountain so long ago, and Jerry was his preferred companion when it came to outdoor adventure. But he was unsure if Jerry, his friend, could possibly think of the sky and stars, Earth, and the green of the living world in the same manner as himself. It was useless to try and combine his two worlds—they did not mix.

And one of the two would triumph, scoop him up in the end, and keep him forever. Which would it be?

He shivered, thinking about his two worlds as he looked to the northeast, to that wonderful, towering spire of ice and rock. He thought about his home and the material things within. There were his parents, whom he alternately worshiped and criticized. There was Stephen, and Mark could communicate with him just fine, but alongside his brother, he felt small and sometimes left out. There was Amy, the innocent young girl, who took the days as they came, who felt she had already lived forever, never thinking of the long, sometimes torturous life ahead. But she looked up to him in a way that made him feel responsible, and this reminded him that he was still a human.

Yes, there was Jerry, the center of his ring of friends, off of whom he could bounce excess thoughts and ideas, never having to worry about highly negative feedback. There was school, and plenty of human activity to keep him busy. Radios, magazines, fishing rods, downtown avenues, the very clothing on his back. All of these things were symbols of mankind, one of Mark's two worlds, and these things enveloped him securely. There was TV, and board games, and there was music from Dad's stereo ....

Ah, yes! But music was different. It could indeed overlap into his other world, the world of Nature. Right where he wanted to, he could change key, and it *worked*.

There was the music of the world itself. He could hear it in the rustling leaves of the alder, from the throats of singing robins, even in the sickly *groak* of a soaring raven. He could hear this music in the tiny, gurgling streams that leaked from the heights of Thunder Mountain, and in the sighing of the air that raced off its slopes and was lost in the infinity of space.

The twinkling of the stars—a silent form of music.

He thought of his pond, and his boulder; they were his own little corner of spacetime. He thought of his mountain, which stood cold and serene through the gap between ridges, waiting for him to touch its white-mantled crown. Yes, unclimbed!

There was the forest, and the entire spectrum of flora displayed there, for eyes such as his to see. From the giant Sitka spruce, down to the modest clutter of willow and gooseberry, and further down, to the dogwood and the tiny, mostly unnamed sprouts that created the soft, damp muskeg. They of the shadows, withdrawn from all but the most searching of minds and souls. He breathed deep; watched the clouds as they took Delphinus for their own, and he loved his Natural World.

He had his worlds in his hands.

And crumbling slightly, in his left one, was the remains of the pie crust. He raised it to his lips and ... something made him start, and he nearly bit his tongue.

He saw something, another vision, and for a moment, his body felt horribly funny, as though his skin had separated from the rest of him. He thought he was somewhere else, or perhaps someone else. Hair and face were wet—it must have been raining—and the hand was bringing something else to the lips. It was sweet, perhaps a berry. And then it was gone, the strange sensation and the strange thought. He stood there on the side of the road, feeling as though something was not quite right anymore.

He looked at the sky once again. "You won't let anything happen to me, will you?" he whispered softly, then ate the remains of the pie crust. As he did so, he sensed some sort of cosmic echo, and could almost see a redness, like a stain of some sort, on the hand that brought the food to his lips, and there was a clanging noise. A moment later, the echo dissipated.

The clouds continued to push across the sky, above the Valley, and race northward to the glacier and the icefield. They took on a menacing look, and for the first time tonight, Mark was uneasy about their ever-thickening form. He began to walk quickly back toward the house, wondering if the clouds were trying to bring a halt to his evening constitutional. They bumped the crests of the mountain peaks, and their base began to lower.

But clouds did that, he told himself, they were doing what came naturally. They reminded him that Nature had balance, that with every rose there was a thorn, and there was a very special reason for this. For every delicious, juicy fruit of the woods, there was another that contained a worm.

And perhaps the rain would fall before he reached the house. Fine! He loved the rain; it was Nature's Tears of Joy. He smiled to himself and began to gallop homeward. He liked what he'd just said, and he repeated it, to store it away for future use. Nature's Tears of Joy. And the stars were Nature's nightlights, so that he might travel safely in and about his World during yet another one of those balance effects, the one known as darkness. But, he reminded himself, the stars were now gone this night ....

This was an important time, he figured, as he opened the front gate. How necessary it all was, everything around him, all these thoughts vortexing into and spiraling out of his mind. Even the strange moment when he had transported, minutes earlier, was a message of some kind, and although it seemed to deposit into him a rather dark sense of impending, he felt that he would soon be allowed access to the riddle's meaning.

That is exactly what would happen. His love of Nature, and his gift of Natural Sight, which took him up and beyond his peers, was for a great purpose, he knew. True, there was much time left, many years of growing to be done still, and maybe something would happen. Something or someone could become dominant. College? Working? Marriage? And would the human world take over?

He mustn't worry about that, he decided. There was time left to understand it all, plenty of time. Shaking his head, he ran to the house and jumped up on the back porch.

But he did worry, just a little, because something had definitely happened back there, a moment ago ....

He opened the door and stepped into the furnace room. Mom was there waiting for him.

"Come here," she said, in a voice quite strange. Mark followed her through the den, and he noticed that she was walking in a tight, awkward motion. She led him into the living room, which was deserted, and sat him into a chair. Then she looked at him, but not steadily.

"I have something to tell you."

"Oh? Good or bad?" It just came out like that.

"Very bad." And then he noticed her face, her eyes, her grip on the nearby sofa. He went rigid.

"There was a phone call while you were gone. Grandmother died this evening." She broke down and wept, and Mark stared at her, then rose up and walked like a boy in a trance, through the hall and into his bedroom.

Stephen was not there. Mark dropped onto his bed, let his face hit the pillow, and shut his eyes tightly. He began to cry, and his bed trembled as he sobbed and retched.

His mind spun, and it brought him visions. A pond, and a massive sheet of ice. The stars, and a great mountain peak. He cried and cried, feeling the softness of the bed, and the hardness of a granite boulder that he instantly damned and wished had never existed.

CHAPTER SEVEN

The afternoon was hot. The blue sky seemed to stretch forever, and the mountain peaks glistened. In the meadows and along the roadsides, lupines nodded in the slight breeze that drifted through the Valley. The moving air was full of sound, the buzzing of bumblebees and the whistling of diving swallows. There were the cries of children playing, for it was summer yet again.

Mark sat on the living room floor, and in his lap was the small, two-person nylon tent. He let his fingers run along the edge of the door flap, feeling the smoothness of the hem and dreaming of the night ahead, when he and Jerry would sleep at the campground, under the stars, in this very tent. He folded it carefully into a small, square package, and put it into the forward compartment of his new rucksack.

He tied on his sleeping bag, then put his canteen into the upper compartment. Next came the food. The sandwiches, the crackers and cheese, the cookies and pudding treats, and finally the spice cake, which was wrapped in a double layer of plastic film.

When he was finished, he slung on the pack to test the weight; decided that he could carry it for a thousand miles if necessary.

"He should be here pretty soon, don't you think?"

Looking up, he saw Mom standing in the foyer, and he nodded. Less than an hour ago, Jerry had called, saying that his mother had volunteered to drive over and pick Mark up, rather than have him hike the mile to the Floyd's house. He'd agreed, seeing that there would be time enough for hiking afterwards—to the campsite.

"Looks like you've got quite a load there," Mom continued. "You won't get tired with it, you're sure?"

Why was she asking all these strange questions, he asked himself, as he adjusted the straps on his pack. Was she just nervous, seeing that this would be his very first camping trip on his own? Now, there had been those two overnighters with Stephen and his scout troop, and he had been thankful for the invitation, but it really wasn't the same thing as tonight. Well, he supposed he could see why she thought there might be mischief, or perhaps a dangerous episode of some sort. Still, it would be a great adventure, and if it turned out all right, then maybe the next step would be the mountains, and ultimately *the* mountain, the summit of which had yet to feel the footsteps of a human.

Ah, there was Mrs. Floyd! Peering out the window as the car drove up, he saw that Jerry was with her. He started to haul the pack out the door, and then put it down again. "Forgot something," he muttered, and ran to his room.

Pulling open a drawer, he reached in and grasped his new spotting scope, which Dad had given him as a present. He slid the instrument out of its simulated leather casing, looked at it for a moment, and smiled. Jerry didn't even know he owned the thing, and he figured he'd just pull it from his pack later on and surprise the heck out of his friend.

He recased the scope and glanced around in a last minute search for things he might need. His gaze traveled across Stephen's half of the room, but he saw nothing of his brother's that interested him.

He started back to the living room and heard Jerry knocking at the front door. As he passed his sister's room, the girl appeared and asked if he was getting ready to leave.

"Yep. See you tomorrow, I guess."

Amy stared at him. "Be careful, and don't let a bear or something eat you alive." She leapt at him and gave him a quick hug.

Strange, he thought.

He put the scope in his pack, hoisted it once again, then walked to the door and saluted his camping partner. Without wasting any further time, he shouted goodbye to Mom and stepped lively to the rock path in front of the house. As he approached the car, Mrs. Floyd waved a greeting from the driver's seat. He returned the wave as he followed Jerry to the trunk, where he stuffed in his pack.

On the ride to Jerry's house, she asked the boys about the day's plans.

"Nothing much," her son answered. "A regular hike, and then the campout by the lake, which I already told you about. What more do you need to know?"

She frowned. "How have you been, Mark?"

Shrugging, he grunted a reply, then added, "Stephen was pretty sick last week. Flu, or something."

Mrs. Floyd shook her head. "You don't sound too excited about this little trip you're taking. I thought you'd be bouncing around in your seats."

"Look, Mother," Jerry sighed. "This isn't a Himalayan expedition." He glanced quickly at Mark, to make sure he'd pronounced it right. Mrs. Floyd laughed but drove the rest of the way in silence.

When they reached Jerry's house, she offered them cold drinks inside, which they politely refused, saying that they'd better get going if they wanted to keep their schedule.

"Don't forget!" Jerry called out as they started off. "Keller gets fed only once more, about dinnertime!"

She smiled at him, and Mark asked, "You changed the thing's name again?"

"Uh, huh. After one of my uncles." And the hike was begun.

They walked north, the sun at their backs. It was indeed hot, almost too hot for early June, Mark thought. Before long, the boys were shedding layers of clothing, and it wasn't much longer before Mark's shoulders ached from the weight of the pack, but he kept his mind on other things and would not admit his discomfort, not to Jerry.

They followed a trail through a stretch of woods, and soon they came out on a long and narrow clearing, with a line of power poles in the center. Beyond was the roar of the river, carrying silty water from the lake down through the Valley and into the saltwater channel. Traveling across the clearing, they came to the loop road, which had turned and was heading west, toward the low hills. They walked along its shoulder, crossed the river on the big steel bridge, and hiked on to the small dirt lane which led to the campground. Here they stopped to rest and take a drink from their canteens.

"There's a path that starts over here," Mark pointed. "It leads to the campground. At least, Stephen said so. But I don't want to spend time looking for it. Let's stay on the road."

Jerry nodded agreement, then glanced past his friend and widened his eyes. "Looks like the gang's out today."

Mark whirled about. The "gang" consisted of four boys, some of their classmates at school, and now that summer was here, they spent their time drifting across the Valley, or their "domain" as they called it, looking for trouble, and if finding none, proceeding to cause it. Mark had more than once been invited to join the "gang", and was already considered a member, as were most of the boys heading into sixth grade. The group approached and hailed greetings.

Mark and Jerry nodded, and then a circle formed as they all began a light discussion, right in the middle of the road.

"Goin' camping?" Allen gawked. "Looks fun. Danny an' me were thinkin' of doin' that, maybe next weekend, on the beach!"

"What do you got in the pack, beer?" Richard.

Jerry laughed and shook his head. "I even left my radio at home."

"Hey!" Scott lifted his voice. "Remember we said we would all go to the movies together. We were thinking, maybe Saturday. I don't know what's showing, but anyway, you guys want to go? Debbie said she would, and I know Lia will too." Robert, who wore a near-perpetual grin, nodded his agreement to the idea.

Mark opened his mouth, but Jerry cut in and said sure, they would love to go, and that they'd be in touch about it later. He looked at Mark, who mumbled incoherently and gave short, jerky nods.

"Well, we're goin' now. We can see you're busy!" And the "gang" moved slowly down the road, making a variety of snorting noises and swaggering as they went. Jerry shook his head after them.

"My mom says if I ever get into trouble with them, I may never see the sun again. Shoot, they don't do much of anything bad!"

"Will she let you go to the movies with them?"

"Yeah, because they won't be able to cause trouble in a theater, will they? And I'm sure it would be fun. Don't you want to go?"

They continued with their hike, and in a short while came to the entrance of the campground. After walking to the far end of the site, near the lakeshore, they hunted around for a good place to pitch the tent, finding at last a clearing surrounded by alder thickets, out of sight of the camp drive. According to Mark, this was perfect, seeing that all campers were supposed to pay a fee, and they had just walked in as though it was their own private property. So, best that a Forest Service attendant not see them.

"Yes, we wouldn't want to get arrested," Jerry said later, as they were devouring their evening meal. "I've got that woodworking demonstration to go to, day after tomorrow, and I wouldn't want to miss it."

"And I've got a game", Mark answered. "Against the best team in the league."

"You should've stuck around Sunday afternoon and seen our game," Jerry said, taking a mighty swing with an imaginary bat. "I got that double on a full count! My dad was shouting from the stands, and I was turning red, there on second base!"

"But you lost the game, stupid."

"Yes."

As they ate, the traffic on the single-lane camp road began to increase. Apparently, a ferry had arrived in town not long ago, and now cars, pick-ups with metal campers, and an assortment of RVs were flooding the grounds, the multitude of tourists looking for spaces to set up housekeeping. The boys finished their dessert and walked about the campground, chatting with the visitors and answering their questions about what it was like to live in this place, in the "far north".

"Some of them expected Eskimos, I guess," Jerry said as they made their way through the lovely campground. Mark nodded, then replied that he felt lucky he was growing up here, and didn't have to be one of those people. Jerry laughed.

It was becoming cooler, but the sky was still blue, even at nine o'clock. Mark presented his spotting scope, and the boys raced down to the lake-front. The glacier leapt into view, spanning the far shore, and icebergs floated on the surface of the water, making for a peaceful yet overpowering scene. Through a gap, *the* mountain was in plain sight, spiraling upward in white splendor. Flopping down onto the white sand, they took turns looking at its summit through the small telescope.

A miniature iceberg, eighteen inches wide, bumped the shore, and the boys raced over to pick it up. Once out of the water, it became crystal clear in color, and it was smooth as glass. It was dreadfully cold, and so first Mark carried it, then Jerry, up the slope of the beach and over to the register box, at the fork in the road. Here they ceremoniously dumped it onto the ground, so that the tourists could bend down and feel a real iceberg when they signed out in the morning. And then they ran back to their campsite to set up their tent for the night.

"Don't you think it'll melt before tomorrow?" Jerry asked as they crawled inside.

"No way. When we first moved here, we had no refrigerator, only an icebox. We went to the glacier and chopped up some of the smaller bergs and used them, because they're packed so hard and last so long. They didn't melt for days."

"But this one's right there in the open, not in an icebox," Jerry argued.

"Trust me. I know what I'm talking about." Mark gave him a wise look. "And I heard somewhere that these things are even flown over to Japan, because it's some sort of fad there, to use Alaskan glacier ice in drinks at the cocktail parties in Tokyo."

"That is *not* true."

"Bet it is." Mark stuck his tongue out. "And anyway, I know about the ice itself. I don't get such good grades in school by luck, you know."

"Oh, yes. You know everything, don't you? Why don't you just skip sixth grade, and go on to seventh? Why don't you go on to college right now! Be a lawyer, or a scientist, or whatever, and become—"

"Oh, shut up!" Mark curled up on his sleeping bag, which was Dacron, with a wild goose picture pattern inside and out. "Maybe you should have brought beer after all, to quiet you down."

"Beer doesn't quiet you down."

"Yeah, it does. Trust me."

"You never tasted beer in your life!" Jerry held his hands to his ears, as if trying to shut out the insane conversation entirely.

"What makes you so sure? I know everything, don't I?"

"Oh, shut up!" Like a momentarily distracted echo.

And a loon sounded, from far away. It was the laugh of an excited sorceress, and it continued, intermittently, for a long time after the sun finally dropped below the horizon. The boys lay in their sleeping bags and stared out the door of their tent, to where the mountains rose above the cluster of the thicket. The summits turned from white to pink, and then to dull gray, as the stars began to show. Capella, and the others.

"So what do you think?" Jerry asked. "Should we go to the movies with everyone else? My parents will be downtown, and I'm sure they'll let me go."

"I haven't been to the movies in so long," Mark answered. "Stephen and I used to go all the time, while Mom and Dad were shopping."

"I really like this. Exciting, isn't it?"

"What's that?"

"The camping trip. I'm having a good time. Except for the mosqui-toes," Jerry added, sitting up to scratch his leg.

"I didn't bring any bug spray," Mark frowned. "And I bet you forgot it, too."

"Let's close the front flap and the netting," Jerry suggested. He reached out, untied the knot, and the boys were in total darkness.

They lay in their bags, and after a short time, Jerry began to snore. Mark lay awake, on his back, and felt the earth below him. He thought about home, and what the others might be doing. It was late, so Amy might already be asleep. Stephen would be watching television, and Mom would be working at her sewing machine. And Dad busy making another fire? No, too warm tonight. He'd be reading, waiting for the TV program to end, so he could send Stephen to his room, then he would get out that new recording of *Ilya Murometz* he had bought last week, but hadn't had time to play.

He sighed. The loon began its laugh once again. Jerry's snoring became louder. And then there was a dull crash, from across the lake. A section of ice had calved from the glacier's snout and dropped into the water.

He closed his eyes and tried to sleep, but sleep did not come for nearly an hour. When it did, Mark had a dream, the first he could remember in a very long time. He dreamed of the upcoming baseball game. His team was winning, but the opponent was catching up fast. Balls were flying everywhere, past his arms and legs, and right through his glove. Figures were streaking around the base paths. Shouts came from the bleachers.

It was the "gang". They were jeering at him.

When he awoke, it was far past dawn, and Jerry was stirring in his own bag. They got up, had a light breakfast of Lorna Doone cookies and vanilla Snack Pack, and took down the tent. After moseying about the lakefront for a while, they decided to head on home. Hoisting their packs, they started across the campground, following the narrow lane that circled past the cars and campers.

Passing the register box, they looked down and saw that the little iceberg had nearly melted away. Mark stared in disbelief, then turned to his companion.

"Jerry. Let's do go to the movies. I think it'll be fun." His friend nodded, and they moved on.

§

He rose from his seat in the dugout, after Ken reached second base. The double had brought home another run, the third of the inning, and now the score was 5–2. Gripping the wire mesh tightly, he yelled for Pat, the next hitter, to pick up his own RBI.

"Got 'em scared now! Keep it goin', keep it goin'!" He settled back, then realizing that he was in the hole, got up and whipped off his cap. He went out to the "corral" and picked up his favorite bat and helmet. And he felt a surge of confidence as he took a few practice swings.

Fourth inning, three-run lead, and they were playing the front-running club! Amazing this was, considering his own team's two-and-four start. He heard the small crowd buzzing; they sensed there was a great upset in the making. Another savage cut at an imaginary pitch, and Mark saw the coach watching him.

"You swung under too much last time, and that's why you popped up. Get that back elbow up more. There you go!"

Pat struck out swinging. Now there were two down, and Mark walked to the on deck circle and stood there as Jim, the leadoff hitter, took a couple of outside fastballs. Then he swung late on a sinker and sliced a foul directly at Mark's head. Mark ducked, but not soon enough, and the ball smacked his helmet with a sharp *crack*. And then he was on the ground, bells ringing, stars flashing, and neon whips looping round and round ....

The coach helped him to his feet. Mark looked about him, and Jim was there, appearing quite shocked. "Gee, I didn't mean to," he said in a small voice.

Mark shook his head, both to clear it and to indicate a sense of forgiving to his teammate. The people in the stands settled back, and Mark could hear Dad say, from the top row, "Not to worry, honey, it will only fire him up".

Jim hit a high changeup, but didn't get solid wood on the slow, spinning pitch. A Texas leaguer dropped behind the shortstop, and the left fielder raced in quickly to grab it on a hop. Now there were runners at the corners, and Mark was the hitter. He walked toward the plate while the fans applauded his recovery from the dramatic episode moments before. He dug into the batter's box, with his peculiar closed stance, and faced the pitcher.

Then he remembered, and backed out of the box. Looking down the foul line, he read the signal from the third base coach, and without acknowledging, reentered the box and prepared to swing away as the coach had instructed.

The pitcher had a strange windup. It was jerky, and he delivered with his arm bent at a ninety-degree angle, releasing the ball with his hand nearly brushing his right ear. The first pitch was slow, but coming in high and outside, and Mark relaxed.

"Make eem pitch to ya!" a voice sang out from the bleachers.

Mark dug in more firmly. Why the hell didn't they all just go home and listen to the game on the radio? If only they realized how much they took the true meaning out of the contest. Put them in the back of your mind, he told himself. Pretend they don't exist. Wake up! Here comes the next pitch!

A called strike, and Mark backed away, staring at the umpire in amazement. The pitch had come in just above his ankles. He stood, looking at the plate for a moment, then at the two runners on base. And he moved into his stance for a third time, remembering to get the elbow up.

The pitcher delivered, and the ball came in waist high. Mark took a quick, whiplike swing and made good contact. The ball shot over the pitcher's head and fell to the right of the center fielder. He raced around first base; heard his teammates screaming as Ken crossed the plate. Out of the corner of his eye, he saw Jim speeding around third and being waved in. He rounded second, and still looking at Jim, realized guiltily that he himself had not paid attention to the base coach.

The ball was coming in to the shortstop, who caught it six feet in front of Mark. He turned, Mark ground to a halt, and for what seemed an eternity, the two boys just stood and looked at each other in surprise.

The shortstop recovered first and headed toward Mark with the ball in his hand. Mark felt like a fool. He was in a pickle, and it was his own fault. Jim was almost home, but before he made it, Mark was tagged out, the shortstop never having to throw the ball. And so the seventh run didn't count.

Sheepishly, he trotted back to the dugout, which was emptying fast as his team took the field. The coach didn't say a word, just shook his head as Mark dropped his helmet to the ground. He snagged his cap and glove, and made his way to first base.

The opposing team scored a run, and then three more in the top half of the sixth, to tie the score. The home team could mount no attack at all in the bottom half, and so the game continued. It was nearly ten o'clock, and the ballpark had no lights, so unless one of the teams emerged victorious within the next thirty minutes or so, the umpires would call the game and continue it at a later date.

"We gotta win it now," Mark spoke to his teammates in a determined tone. They looked uneasy. None of them had ever been in an extra-inning game before, and they glanced at each other nervously. "We'll never get a chance to beat this team again!" he reminded them. The coach made a few defensive changes and installed a new pitcher. In the top half of the eighth, Pat made a bad throw from his second base position, and it scooted past Mark and into the dugout. Everyone tensed, with a runner now at third, and the infield drew close; Mark creeping in front of the base path. There was only one out. The next batter hit a scorching line drive to Mark's right. He fell outward and snagged the ball, then crashed to the ground.

The runner was halfway home when he saw Mark grab the line shot. What Mark did next was pure instinct, and it was the talk of the league thereafter.

He saw Pat closing in to help with the play, and as he hit the ground, he reached for the ball with his left hand, pulled it from his glove, and looped it behind his back to the second baseman. Pat caught it barehanded and threw a perfect strike to third. The runner, trying desperately to tag up, was out by a step.

The stands erupted as the team headed for the bench. It had looked like a big league play, and the coach gave both Mark and Pat a big slap on the rear. It brought the team to life, and they were ready to put the game to rest.

The first batter was hit by an inside pitch, and then Ken walked. They pulled off a double steal, but Ken overran the bag and was tagged out. Next, Pat dribbled a grounder to first, and the runner held as the play was made unassisted. Two outs. Then Jim walked, and Mark could see that the relief pitcher was unsettled. He stepped into the box and cocked his bat.

The first pitch was down the alley. He swung, made contact, and sent a fly ball into the left field corner. The team rose, as did the parents, brothers and sisters, and everyone else present, as the outfielder raced across to pull it in. He dove, missed the ball by a foot, and the game was over.

The team went wild. Pouring out of the dugout, the players threw their glove and caps into the air, then ran gleefully across the diamond to congratulate the losers. And for some reason, Mark wished that—for a moment, anyway—both teams would vanish, leaving him alone to analyze the victory in private.

He went over to the concession stand with the rest of the team, to accept the traditional winners' soda. And then, as dusk became twilight, he walked home with his family. Mom chattered endlessly about the phenomenal play, and Dad winked at him time and again. Stephen grudgingly admitted it was a good performance. Amy didn't understand the game very well, but she skipped along happily, proud of what her brother had done.

"I guess you made up for that awful stunt you pulled earlier on," Dad said to him, as the two sat in the living room, Mark sipping his cream soda. He had removed his uniform top and was resting in his thin jersey. He nodded as Dad got up to pull the shades.

"We just had to win that game."

"Oh, they'll be talking about it for a long time!"

Mark shifted his position. "I don't know, but I get a funny feeling sometimes, when I'm out there. I feel like I'm part of a team, but also that I'm by myself, and I'm not sure anymore who the opponent is."

Dad's eyebrows knitted. "What do you mean?" he asked. "You're out there to have fun, aren't you? Isn't that what Little League is all about?"

The boy shook his head, and cold sweat dropped to his forearms. Dad noticed it. "Ought to get that hair cut again soon," he remarked.

"I know it's for kids to have fun," Mark answered. "But I don't play the game to have fun. I play it to win, like I'm supposed to destroy some enemy trying to get at me. But then … when I win, I don't know what I've just defeated."

The words came out rather loudly, but Dad only nodded, then left the room, and Mark was alone. He emptied his soda and fell back against the headrest. He was so tired he could have slept where he sat. But after a moment, Mom came in and told him to take a shower and get to bed.

Another dream that night. He was having them more often now, and he was afraid to think of why. This time he was running along the loop road. He was running very fast, and he had on his baseball uniform. He ran all the way to the glacier, and when he arrived, he stopped, shook a fist toward *the* mountain, called it his enemy, and began to hike, up onto the glacier and beyond. And he searched for a route to its staggering north-west ridge, approaching it as the dream began to fade. He struggled to keep the picture in focus, but instead he woke up, sighed, and cursed in the dark.

In the morning, he had a late breakfast, and was then surprised when he saw the station wagon pull into the drive. The mystery deepened when he saw Mom walking quickly to the front door and smiling broadly. He peered out of the window for a better view. "What's going on?" he asked.

"Something," Mom answered. She looked at him. "A surprise. Some-thing we decided would be a good idea not to tell you about."

Mark hurried onto the front porch. He saw Dad get out of the car and open the tailgate. And out jumped the surprise.

A dog landed on the ground. It was big and black, with a white belly, its form something like that of a German Shepherd. Mark turned to Mom. "Ours?"

"Yes, she's ours. You like her?"

He bolted down the pathway to the front gate. Dad shouted a greet-ing, and the dog, seeing Mark approach, began to wag her tail. Mark fell on his knees as the dog came trotting into the yard. "What's her name?" he asked excitedly, as the animal licked his face and began to paw him in a sign of friendship.

"Sheka," Dad replied. Mark looked up. "It sounds like a great Alaskan name. That's perfect! She belongs here, all right," he added, as he began to give Sheka a rubdown. He studied her closely, and Dad knelt also, show-ing Mark the trick the dog knew, shaking hands upon request. "She's a malemute. Your mom and I saw her advertised in the paper, and decided that you kids would like to have her."

"Of course! But she'll need a doghouse, won't she?"

Dad nodded. "In fact, we can build it today, if you want to."

And then Amy and Stephen were hurrying out the front door and running for the driveway. Sheka made friends with them all, and for the rest of the day, they played out in the yard, Stephen and Mark assisting with the doghouse, which Dad constructed out of half-inch plywood and two-by-fours, left over from when he'd built the wood rack near the stor-age van. Even though Sheka had a new piece of real estate to call her own, Amy begged to let her spend the first night indoors, and Dad said that would be fine.

Mark went to bed that night with a light head. Yesterday, an upset victory in which he had played a star role, and now, a new dog. And she was such a wonderful pet. Sheka—it sounded perfect, had a ringing quality. His own dog! He'd called Jerry and told him about the new addition, and Jerry had sounded beside himself in his desire to meet her.

And tomorrow, his family was heading downtown to do some shopping, and he was going to the movies with his friends.

§

The plan was to meet in front of the theater at half past one. When the car slowed, Mark glanced at the entrance, but saw no one he recognized. "We're a little early, but I'm sure there'll be someone else here pretty soon."

Mom twisted around in her seat and reminded him that he had better behave himself, and then he was out of the car and moving toward the box office. The air was cool and damp, the wind ripping off the channel and moving through town with a salty bite. It seemed almost like winter, and as Mark stood there shivering, he began to wonder if anyone would actually show up on this blustery day, or if he was a complete moron, waiting while strangers drifted in and out of the theater, rubbing past him. He backed up against the wall, half-wishing that his folks would drive past once more and pick him up.

Then Jerry appeared from out of nowhere, almost as if he had dropped from the leaden sky. He saluted Mark and grinned, the gap between his upper teeth showing. Mark nodded, still shaking from the wind chill.

"No one here yet? Well, I think we're pretty early." Jerry took another one of his many calculated opportunities to look at his new watch.

Mark put his weight on one foot, then the other. "You want to come home with me after the movie? You can meet Sheka. She is really quite a pet! Knows how to shake, and sit up, and never bites."

"Oh yeah! Sure I'll come over and see her." The two boys huddled against the wall, underneath a poster that announced the coming attractions. They waited, and finally saw a group approaching. It consisted of the "gang" members and other familiar faces. Soon they were all as one, staring at each other almost in wonder, as it was the first time they had all seen each other downtown, and away from school.

It must look strange to them too, Mark thought. We see each other in class, and around the neighborhood, but never here, in the middle of town. It's like we're meeting for the first time, and we're not sure what to say to one another.

There was Richard, of course, looking foolish in his blue jean cap, and there was Scott, Allen, and Robert. Stuart, a sixth grader the year before, was also taking part in the big adventure, and then there was Kathy, Lia, Debbie, and Stefany, a new girl in town who lived next door to Allen. They bought their tickets, and then they entered the theater, squinting in the brightness of the lobby, moving straight for the concessions.

"We've been messing around town all morning, Scott and me," Richard said as they joined the crowd that stood waiting for refreshments. "We went to my dad's office, because he works there on Saturdays, and look what he gave me." He flashed a five-dollar bill.

"Said he'd been a good boy lately," Scott hooted. "I wouldn't have given him five cents!"

The girls weren't saying much. Mark looked around and counted. Eleven of them had come to see the picture, which was some sort of historical fiction drama. It looked to be something about a poor girl's rise to fame and fortune, according to the promo posters. Mark stuck a finger in his pocket and felt the money. Indeed, why was he even here? He could be home, playing with Sheka, or building a new ship model, or most anything. And tomorrow! Another baseball game, and he was scheduled to pitch. He hoped today went fast, and at the same time, he wanted to think he belonged to the crowd he was with, to feel he was a part of it all. Another quick look around. The group was breaking up and joining the lines, which paralleled back to the front entrance.

Robert, Lia, and Kathy joined him in his line. He was in front of them, and as they waited, he turned around to make conversation. His eyes fastened on Kathy for a moment, then his gaze traveled past, settling for an instant on Lia, and finally moving on to Robert.

"Think the movie will be any good?"

Robert started to answer, but Lia cut him off. "Of course it will be, Mark. My mom and dad saw it a couple weeks ago, and they talked about it all the next day. That's how I got the idea for going. Remember?"

He shook his head. "No, I don't. I guess you never told me."

Robert laughed and said, "We saw him the other day, and he was going camping with Jerry. By the way, how did your trip go?"

Mark shrugged. How did one talk about a little camping trip? "It was okay. But Jerry snored too much," he added. And Jerry, in the next line, glanced up and frowned as he saw the grinning faces turn in his direction.

"Help you sir?" A fast-talking vendor addressed him. Mark turned around, noticed the open space between himself and the counter, and strode across it, the others in his line following. Studying the price list, he tried to look discriminating, but he knew it was a phony performance.

"I'll have … well … I'll have … I'll have the largest popcorn, and a medium coke. That's all, for now."

"You sure?" the cashier answered with a smirk.

Mark scowled. "Yes, I'm sure." From behind him, Robert said something, but he couldn't make out what.

And then the others in his line ordered, paid the cashier, and waited by a tall green curtain until the rest of the group was finished. Then they quick-trotted up the wide crimson stairs to the loge entrance.

"Did you see how that usher was looking at us?" Stuart jerked his head back down toward the lobby. "Wondered what we were doing here in the first place, I'm sure."

"Well, the movie suggests for parents being with us," Debbie answered him. "And I don't think we look very mature." Lia brushed past her and stood, her eyes roving the auditorium in a critical manner, as though she had just bought the place and was considering some remodeling.

Richard had pulled off his cap and was now peering through the darkness, mumbling to himself. Then he turned and announced, "I don't see eleven seats together anywhere. Look at all the people sitting in twos and threes. Messes the whole thing up for us."

It was true. A large number of couples and small groups filled the seats, and after scouting around for a bit, Mark and his companions began to shake their heads at one another, until a second usher came to them and asked if they were having trouble.

"Yeah, we are," Allen said. "Can'tcha get somebody to move, so we'll have a place for us all? We're a pretty big group."

"Allen! That wasn't very nice." Stefany had a high, thin, quavering voice that caused Mark to choke back a giggle, but she was right, he had to admit. He suddenly felt ashamed to be in company with the blonde-haired Allen.

The usher whispered, "No, I can't do that. You'll have to split your group, half down there in front, and the rest of you over there, in the fifth row."

They nodded and began to spread themselves about the loge. Mark looked around for Jerry, but his friend was already making his way down to the forward section of the balcony. Stuart, Richard, Allen and Stefany were with him, and after a moment, Lia ran after them. Mark shrugged, and then he heard something hitting the floor. Looking down, he saw that he was spilling his popcorn.

He headed over toward the fifth row, and what was left of the group followed him. He made his way to the far wall and sat in the first chair, after carefully setting his snacks on the hard floor. When he looked up, he realized that he was in the wrong row.

Turning red, he got up and moved back to the next row, almost forgetting his soda, and hoping the others hadn't noticed. They had. And there was only one seat left for him. It was between the two girls, Debbie and Kathy. He sat down and forced a grin at the other group, who had turned as one, making signs of mutual recognition from their position at the edge of the balcony. As if we'd not seen each other in ages, Mark thought.

Scott leaned out and looked at him. "We saved the very best seat for you," he said, and gave one of his patented fake laughs. Debbie grinned as well, but Kathy only gave Mark a quick look, then turned her head again.

Out of the corner of his eye, he studied his companions. Scott, sitting on the far left, looked the same as usual, in faded corduroys and a printed cotton shirt, and his hair was in his face. He was always acting nervous, with a foot or a hand in constant motion, and now he was banging his tennis shoe against the seat post in front of him, keeping a quick, steady rhythm.

Seated to Mark's right, Debbie wore a green and white, one-piece dress, and her hair was in a sock bun, held together with so many bobby pins it resembled a metallic bird's nest. Stuck clean through was one of those long rods Mark likened to a knitting needle; he felt that her entire head would function as a deadly weapon. Beyond her, Robert was basically hidden behind his thick, brown-rimmed glasses. His oversized hands, folded across his lap, dominated his appearance. He was looking straight ahead at the big white screen, seemingly entranced, his grin steady.

Kathy sat on Mark's left, her coat draped over the seat back. Secretly, he was glad she was next to him, although they had rarely talked. Only once, in fourth grade, had they been in the same classroom. Last year there had been some teasing about how she was Richard's girlfriend, and Richard had seemed, if anything, to have enjoyed it. Kathy, however, had never once admitted being attached to the boy, and hadn't even spoken to him the past year. Today, she was in one of her quiet moods, which Mark found attractive. She wore white slacks and a short-sleeved magenta blouse, and her dark brown hair was raised over her ears, which were studded with simple black pins. She looked quite grown up for an eleven-year-old, Mark thought. Or was she ten? He couldn't remember, and almost asked her about it, but did not.

The auditorium darkened even more, and the screen lit up. From down below came Allen's deep, mocking voice. "Keep your hands to yourself, Stuart!"

Most of the others laughed, and Mark hoped that no such remark would contain his own name, while he sat in the theater with its four hundred pairs of ears.

And the movie, apparently set around the turn of the century, was not very interesting. It became a long, drawn-out affair, with boring scenes inside a European mansion. The star of the show played a governess who stumbled upon some kind of treasure in the back of a closet, then made her plans for escape to a more glamorous world. And so came the glory days of young men, racehorses, and much wine, with a tragedy bringing the film toward a very sad end. Mark, having finished his popcorn and soda even before the onetime governess had mastered the art of seduction, didn't even bother to try following the plot, and he knew that the others in his group didn't understand the story either.

He observed Lia straightening up, turning her head about, and scanning the occupants in the dark auditorium. Like she had become the rich young countess herself, acting once again as if she owned the theater, with that critical expression. And Richard was causing his own little mischief. He'd brought a number of folded notebook papers with him, and was now in the process of constructing a miniature air force fleet, no doubt for the express purpose of launching his creations into the lower section of the auditorium. A sharp laugh sounded from one of his companions, and Robert whispered across to Mark and the others.

"Glad we're not part of that bunch." They all nodded, and Debbie whispered back, "If the usher comes over, let's all start pointing at them."

Another guffaw from down in front. A small dart of an airplane came hurtling toward them, thrown by Allen. It landed off to their right, as it had too much wing angle. For a moment, no one bothered to pick it up. Finally Robert did so.

"It's got something written on it," he announced. He spread it open, did a quick analysis of the note, and giggled softly. Then he passed it along to Debbie, who also had a pretty good time with it.

Mark said, "Let me see it." Debbie laughed and held the paper above her needle-weaponed head. Scott reached way over and grabbed it.

Mark felt his heart. It was about *him*, he just knew it was. Richard's idea, or perhaps Jerry's. He wanted to try and snatch the note from Scott, but Kathy was between them, so he sweated it out in silence.

Scott grinned as he read the scribbled tale, then handed it to Kathy, who brought it close to her eyes. Mark felt a wave of embarrassment flood him, and he sat back in his seat, dreading what the girl was reading, and worse, how she would giggle when she was through.

But she didn't change her expression at all. When she lowered the paper, her face was the same, with that quiet, soft look in her eyes. She leaned over to where he was sulking and said to him, "It's not funny at all, really. I don't care what the others think."

Sitting up straight, he put his arms on the rests to balance himself. He felt Kathy's arm next to his own, but he didn't pull away. He no longer wanted to read the note, and after a moment, Kathy scrunched it up and put it in her pants pocket. Mark felt himself relaxing once more.

She looked at him. "You like this movie?"

"No. I hate it."

"So do I." She slid down in her seat, and he followed suit. "Tell you what," she said. "Next time Allen goes past my house on his bike, I'll sic my dog on him. Okay?"

He laughed. "All right. That's funny. I got a new dog yesterday."

"Really?"

He nodded. And he looked at her for a moment, then asked, "How old are you? Eleven, or still ten?"

"Ten. But my birthday's in three days. I'm having a party." She fell silent for a minute, and both of them pretended to watch the film. Then she turned to him again.

"Mark, listen. Um … how about if you came to it?"

"Your party? Well, I've never been to a girl's birthday party before. But I guess I will, if you want me to." He could hardly contain himself. Old Richard would hate him now!

"Okay. I was hoping you'd want to." She was smiling, and Mark thought she looked pretty. He said, in a voice too loud, "What time should I be there?"

"Shhh."

And the movie ended soon after.

As they came pouring out of the theater, saying their goodbyes, Mark saw the station wagon pull up, and he galloped over. Hopping inside, he told Dad to wait, that Jerry would be joining them in a moment, after finding his own parents.

"It was a great show" he said quickly, motioning for Stephen to move over.

"Oh, yeah?" Dad looked through the rearview mirror. "While you were in there, we ran into Mrs. Floyd in the bookstore. Another lady was with her, a Mrs. Creighton. She said her daughter was at the movie. You know a Kathy?"

Oh, no, Mark thought. Oh, no. Take your time, Jerry.

CHAPTER EIGHT

At the close of summer, attitudes would change.

Daylight hours shortened, and the cool winds intensified, marking the beginning of a new season, one of wonder. There was metamorphosis in the shady woods and in the meadow. The thick, springy green stalks became limp, yellow slimes, and the forest returned sharper echoes, a hint of the winter stillness to come.

And then arrived the day when the flurries of white appeared, bringing a halt to the weakening cries of autumn. The world almost slept, frozen in its state of shock, with the generation of wilting plants finding solace at last in these dark days of December, when all that moved was the air itself, and with it, the everlasting ravens.

But within this crystal ball of nature, the human world continued to travel. It did not die, to sprout anew the following spring. It remained, moving as always on its self-scripted path in spacetime.

The smell of baking cookies was strong, wafting to every corner of the little blue house. The ambitious "Great Gate of Kiev", from Ravel's orchestral version of Mussorgsky's *Pictures at an Exhibition*, thundered from the living room stereo, vibrating the south windows that were elegant in their frosted ice paintings. The twinkling of the lights on the seven-foot spruce tree weaved a musical pattern of its own, sending the entire visible light spectrum dancing upon the semi-darkness of the walls.

Mark entered the kitchen, where Mom was pulling a sheet of baked cookies from the oven. Amy was at the dinner table, which was covered with numerous small bowls of vanilla icing. Bottles of food coloring were lined up in almost military fashion, as were a number of larger containers full of decorating candies.

"About ready to start? Why don't you help Amy mix the colors. I asked Stephen, a while ago, but he was in a hurry to run over next door to watch that program with Randy."

Mark sat down at the head of the table and began to study the vast layout before him. His head was full of thoughts, the ideas flashing around his brain like strobe lights. Tomorrow was the last day of school, before the short vacation. He would head over to Jerry's for a party, to which most of his friends had also been invited. The day after that was important as well. He would turn a year older. Although he had no party plans for himself, he would nevertheless be royally treated. Dinner at a fine restaurant downtown, a late movie, and a two-week period of freedom on his hands.

His excitement over the forthcoming holidays had built tremendously over the past week. The end of the year was like turning a sharp corner, where the future events—and future dreams—could be brought within reach. Now, as he prepared to create various colors of icing for the scores of mouthwatering cookies, his energy level jumped another notch. Christmas was almost here. Only his birthday had to come first. A powerful way to sweep out the old and ring in the new.

"What do I do?" Amy reached out for the first bowl.

Mark showed her the correct way to add color, and how to mix the primaries to achieve a new trio of hues. After a few minutes, things were getting out of hand, as the girl and her brother mixed two, three, and even more colors to produce some rather sickly wavelength blends. Mom came over to see how they were doing, made an awful face, and pointed at the bowls.

"Come on, Mark! You're going to ruin all the icing before you even get started. Look at that one, more of a mud color than anything else."

Mark laughed. "I'll take the ones with the mud on them to school tomorrow," he said. "I'm supposed to bring two dozen, remember."

"Yes sir," Mom saluted him, and turned back to her pastry board.

The icing process began, and soon Amy was making a mess of things. She put on too much or too little, sprinkled the candies over the table-cloth, and stuck her knife, which was covered with green icing, into a bowl containing yellow. Mark sighed, doing what he could to keep order, but it was like trying to bail water from the Titanic.

After a time, approximately six dozen of the cookies were finished, in about ten different colors. There were snowmen, Christmas trees, bells, diamonds, and stars. There were plain round ones that remained unfrosted, and Mark suggested they leave those for Stephen.

His last cookie split, then crumbled in his hand. "Sheka!"

She came pattering in from the living room, and Mark fed her the snack. As she gobbled it down, he studied the dog and realized for the first time that she was beginning to grow a few red hairs along the line of her back. He pointed this out to Mom.

"Likely the follicles are ruined, ever since you told Amy she could ride her like a horse." Mom sighed, her hands covered with bits of dough, but she smiled all the same.

Amy's face lit up. "I know! I'll make a reindeer out of her." She got up and ran to her room, presumably to look for equipment with which to construct a harness and reins. Mark stared at the multitude of iced cookies, wishing he had not eaten so much for dinner, and then jumped as the phone rang.

Dad was in the process of cueing a new record, so all was quiet for a moment. Mark tiptoed over and lifted the receiver. A man's voice asked him if his parents were home.

Mom came over, wiping her hands on a towel, and took the phone. "Why, yes." A pause, then, "Certainly. Oh, it's all right. He's just playing records. Fine. I'll tell him."

She hung up, and Mark asked, "What was that?"

"That, as you put it, was Mr. Simmons. You know, from where Dad works. He said he thought he might come over for just a little bit. His nephew is in town for the holidays, and he asked if we would all like to meet him."

Dad called out from the living room, and Mom repeated the news. There was a moment of silence, and then Dad came into the den. "But he didn't want to talk to me?"

Mom shrugged. "I guess not. Anything he wants to say, I suppose he can tell you when he gets here."

"Naw, that's not like him. Usually he gets in a 'hello' just about whenever he has the chance."

"Well, yes. He did sound as though he was in a hurry."

Mark went to the living room. His parents could, at times, talk to each other in the most boring way possible, he thought. He got into the rocker, on his knees, and hung his chin over the headrest. The window came at him, then receded, over and over. The fire was burning low. The first movement of Vaughan Williams' *A London Symphony* was playing. The twinkling of the Christmas tree lights reflected off the pane of cold glass, and the scene was one of incredible tranquility. He looked out at the snow that lay deep, what he often thought of as the white darkness.

Somewhere out there was Jerry and the rest of his friends. Out there, too, was *the* mountain, and the pond. He widened his eyes. The pond was frozen, he suddenly realized. He'd never seen it like that, not in a solid state. It had been so long since he'd traveled up the quartz vein, to where the boulder overlooked his private domain. Of course, he said to himself, it was still there.

Then Amy appeared with a blanket, some lace and other frills, and began to turn his pet into a reindeer. He watched her struggle with the harness and bridle assembly, finally getting it the way she liked. She led the dog out into the kitchen, and Mark listened as Mom scolded the girl and told her not to bother Sheka anymore.

He snapped his finger, and the malemute came running to him. He let her lick his face, and he whispered, "Don't worry. At least I know you're still a dog."

A car drove up and parked on the shoulder of the road, where the graded snow was piled high. Mark called out to the kitchen, and then watched as two figures emerged from the vehicle. Dad came into the foyer and turned on the porch light. Now Mark could see the two in more detail, and he recognized Mr. Simmons, but not the young man who accompanied him.

Dad opened the door. "How you doing, Frank?" he sang out, and the two visitors entered the house. "Here, let me get your things, and we'll just put them in the closet here."

In a moment, they were seated in the living room. Frank introduced his nephew, Francis, who said mildly that he preferred to be called Fran. Mom came from the kitchen, where she had been lecturing once more about the "reindeer". Amy followed, saying that she was only trying to make Sheka into a Christmas type of animal, then stopped and stared at the visitors. "Oh. Hello," the little girl said in a small but polite voice.

So the introductions began all over again. Frank then explained the reason for the hurried phone call.

"I was at the hospital. Ree had to check in this evening because her flu was affecting her lungs too much. I'd had to run over there after picking up Fran at a friend's house, and so it's been a hectic day all around."

"Frank! Coming over here wasn't that important then, was it?"

"Well, we were both going to come over, but she insisted that I stick to the plan. You know how she is. Remember the party at Auke Village, don't you? See, we have something for you anyway."

He took out a red envelope from his pocket and handed it to Dad, who slowly and deliberately—to build excitement, Mark reasoned—opened a corner and peeked in.

"Nothing but paper, Frank," he laughed.

Then he ripped the envelope and looked at the contents. There was something for everyone, and they turned out to be gift certificates at a variety of establishments around town. Mark's was good for merchandise at a local hobby shop, and immediately he began pondering what he would use it for.

"How nice," Mom nodded. "Thank you, Frank. Listen, we have something for you, too." She rose and hurried to the kitchen, and Mark heard her filling a box with the newly baked cookies.

"Tell Ree that we hope she gets back home soon," Dad said. "It's nothing really serious, is it?"

Frank shook his head. "She gets the flu often. It was worse than usual this time, and instead of being just a heavy chest cold, her breathing began to clog up, and so we thought it best to have her looked at."

He motioned to Mark and changed the subject. "You and Fran ought to get together. Your dad was telling me how much you looked at the mountains and wanted to climb them. Fran's been up most every one of them, and he can tell you just about all you'd want to know."

Fran shrugged. He was in his late teens, and he had a solid build, like his uncle. He smiled thinly and said to Mark, "I'm going to be living here from next summer on after, and if you want, we'll go hiking together someday. You want to learn to climb?"

Mark nodded, and Fran continued. "Well, don't forget to remind me, and I'll show you how it's done. That is, if your dad and mom will let you.

Climbing's not the easiest thing in the world, you know. See?" And he pulled up his sleeve. A mammoth scar was revealed.

After that, the talk turned to hiking and other forms of recreation, even when Mom returned with the cookies and a note for Mrs. Simmons. Frank accepted gratefully, and after a while longer, the two said their goodbyes and left, Fran giving Mark a smile and a thumbs-up as he went through the doorway.

"Sounds like you got yourself a climbing buddy," Dad remarked as he closed and locked the door. "That Fran's done some pretty tough hiking around here, I'll tell you. If you want to learn what real climbing is all about, I'd get with him!"

"So he can go and get himself killed before he knows what he's doing." Mom gave them a scornful look. Dad returned it, and Mark decided that it was time to duck out and go to his own room.

He went to the kitchen first, however, and nabbed a cookie. He held it in front of him and inspected it. The cookie was in the shape of a Christmas tree, but it was covered with orange icing *and* sprinkled with brown candies. He laughed as he bit off the base of the "trunk". Amy had applied too much icing on the lower half, and he almost choked, but after a few seconds, he managed to get it past his tonsils. He walked to his room, where he was surprised to find Sheka lying in a ball on the floor. He knelt and petted her softly, as she woke and raised her head.

"What's the matter?" he whispered. "Don't you like it when company comes over?" He put his gift certificate in the top drawer of his worktable, then gave Sheka a good rubbing behind the ears before scooting the black malemute out the door.

He arranged his school clothes for the next day, wondering when Mom would call next door to get Stephen home. Then he went out to the bathroom to brush his teeth, and as he was finishing, Amy appeared in her nightgown, asking him to hurry.

His mouth was full of toothpaste. "Uhh, uhh. Ah wuv hehh furff." He spat into the sink, then continued. "Sorry, you waited too long. I'll take all the time I want." And he pretended as though he was just beginning; unscrewed the cap, reached for his brush again. "I'll only be another hour or so."

She called for Mom, and Mark swore under his breath. Mom came to the rescue, and Mark explained that he was only trying to show his sister how he felt when *she* took up the bathroom time herself.

"Oh, Mark, for heaven's sake. Do you think she's going to learn anything that way? I believe you can set a better example. Now hurry up, both of you." Mom gestured at nothing in particular, and walked away.

Mark heard the back door slam, indicating that Stephen was home. He hung his toothbrush on the holder that he and Mom had made, years before. It was composed of yarn and corkboard, and the faces of two ugly old ladies stared out at the bathtub. From their mouths hung the brushes of both Mark and his brother, and in between, a smaller peg had been inserted for Amy. As he looked at it now, he said to the girl, "I'll take a picture of you and put it there, between the others. That way, your brush will hang from the ugliest face of all."

He giggled at his own remark, but Amy puffed out and began to yell for Mom again. He reached forward and stuck a hand over her mouth.

"Sorry," he whispered in her ear. "Just don't shout for Mom, whatever you do. I was only kidding. I didn't mean it." He gave her a pat on the head, and then went to his room.

The next morning he was up early, wide awake and eager to get the last day of school over with. He lugged the plastic container of cookies to his classroom and helped set the decorations for the party his class was to spend the day enjoying.

As the Christmas music filled the room, and the desks at the front became covered with edibles, the atmosphere was one of wild celebration rather than quiet retrospect. Miss Reynolds had to call for order a number of times, and when the students poured out onto the grounds for afternoon recess, she fairly plopped into her desk chair, exhausted.

"I think she's having a hard day," Jerry told Mark on the playground. "Why don't we think of something nice to do for her?"

"Like what?" Richard was butting in on their conversation as usual.

"Like letting us out early, so she won't have to put up with us any longer," Mark laughed. "But that wouldn't be much fun for most of you. I live right across the street, but most of you take the bus."

"And don't forget to be at my house at three-thirty, on the nose," Jerry reminded them. "There's lots more snacks waiting. I won't be able to eat for another week!"

"Scott's coming with me," Richard said. "I hope your mother has gotten to like him by now."

Jerry shrugged, and Mark motioned for him to move away from the group that was now forming. As they departed, he asked his friend what they might really do to give Miss Reynolds a break. Jerry frowned, thinking about it.

"She was going to stay and clean up the chalkboards, and I think also pull the desks to the wall, for the janitor. Why don't we stay and do it for her?" Jerry suggested.

Mark declared it an excellent idea, so upon returning to class, they informed the teacher of their intention, to which she smiled and nodded yes. "I guess the true Christmas spirit has touched someone after all".

Twenty minutes after the final bell had rung, and the happy sixth graders had raced out the doors to the waiting buses, Mark and Jerry were finishing their chores. Miss Reynolds came in, her coat draped over her arm, to check on them.

"Listen, since you have that thing planned at your house, Jerry, why don't you let me drive you over there? You'll be late otherwise."

So to the amazement of all who watched from the windows of the Floyd home, Mark and the host arrived in a black limousine, actually a beat-up Plymouth, with an ever-smiling Miss Reynolds at the wheel.

"Not often you get a ride home with your teacher," Mark said as they bounded up the steps and waved goodbye to her. "Maybe we should have asked her in."

"Maybe we should clean the blackboards more often," Jerry answered.

The others greeted them, and the afternoon partying continued. Mark looked about. Richard was there, and so was Scott, Allen, Pat, and another of his classmates, Rudy. Soon they were all drinking punch and helping to decorate the tree that stood in a corner of the Floyd's spacious living room. It still smelled of the forest, Jerry's dad having cut it the previous evening. Keller, Jerry's cat, purred around them, then proceeded to destroy one of the packages of plastic icicles.

"Hope everyone's having a good time," Mrs. Floyd said as she brought in a platter of tasty snacks.

"Of course," Jerry answered. He raised his cup and signaled the others to do the same. "We are here," he said, in a tone quite deep, "to celebrate the end of school for two solid weeks, and that's good enough reason to have a party. To the vacation!" And the cups met, then were drawn away and emptied.

"Vervee googh" Scott said, his mouth full of cheese and crackers.

"The toast?" Jerry asked him with a silly grin.

Scott finally got the food down his throat. "Well, that too. Good party, Mrs. Floyd," he added. "Best snacks I've ever had. Yummy, yummy, yummy!"

"I don't see any toast on this plate, only crackers."

"Very funny!"

The boys continued laughing and joking well into the late afternoon. Pat spilled his drink all over the rug. Mark stepped on a spare Christmas light. Mrs. Floyd was very patient, it seemed, always cleaning up after them and making them feel like honored guests.

The door swung open, and Mr. Floyd came in, lowering paper sacks to the floor of the foyer. He gave them all the big hello, then stopped to fill up on the snacks himself. "Off the diet for a while," he explained, his cheeks bulging. And laughter rolled through the house.

"Having a wild little party, aren't you?" he asked his son.

"Yes, and you're invited to stay and join us," Jerry replied. "It's a private sort of party, you see."

"Yes indeed," Robert added. "No girls allowed—except for Mrs. Floyd."

"Indeed!" they all chorused, and raised their glasses yet again. Mark thought for just a moment about Kathy's birthday party, nearly six months ago ....

"Well, listen up, gang. We're planning to go sledding on Sunday afternoon," Mr. Floyd informed them. "How about you all coming, and we can have races. We'll meet at the glacier parking lot at about two o'clock, I should think."

Mr. Floyd always came up with the most brilliant ideas.

Soon after, the boys began to leave. Robert's mother came by, and then Richard's dad pulled up and honked for his son, Allen, and Scott to break themselves away from the festivities. Pat and Rudy left together, as they lived just down the block. Finally, Mark alone remained, and although he was used to hanging around his friend's house, he suddenly felt he was in the way, and reached in the closet for his jacket.

"Why don't you stay for dinner, Mark? It'll be later on tonight, but I'm sure you and Jerry can keep yourselves occupied." Mrs. Floyd gave him such an opportunity whenever he visited, but this time Mark only shook his head.

"Well, I think my parents want me at home this time. We're having something fancy, anyway."

"And tomorrow's his birthday!" Jerry shouted, heading for his room.

"You'll be twelve, right?" Mr. Floyd asked, as he picked up Keller and held the cat in his lap, scratching him behind the ears.

Mark nodded, and Jerry returned with a wrapped package in his hands. "Wanted to surprise you," he said, beaming as he handed it to Mark. "Go ahead, I want to see you open it."

They were all watching him, and so he knelt down on the carpet and carefully peeled away the lovely green and gold paper. There was a white cardboard box, and when he opened it, there was another, smaller box inside. He removed its lid and a third box, amid wads of crumpled newspaper, lay at the bottom.

"Getting interesting," he mumbled as the family grinned and crowded around closer, Keller moving up to Mr. Floyd's shoulder.

He opened the third box, and inside was a book. It was a beautiful text, a study of the mountains and glaciers of the Juneau Icefield. It was written and photographed by a mountaineer of national fame, and Mark, after blurting out his thanks, began to leaf through it, stopping at every wonderful picture.

"Thanks again, Jerry," he said again, closing the book and hugging it. "I really gotta go now, but we'll look it over together soon."

His friend nodded, and Mr. Floyd said, "Tell your dad hello for me, Mark. It's been so long since we visited. Maybe you can join us for sledding on Sunday."

"Hope so! Listen, have a good evening," Mark said quickly as he zipped his coat and reached for the doorknob. "And thanks for the party. I really enjoyed coming over." And he jumped down their porch, into the darkness of early night.

The Floyd's hadn't offered him a ride home, as they knew he liked to walk. He started off down the street, his new book secure inside his pile jacket. The air was frosty, and the sky seemed black, the clouds nearly invisible yet blotting out the stars completely. He hurried homeward along the loop road, then across to the narrow clearing where he and Jerry had first met, and on to his own neighborhood.

He reached the house at six-fifteen, and dinner was on the table. His stomach said "no", but he forced himself to fill his plate and partake of the hearty meal. He tried to look at his new text while eating, but after smearing the cover with mashed potatoes, he decided that he'd better put it away. What would Jerry and the book's author think, if they saw the beautiful cover photo of a red sunset behind the glorious, icy peaks, ruined in this way? He promised himself to treat the volume with more respect, as he felt that an important thing was about to happen, and the book had something to do with it.

Dad went to the living room to set up some new stereo equipment, and Stephen tagged along to help him. Mark went to his room, flopped down on the bed, and began to study the book once more. He gazed at the pictures in complete awe. The text was highly readable, and he spent a long time filling himself with knowledge about the wondrous icefield, learning what caused glaciers to advance and then recede, and about how a mountain's appearance gave clues as to how it had been formed.

He was flipping through the last part of the book, searching for pictures that were familiar to him, when he came upon a half-page spread that showed a line of rugged peaks to the east of the Mendenhall Towers. In the center was *the* mountain.

According to the author, the entire line of summits was unnamed. Mark studied the picture for a long time, noting the glacial ice ramp leading to its northwestern ridge, the only possible route, he decided, that one could take all the way to the top. He shook his head defiantly and said to himself that if there was a way, any way at all, then he and Jerry, of all the people on the earth, would seek it out and stand upon the summit.

Thanks, Jerry, he thought. Thanks for giving me the book. It makes the dream nearer than ever ....

Amy tapped on his door, and he motioned for her to come in. She sat on his bed and asked if she could look at the book with him.

"Sure. Look at that! That's the mountain that Jerry and I are going to climb someday." Good for you, he added to himself. You didn't say 'Jerry and *me*'.

They looked through the volume together, and then Amy turned and asked the question that Mark thought would have come from an adult, not a six-year-old. He was totally unprepared.

"Mark, why do you want to go and climb a mountain? Just to get to the top?"

He put his finger on the steep ridge, and as it traveled up the page, he spoke. "Amy, what if I told you that I didn't even know?" He looked at her.

"See, whenever I look at something like a beautiful mountain, I have this feeling, that I want to go and be a part of it." His mouth went dry, and he stopped and shrugged.

What was he saying? Careful, he thought, or you're going to find yourself talking like you did years ago, when you were little, and stupid.

"It's just something that Jerry and I want to do," he said hurriedly. He closed the book and put it down on his pillow. "Do you understand?"

The little girl nodded, her dark brown hair falling into her eyes. Mark started to push her out of the room and tell her to get to bed, but then stopped. He sighed, then reached out and pushed her hair back where it belonged. Instinctively, she wrapped her arms around him and buried her face in his chest.

"Amy," he whispered, as he held her tightly. "Promise me something. Do you hear? Promise me something."

From below, a muffled "What?"

"Promise that whenever Mom and I have an argument over something, that you'll be on my side." He held her out and looked into her eyes. "She never listens to my friends. But she'll listen to you, I think. When I start off to climb that mountain, promise to stand up and tell her that it's all right, and that *you know* there's nothing wrong with doing it. Okay?"

"I will. When are you going to climb up it?"

"I don't know. Whenever I can, I guess."

He drew her close again, hoping that Stephen didn't choose this moment to make an appearance, to see the two of them like this. He felt her pressing against him, felt her heartbeat, and wondered, could he possibly tell her he loved her, as he used to do, long ago? Before he could decide, she wriggled free, pointed her face at him, and kissed him on the cheek.

"Good night, Mark."

§

After but one ride down the bumpy, ice-coated hill, Mark was sore, but he hauled his sled to the top with vigor. Stephen was busy with his own sled, the new one that had appeared under the tree on Christmas morning.

"Something's wrong with the runners," he muttered as Mark ran past, hauling his transport by a white nylon rope. He saw the Floyds drive up to the edge of the parking lot, and then Jerry was pulling his long toboggan from the back seat and dragging it over to the top of the hill. He waved at Mark. "Great day, isn't it?" he yelled.

It was. The sun, low on the horizon, offered only the barest of warmth, but the sky was bright blue. Climbing up the hill, with its deep powder, was enough to make one sweat, even in the almost sub-zero temperature.

"Sorry you couldn't make it last week," Mr. Floyd said as he followed his son over to where the other boys were taking their turns.

"That's all right," Mark answered. "Look at the slope today!" Together they peered over the edge, where Scott had just plunged down with a happy scream. The bottom was nearly sixty feet below, and the trails created by the runners fanned out in almost alluvial fashion. Scott and his sled parted company at the point known as the "jump", where the angle steepened, then lessened for a bit, and the rider literally became airborne. Scott tumbled into the powdery fringe, ate a mouthful of snow, and lay flat on his back, simulating death. Then he leapt up, grinned at the figures waving from above, and started the trek up the worn staircase of foot-prints.

Mark looked at Dad, who was filming the proceedings with their movie camera. Sheka romped at the bottom, waiting for Stephen or his younger brother to come hurtling down the slope, whereupon she would rush them with her fake growls and chase along after the speeding sleds. Far away from the "jump" was a small, flattened granite, which Scott had placed to mark the record distance so far this season. Robert had made it almost that far today, but his sled had died on him only a foot from the speckled rock.

"Mom and Amy stayed home today," Mark told Jerry as they waited for their turns. "Both of them have a cold, and Mom's afraid we'll catch one too, so she ran us out of the house."

"Gee, that's too bad. Sick on Christmas. Well, did you get everything you said you would?"

"Of course. I'm good at guessing about that," Mark laughed. "And did you get your little package in the mail yesterday?"

"Uh, huh. Very cute, Mark."

Stephen stood up, tested the steering on his runners, and then let the sled flop to the snow. He kicked it to the starting grid and lay in a prone position. Digging with his boots, he shot off the precipice and plummeted down the hardpack chute. He had a tremendous burst over the "jump", but then he angled off to the left, far short of the granite, and only Sheka was on hand to congratulate him on his ride.

Robert was next, and likewise missed the marker by a considerable distance. Jerry took his place at the top and crossed himself. "Never know which ride will be your last," he said in a solemn tone. And then he was on his way, riding the "jump" with ease. But then he dug in a toe by accident, the sled performed a one-eighty, and carried by its momentum, actually started back a few feet toward the hill. Dad laughed and lowered his camera. Robert, ascending the frozen stairs with his heavy load, called back down to him.

"Goin' the wrong way, stupid! Granite's over there!"

Jerry picked himself up, and Mark could hear him complaining. "Everyone calls me stupid …." His breath rose in a tower of steam.

Mark waited until everyone had regained the top of the hill, so as to make the situation appear all the more dramatic. He pretended to pull off a heavy cape, then cupped his hands and imitated a crowd's roar. He laid himself down on the sled and worked his way forward until the tips of the runners moved into thin air. After a momentary pause, he dug in suddenly, and was off.

He remained as low as possible, and felt the cold blast rush over him. As he approached the "jump", he glued himself tight to the wood frame, but when the jolt came, he nevertheless gave a partially muted squeak. Then he was gunning his sled forward, correcting his course only slightly, to preserve his speed. He saw, at the top of his vision, the dark form of the approaching granite. He saw that he was going to hit it.

The runners scraped over the rock, making an awful grating noise that, if nothing else, signaled that the record was broken. He felt the sled drop off the rock, and then he was stopped. He had gone eight feet past the old record, and with a whoop, he jumped up to take his bow. Sheka came to meet him, and he dug his face into her back. "What do you think of that, doggie?" he asked her, elated. "I thought so …."

Nobody went further, the entire afternoon.

The shadows lengthened, and the face of the glacier was turning a dull gray, when Dad and Mr. Floyd said that it was time to scoot on home. Mark begged for just one last ride, but Dad said no, that it would only lead to another ride, and another.

"He's right," Jerry said, as they headed for the parking lot to load their sleds. "Once we were here until eleven o'clock, and we had no flashlights or anything. Once you start, you never want to stop. Well, we can come again soon, and I'll break your record by ten feet when we do!"

Mark scoffed, and then said, "Jerry, I've been wanting to ask … you remember that book you gave me for my birthday? It has a really good picture of *the* mountain in it. How it looks from back there, on the glacier."

Both boys turned and looked at the sinister gap, but the towering spire was hidden from this angle. Mark shivered, then continued. "Did you see it in there, and is that why you got it for me?"

Jerry nodded. "My dad saw it and showed me that picture. I thought you'd like it."

"Well, I do! Listen, there's this guy named Fran who's going to show me how to climb, next summer, I hope. Want to come with me?"

Jerry went wide-eyed, but pretended to stay calm. "I guess so. I know my mom won't like it, though." He paused, then said, "Of course, what do I care? We said we'd climb the thing someday, and so we will. Together!"

They said goodbye, then Scott and Robert, along with Mark and Stephen, piled their sleds in the back of the station wagon. As they headed homeward, dropping the boys off at their respective houses, Mark had a good feeling. He watched as his friends grabbed their sleds and waved goodbye, first Robert, and then Scott, and he thought of Jerry, who was probably stepping inside his living room at this very moment.

His friends.

He had so many of them.

Later, when Mark's own sled was inside the storage van, and he was in the living room, helping with the fire, he felt it again. His family, this time.

He didn't *need* them, not to feel alive and well, but it was nice to have them near just the same. Stephen was a brother, and Mom and Dad were the keepers of the house, and from them, of course, he could acquire knowledge and understanding. It was indeed an appealing alternative to the weirdness of his earlier childhood, when his thoughts were so often confused. The woods, the meadow, the creek, the wildlife, and the Northern Lights, all trying to call to him and tell him who and what he was.

And there was little Amy, who learned from him; looked upon him as an idol. He mustn't disappoint her.

He was no longer dreamless at night. And he no longer worried about one of his worlds taking over and pushing the other one away; in fact, he hadn't thought of any such power struggle for a very long time.

The fire roared. The sky was dark. And out there in the distance, still towering above the world of humans, above society and its struggles, was *the* mountain. But Mark wasn't seeing it that way anymore.

Not far away, there was a pond, and there was a boulder. They were there. They existed. They would be a fun place to visit again, someday soon ....

He was pretty sure everything was all right now. He felt the time move, carrying him with it. Everything was all right.

§

Human beings, unable to exist without some degree of rationale, have concocted a method of placing events in an ordinal fashion, and they invent words to describe simple numbers. They decide that "a" is "a", and "b" is not "a". They decide that "now" is "now", and "then" is not "now". They decide that "here" is "here", and "there" is not "here". Words are inadequate for allowing humans to see beyond what they think of as reality, but words are nevertheless what they use.

He moves through time, but his brain is becoming the mind. Many approach the doorstep of arrival, but misunderstand the final gate.

The setting is perfect. It could not be better.

I who witnessed the birth of aspiration … and now they aspire.

Mortals being what they are … having designed their own mortality … will this one fail as well?

No, I do not say what will be. I want the Creator's children to come home, but I will watch. And I will wait.

CHAPTER NINE

The winter was long, and it was cold. Spring arrived late, and the hard-pack remains of the snowdrifts, in dark granular form, stuck to the earth in spotted disarray, well into April. The sun, reaching a higher zenith with each passing day, at last began sending its rays deep into the ground, and the greenness of life began to appear and push upward to greet the sky. The northern migration reached the Valley, with the swallows that darted after flies, and the geese that honked overhead, on their way to the Arctic.

Along the coast, the smashing breakers, which had piled the seaweed high onto the sloping beaches, now decreased in force, becoming gentle ripples that pushed slowly, finger-like, inland with the strong tides. The familiar dark lines of seaweed, paralleling one another along the curving shoreline, became evident once more. Gone was the freezing spray. Here was the new season, the beach and its saltwater shallows populated with flatworms, hermit crabs, and spiny green urchins.

The mountain snows thinned.

Spring fever raced through the community.

Mark Nilsson took his place in the classroom. On his desk was a large paper sack containing an oversized lunch. He was dressed in rough outdoor wear, as were the rest of his classmates. Miss Reynolds appeared from inside the large closet, her hands full. She packed several large carrying baskets with anything she decided could be of use on the class picnic.

It was nine o'clock, but the atmosphere inside was more that of afternoon recess. Mark looked around quickly. The talk was loud and excited. Jerry and Pat were in rapid conversation, interrupted at times by Debbie. In a far corner, another group was huddled together, forming plans of adventure and mischief. He sat and watched them all for a moment, but kept himself removed from the picture.

Only two weeks before, the class had participated in a camping trip, for several days of school in the outdoors, but if anything, the excitement and drama of that excursion had totally faded, and now all that remained between this morning and the end of sixth grade, their graduation from elementary school, was the all-day picnic at Auke Village.

The PA crackled alive, and the principal informed Miss Reynolds that the bus was waiting.

"Everyone have their quarter?" she asked, as the students jumped to their feet and lined up at the door. She brought a small box, and as they filed out into the hall, each added their trip fare, *clink!*

And then they were out the front door of the school and climbing aboard the big yellow bus. Mark was one of the first to hop inside, and he made his way straight to the rear of the vehicle, with the crowd of students pressing behind him. Jerry slid into the seat next to him, and in front of them were Pat and Rudy. The rest of the class grabbed their spots, and then Miss Reynolds took the mic from the driver's hand and spoke.

"Everyone listen for a minute. This is going to be a long bus ride, and I want you to keep yourselves under control. Let's not get too noisy, and let's all keep in our seats while the bus is moving. Is that understood?"

Mark said to Jerry, under his breath, "It reminds me of a stewardess explaining about the oxygen masks while the plane's taxiing out to the runway." He could have added that he knew this from the movies he'd seen, and not from personal experience.

Needless to say, the class was loud and boisterous during the entire trip. The driver sent a few warning glances through his long, angled mirror, and on several occasions Miss Reynolds had to raise her hand for quiet. Then Debbie started to sing "One Hundred Bottles Of Beer On The Wall", to which most everyone joined in. When at last they reached the beach recreation area, they had counted down to thirty-six bottles, and before number thirty-five could be opened and passed around, the door of the bus swung open, and the sixth-graders piled out. Yelling joyously, they went running down well-trodden paths, through the shade of the evergreens, to the open length of sunlit beach.

Mark and Jerry trotted down to the water together. They knelt on the sloping gravel and stuck their fingers into the foam, to test the warmth. There wasn't much, and Mark instinctively put his finger to his mouth.

Jerry did the same. "Yuck! It's salty," he said, screwing up his face.

"No kidding," Mark replied, jumping up to join the others, who were forming lines on the beach for a game of Red Rover. Jerry ran after him.

And for the next hour, the class whooped it up, making the most of their morning away from school. They played games, scouted along the beach for debris that the gentle waves sent them, and went running along the wonderful path system that crisscrossed the line of forest between the highway and the gently breaking surf.

They ate lunch in small groups, scattered about the lovely picnic area. In Mark's group, a contest was underway, as Jerry and another boy were shaking their sodas, preparing to see who could shoot the carbonated jet stream the highest. The sun was bright in the clear sky, causing warm sparkles across the cold water, and a lazy breeze moved onshore throughout the day, keeping everyone free from the insects that thrived in countless numbers throughout the shoreline habitat.

After lunch, there was a large bonfire, constantly fed by the brown paper lunch sacks. And then the games began once more, while some of the children were allowed to roam the recreation area on their own. Mark joined a large group that was making for the main "freeway" through the woods, a wide path that ran clear across the picnic area, then out to a sharp point that stuck obliquely into the saltwater canal. The path intersected with other, less obvious trails that led here and there in almost random fashion.

"Excellent for hide-and-seek, isn't it?" they asked one another. And so a new game began. As one of the seekers, Mark flashed from path to path, searching for Jerry and others behind large spruce, beneath the protective spreads of the fiddlehead ferns, or in dark, gloomy thickets at the crest of small bluffs, with the sparkling canal just below.

He rounded a bend in one of the paths and found Jerry huddled in a pile of driftwood that had been carried up into the forest long ago by a massive winter storm.

"Too easy," he ribbed him.

The pair went in search of more hidden figures, and Mark continued with his light, taunting remarks. Jerry responded with curt glances.

But they had traveled only a short distance down the worn trail when the setting around them began to change. The trees crowded them. The ground became rocky, and the boys' voices came out sharp, the echoes ringing about in an eerie manner. They looked at each other as they walked through the deepening shadows.

"Isn't this where the Indian graves are supposed to be?" Jerry asked. "Someone said they were deep in this part of the woods. I tell you, this place is giving me the creeps!"

Mark nodded. "It is spooky, all right. But it can't be that scary." His friend shook his head.

"Yeah, well what about those things we've heard? You know, the people missing around here? Something like four or five people vanishing near this beach over the years, and others found dead, all torn up. Huh?"

"Come on, Jerry! Think of the thousands of people who have walked through here, on their way out to the point. If they can make it across this hillside, then so can—" He stopped short, and his body was momentarily frozen stiff, as he had a lightning-quick vision of an otter—or was it a man?—rising from behind an old stump. Just as quickly, the vision was gone. He shook his head, and decided not to tell Jerry what had happened.

They hurried on, and then the forest opened up. Simultaneously, a group appeared. Pat was leading them, and as Mark and Jerry approached, he spread his arms and complained. "We went all through that area behind you. How come you could find him, and we couldn't? Jerry, you must have been hidden in a pretty strange place."

"I was," Jerry grinned. He jerked his head back over his shoulder. "I found one of those old Indian graves and jumped right in. I rolled a boulder over me, but Mark here knows all about trailing and tracking, and he found me in no time."

And Mark burst out laughing as he scanned the group in front of him, for he could tell by their faces that many of them believed the spoof that Jerry had just laid on them.

"Come on," he said to his friend. "Let's go out to the point." And he started off down the main path toward the water.

"We're goin' back now!" they yelled after him. "Remember, Miss Reynolds has that surprise dessert for us? We don't want to miss it!"

Mark stopped and looked back, in the shade of an enormous western hemlock. Putting one foot on the other, and trying to balance himself on one of the shallow roots of the tree, he waited as Jerry pondered for a while. Then his friend shrugged and started off with the large group of students.

"Hurry up, or you'll miss it!" he cried as he galloped along with the others.

Mark turned abruptly and walked in hurried fashion, out of the woods and into the sunlight. He didn't care if Jerry came with him or not, he told himself, as he strode along the narrow peninsula, out to the rocky tombola. The point was covered with small trees, and it seemed to stand alone, out in the canal. It had a certain appeal to it, of a sudden, and Mark glanced quickly over his shoulder to make sure that no one else was in sight. Far off to the left, across the curve of the beach, he could see the main gathering, but he was certain they paid not the least bit of attention to him, a lonely figure strolling to the end of the point.

On either side of him, the water hissed, and the natural causeway became narrower still. Finally, he arrived on a strip of grassy beach that was scarcely twenty feet in width. As he continued toward the rounded head of the point and its covering of shrub hemlock, he felt almost as though a door was closing behind him, and he was suddenly cut off from the civilized world. Across the water, he could hear the cries of his school-mates, but they were centuries away from him; totally separated was he from the friends he had laughed with, just minutes before.

The shrubs came up to meet him, and in the far distance, the white peaks of the Chilkat Range soared above the blue-gray waters of the canal. He picked his way through the small trees and continued on, out to the furthest group of rocks. They were slippery and treacherous to walk on, the tide having dropped. He squatted down on the large, flat granite that jutted out further than any other, and he heard the barnacles as they cracked beneath his shoes.

He stared at the water in front of him. It swept in and out, carrying with it shreds of green algae and rockweed, the latter dragging over the gravel bottom. Tiny shrimp darted through the clear, salty liquid, and anemones waved their tentacles and stinging cells, looking, or rather feeling, for something to poison and immobilize.

There was the sound of a motor across the waves. He looked up and saw a small troller gliding by. The crew on board noticed him and motioned greetings. He sat up straight, returned the welcome, and watched as the wake from the craft approached and rolled against the rocks. The water lapped his tennis shoe, and he felt his sock become wet. He jumped to his feet, turned, hopped back across the tops of the sharp, slippery rocks, and continued on to the shrubs.

As he did so, the mountains of the mainland shrank behind the trees and were hidden from view. His subconscious noted this.

He explored the tree-covered tombola for a little while, following every path that ran from shore to rocky shore. And after a while, he knew that he must get back with the others. Soon, it would be time to board the bus and leave the beautiful beach. He began to walk across the thin peninsula, back the way he had come ….

He stopped for a moment, remembering something.

Then he continued, feeling as though this place had been created for him, and him alone. Out there on the point, he had been truly contaminated with his other world, and he realized how much he had missed that feeling.

He returned to the main path and ran through the dark area that supposedly contained the spirits of those who no longer ran. The shouts of his friends became louder, and he hurried down a steep incline to where a number of them were gathered, near the main picnic shelter. They were carrying out some sort of drama, below the crest of a giant, flat boulder, when they saw him approaching.

"Went out to the point, didn't you?" Pat said, as Mark drew near. "We could see you out there, where those little trees are."

So they'd seen him. He shrugged to himself, but it was noticeable. "So what?" he caught himself saying aloud. "I wanted to go out there, and nobody else did. Is that a crime?"

No one answered. "We're doing a little experiment," Debbie announced from the top of the flat rock. "Watch this," she added, as she walked out to the edge and turned her back on the group below. They formed a line on either side and held their arms out to each other. And with a happy screech, Debbie fell backward, with her eyes closed, down into the maze of interlocking hands. Mark's heart skipped a beat. Good grief, that must feel funny!

Pat turned to him. "Miss Reynolds was showing us how to do it. But nobody will, except Debbie and me. Want to try it?" And they all looked at him expectantly, almost critically, he thought, as if the question of friendship rode on his answer.

"Of course I will," he answered sharply, and climbed up onto the rock with ease. They clustered about, and he waited until he was sure all was ready. Then, without any hesitation whatsoever, he straightened up, stiffened, and closed his eyes. He pushed off the edge of the tall rock and fell backwards.

The sickening plunge lasted only a second, but in that second, he thought about how it would feel, when the sensation of freefall was replaced by that of many sturdy arms underneath his back and legs.

As his head struck the hard ground, he was aware of four things. One was the shriek of a gull as it zoomed high over them. Two was the scrabbling of many hands as they clutched around his legs and torso. Three was the frantic voice of a girl yelling, "Why did you do that?" Four was the sharp pain of impact.

Someone had jumped back, allowing his head to strike the gravel. Stunned though he was, he knew that it was Pat, the second baseman on his ball club, who had pulled the evil trick. As he lay on his back, with his teeth clenched and his head spinning, he heard a low-keyed giggle, which trailed off and stopped as Debbie began calling for Miss Reynolds.

Slowly his head cleared. He opened his eyes and saw moving hemlock boughs. He tried to speak, but then a girl's face was directly over his own, and her hair was hanging down and getting into his mouth.

"It's all right! Watch out, Stefany," he growled, and forced himself to sit upright. He turned his head to look for Pat, and as he did so, the pain made him shake. He felt nauseous, but when he saw the boy gloating from a short distance away, he stood up, wavered a moment, then pointed at him.

"Why did you do that, anyway? For fun?"

Pat shrugged, then grinned, putting his hands in his pockets. "Well, it was an experiment," he said in a strange voice. Some of the others around him began to snicker nervously, but a few were giving both boys worried looks, and Mark could sense the falsity in the low giggles.

"Are you sure you're all right?" That quavering, high-pitched voice. Stefany moved toward him, reaching out with her hand.

Mark was still dazed from the blow, but he waved her off. "I'm going to have a coconut on the back of my head, if that's what you're asking." He started wobbling away from the group, but he tripped over a piece of shale and fell over onto his stomach. His mouth opened and filled with beach grit. Stefany began to wail.

As he sat up, spitting the dirt out and cursing himself, and with his head pounding so hard he thought it would burst open, he heard Pat's voice, from directly behind him.

"Mark, I'm sorry, I thought the rest of them would catch you. What's bad about it is, you're supposed to pitch in tomorrow's game, but now I guess it will have to be Jim."

Mark got to his feet and looked Pat in the eye. He forgot the pain, and with all his might, struck Pat a blow to the right side of his face. The boy crashed to the sand, and Mark caught a glimpse of blood as he staggered past, away from the group and around the bend to where the shelters were. He ran into Miss Reynolds, who was running in the other direction. Jerry was with her.

"What happened?" she asked, as she grabbed him and looked into his eyes. He mumbled incoherently, and then let his gaze move to his best friend of the past five years. He smiled a thin smile, and as Jerry opened his mouth, Mark cut in and said "I'll explain later. When I'm feeling better. Then you'll understand just what happened."

§

Two weeks after summer vacation had begun, Fran made a surprise visit. He brought over several books on hiking and a small backpack from which he produced selected items of climbing equipment. He'd just returned from a trip inland, over the icefield to the eastern part of the Coast Range, and Mark listened closely as the adventure was recounted. And then Fran asked if he would like to join him on a short hiking trip, perhaps next weekend?

And Mark had accepted immediately. Mom and Dad gave him the nod, and so Fran got the measurements of Mark's hiking boots—for crampon rental, he told him—and left him with a supply list and a brief outline of where they would go.

Mark wanted Jerry to come along, of course, but his friend had business elsewhere; besides, it was doubtful that Mrs. Floyd would have let her son escape to the world of the mountain peaks. So unfortunate, Mark thought, that she had to be worried about things like this.

Fran picked him up on the morning of the hike, and as they started down the bumpy road in the Simmons' Volkswagen, Mark turned and saw Mom waving from the living room window. Probably thinking I'll break my neck and make the headlines, he thought. And then he settled back and let his eyes roam the car's interior, where crampons lay on the floor and a shiny, coiled rope nestled in the back seat. Exactly *what* was he in for? His excitement built, and he could tell that Fran had noticed.

Eight hours later, they turned into the Nilsson's drive. Mark pushed open the door, climbed out, and asked if Fran would like to come in for a bit. Fran said no, that he had better be getting home himself. Mark waved goodbye, then slung his daypack over his shoulder and began to stagger wearily up to the back porch. He groaned as he climbed the steps, and as he put his hand on the doorknob, he stopped and rested for a moment. He was so tired, and he began to fall asleep where he stood.

Then he shook his head and went inside. He let his pack drop to the floor, then he stumbled out to the dining room. Waving to Mom, he continued on to the comfort of the sofa, letting his head drop. He sat there and blew air down his shirt; heard the refrigerator door open, then close.

Mom came in with a glass of milk. Handing it to him, she said, "Looks like you've had quite a big day. You have fun?"

"Fun?" he asked. "I am dead. Dead with fun."

She nodded. "You look like it. Well, I've got dinner in the oven, so if you're hungry—which I'm sure you are—we'll be eating as soon as your dad gets home."

Amy came into the room, and Mom gave her a shove toward the occupied sofa. "Why don't you get Mark to tell you all about his day?" she asked her. "I've got to go and get the table set." Without further comment, Mom left the two of them alone.

So, she doesn't want to hear about it herself, he thought, as he sipped white liquid from an amber-colored glass. Well then, he didn't want to tell her. Amy sat on the couch next to him, waiting as he put down the milk and wiped his mouth.

"If only you could be there," he began. "And could have seen what I saw."

"Mark! You smell awful!" Amy made a face.

"Thank you, thank you," he said, looking himself over. His clothes were dirty, and his feet, still inside the big hiking boots, were feeling hot.

"It was a long day! We hiked up this trail, way over on the west side of the glacier, and then, guess what? We left the trail and went down right to the front of the ice. He showed me how to wear crampons—those spikes you put on your boots—and then I walked right onto the glacier! It was more fun than you could imagine. There were caves underneath the ice, and we went right into some of them. You could look up and see boulders, stuck deep inside the clear ice, and when the sun struck the walls near the entrance, it made rainbows of colors. I've never had so much fun in my life!" He reached for the glass, and in another couple of gulps, the milk was gone.

"So, are you going up that mountain next?"

He quickly glanced up. "What made you ask that?" he queried the girl. "Oh, I know, I talk about it all the time, don't I?" He snapped his fingers, and Sheka came running from the hall, sniffing as she approached him. Her nose explored every part of him, analyzing the various new scents.

"Tell you what I'll do, I'll get a pack for her, and she can come with me from now on. Dad always says that malemutes love the hard work!" He jumped up and went to change clothes, Sheka following. He vaguely heard his sister calling after him and saying something about why she had asked, and wasn't he going to listen to her answer???, but he didn't catch her exact words.

A few minutes later, he went to the den, picked up the phone, and dialed Jerry's number. As he waited for an answer, he heard Dad come in the door, and at the same time, Stephen's voice.

A click at the other end. Jerry said hello.

"Hey," Mark said. "How come you always know to answer when I call?"

"I knew the first thing you'd do when you got home was to phone and tell me all about it!"

"You're right," Mark told him. "By the way, how did your caulking job go?"

"Okay, I guess. Terry says it will be puttied and painted and ready for the water by next weekend."

"I'm sure he'll let you go out on it, too. Did he pay you?"

"Sure did. But come on, what all did *you* do today?"

"Oh, yeah." Mark scratched his head. And he repeated his story of the hike on the glacier.

When he was finished, he could sense that Jerry's eyes were as wide as saucers. As he waited for his friend to comment, he listened, with his other ear, to the conversation around him.

Dad, it seemed, had approached the neighborhood in the station wagon and had spotted his eldest son walking toward home from a friend's house. And Stephen, seeing and recognizing the car, had stuck his thumb out for a ride. Dad had given him one, but now he was in the process of telling Mom that Stephen was learning a bad habit, and that a lecture was in order.

Mark said, rather loudly, "Be quiet, will you? Can't hear Jerry talk." Dad turned and frowned, but herded Stephen out to the living room.

Jerry spoke up. "Sounds like you guys are having a good time over there."

"We are." Mark's voice softened.

"Well, I gotta hang up. We're fixing to eat. Just let me know when it's time to climb the Big One!" And he haw-hawed in his funny sort of way.

Mark acknowledged and started to say goodbye, but then Jerry added quickly, "Almost forgot. Robert and I are going to the movies next Friday. Why don't you come with us? We're going to stay all afternoon."

Mark sighed. "Don't you get tired of that kind of thing after a while?"

"Oh, c'mon! It's gonna be great. Kathy and Lia might come along, and you know how much fun we always have. Let's go!"

"Maybe." And he put down the phone.

He started for his room, but Dad's voice stopped him. "How did your trip go? Come on, and tell me about it."

Mark stopped in the darkened hallway and half-turned back, calling out, "I'll tell you at dinner. I've already gone over it twice. In fact, Amy can tell you."

"What's the matter? You seemed in a hurry to tell your friend all the news." The dinner bell rang.

Couldn't he have a moment just for himself? His heart was pounding fast, for some unknown reason, and without answering Dad, he pushed open the door and entered his room. He sat on his bed, removed the smelly boots, changed his clothes, and put on fresh socks. Then he leaned back against the wall and let his mind talk to him. He asked himself, why was he behaving this way? A moment ago, he and Jerry were in happy conversation, and then there came a congestion of activity. And he'd sensed something, when Jerry's talk turned to that of the movies. He'd become impatient, had wanted the phone call over and done with, and had raced back here, to his room.

One year ago, he had sat next to Kathy, the quiet girl he liked, and maybe she would be there again, in that theater, but somehow that didn't excite him today. Indeed, the idea of horsing around with his friends or gathering to watch silly movies was now beginning to seem rather dull.

2 ERIC C TRENT

He thought about the hike, the glacier, the clear blue sky, and the great peaks all around him. Fran had been a wonderful teacher, showing him all the finer points of glacier travel, and offering plenty of advice on how to best attack the mountains in this area. He talked of both physical and mental readiness. Mark's lips moved. "You have to put *you* on the edge of yourself." That's what Fran had said.

The dinner bell rang again, but he paid no attention. He let his eyes travel around the room, and they settled for a moment on the small envelope on his desk. Straightening up, he reached over and opened it, pulling out the gift certificate that Frank Simmons had given him, on that day in December, now six months ago. The night he and Fran had met, he nodded to himself. Strange! All this time, he'd not been able to figure out what he would purchase at the hobby shop. He sat now, trying to think what he would like, but couldn't come up with anything. He exhaled loudly, then put the certificate away. He would simply have to go up there, to the hobby store, and look around.

He laughed. He knew that hobby shop inside and out; knew what lay on every shelf, in every glass case. And he couldn't think of what to buy. Maybe Fran could suggest something.

He heard Dad calling for him, and so he left the thought behind, stood up, and went out to the dining room. Sliding into his seat, he noticed that his parents were looking at him expectantly, waiting to hear his recount of the day's events. He sighed, and then began.

After a moment, he began to speed up the pace, and then he realized the excitement of the day was coming back to him. He told them how he had felt, out there on the ice, and how he liked the way Fran had been so patient with him, and how a feeling had grabbed hold of him, that where he'd been and what he'd been doing was like something out of a dream, from his past, from his earlier childhood. And that now he knew what he wanted to do most, and that was to go and play among the mountains, in the land of perpetual snow and ice, to marvel at the fantastic hugeness, bigness of it all ….

He stopped and looked at Mom, then at Dad. He shrugged, took a bite of green beans and said, with his mouth full, "I gesh being up t'er ish sho wonnerful, yuh ne'er wah come down." He swallowed. "Well, I can say one thing for sure—I'm going up there again soon. Very soon."

A quiet pause around the dinner table. "I'm glad you had fun," Mom said. "But all I can think of is the dangerous part of it. All the places where you can fall, places where it's steep and you can lose your balance, and then, goodness knows."

She started to say something else, but stopped. Dad was silent, and Mark could see that while Mom talked, her mind had been working on a further thought.

He said, "It's fun, and I won't worry about the danger. Besides, Jerry will be along with me from now on, I hope. It's part of the big plan, remember?"

When he went to bed that night, visions of the glacier, the icefield, and the silent peaks filled his mind. And there was also something else. Something small, seemingly distant, was making itself heard. He didn't understand where it came from, and he couldn't make it go away. It was that voice—no, not a voice—but it spoke nonetheless. It told him that he was mistaken perhaps, that it could be many years before he set foot on the glacier again. He turned over on his side and shook himself, trying to make the intruder disappear.

You're wrong. I know what I'm going to do.

§

Light rain was forecast, however the clouds remained at a high altitude and were quite thin, allowing the sun's rays to sear through and warm the earth. Mark sat on his bed, dressed in his baseball uniform, and tried to put his mind on the upcoming game, the season's last, but it wasn't easy. He fiddled with the rawhide knots on his fielder's glove.

Last night's fireworks display had been beautiful. Set off from a float- ing barge in the center of the channel, the rockets had boomed loudly, and the sound had echoed from the mountain slopes. The brilliant colors had grabbed hold of him in a mysterious way. He remembered lifting to his toes as each rocket was launched into space, feeling as though he was traveling with them, to the stars. The explosions of strontium, salts, and aluminum powder had helped to comfort his troubled soul, numbed earlier by the news of Fran's death.

He reached for his cap, put it on, and stood up. Walking toward the den, he stretched his left arm, working it in a windmill fashion, to get out any remaining stiffness from his last pitching practice. Mom and Amy were already at the ballpark to watch the first game of the day, but the kitchen radio was still on. Mark listened for a moment while the announcer spoke of the upcoming second game, and he jumped slightly when he heard his own name mentioned as a probable starting pitcher. He reached out and snapped the radio off, then turned and hurried out the front door.

He walked quickly across the street and past the minor league park, where the younger boys were screaming and loose balls were flying all over the enclosed field. He continued on to the major league park, and the familiar mixture of scents—the raked dirt, the toasted bread and boiled franks, the peanuts, and the grape bubble gum—began to fill his nostrils. He spotted his family in the bleachers, waved to them, and then clattered across the painted wood seats to where his teammates were gathered.

He sat down next to Jim, who looked at him from the corner of his eye, while at the same time concentrating on the action. "Well, the big winner shows up at last," he breathed. When Mark didn't answer right away, the other boy turned around.

"What's the matter? You not feeling well? Usually you're the first one here," he pointed out.

Mark sucked in his breath. "Nothing like that. And yes, my arm feels just fine. But I didn't sleep well last night. Stayed up too late."

He didn't mention anything else. He sat and watched as the first game progressed. It was a high-scoring affair, as both clubs were trying out younger pitchers who had not been given the chance to show their talents during the season. At one point, a foul was popped into the stands, and for a second it looked as though Mark had a chance to snag it. But as he stood up, someone cut in from behind and grabbed the ball in the webbing of his glove.

Mark had seen a flash of navy blue and recognized a member of Jerry's team. The boy headed for the press box to return the ball, and Mark looked up and saw Jerry sitting with his teammates. He started to call out to him, but decided not to, as Jerry seemed quiet and absorbed in his own thoughts. Probably wondering if he'll make contact his first time up, Mark reasoned.

Jerry couldn't hit a slow roller off of him, and everyone knew it. Mark had kidded him about it all week, as the inevitable season finale approached, but inside him, there was once more that strange feeling about playing against his best friend. The two teams had squared off three times already this year, and although Mark's club had won two of those encounters, they were firmly entrenched in fourth place, where they'd finished the previous season as well. But Jerry's team could win the championship trophy outright with a victory this afternoon. Mark knew his performance on the mound would go a long way in determining that.

When the first game ended, Mark followed his teammates to the third base dugout, and after waiting for it to clear, the players wearing green and white entered to set up their equipment. Ken put on his catcher's gear and went out to the bullpen. Mark followed, with the coach walking beside him.

"Remember, only three innings today. Sorry I had to use you on Wednesday, but I had no choice. Do your best, and Glenn will relieve you in the fourth."

Mark nodded, then the coach gave him a backslap and left him to his warm-up. Mark had always hated the rules limiting a pitcher to six innings per week, but today he wondered if he could have gone the distance anyway. He tried to think of the game, but the tragedy kept sliding into his consciousness, and it was hard to put it back away, much like how a dirt speck got caught in the eye and continued to drift back to the center, no matter how many times a person blinked.

As he warmed up, he concentrated on his form, on snapping off his unique breaking pitch. Not once did he shoot a glance over to where Jerry and his mates were taking infield practice. He became all business as he loosened up, firing a series of hard fastballs, then letting fly his famous drop-slider, a confusing pitch thrown like a football and with extra mustard. It sank toward the ground in front of Ken, and then the angled spin took over and twisted the path of the ball gently to the right. Ken was prepared, however, and scooped the pitch out of the dirt with learned finesse.

"Gonna ruin your arm, throwing them at our age," he warned Mark for the hundredth time. Mark caught the throwback and replied, "It's the last game of the season, and I lead the league in called third strikes. I know what I'm doing."

Forty-five minutes later, Ken, along with everyone else connected to the team, was glad indeed that Mark was throwing his patented slider with perfection. In the third inning, Mark protected a 3–0 lead, he was pitching no-hit baseball, and his mates were playing without error. Mark felt an oddness, however; this was the final inning he would stand atop a Little League mound, and for some reason, he didn't care.

There were two outs when he walked his first batter. Then the next hitter drove a high fly to the right corner, and the outfielder let the ball drop right through his glove. An error was announced on the loudspeaker, and with runners at second and third, Mark found Jerry waiting in the batter's box.

Jerry wore a faint smile as he cocked his bat. As Mark released the ball, he felt something he could not describe. It was a horrible sensation, and he suddenly felt he was pitching to a total stranger. As the ball approached the plate, he stared after it in disbelief; it was headed straight and true, for the center of the strike zone. He'd thrown his slider, but it *wasn't breaking*.

Jerry was equally surprised, it seemed, and swung late. But the sound of the wood meeting the ball told everyone the story even before they saw the white pill streaking for the fence. Mark whirled around and watched the ball drop between the right and center fielders. He slumped his shoulders and saw, out of the corner of his eye, the runners as they galloped home. He saw Jeff, the center fielder, chasing the ball, stooping and picking it up. He appeared to move with odd slowness.

Jerry came into his picture, rounding second. The throw came to the shortstop, who let it bounce through his legs. Mark raced over and picked up the rolling ball, saw that Jerry was trying for third, and threw to his third baseman with all his might.

And they got Jerry by half a step.

He walked toward the dugout, realizing that it had been a heads-up play, and that he'd finished his Little League pitching career with a flourish, but he felt only painful mystery. Something had happened, and Jerry had smacked that pitch almost out of the park. As the two passed by each other, Jerry brushing the dirt from his pants, Mark did not congratulate him, but only gave him a sharp glance, then turned away and hurried to the shade of the dugout.

His team was still leading 3–2, and Mark had pitched brilliantly, but the reliever was not so fortunate. The team in green played hard the rest of the way, fighting the opponent tooth and nail, but in the end, Jerry's team won 9–7, securing the league championship.

Afterward, the coach called a quick meeting and began to speak to them, but Mark barely heard the words. He sat next to Jeff, who'd combined with him on the spectacular putout earlier. Jeff turned to him and asked, "How did he get such a big hit off you, anyway?"

Mark looked at him. Jeff was new to the team this year, in fact new to the community, and Mark hadn't gotten to know him very well yet. He was a likable type, however, and Mark searched for a polite answer. Before he could open his mouth, Jeff spoke up again, and simultaneously there were cheers, and someone was patting his back.

"Did you hear that? Coach is naming the All-Star team, and you're on it! I knew you'd make it! And listen to that … Jim made it too!"

Mark wasn't paying much attention. He turned and looked at his teammates, who were hollering "Speech!"

"Thanks for the support," he mumbled.

That was all he said. The meeting over, the team rose and filed out of the dugout, many of them glancing at Mark and smiling in admiration. He waved to Mom, in the stands, and he could tell she already knew.

Jerry knew as well. He skipped over to where Mark was walking slowly in the direction of the concession stand.

"Heard you made All-Stars. Way to go, man!"

Mark looked at him, the boy he had known as his best friend for so many years, the boy he'd thrown out in the third inning. He looked at him almost in anger, and Jerry saw the look, stopped his forward motion, and spread his arms.

"Sorry. I mean it was a lucky hit. Swung at the right time, that's all. You pitched good, I mean you … you pitched great. You did, Mark."

Mark gestured for him to follow, and they walked from the crowded snack bar, out to the playground. Here they stopped. Mark took a deep breath, and then told him.

"Fran was killed last morning, up there on the icefield. He fell into a crevasse, and his friend, who was with him, forgot which one it was … couldn't remember when he got back up there, in a helicopter with rescue people."

He looked at Jerry, tears in his eyes. Jerry lowered his head, stared at the ground, and kicked one of the speckled granites. "Yeah, I heard something about it."

Mark waited for him to look up, but Jerry did not. As they stood there, apart from other humans, Mark remembered the gift certificate, and the fireworks, and now he knew what he was going to purchase.

"Jerry. When I was with Fran, up there on the glacier, I felt really great. Like I was being shown the right way or something. I don't know." He swallowed, and his throat ached.

"But when I was downtown last night, watching the fireworks, I got the same feeling. Like I was a part of those wonderful displays, and the great empty space between me and the stars. So I'm going to do something, just for Fran. I'm going to build a rocket, a really good one, and I'm going to shoot it off, toward the stars. I know Fran would like that."

He stopped talking and let his breath come trembling from his lungs. Never since that day, near the edge of the little pond, had his friend heard him talk like this. Would he accept it? *Could* he accept it?

Could his best friend understand him, this time?

Jerry looked up, and he smiled a sickening smile. For a second, Mark sensed that Jerry had indeed accepted the strange thought, the strange dialogue, and forever his strange companion, Mark Nilsson.

"Well," Jerry said in a thin voice. "I got something else I really have to tell you. I only found out on Friday, and that's that I'm leaving."

Mark's body tightened. "Leaving? What do you mean, leaving?"

The boy shrugged. "Leaving. Leaving town. We're going to move, to Anchorage. So, I guess after a week or so, I won't see you again." And the smile withered, then disappeared altogether. "I would have loved to climb that mountain with you, Mark."

The boy in the green uniform vibrated, and the noise of the people nearby made him want to scream. He fixed his glance on Jerry, and before he could stop himself, it came out of him.

"Jerry. I thought maybe of all the people in the world, you understood why I seem so different. I was sure of it. Now, you're just nobody. Go away."

"What are you talking about?" Jerry gave a nervous laugh.

"Get out of here! Get out of my sight! I don't EVER want to see your stupid face again. Ever again!"

Jerry cringed, his neck veins pumping hard.

"I hate you! I hope you die! Now get out of my way, I said get out of my way! Damn you, damn you, damn you!"

Mark ran past him, across the playground, away from the boy in the striped pants and blue jersey. He looked back after a moment and sneered.

"DAMN YOU!!

Running home, he began to cry loudly, until his entire body was in pain. He threw open the gate, waved Sheka aside, and ran to the back porch. He raced up the steps and just stood there until the sobs died away. Then he slung off his mitt, threw his cap to the ground, and kicked off his baseball cleats. He jumped off the porch and threw open the door of the storage van. He grabbed an old pair of tennis shoes and put them on, then hauled out his bike and slammed the door shut. And still in his uniform, he took off, back through the gate, across the drive, and down the road, weaving between the chuck holes, ignoring the fact that Mom and Amy were walking home from the ballpark.

Speeding along, he reached the lake twenty minutes later. The glacier loomed in front of him, its open fissures deep blue in color. The clouds were now thickening, sweeping across the marsh flats, as the boy leapt off his bike and wheeled it to the safety of the bushes.

He ran up the path to the visitor center, his vision still blurry. Hurrying past the building, he started up the wide, sandy trail, coming soon to the gentle slope and the quartz vein.

Reality was the daydream, and the dreamer could not wake.

Mark raced up the tilted rocks and stood at the edge of the little pond. He looked into the glassy pool; saw a boy in a green and white baseball suit. The clouds pushed ever closer.

Now he was running again, through the alders and around to the far side of the pond, where the boulder rose as always. It had waited, he knew, for his return, had waited ever so patiently. As he climbed up and sat, he could almost hear it sigh, almost hear its reassuring breath below him. Then he realized the sound was his own. He took another, much deeper breath.

He looked toward the glacier. Up there was the icefield, where Fran had reentered immortality. Up there was *the* mountain, which was pure and virgin as the earth itself, as the sky and stars themselves.

As he himself.

At his back was the Valley. It contained life, human life, the people he knew. At this moment, he despised them all.

How long would this last? How long before he climbed down, returned home, and called Jerry to say he was sorry?

Mark stood up on his boulder and reached out slowly to his beloved peak, hidden behind the other, lesser mountains. "I am not sorry," he breathed. "I will never be."

As he stood, he noticed the breeze had picked up. That was fine.

Now he recalled the night dream, where he had shaken a fist at *the* mountain and called it his enemy. Could it be true? No, he decided, it must have been a coded message, and certainly he would understand the true meaning at the appointed hour. Someday soon, everything would come into sharp focus. It had to.

The sheet of clouds lowered, slowly and steadily, and pushed against the mountains in front of him. The thunder did not come, it would never come. Then the breeze shifted, and Mark felt his skin crawl as he witnessed, for the first time ever, the wind blowing ripples across the pond, marring the surface and distorting the identity of the one who looked back at him.

CHAPTER TEN
(PALINGENESIS)

Stratus clouds were moving …

… reality had cleared its throat.

CHAPTER ELEVEN

Night had fallen, and the birds quieted. The breeze was faint, barely moving the willow leaves, and the only sound was the spitting of hot coals.

The flames had died away, and the ring of red-orange did little to heat the air around it. In the dark shadows, off to one side, was the makeshift camp shelter, constructed of hemlock boughs. Besides this, the glowing embers, and the two boys who squatted around the circle of stones, there was nothing to disrupt the natural forest scene.

Stephen was quiet, unusually so it seemed, to his younger brother. He was poking the hot ashes with a spruce twig, listening to them sigh, and then watching, as if entranced, as Mark tossed in the rest of the garbage, temporarily bringing the fire to life once more. Neither wore an expression of happiness, wonder, or puzzlement. They sat and looked at the fading cinders, feeling the coolness set in upon them, as their section of planet surface rotated away from its parent star.

Both had settled into their own private thoughts. Mark touched his boot lace and slid his fingers from the knot, slowly out to the plasticized end. He did it over and over as he relived, within his mind, the events of the day.

It was Friday, the end of the first week of school, and during the morning, he and Jeff had made their final plans for tonight's campout. It was an introductory science project, its goal to determine the content, as well as the extent, of human interaction in an unfamiliar setting, in this case, a fake situation where two people were stuck in the wilderness.

And sometime after lunch, Jeff became violently ill, and Mark received notice that he'd been hurried home to bed. Unwilling to give up on what was started, Mark had summoned his older brother to take his place. Now, as he sat there thinking, he wondered if it was such a good idea. There was little to share between them nowadays, and they had scarcely talked since before dinner. Not that either had tried very hard. Mark wondered if it was he who was causing the evening to be so quiet.

He straightened, and then rose and stretched himself. "I'm going for a little walk," he said, buttoning up the front of his coat.

"It's almost completely dark." Stephen looked up quickly. "You better not go too far, or you won't find your way back."

"Oh, come on. I know every foot of the Valley. I am my own compass here!" Mark turned and left, past a rim of blueberry bushes, asking himself as he tramped through the dense foliage beyond, exactly what he'd meant by that.

In front of him, above the treetops, loomed the dark, lower end of Thunder Mountain. Not too far away was the old logging road, where the flagged trail began. Mark passed through stands of tall, thin spruce, the muskeg giving underneath him with moist, squishing noises. He walked until he was two hundred yards or more from the crude little shelter. Then he slowed his pace, which now became more of a stumbling drift through the cool shadows and mossy undulations. And his mind drove itself into the powerful dream state, just as he knew it would.

His legs must have stopped moving, and he felt a strange alien sensation. Suddenly he wasn't entirely sure that he was Mark Nilsson. The eyes that saw … did not seem to be his own.

There was a globe, perhaps not perfectly spherical, but close enough, the equatorial bulge too fine to discern from great distance. The globe was bright blue in color, with splotches of white spreading from the oceans, where moisture had its opportunity to rise and condense. The sphere hung in space, so it appeared, but it was a poor description, for hanging implies suspension. The earth was not suspended. It sought to break free of the sun's pull, yet the sun, not seen in this picture, was therefore unavailable to explain the phenomenon. The backdrop was of total blackness, save for the infinite number of pinprick lights, shining without the hint of a flicker, in the vacuum of empty space. It was impossible to measure distance and time; all one could do was invent objective truths and pretend they were unquestioningly factual.

Even Capella was hopelessly lost in this enormous void.

Now the earth was approaching. It loomed ever larger, and a thin bluish haze, beautifully luminous, became visible, as if the planet wore a gaseous skin. It was the breath of the earth. It melted past, and now the blue sphere was so large, all the stars were gone. Directly in front was a new contrast of colors and distinct formations. Blue met brown in a jagged line, broken and uneven.

Now even closer it was; much of the brown became green, and wisps of white, the ever-present clouds, wafted past. The green flecks became land covered with forest, the millions upon millions of evergreens and deciduous trees covering the earth, as if protecting it. It was a wonderful scene of green, white, and blue. The trees, the clouds, and the vast ocean. Spots of brown were rising above the greenness. White-capped mountain peaks now pushed higher than the eyes that watched, reaching out to where the eyes had just been ....

And now the freefall was ended.

Noise. Music. The birds, and the rushing of a clear brook. The *groak* of a raven as it appeared, mysteriously so, from behind the low ridges. The cold wind as it raced from the peaks, roaring from those dizzying heights and speeding through the cottonwoods below.

Now a chattering sound, and a red squirrel dashing from one small tree to another, running to the edge of the soft hemlock branches and jumping through its own infinite space, in this, the most wonderful playground. It had not a thought in its head, for there was no need for thought. It was truly alive.

And that was when Brian fired.

There was a great city, and its boundaries pushed deep into what had once been wilderness. Freeways looped the outer residential areas and snaked their way into the central business district. The sounds of construction filled the air.

Parks dotted the surface, and their grass was newly mowed. The dirt had been brought in by dump truck, and the big, broadleaf deciduous trees had been planted there, decades before. These parks were encased by sidewalks that ran straight as an arrow, with lines of soft, black tar separating the white squares.

And when the people of the city rose in the morning, they listened to traffic reports on the radio, they poured coffee, they brought in the paper from the front porch, they ate their Rice Krispies and toast, and as their brains processed the news headlines, they nodded to themselves and thought, how good it was, that the news of the world was made up only of printed letters, and that all was well, here in the great city, and all was well with their loved ones, those here at the breakfast table, and those out and beyond, at a distant post office or telephone number.

And on Sunday, the families would drive to the country. They would pass by the very last line of suburban homes, and the road would narrow, becoming poorly maintained. The trees would close in, and the shadows of the forest would dominate.

A car slowed, crunching to a stop on the graded shoulder. The people got out, almost hesitant. They walked cautiously about, looking at the shrubbery along the front line of trees, and they jumped slightly as a twig snapped beneath their feet, or when a strange bird cried its own headlines from the depths of the green.

"How tranquil," the man said.

"Yes, but so eerie," his wife answered.

The boy jumped down into the marshy ditch, yanked a few of the tiny blue flowers, and scurried back to the others, his shoes muddied. "For you, Mother. They'll look nice, at home."

The girl shivered. "I think a bug just bit me. Let's get back into the car now, please!"

They did so, as the eyes watched.

And these families would drive quickly back to the city, to the parks and the black tar, and to the sounds of new construction, smiling as their house came into view.

The eyes blinked, and Mark was looking at the ground in front of him. It was pitch black, but he sensed there was a boggy area just ahead. He looked around him, trying to see though the darkness and get his bearings. And then he knelt down and reached out to the underbrush.

He felt the leaves of a gooseberry plant, and he reached further, rubbing his hands over the damp moss. It was cold. He felt the multitude of plants which made up the colony, felt the life of a complete habitat, a complete city.

And it was just there. Nobody had planted it. No one but himself had ever touched it. And best of all, it didn't care whether humans existed.

He straightened up suddenly. "Is it true?" he asked the dark forms all around him. "Is it true that if I don't need society, then you don't need me, either?"

He knelt again. "You don't want them, but you do want me. Yes?" He lowered his head and kissed the moss. And then he got up, turned, and started back to the campsite, knowing what he would report on Monday.

The trip back seemed twice as long as the journey outward. When at last he reached the shelter, his brother, and the soft glows from the fire pit, he was tired and ready to prepare his bed. He ducked beneath the hemlock boughs, pulled his sleeping bag from its stuff sack, and spread it on the ground, which was covered by smaller, softer green limbs.

"Where'd you go?" Stephen called out.

"Just a little ways. I wanted to do a bit of headwork for my report on Monday." Mark came out of the "tent" and stood near the fire ring for a moment.

"Do you think," he began, and put his hands in his pockets. "Do you think that maybe, if someone lived out here, or spent enough time out here in the woods, that he might go crazy? I mean, to his friends. You think that he might become so attached to his natural world, that he would forget even how to deal with people at all?" Without waiting for an answer, he added, "I think it's happening to me. I think that someday I'll go completely crazy, and never want to talk to another human being as long as I live."

Slowly, Stephen looked up. Throwing his poker stick into the dying coals, he said, "I think it's probably happened before, somewhere."

Mark turned and went back to his sleeping bag. He got inside and closed his eyes—his own eyes—and tried to fall asleep.

It wasn't a good enough answer. Or was it?

§

Three days later, Jeff was still absent from school, unable to hear Mark give his oral report. He returned to school on Tuesday and was given a rundown on how the overnight trip had gone, and what the teacher had thought of Mark's summary.

"After class, I stayed behind and asked him about it. He said the best part of the report was the 'eloquent' way in which I presented it. But he told me that he didn't understand exactly what I was trying to say, only that I said it well. And I know damn well that nobody else in the class had the slightest clue!"

"Hey, if that's how it seemed to you, then you should have said what you did. The idea was to bring in your thoughts of the weekend, and how you got along with someone else. He made that clear."

Mark shook his head. "I could have added something to the report which I know for a fact would have made *it* a lot clearer. But I chose not to do so."

"What's that?"

"I choose not to tell you either."

During the next two classes, he struggled with himself, and then decided before the sixth hour. As he walked into the hall, heading for his locker, Allen approached and asked him if he'd read the chapter on wood-working tools, for today's discussion.

"Yes, but you'll have to talk about it without me," Mark answered. "I've got something to do right now."

He fiddled with his locker combination, and then swung open the door and threw in his notebook. As he slammed it shut, he was aware that Allen was still with him.

"Where you goin'? Listen, I've decided that you're actin' pretty strange today. Must've been that campin' trip you took. What'd you do out there anyway, smoke dope?"

Mark shrugged. "Really, it's just another experiment I've got to try. Don't worry, if it's successful, I'll tell you about it someday. Now, get lost—you'll be late to class."

Allen made a face. "Umm … skipping!" Mark turned and walked down the crowded hall, weaving between the students who gossiped in front of their lockers. He reached the stairs, and as he descended, he put his hand on the cold rail, something he had never done before.

When he reached the bottom, the human traffic was clearing, as the sixth hour classes were ready to start. He looked down the hall to his left, took a couple of breaths, and then walked in that direction. He strode down the center of the hallway, convincing himself that what he was about to do was more important than anything that might be in his way.

He went past the main office and pushed open the door to the counseling services. As he stood looking at the vacated desk in front of him and hearing the staccato beat of a typewriter coming through the wall, he picked his words carefully, and then rehearsed them several times.

A lady entered the room, smiled at him, and asked in a pleasant voice, "Can I help you with something?"

Mark rested his fingers on the desk. "Let's find out," he said in a strong tone. "I'm beginning to wonder if what I have is a disease."

"I see. Tell you what, let's go into the adjoining room, where there isn't so much noise. This way," she motioned, and he straightened up and walked across to a small office.

He sat in the yellow foam chair, scooting it close to where she seated herself, at a plain wooden desk that was barren of materials. Without hesitation, he said, "I've got a unique problem."

She smiled again and brushed back her hair. "All of us do. Every problem that gets discussed here is unique in its own way. That's one of the first things you have to understand, the fact that your problem is likely no worse than that of anyone else who comes to see me. It's just unique to *you*."

Mark gripped the sides of the chair. "That's what you think!" he shot at her. "I'd appreciate it if you wouldn't get into that sort of talk—it doesn't apply in this situation. What I'm about to say, you've never heard before."

She was still smiling.

This isn't starting like it's supposed to.

"Well, all right, I'll accept that. Let's hear about it."

He looked straight at her. "This isn't one of those usual things like 'my parents don't understand me', although I'm sure it will involve that sooner or later." The counselor leaned back in her swivel chair and studied him more intently now; the smile was fading away.

Is this coming out "eloquently"?

"It didn't start with them, and it didn't start with my friends at school either. It began when I was a young child, and though it seemed to disappear for a few years, I knew all along that it would never leave me. In my subconscious, I mean."

He jerked a thumb at himself. "There must be no one that spends more time in the woods than myself. And I don't mean out there chopping trees down. I mean out there, like I belong to the world, and not to the people in it." Here he stopped, and waited for her to comment.

She only nodded, motioning for him to continue. He did so. "Well, I'm sure I'm not the only one around here who can point out the various types of plants that grow in this area, or marvel at how beautiful the mountains and the glaciers really are, but I know I stand apart, separate, as though it's of much greater importance to me than to all others."

The counselor cleared her throat. "And now you're afraid that it will dominate you and take you away from your friends at school, your family at home, and for that matter, society in general. All because you will become foreign to them, a stranger. Right?"

"Yes," he answered quickly. And then he added, after a short pause, "But what frightens me the most is the idea that they—all the people— won't bother me a bit when they turn their backs on me, and when I turn my back on them. I'm scared that I won't be scared."

They looked at each other for a moment. She moistened her lips and said, in a hushed tone, "Listen to the story I'm going to tell you. It happened to a boy who came to see me a few years ago, when I was working at the high school.

"He came in one day, and he said he was having trouble with his studies. He couldn't get his homework done, and when I asked him what he thought the reason was, he gave a rather interesting answer. He said that he felt he no longer cared about his schoolwork, or for that matter, for his classes or his teachers. All that mattered now was his interest in hiking about and enjoying the wilderness. All he wanted was to be in the mountains. Said he would rather do that than be at home with his family. And he was fearful it would ruin him someday.

"But he asked, what could be done? And I told him that he would simply have to make up his own mind on what was best for him in the long run. That he would have to set priorities and long-term goals, and begin working toward those goals. And I added that perhaps the best thing might be to keep himself from the mountains for a while, and that most likely they would loosen their hold on him, and he would see the light go on, concerning other important things. He listened, and a few weeks later he came back to visit me, saying that he had taken my advice, and that he'd just received an 'A' for a paper he had written about George Washington."

She began to smile again. "Soon after, his parents got a divorce, and he went to live with his mother in Seattle. I wondered if that experience would shake him up again, but a couple of years back, he returned and paid me a surprise visit. He'd been working part-time in a sporting goods store, and he was a lift operator at one of the ski areas down there. He told me that he had graduated school and that he'd found his place in society. Not that he'd ever had to give up the mountains for good," she finished.

Mark sat, now slumped down in his chair. Her story buzzed through his head, and as he thought about it, he wondered who it was, just who had felt such a way as this, about the mountain peaks that soared into space, his mind having been touched in the ultimate sense by their beauty and outright holiness.

And now she was telling him that this young man had "cured" himself.

"Are you sure that all those other things are more important than what I mentioned?" he asked her. She shook her head at him.

"I didn't really mean to say it like that. But other things are necessary. You can see that, can't you?"

"Yes, I suppose so." Suddenly he was gripped by a thought—and a feeling—that made him shake. His heart sped up.

"Listen," he said in a forced voice. "Do you remember his name? The one you were just talking about?"

Another shake of the head, and for the second time, the smile was gone. She started to speak, stopped, and then said, barely above a whisper, "No, I can't remember just now. But I guess it doesn't matter."

Mark rose out of his chair and pointed at her in an almost deadly manner. "You do remember. And I know his name myself." He paused, then shouted, "It was Fran!"

He shook his finger at her. "You see, I knew him. He took me up into the mountains one day, just before he was killed. And you didn't think I knew. You wanted to keep it from me, because you thought it would ruin everything you've said so far. Well, tough!"

She looked at him, and then he felt stupid. He pulled back his hand and dropped slowly into the chair. "Sorry," he mumbled. He rested his palms on his knees, looked at them momentarily, and then he grunted.

"I don't usually have such a temper."

"And I'm sorry if I caused a sad remembrance. But perhaps that makes it more clear than ever. He was someone you knew. And he turned out to be quite a happy young man, much different than when I first talked with him." She paused, then asked, "What's your name?"

"Mark."

"What grade are you in?"

"Eighth," he answered.

"You seem like a bright young man. I want you to trust me when I tell you there's lots of time left to iron out any problems you may have. I'm wondering if perhaps you've done a bit of weeding out concerning your friends, more so than most people your age, and have become quite selective. If so, that will take care of much of your troubles.

"But let me say this. You will need friends, and I'm not saying you'll need thousands of them. If you'll just be yourself, the ones that stick with you will *become* your real friends. And the others? Well, they were not destined for you at all."

He nodded, and they continued to talk for a while. He thought he felt a little better, and soon the counselor was relating some of the problems *she* had taken to her own student advisors, many years before.

The noise in the hall built up, and he realized that classes were over. "I have to catch my bus," he said, hopping up from the chair. "Thanks a lot for talking with me. I think maybe I do see things more clearly now."

"Of course," she answered. "Remember what I said. You be yourself, and you'll have no trouble at all keeping both of your worlds, and even more important, keeping them in balance." He nodded, stepped to the outer office, and made his way to the hall, thinking about the counselor's last sentence, and how it seemed familiar to him.

As he began to mingle with the crowd of students making their way to the exits, he sensed Tina behind him. He slowed and let her catch up.

"Hey, I just saw you come out of the counselor's office. You in some kind of trouble?"

"Yes," he informed her. "I tried to commit suicide this morning and got caught. So we've been in there talking."

"You're lying!"

"You hope so." Mark walked with her to the corner, where she would turn to reach her locker. As they neared, she asked him, "What were you really doing in there?" And before he could answer, she said, "You haven't been talking to me at all lately."

"I haven't seen you lately," he pointed out. "Not all summer. And you're in only one of my classes this year."

"Oh, come on. I'm having trouble with math already. I need you to help me with it."

He looked at her. "You want to know the real reason I'm acting funny?" She nodded expectantly, and he looked both ways, putting on an act that made her giggle. "Can't let anyone hear this," he lowered his voice.

He motioned her to the side of the hall, then brought his head close to hers, whispering in her ear. "It's like this. I don't get along with too many people anymore. And you want to know why? Because I'm too smart. I don't mean IQ-wise. I mean my brain reaches out to further dimensions, beyond the known universe, through ripples in time and space, and I see and worship the thread of our existence, unknown to most others."

He was confusing her. He could see it in her eyes. It delighted him, though he did not change his blank expression.

Pulling back from her, he asked, "Now, you promise not to tell anyone?"

Slowly, Tina nodded. "Oh, sure. Cross my heart."

He nodded back. "Yes, I see," he murmured, waving a hand at her bosom. "You have indeed crossed your heart at last. Well, I suppose you *are* getting a little bigger."

"You are sick! Know what I'd like to tell you, Mark?" Without telling him, she whirled around and clacked down the hard floor, away from him. He watched her disappear, thinking of other things he could have said. That she was whiny at times, and that her mood changed too frequently, even for a girl. He could have said that her handwriting was so bad it gave him migraines, and that she had a bit of orange wax in her ear.

§

He was one of the last to board the school bus, and as he drifted toward the rear of the vehicle, he searched for an empty seat. Amazingly, he found one. It was in the seventh row, on the right-hand side, and he slid into it, turning at once to the window.

The line of buses began to move, and as the buildings slid past, he thought about his little visit with the counselor, and what he thought he might do to keep himself in control.

He'd forget about the woods, just for a little while. Forget the meadow and the creek, he told himself. And the pond—it would be all right for the time being. The boulder would look after it. Tonight he'd help Amy with her homework, and tomorrow he'd get with Richard and Jeff, and they could plan some sort of mischief for Saturday.

"Mark! What are you doing tomorrow night?"

Turning, he saw Randy, his next-door neighbor, in the seat behind him, and he shrugged. "Nothing. You got something interesting?"

"Yeah, after dinner tomorrow, we're taking our boat across the bar at high tide, and into town, because it needs work. Want to go with us?"

Mark nodded. "Sure. Call me later tonight, or come over."

There, that wasn't too hard, was it? And it sounded like fun. Cruising over the hazardous bar at the western end of the channel was sure to be exciting.

Keeping both worlds in balance, he told himself. As the bus ran the distance over the narrow, twisting highway, Mark was now content to sink into the green padding and stare at the writing on the back of the seat in front of him.

Some of the tales were actually funny. He'd not seen them before, which made him realize that he'd never sat in this row. He studied the hurriedly scribbled lines, most of which were pretty dirty in nature. One of them had to do with a girl named Wendy, and he wondered if it was possibly the same Wendy he'd known all these years, or was it perhaps another Wendy, from long, long ago? It sounded as if this Wendy was in lots of trouble, the kind that he couldn't, or dared not, picture cute Wendy Shelton to be in.

Keeping both worlds in balance, he told himself. He gazed out the window again and watched the trees go by; saw the long arm of Thunder Mountain approaching.

Beyond it was the Valley.

At the head of the Valley was the glacier, and the soaring peaks of the icefield.

And hidden behind the first row was *the* mountain, which would become visible at precisely the point where the bus would turn into his neighborhood.

He waited with anticipation, eager to tell it with his mind, that his worlds were in balance, that the towering mass of rock and ice was perfectly counterweighted by the moving vehicle on which he rode, by his sister Amy, by his adventures with Richard and Jeff, by all of society.

Even by Wendy Shelton, and silly Tina.

He remembered something he'd once said, years ago, on a November holiday, as he stood at a lonely intersection at night, the very crossing this bus now approached. He had the world in his hands. Both of them, he decided, and he smiled.

Even as he did so, however, he was aware of the joke he was playing on himself. And this joke had no funny ending. His smile quickly faded.

Society; it was all around him, and with each passing day, since Fran had died, and Jerry had vamoosed, he'd felt the cosmic tug, just as he'd felt it during his early years. He was being pulled away from the world, and toward the World. Now was now, and there was no "then". He didn't belong here, he belonged *Here.*

Deep inside, he could not deny it. The teeter-totter was unbalanced; one of the riders was heavier than the other.

§

Winter that year was peculiar; cold and dry at times, the snow topped with a hard crust, alternating with sudden warming trends and melting rains. On those blustery days, it was miserable to be outdoors, and Mark spent much of the dark months working on his model rockets.

He was putting the finishing touches on MN363, a two-stage, high-altitude probe he had designed completely from scratch. It was an interesting rocket. Long and slender, it was nothing like the beautiful *Ganymede.* It had a blunt, ogive nose cone, and the set of four little fins could almost escape one's notice. They were stubby and had flat bases; the rocket could not stand by itself.

The first stage was only four inches tall. The upper stage contained a clear plastic payload, and just below was another set of tiny fins. The entire model was twenty-two inches in height.

He carefully applied the black, ringed decals at the proper places on the fuselage, to give the impression of staging bulkheads. Then, as he held it up and sat on his bed, he realized that he hadn't as yet given it a name. He thought hard for a minute, and as he was trying to come up with something, Mom knocked on his door and pushed it open.

Still looking at the model, he asked with a frown, "What do I call this thing? You got any ideas?"

Mom stood near him, and he saw that she was gazing at the model with approval. "That's quite a rocket, now that it's finished. Are you sure it won't just take off and head into orbit?"

He smiled thinly. "No, I don't think so." And then a strange sensation passed through him, one that caused his hand to grip tightly the rocket's fuselage. For an instant, he thought he had damaged his prize model. He breathed out, very slowly, then breathed in and exhaled a second time. "I think—" he began, then stopped himself. A moment of quiet, and then a voice that came from the bottom of his throat.

"I think it will fly wherever it wants." He had no idea why he had said that, or whether it was his voice, the voice of another, or the voice of something else entirely. He felt a momentary chill, but the sensation lasted but a millisecond. The chill was gone, and he was on his bed once more.

He shrugged. "You want something?"

Before Mom could answer, an outburst of young female laughter came through the wall. A giggly voice yelled out, "Just like recess, just like recess!" The sound of something being knocked over. Mark stood up, let go a sigh, and stabbed his finger toward the wall that separated them from Amy's room.

"Isn't it about time *she* went home?"

Mom shook her head. "She can't, Mark. Her folks won't be back for another hour or so. I'm trying to keep them quiet, but as you can see—and hear—they're in a rowdy state, and I've finally given up, so now I just hope they'll run out of energy soon. Look, I have to finish the other bathroom floor. Will you please take Sheka for a walk? I tried to get them to," she said, nodding in the general direction of the rumpus. "But they want to stay inside." She left the room, and Mark set the rocket on its holder, up on the second shelf. He gazed at it for a moment longer and said, "I'll be right back. And I will think of a wonderful name for you."

He put his hands over his ears as he started down the hall, and made it as far as his sister's room. Her door was flung open, and a red-faced towhead jumped out in front of him. Emily lived next door, and was Randy's sister. She jumped up and down in front of him, grinning. "Mark, Mark, Mark!" she cried. Amy came out into the hall as well, and the two girls began to sing a song full of words Mark didn't understand. He took his hands from his head and reached out for Emily's throat. The girls shrieked in delight and ran back into Amy's room.

"Think I was kidding, do you?" he growled as he continued toward the furnace room. He put on his heavy coat, his rubber boots, and his green balaclava. Then he rattled the chain leash, and within seconds, Sheka had joined him. She danced on the utility room floor, moaning in anticipation, and Mark smiled at her.

"I knew that would wake you up," he said to her. "In fact, let's just go without the leash today". He opened the back door, and she bounded out into the crusty snow, Mark following at a more gingerly pace, as the porch was slippery with frozen rain.

It was cool and windy outside, and the ground was hard, underneath the thin layer of white. The marshy pond behind the yard was covered with only an inch or so of the dark ice, and what remained of last year's sedge lay back in small brown bundles, as if afraid of the frozen water. Mark galloped through the amber-toned rushes that appeared lifeless along the edge of the pool, and Sheka loped beside him, her mouth open and her tongue hanging out. They reached the next road, across the vacant lots, and as they started past the oldest section of the neighborhood, Mark looked at the gray sky and thought once more about his rocket.

He decided that when a name was finally chosen, there would have to be a formal christening before the maiden flight. This rocket was so special! He caught up with Sheka, grabbed her by the neck, and put his face on the top of her head, warming first his right cheek, then his left.

"What do you think?" he asked the black malemute. "This is my first original design. It should have a grand name, one that fits me, and nobody else. A grand name, dog-a-roo!"

She made a low sound in her throat and pawed the ground. Mark looked at her, and then at the sky once more. "Really? Maybe you're right. Yes, I think this is the one that gets to carry that proud name."

Straightening up, he called for the dog to mush on, and together they raced down the street, turned north, and ran the length of a much narrower lane, up to the corner of the schoolyard. And then Mark slowed down, and the steam signals rose as he walked along, Sheka padding beside him.

Indoors, he gave her a quick rubdown, pulled off his outdoor wear, and headed back toward his room to prepare the dark blue enamel with which he would paint the holy word *Capella* on the gleaming white fuse-lage of his model. Halfway down the hall, he stopped and let out a soft moan. The girls' voices were not coming from Amy's room. They were coming from his.

Mark braced himself, then moved down the hallway, turned, and entered a most undesirable parallel universe.

Amy was shouting, "The rocket, the rocket!" She had reached up as high as she could, almost touching the beautiful model. Emily was jump-ing up and down on Mark's bed, yelling "Get it, get it!" Mark clenched his fists, relaxed them, and clenched them again. "You stay away from that!!" he snarled.

Amy drew back her hand, turned around, and said, "Uh, oh." She leapt over to the foot of Stephen's bed and curled up on the floor, as if expecting death to swoop down and grab her. Emily stopped jumping for a moment, then started again, grinning at Mark in a devilish way. She made a pooping sound with her tongue, tilted her head from side to side, and said, "You can't scare us. Hah, ha-hah, ha-hah, hah," she sang.

"All right," Mark said. He wheeled about, strode back up the hall, and went to the kitchen. He climbed up onto the sink counter, opened the window, then reached up, broke off a ten-inch icicle, and brought it inside. After closing the window, he jumped back to the floor, thought for a moment, then transferred the icicle to his right hand. Putting it behind his back, he marched to the bedroom. Amy was sitting on the floor, her eyes wide, and Emily was still using his bed as a trampoline.

"What's going on?" Amy asked him. Emily saw Mark's face, stopped jumping, and let her legs fly out in front of her. She dropped to the bed, landed, and after a few small bounces, settled to rest. "What are you hiding there?" she asked, pointing her finger at his midsection. "What's that in your hand?"

"A steak knife," Mark answered. "And I've been wanting to do this for a long time." He advanced on her, and behind him, Amy let go a high-frequency, vibratory moan. Emily shrank back from him, but he grabbed her and flipped the girl onto her stomach. She kicked her legs and yelled for him to stop, but he ignored her and pulled up her blouse with his left hand. Then he brought down the icicle until it made contact with the base of her neck, and drew the "knife" along the length of her spine.

Emily screamed. Mark stood up, backed away, and said, "Oh, god of gods, look at all the blood, and your backbone is sticking out. Better get to the doctor quick and have that stitched up."

He turned and saw that Amy's mouth was large enough to hold a tennis ball. Emily screamed again, and Mark started out of the room. Mom came running in, blocking his path. "What in the world—?"

"It's nothing," Mark said, brushing past her. "Nothing at all." He walked up the hall, and as he passed the open bathroom, he softball-pitched the icicle inside, heard it shatter against the ceramic tiles, and drop into the tub. He continued to the living room, satisfied that his new rocket was safe from grabby little hands.

That evening, Mom and Dad sat him for a long talk. He didn't listen very closely, as he knew that, deep down, they weren't all that troubled by the incident. Mom had related the story to Dad, and Dad had tried hard not to laugh. And the Mitchells had come by to get their daughter, whose face at that point was still just a bit purple. They'd hauled her away, and then Mom had started murmuring something about psychotherapy.

His parents continued with the obligatory lecture, complete with a point about "never doing that again", and Mark sighed and told them it was highly unlikely that he would ever have to "do that again".

Stephen thought it was hilarious, and he started to call Randy to ask how things were going over there, but Dad stopped him. And that night, Mark went to bed extremely thankful for two things. The forecast for tomorrow was good. And his mattress was still firm.

Next morning, he stepped into the backyard, looked at the sky, and clapped his hands. The clouds were thinning away, and the air was still. It was perfect launch conditions, and his heart sped up as he visualized *Capella* streaking into that deep blue space. T-minus seven hours, twenty-six minutes ....

A door opened, off to his right. He turned in that direction and saw a small blond head appear on the Mitchell's back porch. It was followed by a small body, with hands that waved at him. The head broke into a wide smile.

"Hi, Mark!"

§

He entered the launch time and other important data into his log book, just as he had done before shooting off his earlier models. Someday, he told himself, his book might be read by others who would wonder just exactly what all this was about. He wanted it to look very mysterious.

Dad was at work on this Saturday afternoon, and Mom was out shopping. Stephen had gone with her, and Amy was next door; she and Emily were probably talking in high, chattering fashion about the previous day's "attack". He closed the log book, picked up his launch equipment, and gently lifted the small box that contained his model. He looked at his watch, then moved down the hall and out to the living room, stopping in the foyer to get a coat from the closet. Then he was out the front door with his two packages. Sheka met him in the yard, and together they walked through the gate, past the driveway, and across the street to the playground. *I am alone with my dog, and my Capella,* he thought. He wanted it no other way.

As he had done many times before, he went through the exacting procedure of setting up the firing assembly. From the carry-box he lifted his pride and joy, its white fuselage and dark blue trim almost glowing in the sunlight of late winter. He threaded the launch rod through the rocket's side tube and rested the model upon the blast plate. Then he prepared the igniter.

Everything was ready, and he just sat on the hardpack snow for a moment, looking at the rocket on its pad. The ogive nose pointed at the clear blue sky, and Mark sensed the potential energy stored in the model, waiting for ignition to bring it to life.

Something was not right. He frowned and then realized that the payload section was empty. What to put into it? He scratched his head and decided that, since the rocket was an extension of himself, then perhaps a part of him should travel with it.

He took off his balaclava, yanked a hair from the back of his head, and bent over close to the rocket. Taking off the cone, he flicked in the dark brown strand and watched as it curled up in the bottom of the compartment. He looked at Sheka and motioned her to him. "Want to go with me?" he asked. She let out a low growl, and soon there were two hairs in the clear plastic payload. "Not exactly Laika," he informed the dog. "But then again," he added, "perhaps that's a good thing."

He put in the arming key. There were only thirty seconds remaining until launch time. He had done this so many times before, but there was something distinctly new and fresh about this particular event. His knees shook a little as he counted down to zero, and when at last he pressed the firing button, his eyes were getting watery.

You are mine! You are me! Go, go, to the heavens!

There was a brief, almost agonizing pause while the igniter burned. Then the engine powder reacted, and with a clean *whoosh* that was so quick that Mark scarcely believed it was happening at all, the high-altitude probe *Capella* was streaking upward. Mark grabbed his spotting scope, peered through it with his left eye, and swore to himself for not bringing the binoculars instead. The first stage was quickly spent, and with a second, more distant and muffled sound, the upper stage took off and shot even higher, until Mark could barely see it through the optical instrument. He waited breathlessly, blinking his eyes to clear them. Something was very wrong.

Now it should have been curving over and starting on its downward path, the ejection charge taking over the spotlight and blowing the parachute clear.

It climbed higher. The first stage hit the ground.

Mark strained, blinked, then strained again, and his heart was beating *presto*. He looked and looked, searching for any sign.

He couldn't see it. He clenched his teeth, swallowed, and looked again.

But it was gone forever, in the sky above. A circling raven let out a muted *groak*, and that was all there was. He lowered the spotting scope and looked up with his naked eyes, a useless effort.

It was gone forever.

CHAPTER TWELVE

It was noon, the sun having pushed above the horizon hours before, but the sky was a faded gray, and all was in shadow. The mountains kept the filtered golden rays from spilling into the Valley, and the senses of hearing and smell were of much greater importance. If one listened, one could actually hear the sound of a lone drop of cold water growing in size. After having condensed on a large, yellowing devil's club leaf, one could hear it land with a *ploink* onto the surface of a micro puddle. One could smell the loam, as the stalks in the meadow became slimy and lay down upon the muddy earth.

The boulder too was cold, as it reached into the air above the pond. The alder leaves had parted company with the branches and now dotted the tiny lake, traveling with unseen currents and forming a brown ring along its edges.

Above and to the north was the glacier, the icefield, and the great snow-covered peaks. The most wonderful of all, which soared into the chill of inner space, was capped by the barest layer of white dust, and the others seemed to look upon this as a signal to be ready, when the blanket would lower and cover them as well, sending them to their winter sleep.

Who in the world would think like this? Who looked at Nature in this fashion?

It was what Mark asked himself today, like all other days, and as he sat on the rotted stump, with the town below, he smiled faintly. Down there was human activity, and he had passed through it, moved onward and upward, along the worn path to the top of the wooded cleaver. From here, he could look back and see his two worlds.

After school the day before, he had asked Jeff to accompany him on a hike, and when Jeff announced other plans, he had asked Allen. To which Allen declared that he was canned for the next two weeks, declining, however, to mention just what sort of trouble he was in. And Randy was going to be late-season fishing, Mark knew. So he'd decided to go alone.

Now he was glad he'd made that decision. Up here, he could dream and not be noticed; he could dream out loud if necessary. He stood up, anxious to continue before his legs became stiff, and started up the next series of zigzags. The trail entered the woods again, after which it curved across a large, tilted bowl, where tiny streams ran down the slope and joined together before taking the half-mile plunge to the bottom. Past the bowl, the trail bore almost straight up the narrowing crown of the convex mountain and withered away completely near the top. But up there, no trail was needed.

Within minutes he was sweating, as the trail steepened and twisted near the bowl. He tore off his flannel shirt and stuffed it into the upper compartment of his daypack, and then continued the climb. His hair, which was longer than it had ever been, was damp but attracted no insects; the mosquito season was long over. Indeed, the soaking muskegs were full with next year's eggs, at this late date.

He reached the top of the wooded section and entered the bowl, which was full of yellow grass and heather. Traversing it, he began to get a good view down the channel, in the direction of Grand Island. A blue dot in the water caught his attention, and as he squinted, he realized that it wasn't a small craft, but was only very far away. It was one of the ferries coming into port.

He stood there and remembered a time, over eight years in the past, when he was in the forward lounge of the *Taku* and looking up the channel at his new home, and the big convex peak directly behind it. His six-year-old self had felt a shudder pass through him. Now he felt another, as the strange idea came to him again. He held up his arms and waved at the vessel, which streamed ever closer, the white wakes angling behind and into the distance, their flow interrupted by the jagged shoreline. He knew that no one on board could possibly see him. But perhaps, he thought, they might *perceive* ....

It was possible, he thought, to look at himself backward through that mysterious keyhole, to see himself as a much younger child, so long as the eyes that saw were not the eyes in his head. He and his six-year-old self were viewing each other at this very moment. This he knew, but he didn't know how, nor could he yet comprehend the significance.

He hiked on, and as he went, the town below him continued to shrink in size. Finally the summit came into full view, still a thousand feet above, but looking so close he felt he could reach out and touch it. The sun penetrated the weak cloud cover, the rays peeped over the sagging ridge of the neighboring peak, and instantly he was hotter than before.

Now the boulder is warming up, and the Valley is coming to life, but it won't be the full intensity of a summer's afternoon. The star which gives our planet fuel is dropping lower by the day, and even now, the boulder, the pond, and my mountain are straining for every ray they can get. This is the approach of winter, and soon a new kind of life will make its presence felt, and the warmth of yesterday will be forgotten. And then will come the spring, and there will be sighs ... the sun will rise higher each day, and the full intensity of the winter past will be but a dream.

It certainly was not summer, not with the pretense of dead and dying all around him. It was in fact the first week of October, and it was over a year now since he had talked with that counselor at school.

The clouds! I am rising up to meet them, and they await me. I am sorry for all those below—you are no longer discernible—you cannot imagine the feeling. As the earth tilts upward and rolls into space, so my head expands, and it is filled with Nature's wisdom.

The uphill grade of the mountain decreased, and as the clouds, sheetlike in appearance, floated just overhead, the sun climbed above them and was gone, just minutes after it had saluted him. He began to slip on the damp heather. Once he fell headlong, and as he felt the moisture on his face, and the tickle of bristled stems, he giggled.

And the summit! It rushed to meet him, and he hiked up to the very highest point, an outcropping of granite surrounded by the dense covering of moist flora. Mark sat down upon the rock and let his hand reach out to touch the uppermost little nub. He felt some loose grains of sand and brought them before his eyes. "You are the very top," he said quietly, as he studied the black specks. "Do you realize the fact?" And when they did not answer, he put them back on their perch. They hadn't answered because there was no need. However, he knew they'd heard him.

Swinging around, he took in the fabulous view. He could see across the channel, over the top of Douglas Island, and further, past Eagle Peak. To the right and westward, the silvery stretch of Lynn Canal was visible, and beyond that mighty fjord, the mountains rose and rose in the distance, culminating in the Fairweather Range. The low clouds obscured that mass of snowy behemoths, but the boy felt their presence just the same. He turned around further, his eyes taking in the savage meeting of ice and rock, where forested ridge met bleak nunatak, where organic life halted with a suddenness that made him flinch. The icefield poured down upon him. Staring at it, he nearly rose off into space, so magical was its appearance. In the distance, beyond the first row of summits, he could see Nugget Peak, Split Thumb, and the ice ramp that plunged downhill to become Lemon Glacier. And he could see part of *the* mountain; not its upper slopes, which penetrated the cloud cover, but the flaring east ridge.

It was unclimbable. He had decided it was true, long ago on that day after Fran was killed and his best friend had announced his family's removal from this place. Or was it that long ago? It seemed so, though it had been less than three years, or perhaps, his mind suggested, only this morning, yesterday, or the day before. He glanced to the south, across the peaks, and down the wide body of water that led to Petersburg. He glanced to the northwest where, more than six hundred miles away, Jerry now lived. He was gone, but *the* mountain remained. And it was unclimbable.

He directed his eyes from the view and groped about his daypack for something to eat. As he felt around for the sausage, somewhere down below his spare clothing, he heard the arrival horn of the ferry, and looking down, he saw the ship swing around in front of the town and head for the terminal, which was out of sight, blocked by the lower slopes.

Now that he was stationary, the air was beginning to have a chilling effect on him. He ate quickly, and when he was finished, he put on his rain shell and covered his head. The clouds were lower than ever, and as he looked up at the tallest peaks, he saw that they were being dusted with snow. Quite soon, their rockiness would be hidden below an ever-thickening white blanket.

He walked about the summit, exploring. Mount Juneau was not especially tall, but it was steep and rounded, and it provided an excellent roaming ground. As he dropped below a ledge and started out to the western slopes, he was delighted to see that he was not the only one canvassing the peak. A large black bear was strolling along the ridgeline, coming in his direction. Mark watched for a moment, fascinated by the sight of the wild creature. It was a male, he could tell, and it was probably looking for some last tidbits to add to its fat content. Soon it would enter its den and sleep the months away, awakened in April by the chatter of sparrows and the odor of new, green shoots. Sound and smell were of greater importance here.

Mark shouted a greeting and waved to the bear, which stopped short, peered at him momentarily with its small eyes, and took a whiff. And then with a grunt, it turned quickly and loped off in the direction from which it had come. The boy grinned, the veins pumping in his neck. And he had a remembrance of Doug, running pell-mell through the meadow, screaming bloody murder. He started to laugh through his nostrils and then stopped, as he remembered something else—the little cub. He decided not to bother with the large male anymore, and abruptly changed his course to explore the northern edge of the summit.

The breeze picked up, and shortly thereafter the sprinkling rain began. Mark hardly noticed; he was caught up in the beauty of the rolling meadows, dull as they were at this time of year, the middle of autumn. He wandered about the heights through the early afternoon, encountering a small group of ptarmigan that flapped away from him, startled and confused. If he'd had a mind to, he could easily have stoned them with the rocks that lay on the ground. That was now unacceptable. He wanted to leave them be, and he was content to simply kick his way through the flocks that crossed his path, much like herds of miniature sheep.

At last he was running out of new territory, and so once again he approached the summit. And as he drew near, he began to pretend. He pretended that it was the summit of *the* mountain, and he was staggered by the weight of a heavy pack and bent nearly double by a fierce wind that drove the stinging powder into his red face. The virgin peak was drawing ever closer, and he put his arms out, begging for it … and then he stumbled on a piece of shale, and as he rebalanced himself, the dream was gone.

He sat on the granite. It would never happen, such an event. Never. There was supposed to be two of them climbing toward that moment of triumph, but that was impossible now. It was unclimbable.

And he shivered, feeling more than a bit alone. He looked about at the many peaks, then grabbed his pack and slung it over his shoulder. He was hungry; the sausage hadn't been enough. He began the descent, stopping at a small, clear pool for a drink and to don his poncho, and then hiking rather quickly down to the treeline. The clouds followed him, and soon he was in the fog, with tiny raindrops coming from all directions. The sounds of the town became muffled, and he picked up his pace until he was fairly running along the path, jumping across the gullies, dodging between the spruce and hemlock, and twisting down closer to sea level. His stomach growled yet again, and he tried to ignore it as he cut through the zigzags and jumped over the rotten stump upon which he had sat on the way up. He never stopped to rest as he made his way on down to the bottom.

He reached the larger trail that ran through the narrow valley, and he followed it to the end of the dirt road. And from there he walked all the way to the edge of town. He rounded a bend in the road, and there were the first houses … and like a smack in the face, all that was before, was gone.

There were cars, and paved sidewalks, and parents calling their children in from the rain.

Behind him, the mountains had disappeared, lost in the clouds.

He walked through the narrow, hilly streets, coming at last to the business district. He knew that he must look silly, tramping through town in a bicycle poncho, daypack, and muddy hiking boots. He came to Dad's office building, opened the door to the foyer, and went inside.

There he waited for a moment, until most of the water had dripped from him, and then took off his rain shell and stuffed it into his pack. He took the elevator to the second floor, though the stairwell was less than ten feet away.

He walked through the narrow corridor until he reached the last room on the left. Upon entering, he saw Dad looking out the window with his binoculars. Silently, he walked over and sat in a swivel chair, which was pulled up next to the large drafting table.

Dad turned around. "Hey, you're getting quieter every time." He put the binoculars on the sill and then waved at the schematic diagram he'd drawn earlier.

"Awful boring after a while, if you know what I mean. Ray said there was a cute young thing working down there on the first floor of the phone company, but I haven't spotted her yet. So as long as you don't tell Mom, I'll let you have a look yourself, right?" He snickered, knowing that Mark was aware it was all a joke.

Mark shook his head. "I don't mean to take away your seat, and I'm sorry if I dirtied the place up. But I'm sure you don't mind, and there's no one around to see it except you. When are you planning on leaving, anyway?"

Dad shrugged. "Never should have come in to begin with. This is my third Saturday in a row, and all combined, I've done just about an hour's work. Ha! Shows you just how much I need the others here, so they can come by my desk on Monday and say 'hmm … that's not quite what we have in mind, try it this way', and get me started in another direction." He looked at Mark. "It's pretty nice to know that I'm the only one around this place who can draw a straight line without a ruler."

Mark could have used the same argument.

"All right, enough ballyhooing," Dad continued. "Sorry. Well, Mom brought Amy to town on the bus earlier, and they're out there spending our money. I was going to meet them downstairs in about"—he looked at his watch—"half an hour. You can wait here if you want."

"No. I think I'll just walk around some." Mark saluted and left the room, saying that he'd meet everyone in the foyer.

He sensed that Dad wanted to talk to him about something, but he kept his pace to the elevator. When he stepped out into the rain, he drew back momentarily, as the cool air whipped against his collar. And then he started down the city street, once again pulling on his rain shell.

Waiting around in Dad's office wouldn't have been so exciting, he told himself as he approached the channel. Just a little while ago, I was at the top of that mountain, and I was feeling great. And then I shivered; I felt alone. But once I was returned to the city, I became impatient to be off again, on my own.

So I am strange. There is no other way.

And he wondered, is that what Dad wanted to talk to him about? Couldn't be, now could it? No one had the tiniest inkling of the inner workings of his mind, he was sure of that. Or was it his face? Did his face give away the idea that he was wrapped up in two worlds, the conditions themselves hidden, yet the central fact obvious?

As he mulled this over, he rounded a corner and almost ran down his little sister. Mom was right beside her, and the meeting startled all three of them. For a moment, everyone just stared at each other, the drizzle falling from the sky.

"Good grief, Mark! What a way to tell us you're back from your hike." Mom had dropped her shopping bag on the wet sidewalk.

"Yes, I came down pretty fast."

Amy said, from deep within the hood of her rain parka, "Mom was worried that you might get lost in the clouds. She was talking to Dad about it on the phone."

"I wasn't worried," Mom said. "I only thought it might get so messy that you'd call it off, and then you'd be stuck in town."

"Nuh, uh!" The girl raised her voice. "She said—"

"Hush." Mom patted her head and grabbed the shopping bag. And they all walked together, back to Dad's office. Mark, his stomach growling once more, was becoming more and more sure of what Dad wanted to talk about, as he trailed behind the others.

§

That winter, he became less involved in school activities than ever before. He was at home much of the time, burning excess energy by shoveling snow from the driveway.

He invited Jeff over on the rarest of occasions. One day, he found himself shrugging off the fact that he hadn't called Tina in over a month.

§

Once more the snows came during the night, and when Mark arrived home from school, he knew that his first job would be to shovel the drive and the pathways. As he hopped up to the front porch, he saw last night's paper, wrapped in a clear plastic sack, laying against the foundation. No one had bothered to pick it up. He grabbed it and went inside, where Sheka waited eagerly. He tapped her head with the paper and wandered through the kitchen to the furnace room. Mom saw him and began to say something about the track of snow he was leaving behind. He showed her the paper as he went by, and she stopped and nodded her approval.

The driveway could wait a few minutes, he decided, and after slipping out of his outdoor things, he sat in the living room and spread the newspaper before him. He read a few of the headlines, then the sports pages, and barely glanced at the comics, as they looked rather uninteresting. He scanned the classifieds, wondering to himself why he was doing so. Lastly, he turned to the weather information.

He looked at the map and noted the position and movement of the frontal system. Then he busied himself with yesterday's temperature readings. To him, this was far more entertaining than stories about killings, robberies, road improvements, or bills passed in the state congress. Far more interesting than a major trade in the NBA, what Linus was upset about, or who had what for sale.

It was cold in Fairbanks—twenty-eight below zero. Ketchikan, however, had reported a relatively mild thirty-six. He looked over the list for a very long time; saw that Northway had just experienced a positively absurd twenty-four-hour temperature drop of more than forty degrees.

He folded the paper and sat in the chair for a moment longer. Then he shook his head and went to put on his heavy clothing again.

§

Stephen's radio was on full force, and Mark especially disliked the song that was now playing. "Turn it off, will you? That man's voice makes me want to puke!"

Stephen reached over and lowered the volume. "I heard what happened over at your school," he said. "Too funny, huh? Sherry, was it?" Mark nodded, and his brother turned back to his homework. Mark was supposed to be doing his as well, but the math text, along with the sheets of paper and the sharpened pencil, lay forgotten on the desk. He was curled up on the bed, reading a novel.

It was the story of a sailor and his adventures.

He'd read it before, and when he came to a rather detailed section that he found slightly boring, he let his mind wander between the lines. He began to think about what had happened earlier today, and even the nauseating radio tune faded from his mind.

In chemistry class, he and Richard had been partners for a complicated lab experiment. Everything had gone well at the start, but when it came time to dilute the hydrochloric acid, Richard had made a serious error. Having forgotten which of the two beakers contained the acid, he embarked on a short journey to failure. He began adding distilled water to the acid.

Mark, having gone to the far end of the laboratory to obtain a 100mL graduated cylinder, turned around just in time to see the beaker shooting mist into the air. He opened his mouth, but before he could say a word, the beaker cracked down the middle.

The worktable resembled a bubbling, steaming geyser. Sherry, whose intelligence level was approximately that of a sump pump, looked over, delivered a scream for the ages, then proceeded to demonstrate to the entire galaxy just how stupid she was by running over and pulling the fire alarm. Within moments, the school's entire human population, with the exception of Mark and Richard, was out of the building and crowding the parking lot.

Richard got a fire extinguisher, and ignoring Mark's shouted warning on how utterly pointless this was, emptied the dry powder onto the solution, and soon the mist had settled. Richard, apparently proud of himself, turned around, his face beaming, and accidentally pressed the lever once again, shooting powder right onto Mark's flannel shirt. Mark stumbled backward against the lab case, and it shuddered violently, upsetting beakers, test tubes, and containers of various reagents, some of which fell off their shelf and smashed onto the floor, emptying their contents as the glass shards took off in every direction.

There were really no adjectives to describe the next few minutes. The vice principal and the science teacher came back inside, entered the lab, waved their arms, and demanded answers. The alarm buzzers quieted, sputtered a few times, then died at last. Custodians rushed about. The fire trucks arrived, and the fire trucks left. The worktable was a mess, the top counter pretty much ruined. The two boys were told to go and wait in that dreaded little room with the pebbled, no-see-through glass window in the center of the door.

After a long talk with the principal inside that compact horror chamber, Mark was informed he could return to school the next day, but Richard would have to wait, pending an agreement between the school and the boy's parents, all because he didn't cooperate very well during the interrogation. Excellent, Mark thought. Teach him to think next time, before doing something so idiotic. As for Sherry ....

From outside the door, Mom called his name and asked if he had finished his homework. He replied yes, to which she replied in turn by asking if he would come and help Amy with hers, and to hurry up because it was getting late.

He sighed, then started to ask, through the closed doorway, why it was always him, never Stephen. But the words didn't form. It was no use; Mom had already walked away. He pounded his fist on the pillow, tossed the book aside, and after another deep breath, he got up and stumbled out into the hall. He tapped on his sister's door, pushed it open, and entered the mysterious domain of preteen femaleness.

"What's the problem, dummy?"

Amy looked up from her little desk. "Oh, stop it! Mom says you have to help me with my arimmethic ... arith ... arithmetic."

"Well," he said, "I've got only a few hours to spare." When he saw that she didn't catch his remark, he swallowed hard and pulled up the matching stool, then looked at the assignment with her.

Amy showed him the paper on which she had been working. "See, I don't know how to divide a number this big. We did ones that were smaller, in class today, and then she said we had to do these for tomorrow."

He nodded and picked up a pencil. "You do them just the same way. Watch this," he told her, and then he drew in the problem. "First, how many times does four go into one?"

She screwed up her face. "Four doesn't go into one!"

"Right. So you go on to the next number, just like you would for any two-digit dividend."

"A what?"

He went on. "So, how many times does four go into thirteen?"

After a few seconds of heightened brain activity, Amy replied that it went "about" three times. He waited until she had figured out the remainder, then showed her how to drop the last number, which in this case was seven. "And how many times does four go into seventeen?"

This time her answer was almost immediate. "Four times!" He waited until she wrote it in and subtracted. "And so the answer is thirty-four times, with a remainder of one. Right?"

"Exactly," he told her. "See how simple these things are, once you've done one of them?"

"Well, I couldn't have done it without you helping me," the girl answered, almost reverently. "Will you watch me while I do the next one?"

"Okay." He stayed at the desk while she struggled with the next problem, which was indeed much harder than the first. But after a few moments, she got the idea once again, and solved the problem without much trouble.

And the third problem looked easy. So easy, in fact, that Mark had it figured out in just a few seconds. He waited with anticipation while his sister began to divide, and then he frowned when she stopped her pencil and turned to him.

"I can't do it. I don't know how many times five goes into fifteen!"

He couldn't believe his ears. "What! Five into fifteen—you must be crazy!" he yelled at her. "How old did you say you were, nine? You must have meant nine months, not nine years. Sometimes I really wonder about you, I really do."

He jumped up and headed out of the room. Amy began to cry, and as Mark started up the hallway, he shouted back, "Get your teacher to help you. That's what she's there for." Walking to the living room, he said in a loud voice, "Dumb fool!"

From his easy chair, Dad said angrily, "Mark. Get over here."

He went clammy, but shuffled over past the blazing fire, to where Dad was reading. Mark looked at him, and Dad took off his glasses. "Keep your voice down, will you? Your mom's had a long day, and she just went to bed."

Mark shrugged. "The kid has a pea brain."

"That's no way to talk about your little sister, and you know it. I remember when *you* were nine years old. Do you? We'd be in the den, spending hours looking through your homework with you."

Of course I remember when I am nine years old. I discover the pond, and we get into a discussion right here in this room, and that symphony is playing, the one you love the hell out of. Admit it—you wouldn't expect Amy to talk and feel the way I do when I am nine, would you?

I am way ahead at nine years old, and I am way ahead now.

The silent words frightened him as they flashed through his mind, but he only blinked and said, in a small voice, "I'm not her teacher, and I haven't the patience of one."

He sat on the sofa and looked out the front window, into the black night. Dad read his book for a minute, or as Mark thought, pretended to, then he flopped it shut, set it on the lamp table, removed his glasses once more, and looked over at him. "Listen good. I want to ask you something, and I want you to answer me. And don't be afraid to answer with the truth, you hear?

"Do you think you're just as smart, just as intelligent as anyone, or do you think you're less so? Or do you think you have gifted powers of intellect, which you're reluctant to use? Do you think your mind is unique?"

Mark lowered his gaze and stared at his hands. Why was Dad asking him such a question? At the same time, he sort of expected it. That day when he was in the office, last October, after his mountain hike. He had suspected—was almost sure—that Dad had wanted to spend a few moments on the subject, though he had apparently decided to put off the inevitable until now.

But he's just a little off the track, he thought to himself. *Close, but off the track. He will never understand, no matter what I tell him.*

He looked up at his father. "No, I don't think I'm as smart, less smart, or more so. But I do think I use my mind in a different way than others my age. Some problem with that?"

"Maybe so." Dad adjusted his position in the chair so as to be ready, it seemed, to jump up in anger, arms waving, should he feel it necessary.

"When you boys were little, and Amy was still in her cradle, your Mom used to ask me what I thought you would be like, growing up in this area, and what would become of you when you matured." He cocked his head to one side. "I suppose it's a perfectly normal thing for a mother to worry about, hey? Still, if I was to give my honest opinion, I would have to say that if anything, you might grow up more sophisticated, but less in tune, than she did.

"And she would say 'Charles, what exactly do you mean by that?' Do you know, Mark?"

The boy narrowed his eyes, and his heart sped up, but he tried to look calm. "Sure. You think that kids up here have a better sense of who they are, but at the expense of losing out on experiences that kids have down south, where everything is connected by highway, and a pro baseball team is only miles away."

Now that must have come out "eloquently". Surprise, old man ….

Dad shook his head, and Mark could see that he'd almost laughed. "Not the way I would have put it. Almost, but not quite. But in fact, I think that a certain individual, in a certain place at a certain time, could be affected in a powerful way."

He didn't mention what sort of way. Mark had to ask, "And exactly *what is it* that would affect this individual?"

"Well. When you grow up in a small town in the 'middle of nowhere', as city dwellers would call it, there's more of a closeness between the people. Sometimes that's good, and sometimes it's not. Unconsciously, indeed subconsciously, the dealings between people can have effects that are later blamed wrongly." Dad paused, then leaned toward Mark. "It's not everyone losing a friend in a crevasse, on a glacier that stares them in the face every day, through the front window."

Helplessly, Mark's eyes traveled up to gaze through the pane of glass, and he let the words sink in. Dad was trying to tell him that the people he had known through the years, in this small community, were having some sort of unusual effect on his now maturing behavior. But was he saying that the mountains, the boulder, the pond, the stars, and his love for them, indeed his own private world, was holding him back? That what he really suffered from—if suffer was even the right word—was a lack of diversified social involvement? That he was using Nature to fill the holes?

Never! It could not be true. Dad himself could not know of these things; they were the boy's secret. He had a fleeting remembrance, when the counselor had mentioned that same "disease". And she had told him the "answer", and he had left that little office with the decision to balance his worlds, and that would be enough to carry him through, forever. But that was not to happen, and deep down, he'd always known that. He'd poured that decision into a reservoir, a reservoir with a large hole in the bottom.

No, not now, he told himself, sensing the sweat on his hands and on his forehead. They were wrong, the people at school, the friends who thought him strange, even Dad, who now sat and lectured him; tried to convince him that what he needed was a stronger social base upon which to stand. Was that not his point?

If only you knew. If only you knew how much I know. I wish I had let that snow carry me right off the edge ....

And he was frightened again, as the memory of that thought passed through him like an electric shock. Blue mitten. Mountain meadow. Deer tracks. The past did not happen long ago. It was happening right now. He blinked back tears, and then he got up off the couch. He started for the hall, and then Dad called to him.

"Have you finished your homework?"

"Yes."

"No, you haven't. I can tell when you're fibbing."

The wood smoke grew strong in Mark's nostrils. He turned around and said, in a whisper, "I did all that I could. I'll have to ask the teacher about the rest of it."

Dad pointed at him. "Like you told your sister, a while back? Yes, I heard what you said. Go get your homework, and bring it here. Move!"

That rasping voice. Mark felt his hairs rise, and at the same time he wondered whether to look Dad in the face and tell him to keep his voice down, that Mom was tired and had gone to bed early. He decided against it and went to his room.

Stephen appeared to have fallen asleep, but the light was on. Mark grabbed his supplies and left without turning it off.

From down the hall: "Mark, turn off the light, so your brother can sleep."

Mountain in heaven, what is happening?

He flicked off the switch and started back up the hall, wishing that the corridor would go on forever, that he would never get to the end. But the green whatnot that supported the beautiful oil lamp drew closer and closer, and when he reached it, Mark felt completely subdued. He glided into the living room, moving as though driven by a weak electric motor. As he approached the sofa, Dad stopped him.

"Don't sit down." Mark watched him go to the window and pull the shades. Then he waited as Dad traversed the room, turning off every lamp. Now only the firelight was interacting with the boy's retinas, and Mark thought its glow was wicked as it struck his face, and Dad's.

"Now," the man said. "Go over there, to the fireplace, and put your book, and your paper and pencil, upon the stones."

Mark did so. The warmth of the fire reached out and touched him, and through his teeth he hated it; not the fire itself, he was sure, but the fact that someone was *making* him sit in the face of Nature.

Dad eased back into his chair and crossed his legs. "You have plenty of light. I'm going to sit here and watch you do your homework. When I was your age, that's how I did my homework. Feel lucky you have a pencil, by the way. Abe Lincoln wrote on a piece of wood, using a charred stick. Begin working!"

Mark looked at his hands, and they shook. He opened his math book to the assigned page and labeled his paper. And then he began to work the problems.

The fire hissed at him, spitting orange sparks through the grate and into his lap. He tried to concentrate, tried to finish before he had a chance to ask himself why Dad was making him do this?

He wrote the entire problems, and showed all of his work. The poly-

nomials looked the worst he had ever seen, and the task seemed insur-
mountable. The X and Y symbols went flying past him, across, around
and through his brain, and he struggled, the fire becoming hot at his side.

Now he was nearing the end. He looked at the pendulum clock, and
his eyes widened. He had been working for nearly an hour, an hour that
had taken only minutes, or seconds. The fire was livid as ever, as Dad was
burning hemlock. It sputtered, and the uneven light danced across his
paper, but he held back the tears, and the love he had for the fire again
turned to the hate that he'd felt at the beginning. He solved the last equa-
tion by use of the quadratic formula, paused a moment, and put down the
pencil.

"Are you through?" Dad leaned forward once more.

"Yes." Mark's voice, though soft, was strong and sure.

"Good. Why don't you go on to bed, then. And do something for me.
When you pass by your sister's room, stop and think about it for a minute.
You know what I mean."

Mark looked at him, through the eerie light, and then rose to his
feet. Picking up his algebra book, he turned slowly and left the room. He
wanted to cry, but something told him not to. As he started down the hall,
his lips moved. He offered a near-silent condolence to the fire, saying how
pitiful it was that the beautiful flames had been forced to take part in such
a terrible event.

Amy's room was there. He stopped, looked at the wooden door, the
stained, varnished finish, the brass knob. He had a vision. The door evap-
orated, and what he saw was his sister, at the little desk and struggling
with her homework, with her brother at her side.

He shut his eyes and clutched the book to his chest. He was now
seeing something else. He was watching himself as he helped his sister, as
he gave her light.

And Mark realized that the analogy was his own; he had made it up
completely. It wasn't even what Dad was trying to tell him. Angrily, he
turned from the door and continued down the hall, knowing that Dad
was still in his chair, and that right now he would be smiling, sensing that
Mark had understood the point he was trying to make. Yes, he would be
thinking that Mark felt foolish. And enlightened.

He reached his own room, but paused before entering. Then he heard
a violent pop, as the distant flames bit into a resin cavity. Mark breathed
heavily, in and out, as he put his hand on the doorknob. This entire mess,

it wasn't anyone's fault. This wasn't about fault. It was about complete misunderstanding. A misunderstanding that no human had ever solved, even though many thought they had.

And the words came again, this time from the very center of the mind.

I am not sorry. I will never be.

CHAPTER THIRTEEN

Down the slopes of Thunder Mountain came the bears. They feasted on blueberries and spawning salmon, fortifying themselves with proteins, carbohydrates, and minerals in preparation for their winter slumber. In the tops of trees perched the eagles, their black and white forms massive and quite still. Although they did not often partake in the consumption of rotting carrion, the odor emanating from the dead salmon that lay stiff along the creek banks had lured them.

The land was damp, the rains having beat the soil for many days before moving on and giving the sun yet another chance to dry the forest, something that truly could never be accomplished.

In the meadow, hanging from the limbs of the willows, were the red ribbons. Mark slipped past the two chunks of wood that marked the beginning of his trail, then reached up to grab the nearest marker. He pulled it free and stuffed it into his pocket.

He did the same with every marker until he was far across the creek and hundreds of feet above the floor of the Valley. He removed the final ribbons, below the steep ravine that carried his trail to the junction.

Then he sat on a projecting rock and listened to the creek, far below him. He was surrounded by dark hemlocks and could barely peer out and see into the lowlands. He heard, above the murmur of the stream, the distant sounds of human society. And then, barely audible, came the sound of a dog barking. Was it Sheka?

From directly above, a sooty grouse proceeded to drop its load of excrement on the boy's shoulder. Wordlessly, for there was no one and nothing to blame, he stood up, walked over to where a species of twisted stalk grew in the shadow of an enormous, moss-covered stump, and leaned over. Without pulling a leaf, he scraped his flannel shirt until it was clean.

He returned to the rock, lowered himself, and sat there thinking. He wondered if his trail would be missed. Not that he cared. His flagged trail had been an intrusion upon the mountain, a mistake from long ago, and he wanted the ribbons gone. He could almost hear the mountain sigh with relief as its parasite was removed. He grinned. Its tapeworm. Now only he would follow the path to the summit, and he needn't any markers for that.

The sun's rays were spilling over the lower end of the ridge, and he knew it was past noon. It was time to be getting home, because at one-thirty he was supposed to meet Randy and his cousin; they were going saltwater fishing and had invited him aboard the Mitchell's boat.

The opposing pulls, he felt them yet again. He wanted to be on that vessel, partly because of the human company he would keep, but more strongly because of the company he would keep with the marine swells, the seagulls, and the salty breeze on which the birds soared. His heart sped up momentarily, then resumed its normal pace.

Just a moment longer. Stay here as long as possible, and absorb whatever you can. It will be tomorrow before you can return.

He sat on the rock for another fifteen minutes, without a thought in his head. He simply opened his mind and let the cosmic sensations entangle him.

§

August continued. It was what many people called the dog days, but Sheka felt no additional heat from Sirius. One afternoon, she lay in her favorite corner of the living room, near the open hearth, and out of the corner of her eye, she watched as Mark entered from the hallway and approached her. He curled up on the floor beside the dog and put his face near hers.

"Hello, doggie," he whispered. She reached out with her tongue, and without drawing back from the wet lick, he continued.

"I've been so quiet these days. Have you noticed? Sometimes I believe there is no one left to talk to. No humans, at least. Maybe I can talk to you instead, Sheka."

Her ears went up. "Do you understand me?" he asked the golden-brown eyes. "I always believed that you did. The things I say to myself, when we're out walking—I know you were always listening. I'm afraid that mankind in general has progressed, as they call it, so far that people have lost the ability to communicate with anything but themselves. The key, dear animal, is to sidestep this awful catastrophe by avoiding humans when you feel it necessary.

"You will then collect to yourself a new set of rules, laws, and ideals, and they will be the foundation of a much larger world that humans may someday hope to realize, a forever world that really does exist. And when you do this, it will become clear that these laws and ideals are in fact ancient ones; they were always there, ready to be followed, by those of us who could hear the faint cries from the distant past.

"However, there's a problem, doggie. If you are the only one who manages to unlock this door, and see this light, then it will be upon you to prepare for the onslaught, the criticism that will follow in your wake."

The malamute sneezed loudly.

"I agree with you, one hundred percent. You don't need to think, and I understand how you feel about things. No, you don't need to think. You're not burdened with the problem of time. Lucky are you! May *the* mountain bless you forever."

And after thinking for a moment, he added, "As I was just saying, don't worry about the forever part. I'll take care of that."

He rolled over and looked out the front window. The stratus clouds were pouring over the Valley, heading for the glacier. He jumped to his feet and watched as they covered the sky. They pushed against the mountains on either side of the ice river and descended still further, changing their shape and becoming blurry in appearance.

Here come Nature's Tears of Joy. It seems to me now that the rain and the sun do not quite balance. The rain dominates. It is just what many do not want, but it is what they get.

And it seems to me now that my two worlds are not at all balanced; instead Nature dominates. It is not what they expect, but it is what they will get.

"See you later, doggie," he saluted, and headed for his room. Calling back, he added, "Tomorrow, I think we shall go visit the pond and talk to the boulder. Sound okay to you?" His voice trailed off, but Sheka needed no ribbons to follow it.

§

Slowly, Jeff let out the twine, and Mark stepped backward, holding the enormous box kite. A gust of wind came up, nearly tearing it from his grasp, and as he squeezed the kite in a firmer grip, his little finger punctured the tissue. He looked, saw the tiny hole, and decided not to tell his friend about it.

After the two boys were thirty feet apart, Jeff got an idea. "Next time, why don't you stay put and let me walk backward with the string?"

A moment later, the kite was in the air. It was beautifully designed, and the sunlight struck the golden "wings" with an unusually dazzling effect. It rose higher and higher into the sky, and they took turns holding the line, which sought to drag them along the ground.

"Strong kite we made, Jeff. Look at it pulling me."

"Yes, and look at the clouds piling in from over the canal," Jeff answered him. "We keep the thing up there much longer, it'll get struck by lightning."

Mark scoffed. "Come on, now. Don't tell me you're afraid of a little cloud cover. And just how many times have you seen lightning around here?"

Jeff put his hand to his forehead, to shade his eyes from the still bright sky. "Never, I suppose." He turned to Mark, who was letting out even more line. "Why is that, by the way? There never is any thunder and lightning here, come to think of it. You know the reason?"

Mark handed him the stick. "You fly it for a while. Of course I know the reason."

"Yes, of course. What?"

Mark sighed, then pointed at the advancing weather front. "See those clouds, Jeff? Look at them closely, and tell me, what shape are they?"

"Flat. Sort of diagonal, but flat."

"Exactly. They formed out over the gulf and were carried here by a low-pressure frontal system, and now they're over the land." He stopped and looked at Jeff, who was concentrating on keeping control of the kite. "You can figure that much, can't you?"

"Yeah, yeah. Just you go on."

"Well, the air over the ocean isn't very warm, because the water doesn't heat quickly. And the air over the land isn't much warmer, because we're quite a ways from the equator, and also the snow and ice reflect much of the sun's rays. And so when the clouds move over the land, they aren't pushed up into tall, cumulus forms, like you would see if you were further inland, and under the influence of greater heating effects."

Jeff glanced at him. "So what?"

"All that electricity is built up by the cloud motion, because the water molecules are rubbing on each other. The bottom of the tall cumulus clouds become negatively charged, and the tops have positive charge. That means there's an imbalance between the cloud bottoms and the ground. Okay?" Mark watched the kite for a moment, then looked at Jeff. "You hear? A path opens downward and allows the positive charge from the ground to travel up to the cloud and rebalance everything."

Jeff began to reel in the line. "You mean the lightning bolt is actually going up instead of down? Sounds scary," he said, working the twine around the stick.

"No. The electricity travels up, very quickly," Mark answered. "Just a flow of electrons, called a stroke, but that isn't the light we see. All the surrounding molecules turn into plasma, and that creates the light. But the light isn't really a streak. It isn't going up, down, or anywhere. It's only the stroke that's traveling. It's like a light bulb. The electrons are moving along the filament, but the light isn't. Anyway, a lot of the energy goes into the surrounding molecules, and sound waves are the result. The thunder."

"You sure our kite couldn't do the same thing?"

"I very much doubt it," Mark said. "Look at those clouds. They seem pretty harmless to me."

As he spoke, the clouds covered the sun, and instantly it felt ten degrees cooler. Jeff continued to bring in the kite, which had been nearly one hundred feet in the air.

"Besides, I wouldn't want you to cause something like that anyway," Mark added.

"Why?" Jeff handed him the kite line.

"Because it wouldn't be natural. You would upset a natural process, and I wouldn't stand here and let you do it!"

Mark swore, very much silently. It was too late to change what he had said to his friend. If only he could go back through time, just a few seconds, and stop himself, but he didn't quite know how.

Jeff eyed him curiously. "What the hell's with you?"

Mark paused before speaking, then said, in a raised voice, "Nothing the hell's with me! If you'd think for a change, use your damn brain, which I'm fairly certain you still own, you'd see exactly what I am saying! You understand, do you?"

They stood in the center of the grassy field and looked at each other. For an instant, Mark could have sworn he was on top of Thunder Mountain, and he was seven years old ....

"Listen here, Mark. Just because you know everything there is to know, it doesn't give you the right to tell me when to upset a natural process, and when not to."

Mark glared back. "Didn't you hear what you just said? If you think I know everything, then you'd be wise not to question what I say—and if I tell you it's not right to interfere with Nature, then dammit, you'd better not!"

He shoved the line stick into Jeff's hand, turned, and began to walk.

"Where are you going?" Jeff shouted after him, to which Mark replied hotly, "Away!"

He reached the street in front of Jeff's house and got on his bicycle. Then he looked back to the field, where his friend stood, and he exhaled a second curse, because Jeff was letting out the twine once again, and the kite was rising in the quickening breeze.

He was doing it to make him angry. Jeff didn't care about lightning at all. Not that anything like that would happen, but the fact remained that he wanted to show Mark up.

He took off down the road toward home, almost wishing that the lightning would indeed come, strike Jeff unconscious and put him flat on his back, where perhaps he'd wake up with some sense in his otherwise hollow head.

When he reached the highway, he pedaled even faster, and soon came to the loop road intersection. And then he was flying up into the Valley, with the glacier and the snow peaks moving silently in his direction. As if to greet me, he thought, as he approached the turnoff that led to his neighborhood.

He turned a little too fast, a little too sharply, and too late he saw the oversized lupine hanging into the road. Its petals were long gone, dried up and blown away, but the stalk, and its weighty top, looked as pretty as ever ....

He raised his hand and smacked into the plant at full speed. His motion upset the course of the bike, and the front wheel hit a speckled granite that occupied the shoulder of the dirt road. The lupine was sheared off neatly, part of the lower stalk became entangled in the derailleur, and he went down in a heap.

The bike spun away from him and came to rest in the middle of the road. He felt the lupine against his face.

Oh, no! It was an accident, I didn't mean to kill you! I was angry, you know I was. You know what had happened, don't you? Please tell me you do, that you forgive me!

Only then did he feel the pain in his shoulder. He groaned, sat up, and reached down with his left hand to pick up the stalk. He felt it for a moment, and then he stood up and walked over to the ditch. He laid the stalk down among the wild grass and forget-me-nots that grew in the bottom of the depression, and then turned and went for his bike. The throbbing in his right shoulder became more pronounced, and his hand began to turn a dark purple.

Later, he stepped into the waiting room at the hospital, the doctor right behind him. He stood and looked at his family. Mom was expressionless, and Dad was pretending to be interested in a see-through plastic display of the human body. Stephen was not there, and Amy was staring at him as if he'd just lost a battle with the Northern Lights. The doctor smiled and raised Mark's right arm.

"See, it's not that bad at all. He pinched a nerve when he fell, and sometimes that causes enough discomfort to induce an unusual amount of swelling. But he did strain a few tendons, and actually crimped some tissue, so he'll be sore for a while. You see the shoulder sling he's wearing? It's put on like a harness, right underneath the shirt, and he should wear it, for safety's sake, at least a couple of weeks." He let the arm drop, and Mark gritted his teeth in pain.

Mom and Dad nodded. "Good," Mom answered. "I'm so glad to hear that it was nothing more than that." A false laugh came from her. "He's been running around so much these days, the relaxation should do him good!"

Mark had no words for the doctor or his family. He shut his mind to the room he was in and the ridiculous conversation taking place around him. He thought only of the lupine.

They left for home, and when they arrived, Mark was glad to see that his brother was not around. He let Sheka into his room, where he spent the rest of the evening talking to his pet and crying to himself.

§

Four days later, he ripped the harness from him and flung it under his bed. The thing annoyed him, and he felt as though the entire human population could see it under his shirt. His arm and shoulder felt stiff, but they were without pain, and so he decided he was well enough to ride his bike once again.

He traveled along the highway, in the direction of town. The wind was blowing up the channel, into his face, and so the trip took longer than he expected. He was tired when he reached the edge of the business area, but without resting, he pedaled up a steep hill until he came to the beginning of yet another trail.

This one led up the sloping ridge behind town, then onward and upward, across the narrow valley from the mountain he had hiked the previous year. He hid his bike in the weeds, and then he started up the winding path, into the trees, until he came to a lookout.

The town was far below him, but he could see the movement of people and cars. The boats were large specks gliding along the channel. He paused there only a moment, until the artificial habitat began to stir anger in him, and then he turned and continued his journey.

The path zigzagged endlessly, and he was again tired when at last he reached treeline. The green shapes fell away below him, and after getting his second wind, he raced up the sloping meadows, which were piled high in front of him. He climbed on and on, the noises of town becoming ever fainter, and finally dying altogether. He approached the first in a series of peaks, crossed its shoulder—he knew that *it* did not feel pain—and proceeded along the sagging ridge toward the next one.

Soon he was hiking on packed, granular snow, and his tennis shoes caused him to slip about. And then he was off the snow and atop the second peak, and far below was the deep gorge of Icy Gulch. He felt the wind rushing up to him, felt it roll over the summit and lose itself high above the channel. He sighed deeply, and then he was off again. Twenty minutes later, he reached the third and highest of the summits.

Roberts Peak was flat-topped and covered in heather. He sat down and looked at the scene around him. He could see over the top of Mount

Juneau and on to the icefield. And of course, there was a view of *the* mountain.

The breeze turned quite cool, but there wasn't a cloud in sight. The Fairweather Range, nearly a hundred miles distant to the northwest, stood out bold and white on the horizon. He had a feeling of drunkenness, up there in the heights, and his head felt dizzy with pleasure. He lay down, curled into a ball, and began to fall asleep. He was completely alone.

He wondered, as he closed his eyes, if he would dream. For a couple of years, he had been able to, but now he rarely did, as had been the case when he was a young child. As the afternoon wore on, and he continued to lay unconscious on the top of the mountain, the dream curtain never opened. He felt himself coming out of slumber, and in a rather slow-motion way, he sat up and rubbed his eyes.

He looked about him, and everything was in focus, and yet it wasn't. There was a slight wavering, not of the air, not of the ground, not of the sky, but … a wavering. Of course he hadn't dreamed. There was no need for a dream. This place was where he belonged, wasn't it? He belonged here, in the center of the Natural World, and when such a place was found, there was no more need for dreams. The real dream was all around him, even though it was slightly out of focus.

The wind was no longer brisk. Mark sat and told himself that it was all true, that he wasn't running away from something. He wondered what he would do if someone, say Tina, was to come hiking over the last ridge, look around, and spot him. Would he be angry and tell her to get lost? Or would he let her come on over and sit beside him?

He shook his head to clear it, without success. The very idea was preposterous; he couldn't begin to imagine the odds against it. People hiked in twos or threes, he told himself, with their ugly mongrel bounding along in front of them. That is exactly what he would expect to see, if indeed that was even possible. No, today the mountain was his, and the universe could not allow another to walk its slopes, not while he was here.

He looked around once again, satisfied that he was totally alone. He sat in the heather and gazed out across the channel, to the row of peaks on Admiralty Island. Things began to come back into full focus … and then he caught movement from the corner of his eye.

Over to his right, someone was coming up over the last little hill below the summit plateau. He turned his head. It was Tina. His mouth dropped open as he watched her approach, in her thin cotton jersey and safari shorts. She wore hiking boots and sported her favorite cap, the one with the humorous patch sewn on. Even from a hundred feet away, Mark could make out the hunter with a rifle in one hand and a giant mosquito in the other. Tina had a small knapsack on her back, and a camera hung around her neck.

It is not possible. Look at her, walking right toward me. What are you doing to me, World? What in the name of Capella ....

She didn't call out to him, but only smiled as she recognized him. She drew ever nearer, and he blinked a few times, wiped his eyes, and looked. She was no mirage, she was really there.

Intruding on his day, on top of this mountain. On top of everything. What was he to do now? As she came close, he dropped his head and looked at the clover plant that grew directly in front of him.

This is a Temptation.

He knew that she'd seen his lips move, seen him talking to himself. He didn't care.

And it seemed that she didn't care either. "Hey Mark, guess who's here?" she said in her bright, happy voice, and sat on the ground next to him. "I can't believe I ran into you up here."

Mark looked at her. "Oh," he said, and his own voice sounded foreign. "It's not that big of a town. Have you been up here before?"

"No, this is my first time. Mother ran me out of the house, and Leanne was busy, so I decided to go hiking. And look who I found!" She smiled again, and her blue eyes dazzled.

He smiled in return. Blue eyes were hardly Mark's favorite, but they always did look good on Tina. She used to complain that her eyes dominated her features too much, and he would shake his head in disagreement and say that it was her nose instead. Anger like he had never seen! He wondered if he should try and get away with the remark now, and decided against it. The joke was growing too old, and besides, her nose was perfect.

So what are you supposed to do? Are you supposed to excuse yourself and hurry down the slopes away from her? Are you supposed to sweat it out, make small conversation, until she decides that you're not going to do anything, and she leaves?

He looked around until *the* mountain caught his eye. He strained at it, but the summit appeared to be ignoring him. And nor was Capella in the sky to help him; it was hidden behind the light of the sun.

They are daring me.

He turned back and faced her. Nodding at the camera, he asked, "What have you been taking pictures of?" His voice sounded even more strange, like an auditory version of a lazy river.

She raised the camera and looked at him through the viewer. "Just about everything. Downtown, from the lookout point. The top of the first peak, from treeline. Those cute little puddles, way back there, off to the left." The shutter snapped. "You."

"Funny. I didn't know you were into photography. Well, I certainly do hope you know what you're doing with that shutter speed. I give off a lot of inner light, you know."

She put down the camera. "What is *that*?"

"Forget it." He lay back on the heather. "Did you know that Allen is moving next week? His dad is going to be the contractor for an office building in Vancouver. Can you believe that? With all the engineers in that city, they latch onto one here, and away goes Allen." His voice slowed even more.

She sighed. "No, I didn't know. That is really too bad. Hey, does that mean he has to become a Canadian? Allen … he is soooo nice, too!" The sigh became more of a whine. "Don't you think so?"

Step One of this Temptation.

"Of course. I think he's the cutest guy in the whole world."

She slid down beside him. "Come on! You know what I mean. Well, I suppose we can get along without him."

"Just what you'll say when … I'm gone … right?" He was starting to feel drugged. Things were wavering again.

"Oh, no!" she exclaimed. "You're not going to move, are you? If you did, I'd cry forever. I'd flunk math, flunk biology, oh God! Please don't say that."

The breeze had become warm again, and there was something dreadfully, sickly sweet about the moving air.

"Don't you just love it … up here," he said dreamily. "Away from … all the pressures of life. Just wonderful …."

"Mark, stop it! You're not moving away, are you?"

"Noooooo …."

Tina breathed relief. "God, I was scared." She reached out her arm and briefly touched his shirt sleeve. "I'm so glad." When Mark said nothing, she repeated, "So glad."

Step Two. Time is leaving you behind.

And then he wondered if perhaps it wasn't really a temptation at all, but rather a sweeping gesture on Nature's part, to allow deviance from his otherwise closed shell. It must be! Seeing that nobody could truly realize just how deeply he lived in his Natural World, it logically followed that nobody could detect it when he climbed out for a go with society.

But in *this* particular case … they (the gods of Nature?) were being overdramatic, were they not? He couldn't understand why he felt so light-headed, why the world was moving oddly around him, and why he was unable to talk properly.

You won't let anything happen to me, will You?

He extended his own arm, and eagerly, Tina rolled against him. At the first contact of her body against his ….

She vanished.

The wind became cool once more. Mark knew exactly why, as he sat up straight. He had only just now awakened from sleep. There was nothing wavering. Everything was in sharp focus, and he was completely alone. Tina wasn't gone, nor was she there. The two of them had merely escaped existence—the present—for a moment, to experience reality. He lowered his head.

What are you telling me? Was this Temptation a test of some sort? I'm trying to understand, but I feel I'm running out of cards.

§

At the trailhead, he picked his bike from the cover of the tall weeds, got on, and went wheeling away, through town, and on to the Valley. He tried very hard to concentrate on the ride, but it wasn't easy. The difference between existence and reality was a math problem, one with no simple solution. He thought he'd figured it out, but now he was unsure. And then he realized what had to be done. It was the right time, and he was in the right place. One more night's sleep, and he would know for certain.

Near the loop road intersection, he took a short cut through a ditch, then rode up and over a series of bumpy hills. As he swung around to hit the pavement once more, he saw, in front of him, an oversized lupine, bending over in crazy fashion. He fairly screamed in disbelief, swerved, but not far enough, and ….

Tina's hand brushed his cheek, ever so softly.

That night, he found it very difficult to get to sleep, but after he did, there were no dreams.

§

Morning came, and the window curtains were a fiery golden color, indicating another sunny day. He dressed quickly and went to the kitchen, where Mom was preparing breakfast for Amy, Stephen, and himself.

The radio was on, and it annoyed him, but he said nothing about it. He waited as the eggs were being cooked, and when he had consumed every scrap of breakfast, he surprised Mom, as well as his siblings, by heading over to the sink to do the dishes. He knew that she appreciated this action, but she could not know, of course, that he was giving his thanks by returning Stephen's and Amy's leftovers to the Earth.

And then he was outside, snapping the leash onto Sheka's choke chain. When they were safe within the confinements of the forest, he stopped, sat on a rotted log, and took the dog's muzzle into his hands.

"Listen, doggie. I think you might be noticing a change in me, and I hope that you are not afraid. Remember what we talked about last time? See, it's been welling up in me, and now it will overflow."

He fell silent, and looked into Sheka's eyes. And he wondered if there were any words, any words at all, to say what he meant. His heart sped up, and he realized that it was really happening. For a moment, he tried to fight it.

"Say, wait 'till I tell you about yesterday, doggie! I was all alone, up there on a mountain, and just *who* should appear in a daytime dream …."

No, it wasn't going to work. He stopped himself, and just sat there for a while. Then he got up and pulled hard on the malemute's leash. And he took her home.

"I'll be back later," he told her, and he left for a second time. He told no one else.

§

He began slowly, making his way across the playground. It was where he once enjoyed recess with the other children, in another time, another life. He kicked at the speckled granites, and remembered when he had seen the first of those strange rocks, on that pathway in British Columbia. And he saw that image in a new way. The path, leading onward and upward, out of sight, but he and Daddy stopping, turning and retreating their steps, to rejoin the others.

He paused for a moment. It was still morning, and the air was cool. Ravens soared overhead. The trees looked dark and gaunt, as though asleep, even though the sun glared brightly in the southeast, over the humped ridges of Thunder Mountain.

The peaks loomed, and they reached for heaven. Mark looked around, dizzy. He looked to the south, where the land was flat, covered by the marshes. He looked to the west, where the shrugging hills protected the Valley from the salty waters of Lynn Canal. To the east, where a steep ridge had kept him in shadow for much of his life.

To the north.

You fill my head, to the bursting point. There is no room left for anything else, or anyone else. I am Yours. Receive me into Your kingdom, now!

And he moved. First a step, then another, and suddenly he was running as he had never run before. He galloped across the playground, across the lawns to the corner of the neighborhood. He reached the loop road and streaked past the intersections, raced along the shoulder, with the glacier looming in the distance.

He wore blue jeans, a bone-colored sweatshirt, and tennis shoes. He became sweaty as he ran, but he didn't actually feel his body getting warm. So intent was he, so caught up in the flow of the adventure, and the upcoming Commission, that he felt no discomfort whatsoever. The ground met his running feet in the manner of a tongue pressing against cotton candy. Everything was pure energy.

... sudden vision of a black bear rearing up on its hind legs ... his body passed right through the holographic display....

... just a millisecond, everything went dark, and when that millisecond had passed ....

This was it.

I should have known it then. Yes, for I was being Born. The beaver pond, it was a baptism.

On and on he ran. Thunder Mountain slid by on his right, and the road began to gently curve. Then he was at its end, and the glacier sprawled in front of him. Never had it looked so beautiful. His head swam.

But he didn't pause his forward motion. He ran down the gravel path to the visitor center and bounded up the rocks, preferring their natural smoothness to the artificial, concrete staircase. He reached the observatory and went past, to the wide sandy trail. He raced along it, coming to the quartz vein. Running up the hill, he spread his arms as the pond came into view.

He stood there in exaltation, and looked down upon his private World. He knelt, and he drank from the pool, the clear water tasting like nectar. He hurried to the granite boulder and threw his arms around it.

And then he twisted around and looked at the mountains.

Goodbye, pond! Goodbye, rock! There is still one more leg of my journey, onward to the final destination!

He had the strength of a thousand. He sprinted along the trail, reached a fork, turned to the left, and continued. After a mile and a half, he came to the narrow gorge, near the eastern face of the glacier. He whooped at the marvelous scenery, but his legs did not stop; he turned into the gorge and continued to follow the twisting, rising trail, into the shadows.

In this narrow, forested canyon, the sun was never seen. He had once thought it spooky, but today the gorge exuded an air of holiness; a great natural cathedral. The moss hung from the lower limbs of the spruce, and the trail skirted a number of devil's playgrounds. He ran on and on, smiling at the thought of the devil playing in a church. Here that was possible, because in this church, no devil had fallen from grace. No sin had been committed.

The gap widened into a basin. He raced through it and came at last to where the land rose in front of him. The trail became less maintained, less used, harder to follow. Within half an hour, he had scurried up the steep rise and entered a second basin. To his right, he could see both peaks of Thunder Mountain.

Yes, yes! It is getting near … you remember what you felt the last time you stood between those double peaks, and the time before that, and before that. You feel it now, drawing you in! And it knows that you are almost there!

A second rise was before him, and up it he went, through the trees, the thick underbrush, and the devil's club. The trail began to fade, and soon it was gone completely. He cut to the left, hit the pebbly bank of a small creek, and continued ever upward. Soon he reached a third, much higher basin, and here the trees, which up until now had crowded him, were beginning to thin. A long, narrow ridge jutted into the center of the basin, and above rose a small rock peak. He began circling its base.

The creek was shrinking, and like the path, it was soon gone. Mark was breathing so hard that he should have hyperventilated, but not today; the journey, though near its end, was not yet over.

A long, sloping hill was before him. A cold wind came lashing over the top and whistled through the giant boulders that lay scattered to the right, to the left, and straight ahead. At last he stopped his forward motion, and instantly the sweat chilled on his back and forehead. He was above the trees, nearing the domain of rock and snow. Never had he visited this upper basin, never had there been a reason, not such as this.

A mountain goat appeared on the slope above him. He grinned, and then he was off again, on what he knew would be the final climb. The bright patches of snow glinted as he approached them, and the sun, at his back, now felt beautifully cold as he entered this new domain. The goat was a sign, it was the gatekeeper of this place, and this place was wild and uncontrolled, as he himself now was.

The top neared. He slipped once, then twice, on the cold, muddy shale, and he lay panting, a dozen yards from where the slope leveled. He picked himself up, and deliberately, on hands and knees, he climbed to where he could see over to the far side.

And behold! A wall of black and white, as if the world itself has risen to greet me. I kneel before it, my God of Nature, and pray for acceptance into its Kingdom on Earth!

Directly in front of him, soaring into space, was *the* mountain. Around it were the lesser peaks. Below it, the earth. And above was … nothing! Nothing at all, save Capella in the darkness of night ….

He reached out, as he had done years before. Only this time the peak wasn't out on the horizon, but looming *over* him, with the awesome, deadly southeast ridge plunging downwards, flaring off to his right. The south face looked smooth as glass. And the northwestern ridge, which he knew rose directly to the higher of the twin peaks, was hidden.

He stared at the giant mountain for a long time, feeling its reality as a living entity before him. So close! He gazed at its virgin summit, where only the snows had touched the crown of this, the Preeminent King.

The goat he had seen earlier was visible once more, crossing from one rock ledge to another, at the very base of the miniature range. He watched as it climbed in an almost uncaring, peaceful manner. It finally became lost in a series of gullies that separated two of the lower summits.

He breathed slowly.

There it is, North! It is the culmination of all I have learned, and as I stand here before it, all doubt is gone. There is nothing else to debate; nothing can save me now!

I am not sorry. I realize there will be misunderstandings, and there may be heartbreak for some, and the shedding of tears. The lives of others will be altered as well as my own. But was it not the Plan? I have made it, dear Elders, and I have seen the glory, and I have felt the ultimate bliss of belonging to You ....

Mom and Dad, what can one say—it would be easy to get over, after a time, and besides, there is another son and a daughter to look after. Mark isn't yours, he is Nature's child, born to die in the woods.

Yes, religious angle. Mustn't leave that out. The world around, all of it, is the God ...

Food for next year's weeds. Fantastic.

... all those acquaintances wouldn't care.

... had a rather strange influence on me ...

Loves, and offers the true forgiveness.

The sky was incredibly blue. The wind tugged at him, sought to lift him from the ground and carry him up into those dizzying heights, but he fought the temptation. He was not allowed to travel the slopes of *the* mountain. It was too holy. He continued to gaze at the towering mass of black and white. Someday, and he would know when, he might be granted permission to actually touch it with his fingers. But for now ... and he nodded his understanding.

It was late in the afternoon, but that meant nothing to the boy, as he stood below his Natural Idol. He belonged no more to the world of mankind, to the world of time, and his species' other foolish inventions. Yes, he felt the shirt on his back, and the jeans on his legs, but he shook his head defiantly. Was it not the plan?

The mountain wanted him gone. He was not to remain at its feet for a time longer than this, and so turning, he began the descent of the rocky, windswept hill. He reached the bottom and followed the creek down into the trees, coming soon to the faint beginnings of the trail. He walked slowly through the lower basins and the forested gap, where the glacier, the Valley, and the pond, with its boulder throne, awaited him.

He stopped for a moment, at the quartz vein. And then he hiked up to the pond, circled around to the boulder, and stood atop the granite, facing the lowlands. For a moment, he just stared. And then it came out.

"You!" he shouted. He could have sworn the voice came from the boulder itself.

"Look at me! I have been there, and I have seen! The Mark Nilsson that you once knew is no more, and I say this … you shall have to prepare quickly for the arrival of the Nature Boy. Here I come!"

He left the boulder and ran down the slope to the road. When he arrived, he continued without hesitation toward what had once been known as his home. And as he walked, he thought about just why, after the supreme Commission, he was traveling toward the house, and the faces he knew.

He decided, with a mental shrug, that all would not be good if he was to become too wrapped up in his new life so quickly. In fact, the very dependence he felt when there, in the little blue house, was not gone. It still existed, but in another form. He needed the warmth and security of that place, not to protect him from the elements, but to shelter him in quite another fashion, so that he may carry on a semblance of day-to-day living. The reason for this?

Simple. It is also part of the Plan. I am not yet at liberty to choose my final direction and sally forth. I am still New, I am a Nature Boy, but I must hold on to what I have, as well as accept the Realization. There is room for the past, absolutely room for the past, in my new life, and to discard it too quickly would create an imbalance of its own. That would be a sin, for the past is right here, right now! To let it all go at once??? Think of the messiness that would create. Listen! News flash! Boy goes crazy in the mountains … some sort of modern-day Captain Nemo … will he be vengeful? Will he be kind? We have no further details at this time, but will bring you an update as soon as we hear ….

So I will take it slowly, because a mistake now would be catastrophic.

It had occurred at last. It had been coming on some time, and he had known it, if only on a subconscious level. For years, Nature had tugged at him, begged him to live and learn in the great world that most folks simply called the outdoors, and to not be overwhelmed by the artificial habitats of mankind. There was a time, there must have been, when people every-where thought—no, not thought—felt this way, appreciated Nature and knew they were a part of it.

Something had happened. Humans had stepped forth into an invit-ing world of greater and greater knowledge, and with it came the need to define good and bad, less and more, trust and distrust. They began to *create* the difference between "a" and "b", and they did so in one place, and then in another place, and at one time, and then again, at what was now recognized as a later time. They interacted, they disagreed, and they blotted out completely the subtle indications of Natural Awareness.

And so the species morphed into what was seen today; creatures involved with a world, but practically separate from it. These creatures were to use this world for whatever purpose necessary to obtain a place called Heaven. In the contracted minds of these creatures, there now existed a box that could be viewed from the outside, and everything and everyone could be inside the box or outside the box. The new idea was to get as many as possible to jump inside, because outside was Hell.

It was about complete misunderstanding.

There never really was an "outside" the box. The box was all there was. Even Hell was inside the box; it manifested when the people of this new Earth mistakenly believed they could measure the size and dimensions of the box, invite things in, throw other things out, and objectify their existence using blueprints that were in fact useless. Hell manifested when people began to push and shove one another, and when they taught their beautiful children to fear a wrathful almighty instead of contaminating themselves with a loving one. Hell became real when people lay traps for the devil, completely unaware that the devil was created at the precise moment the traps were set.

Those traps would indeed catch something. They would catch the very people who set them.

The math describing the ancient voices was no longer recognizable to most. People had invented the number zero for the wrong reason.

The splendors of the wondrous Earth became more and more a toy, to be played with and enjoyed whenever the need arose, and to be destroyed when people felt they needed more and more for themselves.

There were hints that all was not lost. The cries of the environmentalists were heard far and wide, but too many of these voices were themselves tainted with the color of political gain. It was still possible that in certain minds and souls there was a trace of what had been. Yes, a very few of those who rallied for the earth believed that all of humankind and all of nature were still wrapped together as one, that people could truly come together, bathe each other with the light of celestial understanding, and make the world whole again. Those people were too few in numbers, and they could not connect. Their minds were unable to intersect. What a pity.

It was too late. Never again could people run naked as one, through the forest. Never could the people endure communal living, surrounded by the great and dominant wilderness, and lead productive lives. Never again would there be love without hate.

This was what Mark thought as he walked along the shoulder of the road in the early evening. He mustn't let the world find out what had happened today, but only that *something* had. Otherwise it would cause uproar, a barrage of criticism from the keepers of the social order.

There would also be something on the edge of approval from just a few, but those few individuals would invariably form their own ideas about what to do next. Their dream of Natural Envelopment differed from his own. They would use him as their model child, their spokesperson, and he wanted none of that. He would not be representing them, because they did not know what he knew.

It is too late! I must believe that I am alone in this, the only one in the World.

Until today, he might have shook with fear if such thoughts entered his mind and swirled around his soul, wonderfully contaminating him. Never again, he told himself firmly. The world of Humans had lost him now, and he was of the Earth and Stars. And if all went well, the people would never even know the reason.

He reached his neighborhood and walked across the playground. Sheka was in the front yard, waiting for him. He spread his arms out to her as he neared, opened his mouth, and imitated her growl. When she responded with a long, drawn-out wail, he smiled. *She* knew!

"Yes," he said aloud as he passed through the front gate. "You know what has happened today, don't you?" He knelt down and patted her, and his voice dropped to a mere whisper.

"It is true," he said to her. "Mark has gone and freaked out at last. And I am not afraid. What I feel is a warmth, not the cold fear that used to grab onto me."

He stepped into the house, and immediately Mom was in front of him, demanding his excuse for such a prolonged absence without notification.

"Like it's the first time it's happened," he murmered. And then, looking around, he noticed that Dan and Stephen weren't home.

"Fishing," Mom said. "See, you could have gone with them. They left about an hour after you did, and won't be back until tomorrow."

He nodded.

"Pretty sorry you aren't going along, am I correct?"

He shook his head. "No. Not at all. I had a pretty good time myself today. So good, in fact, that I'm bushed. I think I'll just take a little nap." As he turned to leave, he added, "I was up at the glacier, and there were quite a few tourists. I got so involved with them, I forgot the time."

He knew that she would believe his lie without question. He went to his room and took off his shoes. And then he lay on his bed; knew for the first time how much energy he'd expended.

His mind register a smell wafting from the oven and making its way down the hall, into his room, to his nose and his olfactory dendrites. Pork roast.

It was New Years Day.

He smiled inwardly as the odor dissipated in his mind, because in the "real" world, it had never been there; from Mom's perspective, the oven was empty and cold.

From now on, his New Year's Day would be this day.

Visions of *the* mountain danced across the ceiling. As he watched them, he began to tremble. It wasn't because of fear, of what might be happening to him, as had often been the case before. Until today, he had been unequal to the strength of his own perceptions. Now he trembled from the knowledge that he was newly assimilated, and not by society's hand.

§

He slept peacefully that night. He slept without dream, and upon awakening, he once again felt himself a tower of strength. He was prepared to walk among the world of Humans, interact with them, yet remain what he had become, indeed what he had always been.

However, new visions appeared as he lay beneath the warm blanket. And they were slightly different.

He could see *the* mountain, but was unsure if the eyes that looked were his. Quite prominent was the southeast ridge, which yesterday had risen directly above him. It looked almost climbable.

Who is gazing at this? Not I! The World tempts me again, but I am not fooled, as is this other ....

CHAPTER FOURTEEN

Gentle rain fell, bathing the forest. The clouds had lowered, blotting out the peaks and the sky. The wind, gusty in the morning hours, had faded away completely.

The earth had received its just due of warmth, in the days past. Its skin was barely moist, unusually so, and the chill moisture was welcomed by every tree, every shrub, and every weed. The human inhabitants, unconditioned to the days of sun and heat, had retreated to the confinement of their homes, where they waited until the cooler marine air, laden with clouds, pushed across the gulf at last, dropping heavenly moisture over the land.

During the spell of dryness, Mark Nilsson had made his First Pilgrimage. It took place exactly one year after his Commission, and while he was up in the basin, he had found himself shaking in disbelief. Time, when forgotten, could become more than just a stranger when finally recalled. He remembered the mountain goat, and he'd scanned the rocky ledges above him, but it was not there. A year, he decided, could in fact make a difference after all, but the difference was not what most people thought it was.

He had spent time at the pond, sitting on his granite boulder and looking through the glassy surface of the water, into the dark, unfathomable depths, while making his resolutions for the New Year. His thoughts were somber in tone.

He had talked to the pond. And he had listened as it answered him. They talked of the world and of the intrusions of his species, the invaders. Once they had not been such, but now all harmony was gone. Most would not care to feel the austere beauty around them, and in regard to the few who did, he could only shrug and say that their attempts were fruitless. They *persisted*, which was absolutely the wrong thing to do; it was just what one must not do. One must allow, but not persist.

Need he any proof, he had asked the still waters of the pond. No, where the true Nature was concerned, proof would be unrecognizable to most others, as much as his thoughts now were. No one would understand him if he explained his personality and his reasons for living. Indeed, he knew that silence was the best policy.

And now, as he lay on his bed, and with the first day of school at hand, he watched as the room grew lighter, and he recounted his thoughts of the present time.

He still attended school because it was part of the Plan. There was still much to learn, and although he felt he comprehended the math of the world, he needed to understand much better the difference between his learning and the learning of his peers. He knew that all would go better if he remained as Human as possible on the outside. So he had launched into high school with great enthusiasm and could in fact say, with a good measure of truth, that his sophomore year had been one of the best. Now, if he could turn the trick again, twice more, he was home free.

And then what? Ah, it didn't matter just now. The answer would come at the proper place in his life.

Now the school year was about to begin, and with it, a new task of social involvement. Was he ready for it? He rose from the bed, leaving the covers rumpled, and exited the room.

§

"You must have eaten three lunches. What you've touched so far wouldn't satisfy a mouse."

Dad spoke from the head of the table, and Mark shook his head. He had vaguely heard what was said, and the voice had been a dull sound, echoic and distant.

His feelings were hurt. After discussing his last composition in private with the language arts teacher, he had left the school and hitchhiked to the glacier. And he had cried, the tears dripping into the pond and sending out numerous concentric rings. He had begged the water for forgiveness, promising to be more careful. Now at home, the event had not yet drained from him.

The assignment had been simple enough: Visit, and then compare in writing, two environments of extremes. Home vs. school, building vs. field, or whatever. And most importantly, the feelings of the individual about these extremes was to be penned as well.

His teacher was the understanding sort, and he favored her above his other instructors. Wishing to surprise her as well as the entire English department, he decided to compare her class to his pond.

It was a risk, but a small one, he figured. If anything, she would smile and say that he'd purposed to great lengths in fashioning his analysis and had gone a little overboard with the language, but in the end, she'd give him an A-plus. And of course, *that* was the ultimate goal. A top grade, earned by the World itself!

He spent the next two days absorbed in his project. There was no rough draft; there never was when he composed. When it was finished, he read it over but once, then he submitted the paper on Friday.

And over the weekend, his teacher must have had quite a time with it, judging from the look she gave him prior to their little meeting. Indeed she had, though not what he expected.

... and wouldn't identify with them. A picture comes to mind, and I daresay it's laughable enough. From the far left corner, I obtain a superior view. Seventeen others sit and play their part in the scene. And my first thought? Well, here is a postcard-sized example of humans at work, as I described earlier.

Some listen intently to the drone of the lecture. Others are deeply involved with their presentation of self, and their roving eyes give them away. In the back row of desks, a number of spitballs are flying about. Kid stuff? Yes, of course, but only because we have defined a kid incorrectly.

I cannot sit alone in this atmosphere and fail to come to the conclusion that five out of six females present are so concerned about themselves, about their appearance, and about their present or prospective boyfriends, that they have in truth acclimatized, where the reality of the class around them can slip in and make itself felt. Walk and chew gum, in other words. 'Everything about me', but ready enough when their name is called. This is their capacity, their load limit. Similar thing with the guys, all about their aggressiveness and their confidence at taking charge, getting something done. If asked to express their feelings for the good earth on which they live, there would result a look of complete bewilderment, and *that* is the point entirely.

They do not know what they are, or what their life is for. Their minds are diversified, but only into certain compartments that involve the storage of human social interaction.

As I have stated, a brain in today's world is, for the most part, incapable of knowing the ultimate, almost sexual pleasure of a true association with Nature. An association, I must add, that makes clear, once and for all, the ultimate horizon of idealistic thought.

So let me tell you of an experience, one which is foreign to most who walk this planet ....

And now what? Mom was telling him to eat his pudding, if nothing else. It was pistachio.

He felt something rise in him, and before he could stop himself, he closed his fingers around the little ceramic dish, which had a beautiful willow design. He violently shoved it from him, and the contents slopped onto the table.

"I don't want the goddamn PUDDING!"

Both Mom and Dad were staring at him incredulously, as if they'd never seen him before. Amy was open-mouthed. Stephen looked quickly from one face to another. Mark breathed heavily, then let his eyes drop to his plate.

"I mean, I'm not hungry. I haven't been feeling too well all day ...."

No! That one is no good, not tonight. Stop before you let it get away from you!

He jumped up from his chair. Dad hollered at him for an explanation and started to get up himself. But Mark was quicker than he'd ever been, and within seconds, he was out the front door and beyond the fence, and with Sheka beside him, he ran for the woods.

When he was deep within the confines of the forest, he slowed, stood for a moment, then let himself fall to the thick moss. Sheka roamed about, but he forgot her momentarily; he was pressing his face against the ground, smelling its sweetness, loving its texture, and hating the world of Humans.

His voice began, and he rolled over and sat up, listening to himself as he babbled.

"I don't care. I don't care. Whatever they say, I will not listen. I do not need their help. All I need is my world, my little world, my big World.

"What did she say? 'Your attitude really does border on egotism.' She can take a flying leap! My paper was wonderful! It was a part of me! I am part of the Earth!" He stopped for a moment and then, much more quietly, he spoke again.

"Oh, Capella, my God Star, I don't want to be angry at anyone, I truly don't. You can save me."

He would have spent the night there, but Sheka was becoming impatient. After a long deliberation, he nodded to her, and together, they started back to the house.

§

The next afternoon, he was straightening his room when suddenly he stopped, thought a moment, and went to the closet. He began pulling things from the corner, and soon there was a large pile on the floor. He stared at the memories of childhood, and then he began to destroy the items one by one. He took his old baseball glove and went to work on it with his razor blade knife, which he had once used to cut the balsa fins for his models. He ripped and shredded the mitt until it became an unrecognizable tangle of leather, then threw it into the yard for Sheka to play with. His baseball bat disappeared into the ash can, along with various other things that were now garbage. They were ignited and reduced to cinders.

He searched through his record collection, shattering those which he felt in his mind were too Human. He placed the others in his trunk and locked it shut.

He threw away books, posters, and playing cards. He reached across his desk, and his hands gripped the text of the Juneau Icefield. He looked at it in anger, for it reminded him of his biggest blunder, the biggest mistake in all his life. He began to hate the boy who had given him the book, and he started to toss it into the pile of trash, but then he stopped. He could not make himself do it. There was a picture of *the* mountain between the hard covers. Carefully, he laid it down.

Mom would never know what was happening. She would come home from her work, at the elementary school where Amy now sat in the same fifth-grade classroom he once did. And Mom would smile as she surveyed the bedroom. As long as it looked clean, she would be satisfied. As long as it looked as though *Mark* lived there, he would be satisfied as well.

He looked up, and through the window, he saw that it was snowing. Having grown colder by the hour, it did not surprise him, nevertheless he felt a thrill as he related himself to the wildness, the unpredictable wildness of Nature. He let his eyes travel around his room. Could anyone possibly doubt that he was a part of it all? No, and he smiled, for it was his opinion that no one possessed what it took to diagnose him.

He had weathered the first, and was forgiven. Now, would there be a second, and a third, and so on?

§

And now I see it the way I should. A time frequency, and a frequency of space. Only a year ago last August was the Commission, but this was already deep inside me, because three years earlier, I was born the first and only time.

§

Seemingly, there was but the coldness of it all, amplified by the steady breeze that rippled the waters of the canal, the breakers striking the beach at an oblique angle. The coastlines were rough; the sands, quite scarce even in summer, were gone completely, having sunk to the lower reaches of the tide.

But now could be heard a grating rustle, as the wind touched the dry yellow stalks that bobbed in the crusted snow, above the ragged line of seaweed. The surf's mist and spray had worked upon the edge of the snow and rounded it, so that it resembled beds of soap suds.

Above, the sky was clear, save for thin streaks of cirrus clouds. They sported mare's tails, which indicated an increase in high-altitude winds and the likelihood of an approaching weather front.

The sun rode the tops of island peaks to the south. The ball of fire was eleven degrees of declination above the horizon at this, the noon hour. Even without a calendar, a rudimentary estimate of the date was still possible.

Gulls flew in pairs, or alone. They skimmed the surface of the canal, interested in just about any dark shape that caught their roving eyes. Their cries were muffled, coming out like the voice of a sickened eagle.

A troller plied the canal, heading north. It was on its way to Haines, and the business at hand was not fishing, but rather the transport of passengers. And off to the left, a much smaller, open boat was braving the wake of the larger craft, and the freezing spray fell upon the lone occupant.

The mountains shone, and their whiteness was almost blinding. Out across the canal stood the Chilkat Range, and their summits, though not extremely high, caught the crystalline clouds whenever they poured in from the gulf. Their timberline was five hundred feet lower than the mountains on this side of the water. They took the brunt of every fierce winter storm and helped tame the violent fronts before they reached the Valley.

The wakes from the troller hit the shore, and with a *ssshhh!*, they traveled up the beach in the same direction as the vessel itself. They pounded the black rocks in the distance, and the miniature forms of water spouts, chaotic in their upward surge, sent yet another thin wave of mist into the air, to be blown inland to the amber-colored remains of life.

Those rocks were covered with white specks, as countless barnacles clung to their home with amazing strength. The icy cold of the saltwater, and the battering of the surf when the wind was high, could not dislodge them. At the bottom of the shallows, the crabs and the shrimp, along with a few pricklebacks, were swept in and out but refused to die; indeed they flourished in this seemingly desolate environment.

The cries of the soaring gulls increased in amplitude. A pair of them had discovered an Irish Lord, floating stiffly upon the swells. Within seconds, a dozen of the birds had gathered, bobbing and taking turns pecking at the dead fish. When at last it was considered hopeless, the meat being almost frozen, they opened their beaks and fluted their disapproval, then one by one, they took off, fanned out, and disappeared as mysteriously as they had conglomerated.

A roar was heard. It was a distant rumble, and then, from over the peninsula to the east, a jet glinted in the sunlight and rose on its cold, silver wings. It traveled above the canal, rising steadily until only the exhaust trail was visible. The roar became a crackling, explosive sound that ripped through the skin of every living thing. And then the noise began to fade, as the arc of the sound waves lessened degree by degree, and the dispersing exhaust trail became ever more faint. And finally the dark streak itself became one of pure white, formed by the water created in the jet's engines.

Quieter now. The tiny breakers still raced up and smacked the shore, and the breeze continued to set the yellow stalks in motion. But after the jet, all was quiet but for the music of the natural world.

Two hundred yards from shore, a herring jumped. This helped scatter the copepods and phytoplankton, making it easier for the fish to detect and consume them. The concentric rings formed by this action became larger and more distorted as the swells went to work on them.

A smell came in on the breeze. From where, it was impossible to know, but it was strong and rank. It certainly had the properties of marine origin, as it carried the odor of salty rot. It lasted for about two minutes, growing more and more pungent, then at last clearing, and all became a dry cold once more.

For a spell, there was no further activity. The scene was unchanging, and the breakers continued to hit the shore as they had done for thousands of years, ever since the great ice had melted and allowed the ocean to rise, deepening the great fjord.

But after a moment, another interruption. A dark blue shape glided from behind a distant island. It was one of the ferries, and like the troller, it was on its way to Haines. It moved with deceptive speed across the expanse of water, finally sliding behind another, larger island. Soon it would catch up to the fishing vessel and pass it by. It was an instrument of homo sapiens, but for a moment, it had looked as though it belonged there, in the canal ….

Mark stood up. It had looked so peaceful, so … in its place, that ferry-liner. It had moved him, though something inside told him it shouldn't have. He scanned the water in front of him; noticed that the small open boat had vanished.

His nostrils cleared of the strange smell brought by the wind. He felt the stiffness in his legs as he turned to make for the highway, which curved through the trees. When he reached it, having followed the path, now snow-covered, along which he had run, years earlier on the class picnic, he stuck out his hand and began to hitchhike.

A Ford crunched by him, and he walked after it, listening for a second opportunity. It soon came, in the form of a battered old wagon, which also went past without slowing. The third car, a Volkswagen with chains on the tires, stopped, and the driver unlocked the passenger door.

Mark got in and told the young man at the wheel where he was going.

And fifteen minutes later he was deposited in front of his house; the driver lived just three blocks away.

He went to bed that night, confident that Nature would give him just about anything he wanted. He had made it, and now he deserved an almost limitless reward.

In the morning, the radio was on as he sat and ate his breakfast. The local news was being reported, and the top story was about a dead body pulled from the beach near Auke Village at sunrise; the victim's capsized runabout was there as well. Apparently, drowning wasn't the cause of death, as the deceased had numerous, unexplained wounds on the face, neck, and trunk.

§

It was still dark when they pulled into Jeff's drive. The headlights flashed across the living room windows, and immediately after, Jeff opened the front door and hauled out his pack. From the way he was carrying it, Mark figured he must have brought a ton of useless gear. He hopped out to open the trunk.

Their exhaled breath became steam, rising like towers of exhaust from a factory. It was twenty degrees above zero, and Mark had yet to cover himself with his parka. He fidgeted with the key, and then Jeff dumped his load of supplies into the rear of the new sedan.

"Nice car," he said, as they took off toward the loop road. Mark sat next to him and nodded. Why, he wondered, did people bother to make such a comment as that? If everyone in the world owned a different type of automobile, he could begin to understand. But when there were at least a hundred of the make and model in this town alone, it made the phrase stupid. If they were just trying to be nice, he'd rather they not say anything at all.

Mom asked, as she drove, "You still haven't told me what time you want to be picked up tomorrow. You better hurry and decide."

The boys looked at each other. "It's a hard thing to figure out," Mark answered. "But let's say, about six in the evening."

"Sure? It'll have been dark for over an hour."

"Absolutely sure."

Moments later, they arrived at the turnoff to the campground, and then they were bumping along the poorly cleared road. Balls of ice, created when a grader plowed its way through, were scattered about, and it was nearly impossible to steer clear of them all. Finally, they came to the dead end.

The boys jumped out, Mark finally wearing his down parka. In a moment, they were ready and waved goodbye, to which Mom answered, adding that they had better watch out for themselves. Then she was gone, and the twin red lights disappeared around a bend in the road.

The cold was overpowering; though clear, it was unseasonably humid.

As they started up the trail, Mark remembered the time when he and Jerry had camped near the lakeshore, only a quarter-mile from where he and Jeff now crunched along in silence. A number of times since then, he had come to this area to explore. He had hiked the trail when Fran had taken him up onto the glacier, and he had traveled it alone as well. The path led along the west side of the frozen river of ice, and it ended high on the north ridge of a peak that rose still further to the west.

But never had he been here in winter. He had gotten the idea only two days before, and had for some unknown reason decided to tell Jeff his plan. And of course his one-time closest friend had suggested that he would like to accompany the Wild Boy. Mark grinned as he walked the frozen, twisting trail, cut through by only a few prints and a line of ski tracks.

Jeff hadn't really called him that. It had come from Mark's own mind, slipping into his thoughts of the moment without coercion. So, at last he was becoming used to the idea; the heart palpations and waves of uncertainty were truly disappearing forever.

The sun would rise shortly, but even without its light, the trail was a shining white in the otherwise blackness of the forest cover. After a while, the path skirted the lakeshore and followed the beach to within a half-mile of the ice itself. The two had not spoken a dozen words since the start of the hike, and Mark wondered if the fact was bothering his companion. If so, too bad! He'd wanted to come. Mark let the quiet do wonders for his mind, and the chill air current, moving softly through the dark green spruce, was noise enough for him. It was Nature's Music, and his breath kept the beat.

The trail cut to the left and began a series of rises that carried the hikers above the level of the glacier. The sky was becoming lighter now, and the milky white reflected off the thin layer of fog that had formed over the mass of ice during the night. The daylight brought no instant heat, rather it seemed to deepen the sensation of cold. Mark recognized it as one's tendency to associate the day with warmth, and the night with chill. Nature could confuse the brain in this way; when warmth was expected and not received, the opposite effect was experienced in its place.

They came to the shoulder of the long ridge, having had no trouble thus far with the snow, which was compact and did not give under their weight. The tracks had stopped when the going became steep, and now they'd gone further than anyone had traveled since the snows had first fallen, back in the middle of October.

The trail continued to loop past the ridge, and the boys gained even more altitude. They began to struggle as the snow finally deepened, and it took them a full two hours to cover the last mile, where the "path" jutted out onto a high rock bench, with the glacier tumbling crazily below them.

"What a view, huh?" Jeff said when they came to the point and stood, marveling at the vast surge of the glacier, with the veil of fog lifting and fading into the air above.

"Yes. It certainly is. Makes you wonder why people live in cities, doesn't it?"

Careful, he told himself. Don't be stupid.

They found a good level spot and tramped about, packing the snow down firmly. Mark set up the two-person tent, the one he had owned for years. And then they arranged their supplies and began to prepare lunch.

It was a big meal, consisting of leftovers from previous hikes. Packages of freeze-dried foods had been building up in Mark's supply box for a long time, and he had brought a number of them along today, simply grabbing one after another without bothering to check the contents. As it turned out, the meal was pretty good, more than enough for both of them. As Mark put away the small campstove, Jeff started to dig a hole in the snow, evidently to dump what he could not finish.

"No! Don't do that, you hear? Don't pollute this place. You eat everything in that dish. You'll give it back when you sit on the pot!"

Later, they walked up the slope to take some pictures of the scenery, with their campsite far below. The daylight was short-lived, and before long, the sun was beginning to drop toward the ridge, to disappear behind the two boys. Instantly the wind picked up and wailed across the snowswept heights. Years ago, it might have sounded lonely to Mark, but now he listened eagerly to the high-pitched moan. Looking at Jeff's face, he thought that if anything, his companion worried at the noise. Mark grinned inwardly.

They returned to the camp and crawled inside their sleeping bags. It was still only late afternoon, but darkness was at hand, and soon it would be too dangerous to wander about. They passed the time telling stories and discussing the days at school. After a while, Jeff sat up and abruptly changed the subject from the recent quiz in auto shop to something that had Mark sighing in frustration.

"You do realize, don't you, that if you don't start spending more time with Tina, she's going to look for attention elsewhere."

Mark looked at him, his eyes barely sticking out from his fiberdown bag. "Is that all you have to say about it? No, I didn't think so. Go on, let's hear it all!"

"I asked her what was wrong with you two, during art class." Jeff's face was red with cold; he'd stuck his head through the tent flap to peek at the dark surroundings. He let the flap drop, turned around, and the red face now split into a sickly grin. "She said you were losing your interest in her, like she was starting to feel she was ugly, as if—"

"As if what?" Mark interrupted in a stern voice. And then he added, with a volley of steam, "Listen here, you asshole! I told you that you could come up here with me because I thought you'd like to go camping, not to give me a hard time! If you want to BS, well do so, but not about me, not about Tina, and for that matter, not about anybody I know! Do you hear me?"

"I hear you, I hear you," Jeff answered, the smile gone. "And so can half the people down there," he added, jerking his thumb toward the Valley. "God, I never met a touchier bastard in all my life."

They quieted down, and after a while, they both fell asleep. Mark knew, as he faded into unconsciousness, that he was going to do something he almost never did.

He dreamed. He was bathing himself in the pond, and Sheka was there as well. It must have been a very hot summer day, because the water was warm. The pool was bottomless, yet it buoyed him, and he splashed himself and his pet gleefully. And when they were clean and refreshed, he lowered his head and began to drink the water. He believed it had magical qualities and could never become dirty. It was the purest substance in the universe. It was the blood of the World, and that was the blood he must now drink.

And the Gods of the Earth are watching me! The boulder, the towering peak that is mine, even Capella, through the light of day. They watch us. Sheka, let us sing....

And he was awake. Jeff was shaking him, and he sat up quickly. A penlight was shining in Jeff's hand.

"What the hell is your problem?" Jeff asked, peering into Mark's eyes. "I woke up, heard noises, and then I looked over, and you were tossing and turning and talking in your sleep like I couldn't believe! Something about a pond, and the gods that watch you, and drinking blood! Have you seen your doctor lately?"

Mark looked back at him as he gained full consciousness, and when he realized what had happened, he opened his mouth to shout.

Jeff drew back, as if he was about to be attacked. When Mark saw this, he stopped himself, then said, in a small voice, "I wouldn't worry. It was just a bad dream."

Jeff continued to eyeball him in a strange way. "Uh, uh. You should have heard yourself. Only an insane freak would talk—"

"Shut up, damn you!" Mark kicked his way out of his bag; the penlight flickered off. As he prepared to launch a blow through the darkness, he upset a corner of the tent. He heard the stake pull out of the snow, and then Jeff's voice cut in again.

"My God, he's going crazy!"

Mark felt hate running through him. He wanted far away from Jeff, and he groped for his own flashlight. Turning it on, he saw the other boy's face more plainly than before, but without wasting words, he pulled his boots on.

"Where in hell are you going?"

"Never to worry." Mark tied the frozen laces, snapped on his parka, and put on his wool mittens. And then he flung open the tent flap, and as he stepped out into the night, he kicked snow backward, and Jeff swore again.

"At least fix the tent."

Without answering, Mark stumbled away, following the sets of footprints. He came to a break in the stubby alders and fought his way down the slope, his flashlight beam darting crazily against the snow. The moon had risen above Thunder Mountain, and although in waning crescent phase, it created an eerie glow upon the surface, both near the camp-site and far into the distance, where the dark shapes of other peaks rose skyward, their snows almost blue-looking in the night.

He stumbled and rolled down a steep incline. Before he could let out so much as a squeak, he hit the bottom, and the flashlight was gone from his hand. He looked for its beam, both above and below him, but it was no use.

He groped about, then finally started off again, parallel with the ridge. Forget the flashlight, he grumbled to himself. The moon will be your guide, as was meant.

Another drop-off appeared, and he failed to see the overhang of crusty snow. He fell through it and was again rolling down the slope. He hit something hard, and when he stopped, he expected to see the dark shapes of rock all around him. He did not.

It was the glacier. He had rolled right down to the edge of the glacier. He removed his left mitten, reached his hand out, and touched the packed ice. Snow had fought its way down his neck and into his boots, but he scarcely noticed. He touched the ice again and again, his mind clearing and forming but a single idea. This ice was part of the glacier, part of a living entity that moved just as he moved, even responded to stimuli, if one could only think about it the right way ....

In the dim light of moonglow, he saw a dark circle below his face and realized that it was blood, dripping from his lip. He had cut himself badly but hadn't even felt it. He watched as the blood sank into the ice, and he smiled.

Up above was Jeff, wondering, he was sure, what the hell was going on out in the darkness.

If he told him, upon returning to the tent, it would be disastrous for both. So he would not tell. He would lie here in the soft snow, for just a little while. He would lie here and watch the moon slowly make its low arc across the sky. He was pressed against a fourteen-mile river of ice, but inside he was warm as a spirit could ever be.

§

Downtown, he ran into Frank Simmons outside a coffee shop. They sat down for doughnuts, and as they ate, their conversation turned to hiking, and the mountains.

Suddenly Frank said, in a lowered voice, "There's something you don't know. But I'll tell you now. You know when Fran was ... up there for the last time? He was on his way up a mountain, with a friend of his. It was an unclimbed peak." He paused, then took a bite of pastry.

"And it still is. Sometimes I think—"

CHAPTER FIFTEEN

Through centuries, the land had cleared itself of ice, then life was presented in slightly new fashion. It was a true palingenesis, displayed at first in the most humble, innocent way possible. Gradually, as flora and fauna increased in number and variety, the land was rejuvenated with a firm soil base, and from that was spawned the more complex organisms. Today, it was difficult to imagine that the current landscape was comparatively young.

There were clues. The speckled granites, the sharp ridges, the U-shaped valleys, and the pater-noster lakes. But these were for the unfiltered eyes to see; the majority of eyes were far too conditioned.

More importantly, those eyes were uncaring of such things.

This is the argument Mark Nilsson would present, if argument was in the makings. Indeed, he'd now gone further in believing that the earth was both young and old; that time and space were a consequence of physical universe creation, and that any given moment was the only moment, even as one moved through that moment.

There was indeed the illusion that time passed; the truth of oneself passing in time was a truth rarely identified by most individuals. As Mark passed through the year, and as the next year approached, he felt a strong inner peace within himself. However, coupled with this peace was an uncomfortable nagging, one that he could not—try as he might—command to disappear. It was a horrid concern, a feeling that his knowledge, his secret, would be revealed and spread upon the community like sweet butter on stale, moldy bread. And the mold would contaminate the butter.

He sat at his desk, situated near the rear of the small office, and noticed the time. He had lapsed into an almost unconscious state and had remained there, he now saw, for more than twenty minutes, time that had never really passed at all. He sighed, then resumed the task of scanning papers, of reading them lightly and making corrections. When he was finished, he shoved them into the top right drawer and grabbed his coat to leave.

Today was payday, but that was unexciting. Since the school year had begun, his workday was but three hours in length, and his savings had become a thing of the past. Today's check, already cashed and the bills in his wallet, meant only one thing to him, and that was the purchase of a new pair of hiking boots.

He turned off the light, then closed and locked the door. It was drizzling as he walked across the street and reported out to his manager. Moments later, he was on the bus for home. It was a long, dreary trip along the old, battered highway, the same road upon which his family had driven, so long ago, when they'd disembarked from the *Taku*. The bus stopped at every side street, and by the time it reached Mark's neighborhood, only a few passengers remained aboard.

The rain increased, and Mark snapped his hood as he rose from his seat. He stepped onto the pavement, stood for a moment, and then walked home, slowly and deliberately. He wanted the rain to soak him completely, to wash away the day's filth, to cleanse his mind and his body. It was a cold rain, but the snows had yet to touch the crown of Thunder Mountain.

He entered the house, took off his wet garments and laid back on his bed to rest. After but a moment, there was a knock, then another, and Mom peeked through the doorway.

"You awake? Listen, I've got two things to tell you. First, I got a call from Stephen. He's going to be home for Christmas, maybe for a week. He's going to get a new base assignment soon after that."

"I know."

There was a pause, then Mom asked, "How could you know?"

Mark wished he was asleep. "I just know. And the other thing?"

"Other thing? Oh, Terry called and said he was going to fly over to Excursion Inlet to get his boat. He couldn't get anyone to accompany him, and asked if you thought maybe you'd like to go."

He rolled over and looked up at the crack in the door. "When is he leaving?"

"Tomorrow morning, about eight o'clock. But you better hurry and call him back, if you want to join him."

He heard her move away, and he sat up, looking across the room. The other bed was empty; had been for months. Stephen had joined the U.S. Navy.

§

Here was an excellent opportunity, he decided. He could get away and see new sights, experience a new part of his limitless domain. Of course, he wouldn't be alone, but that was all right. He would be looking at his Natural World from a different perspective, and he was lightheaded as he stepped down the ramp to where the Cessna bobbed in the water.

Terry had lived in the Valley for most of his life. He was ten years older than Mark and had recently married. Having worked with Dad for a brief stint, he'd come to be known around the dinner table. In August, he'd invited Mark to accompany him on a weekend fishing trip, but Mark declined, as he already had something scheduled … his Second Pilgrimage. On this occasion, however, he figured the timing was just about right.

"Can't trust anyone these days," Terry had said over the phone the night before. "Headed over to the inlet and was joined by my cousins the next morning. When I got the call to return—you know, the power failure—they said sure, they'd bring the boat back with them. I'd been at the lodge and flew back immediately, and it wasn't long until I found out the cousins had left themselves, for a trip into Glacier Bay. They left the boat tied at the upper dock and called me in the middle of the week, about the time I was going totally crazy with worry.

"Then I find out they're back in L.A., and the boat's sitting over there, waiting for someone to come and raid it, or worse. Want to go and get it with me?"

So now they were loading supplies and climbing into the plane, and the pilot was starting the engine. Mark had never in his life taken off from the water, and when the door was slammed shut and locked, he felt like he would burst in his anticipation. He'd been given the choice of the front or rear seat, and had decided on the position of copilot, from where he felt he could obtain a better view.

They taxied out into the channel, past a string of black markers, and the pilot spoke into his radio headset. Mark glanced back at Terry, who grinned through his tangled beard and gave the thumbs-up sign.

It had rained the entire night, but the clouds had remained above the lesser peaks. The wind had died in the early morning hours, and as the pilot switched over to the handset and adjusted the flaps, he said, in a voice that Mark graded as semi-cheerful, "Guess we can be glad for the weather report. Supposed to clear up by afternoon."

With that, he turned the plane until it faced the northwest end of the channel. And then he pushed the throttle forward, and the floats rose in the water. Mark leaned forward, his feet pushing hard against the cabin floor, as the Cessna accelerated.

They bounced along for a quarter-mile, and then they were out of the water. Instantly the pilot drew back the throttle and reached overhead to crank the flaps into a more level position. There was sense of relaxation, and for a moment, Mark thought the plane was dropping back to the water. But he looked down and to the right, and the surface of the planet was leaving him.

What a thrill, he said to himself. They raced upward to the clouds and the forested ridges. Thunder Mountain's double summits went sliding by, and then the vast sprawl of the glacier appeared. The icefield was hidden beneath a blanket of white moisture, and Mark thought it a pity, for he had always wanted to get an aerial view of it, perhaps even get a glimpse of *the* mountain.

They turned to the west and zoomed over the expanse of Lynn Canal. And then the pilot said, over the noise of the engine, "Feel like taking a chance today? Good! Think maybe we'll just whip through the Chilkats and save ourselves a couple gallons of fuel." He turned the plane again, and Mark could see that he was aiming for a long, narrow gap in the range, above a lower valley that contained Teardrop Lake.

Mark had been there only last year. He and Dad had taken the little Gamefisher across the canal, braving high winds and bad weather. They had hiked up to the lake to do some trout fishing, and while the catch that day was nothing spectacular, they had returned to their beach camp to find it in total chaos. A brown bear had spotted them, reared up onto its hind legs, then loped away, into the trees and out of sight, a food bag in its mouth.

After cleaning up and resorting the supplies, Mark and Dad had gotten into a big fight. Dad was of the opinion that they should start directly for home, that the outing was ruined. Mark had pointed out that it was just an act of nature, and that the bear was only trying to keep itself alive, and that if Dad would only see it that way, he wouldn't have to be so upset about it all. Besides, all they had lost was the hamburger fixings.

He watched now, as the lake approached and then glided beneath the wings. They came to the pass and started through it, and as they neared the far end, Mark saw the black clouds pressing in.

So did the pilot. Shaking his head, he said something, but the engine and propeller noise was too loud for Mark to even guess what it was. He had a feeling, however, that the pilot remained just as relaxed and confident as ever.

There was sudden turbulence, and before anyone could react, the plane spun downward, and a finger of cloud came from out of nowhere and wrapped itself around them. The pilot turned the Cessna and began to climb once again. Mark realized that it was a one-way street—they couldn't go back the way they had come.

Like I always used to do.

The wind continued to buffet the small plane. Mark didn't turn his head anymore, but he figured the smile was gone from Terry's face. Probably airsick, he thought. He continued to focus his eyes on the front windows, his excitement at being caught in the elements almost too much to bear.

Without warning, the plane dropped over one hundred feet in a matter of seconds, then twisted and leveled out. Mark yelped with pleasure as his safety belt grabbed and held him, and he pictured the Cessna crashing into the tall, dark spruce that covered the floor of the narrow valley below them. Instead they broke through the cloud cover, and directly ahead, Mark saw a sliver of water. It was Excursion Inlet, and beyond it, the sky was blue, with the Fairweather Range surging like a white tide on the horizon.

The pilot swung the plane around and dropped the flaps, making for the eastern beach. They sunk through the lower mists, and the slopes rose on either side of the Cessna. In a moment they were skimming the surface of the quiet little fjord, and then they touched down lightly, sending up the barest amount of spray. Slowly, the plane taxied to the upper dock piers.

Terry's fishing troller was tied up at a long, narrow mooring, and a few buildings were visible through the trees. The pilot asked Mark to open the door, get out on the pontoon, and be ready to jump onto the dock with the wing rope.

Mark did as he was instructed, and as he stood on the float, he felt as though he were a part of the plane itself. He wasn't securing an aircraft to a dock. No, he was simply exploring—as a huge bird—this new territory. He wouldn't say anything to the others; these few moments were not for them.

He jumped to the creaky old dock, and the pilot brought the plane horizontal before cutting the engine. Terry climbed out and began to unload their few supplies, while Mark and the pilot looped the ropes around the metal cleats. And then they went up the ramp and onto the sand. Terry led the way to one of the shacks, saying it was time for some hot coffee.

Once indoors and out of the sprinkling rain, they related their feelings about the short flight. Mark listened to the pilot, understanding that the plane had been in quite capable hands, and what would have seemed a nightmare to many was actually great fun, exactly what the pilot himself called "Just another in a string of death-defying adventures in the sky".

Mark also knew that the pilot did not make the intersection between the plane and the Natural World in any sort of fashion similar to his own.

After the refreshments, Mark and Terry said farewell to the pilot, helped shove the plane away from the dock, and watched as the Cessna raced away from them, climbing once more to the clouds. And then Mark and his companion went over to inspect the *Katzehin*.

Terry's cousins had left a note. It was scribbled on the back of a folded marine chart that was rubber-banded to the steering wheel. Terry read it, cursed, shoved it into a drawer, then looked about the vessel to make sure nothing was missing.

"Who would come and take anything in the first place?" Mark asked him, although he already knew the answer. "It doesn't look as though many people have been here, not for a long time. Did you see all the dust in that little cabin?"

"Hunters," Terry answered from down below, in the cramped sleeping quarters. "That's what made this area so popular, decades ago. There's good hunting up this way, but the season's been shortened, and a lot of areas closed off. We're very close to the protected area—you know, Glacier Bay—but enough hunters still use the dock, so I was worried they might want to climb aboard for a look."

He came up to where Mark waited on top of the engine box. "Guess we're safe. I haven't checked the gas yet, but I'm sure no one's tried to siphon it off." He got out his spare keys, and soon there was a sputtering as the engine caught and held. Terry yelled his approval, Mark untied the troller, and the bearded captain swung the *Katzehin* into open water.

The rain had stopped, and the patch of blue sky was growing from the west. Mark shivered in the cool breeze, caused by the craft's forward motion, and he made his way to the bow, where he sat and hugged his legs against his chest. He watched the scenery as it slid past, along with the floating rockweed. The boat was going at top speed, which Mark judged was only about ten knots, and at that rate, he figured, it would take them seven hours to reach Auke Bay.

He let the movement and the vibrations affect his mind, and after a while he had nearly fallen asleep there in the bow, with the cold wind striking his face. He thought to himself about being part of the plane this morning, and now he was part of the boat. The elements could never bother him; he was part of Nature itself. If Terry called to him at this moment, he probably wouldn't answer.

They approached the mouth of the inlet, and Terry began to sing as he held the steering wheel. "Big, big waves, nah nah nah, you're no match for me …." Mark looked up and saw that the water was getting rougher in the distance. They entered Icy Strait, and Terry steered the boat east, continuing to add lines to his odd tune. "Mark and Terry, out to sea, what-will-become-of-him-and-me?"

Mark grinned to himself. The young man was a nut case, but that was all right; at least he could handle a fishing boat.

The waves increased in strength, and Terry called for him to put on his life jacket. Mark did so, and then the *Katzehin* was pitching and rolling in the whitecapped swells. A large wave smashed the troller, and Mark was knocked to the deck. The wheel spun out of Terry's hand for a second, and the boat lurched crazily to starboard.

As Mark scrambled to his feet and headed past the wheelhouse, a wall of spray broke over the side and caught him squarely in the eyes. He yelled as the saltwater, only a few degrees above freezing, stung him into momentary blindness. He reached about helplessly, feeling for a handhold. Finding none, he stood up, with his eyes shut tight, and banged his head against the starboard outrigger. A moment of pain, and then his eyes reopened.

Another wave hit. It was like being rammed by a freight train. Mark stumbled around, barely avoiding the fish well, and made his way down to the passenger hold. He lay there and waited until his vision cleared, and then he began to giggle as he listened to Terry's singing, between the whooshing noises of waterspray.

Crazy, you say? The elements can be rough, and while others fight them, I lay calmly, accepting what is. Once I was apprehensive, but now I feel one with the Earth, one with the sky and stars. This is the great music of Nature, and the one singing at the wheel does not know the symphony he complements..

Then the sea began to calm, the vibrations lessened, and the boat's shudders faded away. Mark came back on deck and saw that they were rounding Point Couverden. Icy Strait was left behind, and they were beginning the next phase of the trip, up Lynn Canal.

He entered the wheelhouse to join Terry for coffee and sandwiches, which they had prepared earlier. Terry possessed an incredibly huge thermos; he carried it everywhere he went. Mark asked him about it, and Terry smiled as he washed down a bite of bread, bologna and cheese.

"Yes, I know," he answered, holding the thermos in his left hand and steering with his right. "When I was little, my folks never let me drink coffee. When I was older, though, I decided to get back at them, and before I knew it, I was a coffee freak. I felt rather important as well, because none of my friends ever drank coffee. I felt grown up when I was around them, with a cup of steaming coffee in my hand, while they drank pop."

He waved the big thermos around by its gigantic side handle, and Mark guessed it held about a gallon of liquid. "And now, if anyone asks me why I drink so much coffee, I'm content to say that I'm addicted to it. It's an easy way to defend myself, I suppose!"

Mark ate the rest of his lunch in silence.

They continued north, up the canal. Mark remembered that this was the deepest part of the big fjord, and mentioned it to Terry. The young man nodded, saying that it about three hundred and fifty fathoms to the bottom. "Around twenty-one hundred feet," he added, and the two looked over the side, as if they could somehow confirm the fact by doing so. Mark crept up to the bow once again, and Terry resumed his drawling tune, voicing something about the two of them driving the great highway of water. "We're on our way, sailing away, nah nah nah … Mark and Terry," he laughed. "Emmmm … and Teeee …." The sky had brightened considerably.

Mark watched the shore as they passed Funter Bay, and soon afterward, they rounded the lighthouse at Point Retreat. He stood up to get a better view, and then ….

He felt a *push*.

It didn't come from any particular direction; followed no vector. It was just a *push*, and Mark sensed that his Earth was talking to him. It was trying to tell him something, but he couldn't figure out what.

A huge number of seagulls came flying in from the west, and they zoomed over the troller at frightening speed. Another flock approached from the east, and likewise passed over the *Katzehin* at a greatly accelerated rate. Terry looked at them, scratched his head, and turned to Mark, who had left the bow and was moving aft, staring at the birds as they shrank in the distance.

"Strangest thing I've seen in some time. They don't usually do that."

Mark felt his heartbeat gaining strength and quickening its rhythm. "It was something, all right," he said. "I felt it …." He stopped, and Terry looked at him curiously. "What do you mean? Did you see something that I—" Terry never finished the sentence.

An explosion of spray to port, and then a large humpback whale breached less than forty feet from the troller. Terry yelled and grabbed the wheel, then pulled back on the throttle. The whale blew out a tremendous amount of air with a *pfffing* noise, its blowhole tightened, and the animal then dropped below the surface, its tail slapping the water. The wave created from its appearance struck the boat and turned it to starboard; Terry throttled forward again and swore.

Mark had seen the creature's eye, and it had stared directly into his. He held his hands together and said, in a quavering voice, "That was … incredible. Has that happened before?"

"Never!" Terry looked angry. "It didn't even seem to know we were here. Damndest thing I've ever seen!" He regained course, and Mark looked back over the stern, remembering the strange sensation, and then the gulls, and now this, a solitary humpback whale, tarrying in northern waters so late in the year, having yet to begin its migration to the lower latitudes. He knew his World was speaking to him.

Quite suddenly the mainland came into view, with the glacier and the peaks directly in front of them. Soon they were nearing Portland Island, and Mark saw, for just an instant, a patch of white in the northern meadow. It was the Easter rabbit, which he had seen with Dad, over four and one-half years ago.

He didn't point it out to Terry. He didn't see why he should. Terry probably wouldn't see it as a rabbit anyway. Mark watched as it melted away behind yellowed shrubs, and then it was gone. The boat was heading to the southeast, and soon it would come around the opposite end of the island and enter Auke Bay.

And then he saw, out of the corner of his eye, something quite odd. A large swell was coming at them from the west. Mark looked for a boat, perhaps a tug hauling a barge, but saw nothing. He called to Terry and pointed. The two watched as the lone wave drew closer and closer to the troller. It was about three feet in height, and Mark thought it was moving in an oily fashion. It struck the *Katzehin*, raised the boat slightly, and continued on in the direction of the bay. Terry shook his head and twisted his beard as the wave receded into the distance.

"Strangest thing I've seen in a long time," he murmured. Mark smiled, turned to his companion, and replied, "Didn't you just say that a while back?"

"Yes. Very interesting day."

Mark knew that. He knew something exciting was happening with his World, and whatever it was, he had sensed it and Terry had not. He sat once more, watching as they passed Coghlan Island and headed into Auke Bay, while the mass of the glacier became hidden behind the trees of the lowlands.

They came to one of the large docks, near the main launching ramp, and Terry slowed the craft and shouted. Mark looked at him, then followed the pointing arm with his eyes. A boat was on its side, on the ramp itself, and the car, along with its trailer, was half-submerged. People were standing around it, others were waving at Mark, and a few men were running down the planks in their direction. In the far distance, there were flashes of blue and red.

The troller bumped the pilings. Mark hopped off, began to tie up, then heard a familiar voice. Letting the dock hands take over, he walked past them and waved at Terry's wife, who was running straight at him.

"Hi." He stopped and looked at her. "What's going on? What caused that?" he asked, pointing at the damaged boat and car. "And why the emergency vehicle?"

Instead of answering, she grabbed Mark by the coat sleeve and tried to drag him back to the troller. Terry waved at them with his big thermos and began to say something about how good it was to see his beautiful honey-honey again, but she stopped him with a shake of her head.

"Didn't you have the radio on, or the two-way?" she yelled. Terry climbed onto the dock and came to her, arms wide. Mark reached over with his free hand and gently tried to loosen the vise-like grip on his cuff.

"What's wrong?" Terry asked as he kissed her cheek. "Who were those idiots?" he added, waving to the mess on the launching ramp.

"I'm trying to tell you! There was an earthquake, just a couple of hours ago. It caused that," she jerked her head. "And a lot more. Emergency power only, like the radio stations."

Mark let out his breath, very slowly. Of course … it all made perfect sense. His World had told him with a *push*, a flight of gulls, and the eyeball of a marine mammal. The signature on this message was the large swell from the west. "Jen," he said, most politely. "Can I have my hand back?"

§

He stood in the center of the backyard, straddling the long, narrow fissure that ran clear to the fence and beyond, to the woods. With his boot, he nudged a pebble to the edge of the crevice and watched it drop down to the bottom. And he took in a deep breath, looked up at the trees, at the top of Thunder Mountain, and at the clearing sky.

He was one with the Earth. They would never understand it all, those people in the house, or those in other houses, in this town or any other. He felt the sea motion, it rocked him slightly even as he stood now on "solid" ground, and he felt the salt spray as it washed over him. He felt the flight of the seagulls and the lurch of the whale, and he was part of them; had sensed what they had sensed.

Turning, he walked to the house and entered via the back door. Listening for voices, he crept through the dining area, came to the foyer, and peeked around the corner, his right hand touching the whatnot.

They were still picking things up from the floor. Dad and Mom and Amy. He watched as they gathered up broken glass, twisted picture frames, and figurines. Mom was saying something about the vacuum cleaner and about how the power would likely come back on in a little while so that she could use it to clean up a bit better. Dad was putting things back on top of the stereo cabinet, and he was muttering something about the local power company and not getting hopes too high. Amy was kneeling on the floor, facing away from him. Her long brown hair was touching the carpet, and Mark couldn't tell if she was repotting the African violet, or just crying silently.

He walked in and started to tell them he would help, but his mouth would not open. Dad saw him and grunted, "Guess you're pretty sorry you missed it all, huh?"

I miss nothing. I feel the Earth, I feel when it moves, when it shudders, and when it is happy, and when it is sad. I can tell you more about what has happened than you will ever understand, so there's no point in explaining it to you ....

He started; Mom was shaking him. "What's the matter with you? Your eyes! What just happened?"

He saw Dad looking in his direction. Amy turned to gaze at him, and he had his answer about what she'd been doing. Then he looked past them and saw the wall clock. It had survived without falling from its peg, but the pendulum hung motionless. He smiled; the s-waves had traveled through this house, sending the clock in horizontal undulations that canceled out the swing of ....

"Nothing is the matter. I already told you, I had a great day with Terry. And the Earth has moved, and you're upset about it, and I am not." He remembered the pilot's words. "You've just had yourselves another in a string of death-defying adventures." He giggled, becoming drunk on the atmosphere of his planet. He laughed harder and harder, sinking to the floor and vibrating as the spasms racked his body, and he cared not in the slightest what the family members thought, because at this moment, they were not his.

§

He'd liked all of it. After a night's sleep, he lay in bed and wished it was going to happen again. The plane trip, the wild waves, Terry's hopeless attempts at song, and all the rest. He wasn't supposed to remember just the Natural elements, he decided. He must remember it all. Comparison, analysis, just like the paramecium under a microscope ....

Most likely it was because yesterday had been in such violent, stark contrast to the usual routine of living. It had appealed to him, even the parts associated with Humans. There was a reason for that, but he wasn't going to waste his mind power. He knew very well that the comparison was important; was necessary for him to appear "normal" in the eyes of others.

After breakfast, he went outside into the chill air and got the large, double-headed axe from the storage van. Dad had cut a few hemlocks the week before, and Mark found himself staring at a half-cord of wood, ready to be split. He needed a release of energy, and here was the perfect job.

A difficult job, for sure. Spruce was much softer and would have been easier to work with. He set the first round on the chopping block and turned it until he was satisfied with its position. Then he stood back, measured the distance with the axe held outright, and swung.

The wood was fresh and soaking, and when the blade bit into the round, water was compressed and formed a line of foam on the surface, around the head of the axe. The contact had been quick, producing a dull thumping noise, and Mark knew immediately there would be trouble.

It took him twenty seconds to work the axe from the round, and then he went and got the sledgehammer and the wedge. He stuck the latter into the small split he'd made and struck with all his might, the hammer impacting the wedge with the sound of a gunshot. The wedge disappeared into the round of hemlock, which remained in one piece.

Mountain's sakes!!

Dad came to the back door and peered out to see what was going on. Mark saw him from the corner of his eye, and when the door opened, the boy was so angry that he shouted without thinking.

"Why the hell can't we get a splitting mall, like a normal person would have!"

Dad folded his arms and looked at him from the porch. Mark took a breath, set his jaw, and put the wood on the ground, where he would try and tap loose the wedge.

"And I'd just come out here to tell you I approve of your splitting the rounds, without me having to remind you. If that's your attitude, I'd rather do it myself. I fear for my equipment."

Dad's voice wasn't harsh, but Mark knew that could change with his very next comment. He shrugged, and as he went to work on the stuck wedge, he said "Sorry, but sometimes you can get discouraged when you foul things up on the very first piece."

Like a normal person?

Dad seemed to understand, and nodded as he turned to go back inside. Mark worked loose the wedge, and then split the round in half with the next mighty swing of the axe. And then he continued until he had split thirty rounds, into seven or eight pieces each. When at last he felt he couldn't take another swing, he stacked the freshly chopped wood and went inside for lunch.

Afterwards he went for a walk, taking Sheka with him. He headed over to the meadow, near Jordan Creek, following his own trail and wondering, how many people had taken this path in recent years not knowing, much less caring, about its origin? It was well-worn, leading through the meadow to the creek and continuing on past the old fishing hole, where he'd caught his first Dolly Varden. The pool no longer existed. The beavers' activity, though measurably less in recent years, had altered the flow of the stream to such an extent that it hardly resembled the place of long ago, when Doug had run, screaming ....

He went to the largest of the stick dams, crossed, and made his way to the very base of Thunder Mountain. He knelt and put his finger on the exact point where the angle steepened. But no longer did he wonder how many people had ever done *this*.

Sheka came over to him, from where she'd been nosing about, and he showed her the very beginning of the mountain. He grabbed her paw and stuck it where his finger had been, so that she too might sense the strangeness of the mountain that soared directly out of the Earth.

"I am sure that you understand it more than people do," he said quietly into her ear.

As he knelt there, he remembered the day, years before, when he'd slipped on the bank of the creek and seen the vision of the bear that had stood on the end of the dam, just as he fell into the water of the beaver pond. He remembered how he had felt after climbing out. Curiously at ease, he had been. And then he thought about his Second Pilgrimage, only two months in the past.

That day had been cold and damp, with the clouds hanging low on the peaks. He had struggled up the trail, through the gap and into the upper basins, to the lower reaches of his mountain God. And upon his arrival, the clouds had parted, as if by magic, though Mark was certain the Hidden Observer wouldn't put it quite like that. And he had knelt, as he was doing now, and had given thanks that the World had kept him safe for another year.

And again, while he'd stood there in the heights, time had been forgotten. And he'd viewed the southeast ridge of *the* mountain through eyes that did not seem his own, much like the vision he'd experienced the morning after the Commission. It was dusk before he'd returned to the house. He'd been given a new message, he was sure of it, but its details were a mystery.

There was a noise above him. He straightened, and as he did so, he heard voices. He drew Sheka next to him and peered into the trees, through the spruce boughs. The dog had her ears stiffened, and he watched her intently, musing on the possibility that she too was angered by the intrusion.

The voices again. And then Mark saw the form of two men, apparently a father and son, coming over the crest of the knoll above him. They carried rifles and wore small-frame packs. Pretending not to notice them, he walked about as if looking for something as they neared.

"Howdy," the older of the two called out, as they dropped to the floor of the Valley. They waved greetings, to which Mark gave a nod.

"Pretty cold up there," the younger man said. "We thought we could get ourselves a few ptarmigan, because of the early snow. Most of them are still splotched with brown, and they stand out easier." He motioned to the pack his father carried. "And we got some, all right!"

Mark nodded again. "How far down is the snow?" he asked. It was a stupid question; he knew exactly how far down the snow was. "Is it yet as far as the lower ridgetop, where you make that long traverse?" His mind showed him a picture of the silly blue mitten, which still hung on the small hemlock.

They nodded back. "Right to that point, in fact. Sounds like you've been up there recently."

"Not really. It's been a while," he sighed.

"Well, I'll tell you," the older man said. "I'm sure glad someone got the bright idea to put in this new trail. It sure makes the trip up there a heck of a lot shorter. Used to be ribbons marking the way, but some asshole forest ranger must have yanked them. Guess they didn't want another path tearing up the precious landscape. Huh! Since I found this path, Russ and I take it up there every year for our annual ptarmigan supply!"

Mark stood still, and then waved upward. "It's not that great of a trail. When I started it, I sent it straight up the ridge, aiming to connect it with the old one. Should have angled it off to the left, where it would hit the upper meadow, saving even more time, and making it easier on the legs."

They looked at him in disbelief. "You mean," said the younger of the two, who Mark decided was Russ, "that you started this path yourself? I can hardly believe it!"

"Why is that?" Mark's answer was barely audible. Above them, a raven let out a *groak*.

"I don't know," the young man shrugged. "I didn't know that anyone as young as me, or you, would ever bother to start a little old trail. It's more something for ...."

And Russ could think of nothing, Mark could tell. They told him to take care, and then they were off to the beaver dam and the meadow.

He shivered, petted his dog, and listened to them as they crashed through the underbrush; listened to their fading voices. When he knew they were almost out of earshot, he cupped his hands to his mouth.

"Yes! It was me who started that trail! And it was me who pulled the ribbons, do you hear? Damn you, anyway, this is my trail, and this is my domain! Don't you ever be coming back! Either of you! Don't you ever come back!"

§

That winter, the cold dry air failed to push its way down from the Yukon and through the coastal mountain ranges, and the weather remained warm. The temperature rarely fell below freezing, often reaching the upper forties in the afternoon.

To many, it was like spring in January. To Mark Nilsson, it was alarming.

Yes, he reasoned, Nature could act in strange ways, but until now he had always felt he understood. However, the warm clear nights he understood not at all. And he searched his mind, trying to decide what Nature was telling him.

One day he became involved in a verbal fight in the school library. He was suspended for the remainder of the week, after having cursed the librarian to the point of tears. He didn't care. What he'd said to her about Nature was the absolute truth.

And then there was the incident at Windfall Lake. During a rare three-day freeze, he'd decided to hike up there and do a little exploring. Two people he spied, at the far end of the lake, cutting holes and lowering their lines, while a large shepherd romped about them. With a horrid cracking sound, the ice split open in numerous places, and the two men and dog plunged into the freezing water.

Mark raced over and noticed the solid ice reaching to within a yard of where they splashed around. He dropped to a prone position, and extending his arms, grabbed first the struggling dog and helped it onto the ice. After making sure it was all right, he then turned his attention to the ones wearing clothes.

And that had gotten all over town.

§

For the next few weeks, he felt as though the eyes of the entire community were on him. His grades began to slip. He could almost see the near future, when the word had spread to the furthest corner of town, warning everyone to watch out for the Nature Boy.

At his afternoon job, he fouled up the paperwork on more than one occasion. He began to skip dinner, arriving home emotionally tired almost to the point of keeling over as he stepped into the furnace room. Sheka was always there to greet him, however, and the feel of her wet tongue against his dangling fingers was somewhat reassuring.

§

On a sunny day in late March, he decided to visit the pond. Sheka's nose felt rather warm, so he left her at the house. He chose to walk the distance instead of riding his bike, which lay forgotten in the storage van. Besides, he was sure the tires would be flat.

He hurried along, dressed in a pair of jeans and a sweatshirt. The birds of winter and spring, the year-rounders, having discovered the premature explosion of gnats and mosquitoes, were darting cheerfully past, and the sun, which rode the treetops in back of his neighborhood, felt a bit too strong for his liking.

The mountains rose as always. Their very presence eased his troubled mind, and the memory of what had just occurred was soon dissolved.

Amy had discovered one of his journals, and she had read the greater part of it before he caught her. He had not bothered to ask her if she understood it, and had simply thrown her physically from his room. Dad had retaliated by pointing him out of the house, telling him to go and cool off for a while before returning.

Mark approached the glacier and felt the massiveness of the scene close in around him. He ran to the parking lot and beyond, to the rock ridges. He hurried up the slope, past the observatory, and continued on to the quartz vein. And then he stopped, listened, and froze.

Someone was at his pond; he heard laughter.

He crouched, realized the uselessness of this action, and straightened up. He listened intently, as the anger built within him, but he could not identify the voices, as they were muffled by the rocks' echoic effect.

He stood in the quartz gully and tried to decide what to do. If he turned and left, that would indicate retreat, and never could he retreat from anything that was *his*. But if he walked up the slope and confronted the intruders, what would he say to them?

He made up his mind, and began to ascend the gully. As he went, he wondered to himself, just who would be up there at this time of the year, and what would they be doing? As he approached the top, his mind pounded as he thought about the previous October, when those ptarmigan hunter goofballs had disrupted his solitude. He looked nonchalant, almost doped up, as he stepped over the last line of cobbles, near the pond's edge. The tiny alders fell away, and he saw the water, the boulder, and in the distance, the Valley.

And he saw Kathy. She was standing near the boulder, watching as her little sister attempted to climb to its summit. Mark felt his jaw drop, and he couldn't help himself. He just stood and stared.

Kathy turned and spotted him. Smiling, she waved a greeting, and Mark gave a nod of his head.

"Howdy," she called out.

You are doing this to me. You are making me talk to those hunters again—why???

Kathy motioned to the little girl, who now stood atop the holy granite. In her filthy overalls, the child sat down upon Mark's throne.

"Isn't she fabulous? If Mom could see her, she'd faint. But she told me to take her out of the house and let her have a good time, so I did. And here we are!"

Mark walked around the pond, still unbelieving. His throat worked, and his voice came out as a modified squeak. "So what brings you up here, of all places?"

It must have sounded rude, but she seemed not to notice. Shrugging, she replied, "I needed to get away, and like I said, Mom was having one of her headache days. So I decided to bring Julie to the glacier and let her roam around. I haven't been here myself in, oh my, ages! I'd almost forgotten how beautiful it is. So anyway, we were walking down the path, and she ran up this hill, and before I could catch up with her, she called down for me to come and see the pretty lake.

"And I must say, it is very pretty indeed," she added, staring into the clear pool. "When I first saw it, I got this funny impression. I thought it looked just like a real lake. With mountains and all … sorry. Sound silly, don't I?"

Mark felt the sting of tears, and muttered, "Not really. I'm sure you're not the only one who's felt this way."

He turned and looked at the young woman who had invaded his domain, the same person he'd sat beside in the movie theater, so long ago. To his surprise, he saw that she was wearing black ear pins, perhaps the same ones ….

"I'm sorry," he began, and then his mouth stumbled. After a moment, he started again. "I'm sorry I haven't seemed so friendly over the past few years. I guess I have my moments, when I'm too into myself." He made a chuckling sound, knowing the laugh was made of plastic.

"Because I always did like you," he heard himself say. He began to shake.

"Mark! I want to ask you something. You don't have to say yes, but I was wondering if you'd come over next week and hear me recite. I don't know why, but I think you'd give the most honest review."

He accepted, though he felt no compulsion to do so. For a while they talked, and they watched as Julie tossed pebbles into the water. When he could stand it no longer, he forced a goodbye, and then he ran down the path to the road. He took off through the parking lot, which was occupied by a single car. Then he raced along the shoulder of the road, away from the glacier, and on down the Valley.

By the time he reached the house, he knew. He was shaking because he knew. The messages, delivered through a most friendly and most understanding entity, the Hidden Observer itself, were becoming crystal clear.

And that was what frightened him, because he absolutely knew what the voices were telling him.

When he'd struck Pat's cheek with his fist, long ago on the class picnic, he knew he would never get around to explaining it to Miss Reynolds. There was no point. She would never understand.

When he sat on the mountain heather and witnessed his six-year-old self arrive on the *Taku*, and when his six-year-old self stared back, into his then fourteen-year-old eyes, there was no way to explain that to anyone at all.

When the open boat and its lone occupant vanished, just offshore from the Tlingit burial ground, he knew what was coming, if only in the deepest cavity of his mind. He knew exactly what spirit haunted that place, and what it could do to the unwary.

And now, with his own World having been invaded … this was no fun game of countries and war, as had been the case when he and Jerry roamed the granite hills near his pond.

Countries and war.

In seventh grade, it was that bimbo airhead. Today, it was a girl he'd always liked.

This was not a temptation. This was a gentle warning.

CHAPTER SIXTEEN

The swallows arrived, and spring was officially underway. The air was warm, and the rainfall was mostly in the form of quiet drizzles. The snows of winter retreated up the mountain slopes, and the green shoots of the upper meadows, unable to wait another day, sprouted as one.

The spreading wood ferns unrolled, and in the shadows of giant stumps, the wild spinach became lush. The blueberry blossoms appeared and then, in a twinkling, they were gone. Out in the meadow, at the base of Thunder Mountain, the amber grasses of autumn had curled and faded, covered by snow during the winter and now resembling a slimy skin, while a new coat of weedy flora rose to meet the unseasonably warm weather.

During the last week of school, Mark had felt a growing numbness inside. It was a moment of truth, many of his peers would say, concerning the upcoming ceremonies of graduation, but he saw himself approaching the edge of a great precipice. What lay beyond, he dared not imagine. He tried to keep his mind on his World within, but it was becoming a much harder task, with each passing day.

He turned the combination lock, opened the door, and threw in his books. Beside him, Jeff did the same. Mark waited for him to react in some way to his last sentence, but instead there was a great cry, and Jeff reached down and picked up something from the floor of his locker.

"Look at this! I was supposed to mail this a week ago, and I must have stuffed a blank one in the envelope by mistake. I'm going to die!"

Mark looked. It was a college application, and inside himself, he gave a little smile. He pictured the faces in some distant admissions office when they opened up a blank application.

"Don't worry. You still have time. Though I'm not too confident of your GPA, if you want to know the truth."

Thanks a lot, Jeff's look told him. Mark hauled out the little daypack, which contained tennis shoes, an extra t-shirt, and his personalized set of ball point pens, which he used at work. He slammed the door shut, started off down the hall, and shouted best regards over his shoulder.

And three hours later, he was riding home with Dad. He stared out the sedan's window, his mind on what had happened in the school cafeteria.

Passing by there after his final class, he had stopped, for through the window of the cafeteria door, he saw one of the janitors mopping. He observed the elderly man, a native Tlingit, and followed the sweeping motions over the wet floor. Then he watched his hand push open the door, and he watched his legs take him across the room to where the old man created the s-shapes of water and disinfectant.

"May I ask you something?"

The janitor raised his head and nodded. Mark sucked his tongue for a few seconds, and then he talked. When he was finished, the custodian paused his mopping, then smiled a faint smile and beckoned Mark to come closer.

"See what I do?" The gnarled fingers moved about. "It is called work, and for all my life I have worked. It is not the work of my ancestors, but it is work all the same. Long ago, my people worked to make clothes, we worked to bring in the catch of salmon, we worked to carve our World's history into the living trees. Our work was our life's calendar.

"And now I do this work, because I am alive only because I do so. I am not yet ready to give my spirit to the earth and sky, or to any animal, so that I may revisit. Yes, I still search for answers, and for"—his voice lowered to just above a whisper—"the truth created by Kah-shu-goon-yah. I can still hear the faint voices of the spirits who lived on this land many centuries before my people, even though history does not record their existence. They cry out across all of time, and I can hear them today."

He stopped and looked into Mark's eyes for a moment, then continued.

"You hear them, don't you? That is good." A pause. "I believe Kush-Ta-Ka will harm you never."

Mark nodded, mumbled thanks, and turned back to the cafeteria door, his mind on fire. Only when he reached the hall did it occur to him that he had just walked over the surface of wet floor, and the old Tlingit would have to mop it again. He felt tears on his cheeks, and tried to wipe them before anyone else noticed. He knew how awful his thoughts could be at times, such ugly thoughts concerning the other people occupying the same planet as himself. He knew the old man in the cafeteria deserved much better from him. That man, that custodian, was a descendant of the people who had populated this area for thousands of years, people who knew as much about life and spirits as anyone else.

He had reached his locker to find Jeff there, and he had told him what the janitor had said, and Jeff had replied with something senseless, and Mark had replied in turn, and then Jeff had noticed the college application down there among his things ….

"What?" He turned his head. Dad had asked him something, but he didn't catch the words.

"I said, did you ever go ahead and apply for the other two scholarships? You had mentioned something about today being the deadline."

They were headed down the new expressway, toward the Valley. Mark let his eyes travel to the window once more, to watch the saltwater marsh. "Didn't figure I had a chance. From reading over the material, I decided that I didn't even qualify."

He knew Dad was putting on his usual frown, though he didn't look around to see. His eyes left the marsh and followed a thin line of hemlock that marched up the eastern face of Thunder Mountain. He wished he was there, not in the passenger seat of this car.

"But you're still certain of your choice?" Dad continued to shoot questions, and Mark became irritated. He knew that it showed, right through the back of his head, but he didn't care.

"Truly, it would be better if you and Mom didn't keep after me about it. It's starting to sound like a soap opera, and it's driving me up the wall, through the ceiling, and across the attic!"

A moment later they were at the house. Mark had hardly entered when the phone rang, and Mom announced that it was for him.

"Tell them to call back later," he said as he passed through the den.

As he reached his room, he heard Mom say, in a light voice, "It's a girl!"

"I don't care if it's the president," he muttered aloud. He threw himself on his bed and wished he'd lived his physical life hundreds of centuries ago, long before even the Tlingit people had first seen the magnificent peaks that rose above them in silent splendor.

§

Graduation went smoothly. Afterward, he regained his full-time status at work, and a few weeks later he was surprised when awarded a two-day vacation. Gladly he took it, making plans to get away for a while. He headed out from the Auke Bay ferry terminal aboard the *Columbia*, with Sitka as his destination.

Much of the eight-hour trip was in darkness. That suited him fine. He stood by the vessel's stern, watching the phosphorescent wake streaming behind. The mountains were like black ghosts, sliding by to starboard and port. He realized, after a while, that the ship were heading through that deepest section of Lynn Canal, where it was over three hundred fathoms to the bottom.

The railing was cold, but he didn't notice. He hugged it tightly and continued to stare out into the night. He felt hypnotized, and was at the point of falling asleep, when he became aware of someone beside him.

She was about a year younger than himself, he supposed. Her hair was short and black, and apparently she was just as immune to the cold night air as himself, for she wore nothing over her print t-shirt. He nodded to her and waved out over the water.

"Lonely, but beautiful just the same. Know what I mean?"

And she surprised him by saying, "Yes. Exactly what I was thinking myself. Where are you going?"

"To Sitka."

"Really?" She turned and faced him. "That's where I live. You know people there?"

"Well, no. Some friends of ours moved over there when I was very young, but I haven't kept in touch." He smiled to himself. He wasn't a local, so what would she say next?

"You must be from Juneau."

"How could you know that?" he asked, intrigued.

"I just do. I don't know how to explain it, but every town in the panhandle has its own personality, to me anyway. You fit Juneau best, I say."

He could tell she was having fun. And he drew in his breath, his mind working quickly. If it was all right with his Gods, he would have a little fun himself. Why not let her know? Most likely he would never see her again. In this case, he figured, there was nothing to lose.

"So, you can tell that much about me, huh?" He looked into her eyes, which were as dark as the night itself. "I hate to disappoint you, but you've seen only a part of me. And what you saw was a false covering. I'm not what you think I am, not at all."

She was grinning back at him. "What do you mean by that?" she asked, trying to hold back a laugh.

"It'll take time to explain. Here, let's walk and talk." He motioned her away from the stern, and they walked up the portside deck.

"By the way, did you get on the ship at Auke Bay?" he asked as they pushed their way against the headwind, slowly making their way forward.

"Yeah. My mother had to attend a business seminar, and she asked me to come along with her. It gave me a chance to get away for a while."

"I see. And tell me, what do you think of my town?"

She was quiet for a moment, then said, "I think it's all right, but it seems big to me. I'm used to something a lot quieter. But I guess it's a good place to make friends."

He slowed his step. "Is that all?"

"I guess," she said again. "What were you expecting?"

He spread his arms. "That's just it. You come to my town, and what do you see? You see a town, that's all. You didn't see the majestic peaks, or the sprawling glaciers, did you? You didn't feel the overwhelming power of Nature around you, how it closes in, embraces the community, reminds the lowly Humans that It … that's right, It … capital 'I' … is the one that dominates."

He paused, then said "You didn't see that, did you?"

When she started to answer, he cut her off. "No, of course you didn't. You were going to say that it isn't in your mind to think such things. The excitement of the trip itself, new places, new people, new streets, new stores, new snack shops. What room is left for the World itself?"

They went inside and walked through the darkened passageways. She was silent, as if trying to figure him out, and as he watched her, he became more and more impatient.

"No, don't try to present an argument. There isn't a single one you'll find successful. You see, you have met what society calls a Nature Boy. His World is that of the plants, the animals, and the soaring mountains. And the stars that surround him, from which he is made. His mind feels the Earth at work. It gives him strength. He is all but severed from the world of homo sapiens."

"Well," she said. "At least I can say this about you. You're certainly not the usual type of guy that I meet. I can already tell that your brain works on the level I wish most others' would."

He could hardly believe what he was hearing. He had expected to receive nothing but a look of bewilderment, as she would be completely baffled by his speech.

"Come here," he said, a bit loudly, and escorted her back outside, onto the starboard deck. The *Columbia* was heading due south, nearing the end of Lynn Canal, and the mountains to the west were low on the horizon. The stars hung brightly in the blackness of space.

"You see that? Up there. That bright yellow star—you see which one I mean?"

"Uh, yes." She put a hand above her eyes to block out the ship's lights.

"The name of that star is Capella. It's part of the constellation of Auriga. It, like the sun, will soon be nearing the end of its Class G position in the Main Sequence. Do you follow me?"

"No"

"And do you see that hazy line, running across the entire arc of the sky?" He demonstrated with his arm. "Right there?"

"Yeah, I can see it."

"That's the Milky Way. Our galaxy. It's composed of over a hundred billion stars. And beyond are a hundred billion more galaxies. Most people can't begin to imagine numbers that large, but I can. And the reason is simple. I know that I am, in fact, composed of every atom of every one of—"

"Really, that's the Milky Way? You mean all that fuzzy line is billions of stars? No one's ever shown that to me before!"

What is going on?

"Yes," he said, feeling subdued. "You're looking through the plane of the galaxy." He felt his hands shaking. He was getting ready to come apart.

The ferry turned sharply, and for a moment they were bracing themselves against the railing. When the force lessened, Mark looked at her and groped for something new to say, something to wipe that smile off her face.

"Do you have a dog?"

She nodded. "Rinky, that's his name. I've had him for about five years."

"That's good. How many times, in the past five years, have you sat down with Rinky and had a good talk with him?"

"I talk to him every day. Oh, I see what you mean, really talk to him, like he's another person? Well, I'd feel a little foolish. But if you're saying that's what you do with your dog, it's fine with me!" She smiled more brightly than before, and her face looked prettier than ever.

That's it! If she insists on relating to me, I am prepared to go all the way.

He drew close to her and said, in a low voice that came from deep within, "All right. If that's the way you see it, I congratulate you. Now you try to picture this."

He paused for effect, then continued. "I want you to think about someone. Not just anyone. I want you to think about someone who means something to you. Go ahead, think the dearest thoughts you possibly can. Well? Are you thinking?"

She nodded; did in fact appear to be in some sort of reverie.

"Must be someone nice."

"Oh yes. It is."

"Good. Now let's say this trip is over, you've arrived back home, and then soon afterward, you find out this person has died."

He stopped and waited for her reaction. It didn't take long; the smile disappeared, and she took a step backwards.

"What! What do you mean?"

"Didn't you hear me? I said died. Dee–Eye–Eee–Dee."

She looked startled, confused, and full of anxiety, all at the same time. Mark nodded to her for a full ten seconds before continuing.

"You see, it sounds awful, doesn't it? Now, I didn't mean to hurt your feelings, or scare you. But why don't you ask me the same thing?"

She looked at him, the black eyes slowly returning to their normal shape. "How would it affect you?" He could tell that she already knew the answer.

He said slowly, deliberately, "Because, in the first place, I am no longer burdened by such thoughts as caring for others. What I care about is this!" And he spread his arms once more, taking in the entire dark world around them.

"Listen to me. I tell you the truth, but whether you choose to believe me isn't even important. But ask me this, will you? Ask me what would happen, and what would I do, if suddenly Capella exploded, and was no longer there? What would I do? I don't know." And his voice began to quaver. He breathed once, then twice. "I might not … might not understand how to live anymore."

He stopped, and then said, "What do you think of that?"

She looked up at the night sky, and in a voice as shaky as his own, replied "I don't even see it now."

He turned, craned his neck, and looked for himself. And he gasped. Capella was hidden behind a small, dark cloud.

He turned back, staring with an expression on his face that he knew must have scared her. But why did she not run from him? It was unreal.

And so he ran from *her*. He ran up the deck until the curve of the vessel took him from her sight. He ran indoors, down the stairs, past the staterooms, and on to the furthest corner of the ship. He slumped down at the end of the passageway, burying his head in his hands.

Six years earlier, Fran had died, and Mark had felt miserable. Was he saying that if the tragedy had occurred this year, he wouldn't have been upset, not in the slightest? He knew the answer, so why was he asking himself the question?

The ship's vibrating motion had a gentling touch on his nerves, and on his mind. He fell asleep and remained so for a long time.

When he awoke, he was startled and got up quickly. It was morning, he knew,, and he made his way back to the outer deck. He stood and looked at the shoreline, searching for the familiar landmarks that would tell him the ship's position. The ferry was entering Neva Strait, and just ahead was Whitestone Narrows. As he hugged the railing, with the cool morning air rushing past him, he thought about what he'd said last night, to that girl.

He wondered if he should feel ashamed, then shook his head. No, he should not! She'd asked for it, grinning at him like that, as if she could handle anything he could dish out. Well, now she knew!

And then he saw her walking up the deck. She stopped a couple of yards from him and grabbed the rail herself, as if she had not spotted and recognized him. They looked at the water, watched as the rolling bow waves took off and angled into the distance, only to smash against the rocky shore.

Finally, it was she who spoke. "By the way, my name is Paula. I didn't get yours."

"Mark."

She slid along the rail until she was beside him. "You can never convince me. I still think you're normal enough for me to like. More than most guys I've ever known. More than my boyfriend—" she made a face. "I mean, my ex-boyfriend."

He watched the seaweed float past the ship. "Yes, that would make a difference."

And he turned to her. "Unfortunately, it shall never happen that I'll meet another like me. I think there may be a few more …." He hesitated, grabbing the railing a bit more tightly. "But … we can't find each other." The memory of the strange dream, with the line of people streaming toward *the* mountain, flashed through his soul. "I can't describe that. I wish I could, but I can't. I'm afraid this world is too far gone."

And then she said something that truly caught him by surprise. "Well perhaps, if we're lucky, we can start over. Maybe not here on Earth, but perhaps up there near that star … Capella, wasn't it?"

Mark had no choice but to wear a smile, if only a tight one. And a short while later, the *Columbia* blew the arrival horn and pulled up to the Sitka terminal. Mark and Paula said their goodbyes, and she started off in search of her mother. Then she stopped, came back, and said something else. "Last night, it was you I was thinking of."

His eyes widened; he couldn't say a word.

"You told me to think of someone nice, so I did." She turned and was gone.

Mark took a bus downtown and spent the next few hours poking about on the beaches, following the trails in the city parks, and walking through the streets. In the early evening, he returned to the terminal and caught the *Matanuska* for home.

§

He stood on the ship's promenade deck, looking for Capella, but it wasn't visible in the cloudy sky. Astronomers would tell him that if indeed he was to see his star explode, the event itself had occurred more than forty years ago, long before the date on his birth certificate.

He knew better. There was no explaining it in words, but he knew the truth. He knew the explosion would occur at the instant he witnessed it, for time meant absolutely nothing to waves of light, nor to the faint voices he detected, the voices his own species would deem ancient and unimportant. Birth and rebirth were forever entwined.

§

All was quiet at the pond. Mark sat on the granite rock, looking into the water. Behind him, the clouds were pushing up into the Valley, and they were tall, with flat bases. The air was unusually warm and sticky, and the wind was aloft, doing very little to rustle the leaves of the alder shrubs.

Hundreds of yards away, across hills and ravines, was the boulder canyon, where Steep Creek rushed between the vertical walls. But he could not hear it, or would not hear it, from where he sat and was one with his World.

For just a moment, Kathy had visualized the pond as something different. But only for a moment. He alone saw what it saw, and he alone could listen as it spoke to him.

He looked up and gazed over Mendenhall Lake, to the face of the glacier. As he stared at it, a huge section gave way and calved into the water. There was an eerie pause as the ice dropped out of sight, and then suddenly the white surge leaped upward, and the sound raced through him and echoed about the little rock hills. The newly formed berg came back to the surface, bobbed softly for a time, then slowly began to drift to the center of the lake.

His heart slowed down, and his hands, which had clutched the boulder tightly, relaxed. He wiped his brow, and at the same time, he felt the sun go cold against his back. Twisting, he saw the dark forms of the clouds bumping along Thunder Mountain. As he watched them, he felt a great unease. There was something foreign about those clouds, and as he puzzled over what it might be, they boiled overhead and continued on, northward over the glacier.

Now there was a slight wind factor, and his chilled skin moisture set him to shivering. He heard another booming sound, and turning around again, he looked for the inevitable water surge.

There was none. He waited, thinking he'd missed it, when yet another boom, like the sound of cannon, rocked through him.

And he stared upward, unbelieving. A quick flash of yellow light he saw, above the ice. And then the sound hit him. He slid off the boulder, stood, and shivered once more. His shaking continued as he made his way down the path, and then to the road, on his way back to the house.

It was the thunder that could never come.

§

At lunch hour, he hurried from the office and ran down to the waterfront. He found himself a secluded place near the end of an old wharf, sat down, and ate his sandwich. He gazed at the peaks across the channel, and he looked at their wavering reflections in the gray-green water. And he remembered what had happened yesterday at the pond, and what he'd said to Sheka, after returning to the house.

"Come here, doggie. That's it, here, I'll rub your ears while we talk. You see, I'm scared, and I don't know what it is, what is happening all around me. My Gods, I made my break, and I became one with Nature, and suddenly it seems like the people understand me anyway! What is it, Sheka, tell me if you can."

He had started to cry. "And then Nature itself pulls a trick on me, as if it's telling me something. But I don't know what. Just when I needed it most …."

After he finished eating, he crumpled the brown paper bag, stuffed it into the large pocket on his sweater, and got up. He felt the creosote stick to his pants, but didn't stop to pick it off. He walked along the wharf, passed by the couples and small groups who sat and laughed with one another, and then he headed toward the main business district. He hadn't gone two blocks when he ran into Scott.

"Well, speak of the devil," Scott motioned to him. "Richard and I were just talking about you. We were over at the cleaners, where he's trying to get a job. I told him that they'd first have to run *him* through, once or twice, before considering!

"But anyway, where have you been lately? Was trying to find you last week, even called you once, but it rang, and rang, and rang. Oh, wait! You all were at the fair in Haines, weren't you?"

"The others were." Mark's reply was murmured, and he was looking at the sidewalk. "I went camping over the weekend. I got back when they did, and they were angry because of the crowds, and then my sister wandered off, and they couldn't find her." He paused, then glanced up.

"So, what were you so excited about, that you needed to get hold of me?"

"Wasn't just me. Oh, I thought maybe you'd like to go over to Admiralty and do some trout fishing. We went there last weekend and got some really nice rainbows." He spread his hands to demonstrate the length.

"But like I was going to say, you remember Jerry? Well, he was in town last week. I didn't see him, but Richard noticed him, across a parking lot. Said he was more than six feet tall! Don't know if he was here for more than a day."

"That's all right," Mark said under his breath. "Well, I better get back to work." He glanced at his watch and saw that it was only half past twelve. He cursed inwardly.

Scott didn't seem to notice. "Sure. See you around later, Mark. But just in case I don't, take care, you hear? Good luck at college!" And then Scott was gone, around the corner where the old theater remained open for business.

Mark remained still for a moment, right there on the sidewalk. The sun broke through the clouds, and in the distance, the droning sound of a float plane, as it raced down the channel, reached his ears. He turned on his heel and walked back to his office. He didn't have anything else to do.

And later, he was at the house. Dinner was already prepared, as Mom had assigned Amy the housework. He ate with the family and tried to ignore the sinking feeling that had been growing stronger inside, with each passing day. He stopped chewing for a moment. Was it really days? Or was it weeks, or years?

He went to the living room and curled up in the rocker, with the evening paper before him. He picked it up and began to hunt for the weather page, then stopped and tossed the paper aside.

Dad cued a record. It was Stravinsky's *Firebird,* and Mark let himself drift along with the music. In his mind, he pictured the scene; saw a young man about to kill a lovely bird so that he might possess the wonderful feathers. And the bird's pleading, and when spared, rewarding the man with just one of the feathers, which would protect him against evil. And of course evil did appear, but the young man wore that coat of protection and was able to dispose of the sorcerer.

As he listened to the suite, he wondered about his own World, and whether it really protected him. He began to understand just how scared he really was, and he curled himself tighter in the rocking chair.

Dad saw him shifting uncomfortably from one position to another and said, over the loudening end passage of the suite, "What's the matter with you? Have a bad day at work? Something's definitely got you itched."

Mark found himself replying, "Every day's a bad day at work. I must go and do what they wish. Can't you see what that does to me? Not to other people, I said. To me!"

He wasn't sure Dad had heard everything, over the noise of the glorious brass. And Dad showed no reaction.

A few minutes later, while looking for another selection, Dad asked him something else. "I've been wondering, why haven't you been working on your rockets anymore? You were getting pretty good at your designs. That one you had was pretty spectacular. So much in fact, it took off and never came back, right?" He turned and grinned. "You make them any better than that, you're going to have to go out to Eagle Beach to launch them, where there's plenty of room."

"I loved that rocket!" Mark shouted. "And all you can do is to make fun of it? Mountain alive, look at you, sitting there grinning. You'd never in your life begin to understand what that rocket was, or what it meant! So you think you can picture just about anything I might have to tell you about, hey? Because you've probably had a similar thing happen to you, long ago, or perhaps the other day?" Mark trembled as he spoke, knowing exactly why he could remember those very words Dad had spoken, nine years in the past *as other people measured time*. He could see that Dad was stupefied, and so he continued, very much recklessly.

"No, you know nothing of a pond, and a boulder … that lie in a very reclusive location, where I'm sure you've never been! And even if you have, what would you make of it? Nothing that would be of interest to me! Could you know, even begin to know, how important that pond and that granite boulder are, to your second son? So important, I'll tell you, that maybe we'd better alter our thinking to the point where we speculate that perhaps you have only *one son*, only one in the world!"

He jumped to his feet, turned and stumbled on the carpet. Mom and Amy were in the den, looking at him incredulously. He expected to hear Dad's roaring voice, telling him to get back in the living room, to sit down and listen carefully. He heard not a thing. There was horrible silence as he bolted past his mother and sister, tripped over a chair leg as he ran through the dining area, and fought with the back door knob. He jumped off the porch, Sheka came to meet him, and together they left the yard, left the neighborhood, and moved into the shadows of twilight.

They were not heading for the pond. They were going to the meadow.

When they arrived, he was panting as hard as the dog. As he caught his breath, he saw something large and yellow in front of him. It was a frontloader, and nearby, another hunk of yellow machinery. It was a backhoe. And further away, a bulldozer. Red and yellow tape he saw, in the distance, as far as Jordan Creek.

Neighborhood expansion; the meadow would exist no more. Gone forever would be the birds, the ermine tracks, the rabbit grounds, the entrance to his trail. Maybe the creek itself. He fell to the ground, with his eyes shut, and felt the Earth with his hands. He dug into the moss and sobbed, while Sheka whined and licked his ears.

§

He stopped writing in his journals and ripped them up. He tore the papers to shreds, tossed them into the fireplace, and set the pile ablaze.

The next day, he played sick from work and spent the afternoon wandering about the Valley. Most of the time he was either crying or very close to it. He stared at Thunder Mountain, the glacier, the mighty peaks around it, and the tall spruce that swayed ever so gently in the cool breeze. He blinked and looked at the flat clouds that brought the drizzle into the Valley. Soaked to the skin, he listened to the birds as they darted for cover.

He dared not look at *the* mountain. He waited until he knew it was covered by the blanket of gray, then sighed a lonely sigh.

He entered the woods and slopped through a mucky bog until he reached a point well out of sight of the loop road. He stopped and sat himself on a rotted log. It was still raining, and giant drops pelted him as they dripped from the upper branches of the towering evergreens. The air was dank, even in its wetness, with a musty odor that no amount of precipitation could wash away.

He ran his hand along the log, then dug his nails into the orange-colored rot. He brought his hand to his face, looking at the organic matter. He prayed to it, silently, asked it to come to the rescue and save him. In his entire life, he had never felt more empty.

In front of him was a blueberry bush, ripe with fruit. He picked one of the purple spheres, brought it close to his eyes, and observed it. He held it between two fingers and slowly squished it until the red pulp, with the tiny seeds, ran over his palm. He watched the stain develop, studied it for a long time, then drew the berry to his mouth, tasting its watery goodness.

As he did so, he felt a shock pass through him, and suddenly there was a fleeting vision, of another place and another time, when he was bringing something else close to his lips—maybe bread—and it was much colder than today … and then a clanging sound, like a bell ….

Then it was gone, and as he swallowed the berry, he wondered if his Gods watched him. Could the Hidden Observer feel sorrow, a deep sadness that manifested itself, in diluted form, within the souls of people, plants, and animals? Or was this Hidden Observer nothing more than a lifeline thrown by the Creator, a celestial rope with a monitor—some sort of camera—attached? Could the Hidden Observer weep, or was it the ancient voices shedding those tears, tears made not of water but of consciousness itself?

Mark knew that earthly languages, specifically words, were inadequate to describe what the ancient voices were saying. A perfect setting, a final gate, a portal that most could never pass through. Worry, concern, and aspiration with its pitfalls. Was the Hidden Observer unable to change things for the better; could it do nothing more than watch, wait, and allow the voices to touch whatever they could?

His brown hair was streaked down his forehead and into his eyes. He sat on the log, his mind going blank as he hunched over, the raindrops pelting his back, until he began to ache and grow stiff. Then he rose, wiped his eyes, and slogged his way back to the loop road. Walking along its shoulder, he was splashed by every passing car. He walked until he felt ready to drop; the rain increased. He shivered, and the salty tears flew in all directions, mingling with the fresh water that fell from the sky, Nature's own tears, the Tears of Joy. After a couple of hours, he found that he had wandered back to the house, and the rain had stopped.

As he climbed onto the back porch, he heard the sound of heavy equipment in the meadow.

The house was cold. Dad was on vacation, and the family had gone downtown to shop and see a movie. He made a fire, and then went to the kitchen and cooked himself something to eat. And then, when he had warmed himself and filled his stomach, he went to bed. He cried to his pillow until he was asleep, then woke with a start. He hurried to the back door and called for Sheka, who came running. He let her in, and then he returned to bed, with the red berry stain on his hand.

When he awoke once more, it was dawn. He thought he had dreamed, but he couldn't remember what it was about. That was all right. If it was a nightmare, it was faded and gone, redistributed to someone else. If it contained another warning, he didn't want to know.

§

As he stepped off the bus, he could hear the arrival horn of the *Taku*. He hurried to the waterfront, where he stood and watched as the vessel swung around in a giant arc and head for the terminal, just as it had done that unforgettable first day, when he'd looked out from its forward lounge and seen a town, a mountain, and a keyhole in the world itself.

He stood there for a long time. Then behind him, there was the sound of a car horn. He turned and saw Jeff waving at him. He went over and got into the compact, and Jeff told him to check his watch more often, or else he'd be looking for another job.

"And besides, I've got some hot news."

Mark knew that his voice would be tired, sounding as though it came from far away. His throat was sore, and he mumbled but one word. "What?"

"I got accepted! I'm on my way to Corvallis!" Jeff beamed proudly and rapped the horn again.

"Oh, that's hot."

Jeff looked at him, then turned back quickly as he wheeled around the corner. "You look like you've been sick. You think you should even be working today?"

Mark swallowed, and grimaced. "So I look sick. You used to say that every day. When I thought I looked just fine. What gives?"

"Good lord, Mark! I'm sorry, but I can't act like an eighth grader all my life."

The words might have stung him, at some other time, or in some other place. Today, he gave no sign of even having heard the comment. Jeff braked the car to a halt, outside Mark's office.

"Well, take medicine. Other than that, you sound hopeless." Jeff saluted him, and Mark opened the passenger door, stepped outside and turned. He shut the car door and looked through the open window.

"Did you hear what you just said?" The words came out in a flat monotone, and they seemed to take a long time to travel the four feet that separated the young men. "You just made a very astute observation. Because I am hopeless. Please do not cry for me. I've already done enough of that for hundreds, maybe thousands. Bye, Jeff." And the car slid away. Mark stood there, and once again he was trembling.

He turned for a last look at the peaks before he went indoors. The clouds were high, and the forecast for tomorrow was good. He nodded to himself as he opened the glass door.

The morning dragged by. The papers began to pile up, and he scanned the reports as carefully as possible, looking for errors. He was so good at that, wasn't he? He nursed on a soft drink and fought the urge to dream.

When lunchtime came, he walked along the streets. He wasn't hungry, merely content to drift along, glancing now and then at the window displays, their artificial contents sneering at him. He saw Tina, and they talked for a moment. She too was concerned about his state of health, and he grumbled to her that he would be just fine in the morning. She told him that she had finally made up her mind on what to do this fall. She would not attend school. She figured she'd just work for a year, and then make up her mind again. And didn't he agree that it was—for her at least—the best thing to do?

"Oh, of course. Take care, Tina. I'd kiss you, but I don't want to spread disease."

"Mark! It's just a sore throat."

But that wasn't what he meant. He wandered away from her, and eventually he was back at the office. And once again he delved into the stacks of paper. He had been at work for an hour when his phone rang. It was his boss. He was informed that next week he would be training several others to type the daily reports. Yes, he was told, that was in addition to his proofreading duties. Sorry, he was told, there would be no additional pay. It was just the way things had to be this time.

He put the receiver down on its cradle. And he continued to scan the papers, one by one. Outside, a homeless man walked slowly by the window, then stopped, and Mark watched him vomit onto the sidewalk. He sipped his cola, which irritated his throat all the more. And his mind waited calmly, for what was to come.

Finally, it was half past four. He knew so because he had just looked at the clock. And suddenly, for an instant, he was back in the first grade, and he was watching the big clock on the wall, telling time by the hand positions, understanding in a manner unknown to adults that he—not time—

was the mover. His mind had moved quickly back then, and then it had moved more slowly, even as his sled moved faster down the snow-covered slope, and now his mind was moving more quickly than ever before. He breathed heavily, felt another crying period coming on, and struggled to keep himself in control.

How he wished it to be true. He'd do anything to move back in time, when he was sitting at the little desk in his elementary school, laughing with the other boys and girls as he experienced life completely free of contaminant nightmares. Not here, in a tug-of-war between two worlds. He nearly choked, then got up quickly, grabbed his jacket, and left.

He walked across the street, which was heavy with rush hour traffic. Entering the building on the other side, he went straight to the desk of his manager, who looked up at him, surprised.

"I'm sorry," Mark said thickly. "But I can't come here anymore."

The man's eyes narrowed, and he put a hand on his necktie. "What do you mean, Mark?"

"Can't you hear? I said I QUIT!!" And Mark left before any more could be spoken. Outside, the sun was breaking through the clouds, and its beams hit him in the face. He ran up the street, turned the corner, and raced along for several blocks, jumping in front of cars and ignoring the honks of afternoon commuters. He galloped along until he was across town from the office, and then he slowed and finally stopped, resting for a moment against a heavy brick wall.

Out of the corner of his eye, he spotted the red sedan and could see Dad at the wheel. The car went past him, and he was glad he'd escaped notice. He leaned against the cold brick and felt the pounding in his raw throat. Finally he walked away, heading for the nearest bus stop.

He was almost there when he heard his name called. Looking over his shoulder, he saw Debbie and Stefany across the street. They were waving at him, and as he watched, they looked for traffic, then raced across to him.

"Mark, I'm so glad we got a chance to see you again before we left!"

He nodded, and mumbled, "Hello."

"Really," Debbie added. "You're certainly invited to the party tomorrow night, at my place. It'll be fun, yeah?"

He looked at her but didn't reply.

"Mark, are you okay? You don't look too well." Puberty had done nothing to Stefany's weird voice.

"I'm fine," he answered. Stefany took a step toward him, her hand coming up slightly. That also hadn't changed.

"Debbie," he said in a low voice. "Can I ask you something?"

"Sure, what is it?" She looked at him questioningly, and so did Stefany.

"You've known me a long time. And you never did like me very much. No, I'm not going to ask you why. What I want to know is why you're acting so friendly now. And you, Stefany. Talking to me one day, then managing to avoid me in the halls for weeks on end. Look at you now. Acting so sad that we're all going separate ways in the near future. What's the matter? You see something in me that you missed before?"

The girls were silent for a moment. Then Debbie moistened her lips and said, quite deliberately, "I guess we've grown up, Mark. To be honest, I must say that you're a hell of a neat guy. Somewhat mysterious, but neat. And maybe that's just it. What we thought was strange then, we respect now. Isn't that what happens when you find yourself maturing? Mark?"

He looked in her direction, then toward her companion. Through all the years he'd known her, Stefany's legs were absolutely gorgeous beyond description. Today he saw the pavement behind her.

His bus would be arriving in a moment. If he was going to say something, he knew it would have to be fast. So he said it, quickly.

"No. You're so wrong it's pitiful. Look at yourselves. What's changed? All that's on your brain is your party tomorrow night. Easy, isn't it, to stand here and sound intellectual as hell, because you know I expect it from you. But in twenty-four hours, well? You'll probably be stoned out, or worse. Am I not right? Now, excuse me, I have a bus to catch."

Debbie shook her head at the street, and grabbing Stefany by the arm, she started away. The other girl cast a look back in Mark's direction, and she tried to say something. Mark saw a pleading in her eyes.

He turned away, walked to the curb as the bus pulled up, and joined the line of commuters. He dug into his pocked for the correct change, and by the time the coins clinked into the farebox, he had regained his normal breath. The ache in his throat was gone. The clouds were nearly so.

§

He sat in the seventh row, on the right-hand side of the bus. It was an express, and it carried him along the causeway toward the Valley. Thunder Mountain rushed forward to meet him.

For now, he'd forget the woods, the towering evergreens and the flora that lived in their shadow. He'd forget what was left of the meadow, and the creek, and he would forget the pond. The pond. It would be all right for the time being, and so would the granite boulder. They would look after themselves, and they would know he was doing what had to be done.

He was far from crying now. The sun felt warm, as its rays passed with ease through the glass windows, heating the air inside the bus. The sky was blue and infinite. The forest had never looked greener. The ravens had never soared higher.

Something … someone had said, long ago. It was about keeping both worlds in balance. He wondered now what it meant. Even so, the bus ride seemed familiar in some way. He tried hard to remember, but finally he gave up and watched the trees go by; watched the long arm of Thunder Mountain approaching.

Behind it was the Valley.

At the head of the Valley was the glacier, and the soaring peaks of the icefield.

And hidden, behind the lesser summits, was *the* mountain.

Tomorrow was the eve of the Pilgrimage, the third anniversary, when he was to approach its base, as he had twice done, after his Commission.

But those had been baby steps, a priming of sorts. Tomorrow he would approach his Gods once more, and he would go to that place, and that time, *when the living and the dead were in constant embrace, the difference between the two impossible to calculate.* Tomorrow ….

He was going North.

CHAPTER SEVENTEEN

The air was still, but through it, ravens managed to soar. The sound of the rushing waterfalls that streaked the west face of Thunder Mountain could be heard across the Valley. The sun had only just risen, and it remained hidden behind the ridge's main bulk. All was in shadow, and the void above was a milky blue.

There was also was the sound of barking dogs and the purr of warming autos. Here and there, a gate creaked. And a shout could be heard as well—a forgotten lunch sack. But for eyes that could truly see, and ears that could truly hear, the world was quiet. An ominous quiet, the cosmic calm before the presumptive storm.

The Nilsson's back door opened, and Mark stepped onto the porch. He wore his finest wool trousers, his faded wool sweater, and a new pair of leather boots. He pulled the heavy backpack after him, then hoisted it onto his shoulders. After adjusting the straps, he lowered himself down to the gravel.

And then he was through the gate, walking rapidly down the narrow dirt road. Immediately he felt tired, and the stiff boots cut into his ankles. The weight pressing down on his back seemed at first unbearable. But after a short distance, his wind came to him, and he felt the pains dissolve. He swallowed hard, testing the condition of his throat. It was fine.

He had left shortly after Dad. The others were not yet awake, and the note he had laid on the dining table was minimal in content. He had spoken with Sheka and asked for her blessing on this venture. And that was all. He had packed in his room the evening before, and he had eaten no breakfast. Impatient to be off, he'd stuffed a variety of food provisions along with his other equipment, then hurried on his way.

As he walked, he tried to remember exactly when the decision had come. Yesterday at work, the feelings of being an outcast, seemingly mocked by the world and his own World, had built to a climax. But had he known before? And as his brain fought with his mind, his memory became clouded, and his past was lost in a swirling fog.

He reached the loop road and walked along its left shoulder. He faced the morning traffic, and he looked at not a single face behind a single wheel. He became oblivious to the road, the noise of the cars, even the spruce trees that glided past him in their silent majesty.

The meadow was gone. The pond was not a secret. Capella had left him. All that remained was *the* mountain.

He turned at the next intersection and walked through a quiet neighborhood. After a block and a half, he stopped. He stared at the yellow house on his right. And then he walked up the drive and threw his pack onto the concrete porch. He picked up the knocker, and it dropped with a dull thud.

After a few seconds, the door opened, and Ree Simmons looked out at him with surprise on her face. She was in her nightrobe, and from within the house came the smells of breakfast.

"Mark! What is it? What can I do for you?" She saw his rough outfit and the backpack. Puzzled, she raised her hand in an attempt to push back her unruly, graying hair.

"I want Fran's stuff."

At the sound of the name, she drew back, then grasped the doorknob tightly. "I don't understand. Please, what are you talking about?"

Mark felt a sneer cross his lips. "I want his climbing gear!" he yelled at her. "Don't give me that stupid look! I know it's still here—all of it! Probably in those red wooden boxes, am I right? Go get them and bring them here! And hurry, will you? I said, go get them!"

He saw tears in her eyes, and the whistle of a teapot added to the nightmarish scene. Ree put her hands to her face, then turned and ran through the foyer, out of sight. He waited, listening to the sound of a closet being opened, and then the scraping of wooden crates. He stood rooted to the porch, and his breath came from him in a loud, rippling way that was foreign even to him.

The teapot went silent, and then Ree was back, dragging the boxes by their long straps of black webbing. "Here," she said, crying and wiping her eyes. Mark felt gladness only that she was home alone.

He stepped into the foyer and began to hunt through the boxes, looking for anything he felt he might need. The crampons lay on top of one pile of debris, in the first box. He yanked them out and realized, as he did so, that there was very little chance they would fit his own boots. He searched for the L-wrench and pulled it from the crate's bottom, which was covered with dirt.

He grabbed the carbon battery headlight and Fran's balaclava. And when he thought he'd found everything he wanted, he stood up. Ree was leaning against the wall, watching him and sobbing quietly. And her voice, though soft and broken, made him jump.

"You want his ice axe too?"

Moments later he was off once again, hiking along the loop road. The shadows were just as long, and the air was just as cool, but he couldn't possibly have noticed. In his mind was nothing but *the* mountain, and he hiked through the Valley at a quick pace, heading for the turnoff to the campground. He followed the old familiar trail away from the pavement, through the clearing, and along the line of power poles. He approached the river, crossed on the steel bridge, and soon came to the well-traveled lane.

Passing him now were the cars and campers of tourists driving to and from the giant campground. He walked past the entrance, then onward until he came to the turnaround, near the west shore of the lake. He had walked a full three miles, and now he pulled his load from his back and rested, sitting on the white silt beach.

Almost without considering, he had chosen the northwest ridge. From the picture in the book, he had seen how it swooped upward, an enormous ramp of snow and ice, and how the spiny ridge took over and spiraled on toward the summit, curling sharply at the peak's shoulder. It looked dangerous, but not nearly as steep or as shear as all other routes, especially those visible from the south. In fact, he thought, perhaps there were no other possibilities at all, not even the great towering southeast buttress, under which he had stood, twice before.

When he had gazed at his mountain God with eyes that—for a moment—were not his.

He dug into his pack and brought out a few of the sausage sticks. He bit at them furiously, and he let his mind contract a little. His thoughts now centered on the route ahead of him, and he went over his plan once more. First would come the hike, over the trail and along the west side of the glacier. From there, he would climb onto the glacier itself and make his way to the second icefall. After passing around or through this major obstacle, he would attain the upper glacial plain, which was perpetually covered by snow. There were very few crevasses, according to the pictures in the text and from what Fran had told him. Never had he seen it for himself; Fran had not taken him above the second icefall.

Further along, the glacier split into two main tributaries, and the eastern fork rose in front of the Towers and beyond, to the base of *the* mountain. Up there, in the great basin of snow, he would camp. And at dawn tomorrow, the climb would begin.

Beyond that, he dared not think about.

He got up with a grunt, put on his pack, and was off. The trail was flat, and it followed the lakeshore past rows of thin willow shrubs. Alder trees came next, and finally the dark spruce. After a mile, the trail began to ascend, and he approached the white mass of the glacier. The sun broke over the top of Thunder Mountain, which was far to his right and behind him. The sky brightened, and the haze was gone. There was not the faintest wisp of cloud in the blue dome above him.

He continued on at a rapid pace that surprised him. He felt his energy growing, and he began to take shortcuts between the zigzags in the trail. He fairly leapt along, and had just rounded a bend in the path, when he encountered a couple of hikers coming the other way.

He stopped quickly, and an almost nauseous feeling swept over him. He'd forgotten there were others on his Earth.

"Hellooo!" the shorter of the two yodeled out. He didn't return the greeting.

"Looks like you're going mountain climbing," said the other. "You really like doing that sort of thing? I always thought mountains were something to be admired from down here in the thick air! Ha, ha! This trail goes high enough for me."

Mark remained silent. "We camped up there near the end of the trail," the shorter one said, waving to where the path looped upward into the dark forest. "Man, you can *feel* that great block of ice down below you! Know what I mean?"

Mark nodded. He coughed and said, in a husky voice, "Just move out of the way."

They looked at him in astonishment, then slid to either side of the path. He bolted past them and continued up into the trees and out of their sight, never looking back over his shoulder.

He reached the end of the trail much earlier than he expected. He stepped out onto the ledge, near the spot where he had camped with Jeff, on that winter night. Below was the glacier. He dropped down to its level, set his pack against a large, speckled erratic, and put his hands over his face. The cool air near the surface of the ice condensed the sweat on his forehead, as he sat and prayed.

I thank You, dear mountain God, for seeing me safely through, to this point. Yes, I am coming to You, to my last refuge. Your snowy crown has awaited me for all of time, and this day and tomorrow have been prepared, I know, for Your child of Nature. We are all that is left. Please guide me to Your holy summit, where I shall gain the ultimate Knowledge, know the ultimate Truth, that yet eludes me. Go with me! Be with me!

He took many of the contents from his pack and set about resorting his gear. And then he lifted the crampons and pulled off their rubber protectors. Dropping them to the cold gravel, he reached out with his left foot and placed his boot in the proper position.

The fit was almost perfect. After a minor adjustment with the wrench, he was satisfied, and repeated with the right crampon. He fastened their harnesses as tight as he could, then pulled out the sunglasses and put them on. He rolled up his sleeves and untied the ice axe from his backpack. Then he picked up his load and shouldered it once more, grabbed the axe, put his hand through the loop on the wrist strap, and all was ready.

Yes, Fran, I am ready to go. You would be proud of me, for I am only doing as you taught. I am putting myself on the edge of myself. And if you could only know why ....

Moving forward, he walked across the gravel to the river of ice, then climbed up the first steep wall to the plateau. From a distance, this area looked flat, but it was actually ribbed with deep crevasses. He began to hike over the ice, sticking near the left perimeter which, he knew from experience, was the safest area for travel. It contained the fewest crevasses because it moved at a much slower pace than other parts of this great frozen mass. Because of this, there were areas of gentle slopes, rounded and worn from the rains, and this made the trip easier and quicker.

The crampons bit into the packed ice crystals, and he marched on at a relatively smooth pace, though not nearly as fast as he had traveled along the wooded trail. His pack became heavy once more, and whenever he came to a small crevasse and jumped across to the far side, the weight smashed down on his back with force.

The sun's rays, reflecting off the surface, warmed the air around him. Up here in the world of ice, the temperature approached freezing even on summer nights, and the surface of the glacier was hard and crunchy. As he picked his way along, however, he became aware of the sun's work on the frozen torrent. This became more and more apparent as he encountered, with increasing frequency, small puddles in the indentations. They were a light blue color, and very pretty. He stopped at one of the miniature pools for a long drink, and the cold water felt good against his throat.

Ahead was the second icefall. He had long before passed by the first one, while still on the forest trail. A slanting ridge of ice, uniformly level but tilted like a gentle ramp, swerved around and to his right, and it was from there he could gain access to the upper reaches of the glacier. After studying it, and doing some rough measuring, he decided he could save time and energy by climbing through the icefall itself. There appeared to be several routes through the uplift, with its many jagged towers lifting high above the glacial plain.

He started toward the obstacle. It loomed ever closer, and as he neared, he saw an easy passage near its left border, where it rubbed the mountainside. It was like a staircase of rock, and up it he climbed. As he neared the top, he looked back and shivered. The Valley was far in the distance, and it seemed withdrawn from the world of whiteness that was now all around him.

He then climbed over a short ramp of ice, and when he hit the top, the upper plateau sprang into view. It was a startling, beautiful sight, and he moved forward eagerly. As he did so, a large crevasse, hundreds of yards long and twenty feet wide, yawned in front of him. He stopped and drew himself back, for he had happened upon it with such astonishing suddenness, and he grunted his surprise.

Far below, in the blue depths of the crevasse, was the sound of running water. Huge granite boulders could be seen, held tightly within the transparent walls. He looked right and left, then became impatient because he saw no means of crossing the wide gap in the ice. He spotted one, very thin snow bridge in the distance, but it didn't look safe enough to risk. He walked over to its edge, took a few steps out onto the tongue of snow, and stuck in his axe.

He felt it sink completely through. He inhaled deeply and looked further to the left, where the crevasse ended with authority as it met sheer walls of black rock.

And so he took off the heavy pack and slid it onto the bridge in front of him. Then he crawled out behind, and digging with the front prongs of his crampons, began to slide himself and his pack across the bridge of snow. It was the most dangerous thing he had ever done in his entire life, but he remained calm. There was no turning back, no matter what the obstacle might be. As he reached the far side, he told himself that he could risk death a hundred times in the coming hours, but that somehow he would persevere.

The Hidden Observer watches me, and is not surprised.

He stood up and brushed the granular snow from his wool pants, then put on his pack. After readjusting his pack straps, he continued his hike, up the gently tilted glacial plain.

The surface of the ice was now less rippled, nearly devoid of crevasses. There were regions of hummocked terrain, especially near areas where the mountain ridges plunged into the ice. The snow covering was becoming slushy, and he sank two inches with every step. It was beginning to tell on him, and the sweat was pouring down his back. With relief, he saw a black dot appear in front of him, right in the middle of the ice river, and it grew much larger as he neared. It was Lunch Rock, exactly where Fran had described it years ago, and he headed in its direction, worn out from hiking and badly needing a rest.

He reached the flat-topped rock, which was the size of his bedroom, and sat upon it, drinking from his water bottle and eating a snack of raisins. It was getting on toward the noon hour, and the sun was turning the lower icefield into a reflector oven.

He looked around. Even with the filtering effect of his sunglasses, the environs surrounding him were bleach white and midnight black. The granite bit through the surface of the ice, and the peaks rose in their silent splendor, but on this day, something about them was different. They frowned at him. Looking wildly from one to another, he shook his fist at them, and his voice came as a shriek.

"The true test! You have never been satisfied, have you? Now you will attempt to burn me with the sun, swallow me alive, or send a roaring tide of white death from your naked slopes to where I struggle. No! You will not get me, for I make my Pilgrimage!"

He listened to himself defying his World. And he wanted to be moving on.

Two hours later, he was nearing the fork in the glacier. He was burning badly, even though he had applied an extra heavy amount of sunscreen, which now dripped from his nose. The salt from his hair stung his eyes, and his sunglasses began to fog up. He tripped over the front prongs of his crampons and went down in a heap, the forty-pound pack driving his face into the slop. He lay there gasping, and then slowly rose to his feet and continued. He shook his head and willed himself to concentrate, to be on constant lookout for the crevasses. Ahead, the Towers rose above him like a blockade; they resembled giant teeth rising out of the ice, and he grinned fiercely back at them as he began his traverse to the right side of the glacier. Never would he be stopped! There was nothing the World could do to tempt him, to keep him from his goal, from reaching at last the kingdom of his mountain God.

He traveled around a long, gently sloping ridge and hiked eastward. Miles in front of him, Snowdrift Peak appeared to leap directly out of the ice, and it became an important landmark, for it appeared in the very same picture as *the* mountain, in the wonderful text that Jerry had given him.

On he went, the heat becoming almost unbearable. The scene became wilder by the minute, as the black rock became streaked with gray, looking almost hellish against the unending white. He stopped to wipe off his sunglasses, and as he took them from his eyes, he reeled backwards, the light nearly blinding him. He collapsed once again to the surface of the glacier, and the glasses dropped from his hand. He spent the next moments groping about with his eyes shut, the flashing on his retinas all but driving him mad.

Searching with his fingers, he retrieved his glasses and put them on again. And he continued up the east fork of the glacier, which began to rise at about a fifteen-degree angle.

Lesser peaks glided by him, but he barely noticed them. He felt tired, so tired he thought that he might drop at any moment and fall asleep right on the gray, slushy ice, and never wake up.

The grade steepened, and the glacier began to narrow. Ahead, a number of small icefalls rose above the snowpack. He began to weave his way through them, occasionally being forced to backtrack and try a new route. Stepping onto one small ramp that lead around a maze of ice penitentes, he suddenly dropped through the surface. Without making a sound, he threw his arms to his sides, and the snow came up and smacked the bottom of his chin. His lower teeth sank into his upper gum, and he felt his legs dangling free. His jaws were suddenly warm, and he spat a mouthful of blood onto the snow in front of him.

And he became frightened at last. He stiffened up, and without moving a muscle, tried to keep calm and find a way out of the trap. He decided to bring one leg up, very slowly, while keeping his arms spread. If he could raise himself by digging in a knee, then perhaps he could get enough slack to reach out and bury his axe in firmer snow.

He tried, and felt his knee working into the side of the shaft he had created. When he could raise his leg no further, he shut his eyes, said a quick prayer to *the* mountain, and pushed upward. There was a slight give as the snow compressed, and he squeaked out loud, but then his knee held, and he chopped about with the axe, finally getting it secured. He pulled his way up out of the hole, in a slow and deliberate fashion, and then rolled away quickly.

After resting a moment, he stood up, with his gums pounding and the blood trickling down his chin. He carefully tightened the pack straps, then started off once more to find a route through the set of miniature icefalls.

After a while, he came to another level plane of snow, much smaller than the broad highway of the glacier itself. He had gained two thousand feet of altitude since leaving the forest trail and was now entering the icefield proper. He curved off to the right, and quite suddenly *the* mountain sprang into view, at the extreme upper reach of the narrow snowfield. He stopped for a moment and looked at the wide ramp of snow at its base, at the rising tower of ice and granite, and lastly, at its virgin summit. His eyes closed, then reopened, and he stared at the peak once more.

It looked oddly small. He was truly amazed that it did; almost expected something more, perhaps an added touch of holiness, such as a fogbow around its top. But it stood there in the distance, almost meek in its appearance from this, the northwestern view. And for a moment, he was angered. Then he started toward it, to the ramp of snow leading to the jagged rib which spiraled up to the high shoulder and was lost in the white puff of the gentle summit ridge.

It raced to meet him as he struggled through the snow basin. After a time, he was completely in shadow, hemmed in by the rock walls to either side. They slanted up and away from him, separating into a myriad of lesser peaks only high enough to keep the sun from melting the surface of this tiny glacial arm.

The mountain God nears more quickly than I would believe. I think there should be a majestic scene, a dramatic approach, but there is none. I am sure there is a reason! But for now, I am mildly disturbed, as it looks so small, so lifeless, so ungodlike!

Indeed, the peak appeared somewhat lacking in stature from the northwest, where the great icefield met its slopes far above the base. He hiked a few hundred yards more, and then he stopped. With a feeling of wonder, he saw that he was there. In front of him was the snow ramp, and above him, towering into the great blue sky, where his favorite star had vanished, was the final destination, the goal of his lifetime. It was his home, and the home of his God. It was North.

There was not a sound. The silence, here on the icefield, was over-powering. The sun remained hidden behind the rock walls, but the winds of late afternoon did not come, and the shadows too were deafening in their quietude, as they lay across black rock and white snow. Above, the sky was empty, without ravens and without clouds. He was completely alone with *the* mountain, and he shook with astonishment, but not with fear, as he stood at the base of this wondrous peak for the third and final time.

He looked at the summit for a while longer, and he wondered aloud if he could possibly make it. Never climbed! And then the impact of the words hit him, and he began to face the fact of what lay before him. Shaking harder, he began to doubt himself, to doubt his ability to stand on that shining crown.

His gum ached, swollen so badly he could hardly close his mouth. He sucked at the ragged line of flesh where he had impaled himself behind his front teeth, then looked about for a place to set up the tent. His eyes picked out a bit of red striping, something horribly out of place. It was located at the meeting of rock and snow, about fifty paces from where he stood. For a moment, he was frozen solid, and then he felt his legs begin to move.

Walking slowly toward it, he felt something happening to his throat. It was becoming constricted, as though large towels were wrapped around his neck, tightening. He reached the edge of the rock wall and gaped.

Held firmly in place by granite, ice, and snow, was *Capella's* parachute.

Mark bent down, his heart pounding. He crouched, and his quavering legs nearly prevented him from keeping his balance. It was there. Faded but still recognizable, its bright red and white stripes unmistakable, was all that remained of the high-altitude probe, launched by his very hand, more than four years ago.

The rocket itself had long since decomposed and disintegrated, likely separated from the chute strings during the nose cone ejection. Lost too was the payload section and the two strands of hair it contained, as it was fastened to the nose cone. But the parachute had survived, carried by the winds above the Valley to settle here, at the base of *the* mountain. The grip on Mark's throat lessened, then relaxed its hold completely, replaced by an expansion of the mind.

I think it will fly wherever it wants.

It wasn't gone forever. It had merely traveled here, to this place, to meet him once again. If any proof was required, it was right there in front of him. He was truly on a journey of destiny, and his lips pursed a silent kiss. He didn't reach for the weathered plastic. Instead, he got to his feet, turned, and walked away, glancing back only once to convince himself it wasn't some sort of quantum trick. And then he scanned the immediate area for a suitable place to set up the tent.

My star has never left me. It has guided me to this place. And tomorrow, the pieces of the puzzle will fit together at last. There will be no more mystery, no more crying, no more warnings, and no more doubt.

He selected a level site, out in the open and away from the rock walls. Fran had once told him that here on the icefield, the sudden winds could be devastating, whipping around corners in a manner that confused even the most experienced of mountaineers. Often the areas nearest the rock were the least-sheltered during these unexpected gusts. So Mark tramped down a rectangular patch of snow, in front of the giant ramp that led to the ridge he would ascend in the morning.

Next he erected the tent and pushed the stakes deep into the grainy snow. He secured the guy line with his ice axe, removed his crampons, and then proceeded to set up housekeeping inside. By the time he had unpacked and readied himself for his evening meal, he had grown quite tired. Lying down on his sleeping bag, he dozed for what he thought would be a matter of minutes.

He saw himself, and he was but a small child. He was running about the playground with his friends. There was the echo of laughter, and the ones who cried his name. And then the ringing of the bell. The children were lining up, eagerly awaiting the signal to file indoors to their classrooms, to the joy and fun of learning.

And then he was on Daddy's lap, reading the little book that he'd brought home.

And then he was alone, in the woods, and he was picking a sedge from the grasses of the meadow, and he was looking at it carefully, astounded at the regularity of its stalk, so triangular, so sharp to the touch.

And then he was older, and he saw the pretty girl in the front row of his biology class. He felt desire, and then it was quickly gone.

He was alone again, and he sat on a rotted log. He put a berry to his mouth and tasted its watery goodness. And then, as recognition of the vision came to him, he struggled to awaken, and as he did so, there was a flash of light, and the scenes began to reverse themselves, and he watched in terror as he grew younger, ever younger, and his brain shrank until the house became home, and Mom became Mama, and then, with a scream of horror, he sat upright in the little blue tent and fought to settle his whirling mind.

Why am I dreaming again?

Kicking his bag from him, he scrambled outside. It was cool, and glancing at his watch, he saw that it was past eight o'clock. The shadows had stretched down the length of the snowfield, and he turned and gazed upward, at the dark mammoth that stood high in space. It didn't appear to be staring back at him.

His stomach growled, and he set about preparing dinner. His hands shook as he primed the little gas stove, and he wasted a dozen matches before lighting it properly. He melted snow, and while waiting for it to boil, he ate the remaining sausage sticks. When the water was hot enough, he poured it into the large metal plate, mixing it with one of the freeze-dried dinners he had brought with him. The smell of the casserole became strong in his nose. He sat and sniffed the concoction as it rehydrated, the scent beginning to work on his mind as well as his salivary glands, the latter having reset from the taste of sausage.

He reached out a finger and let it dip into the meal. And he brought it back out and looked at it closely. Here was food, here in the most desolate place he'd ever known, where there was no "living" thing but himself. He began thinking of a place, a place that was not in the mountains and not in the meadow. It was a place where, for the past eighteen years, he had eaten his dinner. It was a place that, as a child, he had called home, and had later referenced as the house.

He brought the finger to his lips and tasted the drippy casserole. It was turkey flavor. And then he took his spoon and shoved it into the food, lifting out a generous bite. He put it in his mouth, and despite the pain in his gums, ate the food until it was gone. As he swallowed the final mouthful and felt the warm glow in his stomach, the tears blurred his vision. He lowered his head and began to whisper the blessing.

After he was finished, he looked through the tent flap and took in the view. And then he was filled with wonder, as he saw where he really was, seemingly viewing it for the first time, and he could not make himself believe it. He wasn't down in the Valley, he wasn't along the beach, and he wasn't in the meadow. He was on the icefield. He exited the tent, stood up, and ran out into the middle of the snow basin. He stopped and spun around once, and then a second time, and was filled with astonishment.

The black rocks and the white snow surrounded him, engulfed him, and they were absent of the life pulse he had grown up with, down in the lowlands. Here was Nature, but it seemed dead and uncaring. He felt an odd sort of loneliness that chilled him to the bone, and yet he raised his arms and shouted to the peaks in defiance.

"I can belong here as well, and tomorrow I will prove it!"

He continued to gaze at the cold, awesome scenery around him. The sky turned from blue to a steely gray as the sun dropped below the distant horizon, unseen by the young man in the mountains.

He had a sudden wild urge to look upon the Valley after dark. He wasn't sure why, or exactly what he would see, but after a moment's consideration, he grabbed his parka and the headlight. There was a small slit, back toward the lower end of the basin, and from there, he knew it was possible to climb a small rock ridge and gaze out into the lowlands. He raced down the snow-filled arm of the glacier, then paused as he studied the tiny ridge in front of him. And then, using his bare hands, he scurried up onto the rock, which was without moss or even the tiniest patch of lichen.

By the time he obtained the ridgeline, the sky had gone completely dark, and he turned on the headlight. He walked through a narrow gorge and approached a short hump of snow at the far end. When he reached this white knoll, he paused, turned off the light, and crept slowly up to the top.

Below him was the main branch of the glacier, and it was far below indeed. A series of icefalls lay between him and the massive, tumbling fury. His gaze traveled on to the dark oval of the lake, and then beyond, to where the Valley was bordered by the long arm of Thunder Mountain on one side, and low hills on the other.

The Valley was filled with hundreds of tiny lights, and as he looked at them, he exhaled slowly. It resembled a miniature galaxy in the great void of empty space, and as the multitude of pinprick lights worked upon his retinas, the dark forms of land disappeared. It looked like something from heaven, and the word came to his lips. Beautiful. And as he said it, he was surprised and could not believe himself. The lights were artificial, and they represented Humans.

But he continued to stare at them. He knew that somewhere down there was the family, and Sheka. And there were the others he knew, there was the pond and the boulder, and there was the creek. There was the meadow, undergoing rapid development. It was all there, in that U-shaped lowland, and from here, it looked so small, so interlaced with itself. He felt a lump in his throat. He was up here alone.

He looked up, at the real stars. Here in the cold, dry mountain air, they appeared a hundred times brighter, and he could barely tell one from another. His own star Capella he saw; it had come back to him. Tonight, however, it seemed to twinkle a bit less. He saw the constellation of Delphinus, rising in the east, and he saw the great expanse of the Milky Way as it curved across the black sky.

Mark shivered and began to feel very tired. He threw one last wondrous glance at the Valley, and as he did so, he thought to himself, could there possibly be someone, anyone, standing on their front porch, gazing at the dark shadows of the mountains and wondering, could there possibly be someone up there, in the heights, shivering in the cold and looking at the Valley, which blazed with light, and wondering ....

He turned and made his way back to the small rock ridge. Even with the headlight to assist him, it was not easy going, and now the air began to move. A cold breeze began to sweep across the face of the granite. He lowered himself carefully, with his back to the sky, and when he reached the bottom he turned. And he gasped.

High in the sky in front of him, the Northern Lights began to weave their silent magic. He was hypnotized by the display, and he walked like a specter, out from the rock and into the middle of the snow basin, shutting off the headlight as he went. He watched as the curtains danced and mingled with one another, green with gold, and blue with gray. They brightened and dulled, over and over again. He began to grow afraid as he watched, and felt himself backing up slowly, in the direction of his campsite. An unusually large curtain began to take form, directly above him, and it suddenly shafted upward and seemed to be advancing on him. He stopped moving, and then he began to shrink down, finally dropping to his knees. His headlight fell to the snow, and he tried to cover his eyes against the indescribable beauty of the scene around him, but his hands would not obey him.

A magical scene it was indeed. The mountains and the snow, illuminated only just barely thanks to the billions of stars, while the auroras bore down from the heavens in their wild brilliance, casting a spell upon the Nature Boy who lay there on a surface of pure white, crying for his mountain to save him.

"Yes, I know that You have frightened me! Was it not the Plan? I lay here, on the face of the Earth, and I am at Your mercy! But I am strong, and I will come to You, after I have slept!"

He stood up and ran for his tent. "Go away!" he yelled at the Lights, as they played their symphony above him. "Leave me be!" he sobbed, as he crawled inside the nylon structure. "Tomorrow I will prove my worth! Tomorrow at last!"

The Northern Lights faded suddenly and were gone, their disappearing act witnessed only by the Hidden Observer. Mark had buried his head inside the warm and fluffy depths of his sleeping bag. He lay there and tried to lose consciousness, shivering against a cold that did not come from the night air.

And will You take me tonight, or dare You wait for the morning?

CHAPTER EIGHTEEN

Black skies lightened to thin gray, and finally a pale blue. Down in the Valley, a sparrow chirped. Wispy fog banks lifted from the base of the hills and disappeared into the strengthening light.

The mountain peaks remained in shadow, and small gusts of wind wrapped around them. The resulting sound was lonely and cold, and excepting the eyes that truly saw, the world above seemed lifeless and unyielding.

The little blue tent shook in the breeze, its sides flapping like a ship's colors under full sail. The stakes had frozen themselves into the now solid ice, and the ropes were stiff. The morning light had brought not warmth, only the sensation of deepening cold, and the life within the tent struggled for comfort.

Mark had not dreamed once during the night. He thought about that as he prepared the hot cereal and the powdered fruit drink. He let the stove continue to burn after the water had boiled, spreading his hands, then his entire arms, and finally his upper body over the roaring blue flame. When the breakfast was eaten, he scrubbed the utensils with snow, and then he put on his boots and stepped out into his Natural World.

He gazed at *the* mountain, and then he brought the spotting scope to his eyes. As he stood there, the route suddenly looked impossible. There were narrow chimneys of ice, and there were sections near the peak's shoulder that appeared to offer no passage at all. But then a gust of wind hit his face, and he quickly lowered the scope and put it into the small daypack he had brought with him.

As he set about gathering his supplies, his mind began to blank out on him. Shaking his head, he ordered it to come back. He decided to leave the stove and the prepared foods behind, as well as the headlight, as he was not considering the idea of having to spend the night on the peak, at least not if he intended to return. Besides, if he didn't? He left behind also the spare socks, t-shirts, and gloves. When he finished packing, he looked inside the small daypack, and all it contained was at the very bottom. A few quick snacks, the water bottle, the balaclava, the wool mittens, the sunglasses, the scope, and the small tube of sunscreen.

It was six o'clock, and the wind died. All was silent, so much in fact that he thought he could hear things, perhaps voices, all around him. He stood up straight, turned around once, and then stared at the white ramp in front of him, with its great central peak. His God. *The* mountain.

"Yes, I am still here!" he shouted at its pale white crest. "And soon, I will stand atop Your crown, and will have proven my worth, that I am one with You, the God of Nature, and I will receive my just reward! Will You then take me with You? I am not afraid!"

He snapped the parka around him, then removed the ice axe from the taut-line. He used the axe to drive a metal stake into the snow, then secured the line. Looking at the tent, he decided that it would be all right until he returned.

If he ever returned.

He put on the crampons, slung on his daypack, and then he was ready to go. He walked away from the tent, with the pack on his back, the ice axe in his hand, and *the* mountain before him.

Immediately, a new blast of wind came down from the heights and almost knocked him off his feet. He leaned forward until the gust had passed, and presently all was still again. He looked up, grinning angrily.

Try as You may, I am not thwarted, and I am coming! You went too far with this one, and now I am sure You can see that. All the years behind me— think of them! Look at the people and their world, and look at me; I went far over the brink and into the Earth, and out to the stars. I am one with You, and Your attempts to challenge me, Your experiments of intimidation, were all for naught. I have passed the tests, all of them, and still You are not satis-

fied? That's right, You above are the true test, the final obstacle. You are the North I saw, oh so many nights ago, when the stars called to me! And truly, I am not angry, I never was.

Don't You love me?

Ahead of him, the basin came to an abrupt end, and the broad ramp leading to the northwest ridge loomed ever closer. He moved quickly toward it, and when he arrived, he stopped and looked closely at his feet. There was no gradual steepening, none at all.

And so he took his first step on *the* mountain. As he did so, feeling his boot and its shiny steel crampon dig into the hard snow, his head began to pound. He almost expected a shower of sparks to come flying from the summit, and the earth tremble and swallow him alive. He felt his upper gum aching, and he pushed on, up the great white fan of packed snow.

The surface was sun-cupped, even here on the northwestern side. The sun itself would later appear over the shoulder of the towering giant, and then, come the afternoon, the entire range would be bathed in light. He struggled through the uneven snow, slipping often as he gained altitude. After a time, he stopped and looked back in the direction from where he'd come.

Far in the distance below, and barely discernable, was the blue speck of the tent. He could just barely see the line of prints he had made, and they followed a relatively straight line to where he now stood. He looked at those prints, then out and beyond, to the lower end of the snow basin, and to the wild black and gray ridges to either side. The scene was one of unimaginable beauty, and he had ruined an otherwise virgin territory with his footprints.

No! I cannot look at it that way—it is not true! I am Nature! I am meant to be here at last, and damn it all, look at me! If I was of the people, could I stand where I now stand, and feel what I now feel, and anxious as I am, persevere? Of course not! It is true that I am concerned, but am I weak? As I approach my wondrous mountain God, I am humble, but I will not fall short of the ultimate goal!

After a time, he approached the upper end of the snow ramp, and the black ridge knifed up before him. It was cold and foreboding, but he did not pause to look at it anymore, and instead kept his eyes just ahead of his feet. There were a series of crevasses in front of him, where the icefield pulled down and away from the rock. He wove between them, seemingly oblivious to the danger they presented.

He came to a rather large crevasse, the upper side of which towered above his head. A shining block of ice had caved in the weakest section, and he climbed up on the newly formed bridge and continued upward.

And the sun burst into view. It was rising fast in the southeast, sending its rays through a gap on the extreme left side of the range. He sensed its heat, and for a moment became uncomfortably warm, but soon recognized the effect as purely psychological, and so he concentrated once more on the rising snow before him.

Soon, the slope narrowed and became hard, as he crept within the confines of the peak's perpetual shadow. He crossed boulders that lay stuck fast into the ice, and then climbed onto a small knoll of granite. He was on the ridge itself, and here he sat and rested.

From his perch, he could see for miles to the north. He saw the incredible mass of the icefield, also the countless nunataks that bit through the ice and stabbed the sky. He saw much of the route he had taken the day before, and far to his left, the wide silver band of Lynn Canal drew his attention. The Valley itself was hidden, as was the long arm of Thunder Mountain.

He ate a few crackers, washing them down with the fruit punch he carried in the water bottle. As he wiped his brow and felt the food and drink settle into his stomach, he pictured himself at the house, dreaming of a time when he would sit as he now did, high in the mountains. Is this what he'd had in mind? And he shook his head, as if answering an invisible questioner. He craned his neck and looked up at the ridge, which twisted out of his view. In those days of dreaming, he'd not been alone. Someone had been with him, and they had climbed *the* mountain together.

And he asked himself, had he ever dreamed of being here alone? On that day when he first saw what would become his great snowy God, the thought of being alone with it never occurred to him. And with that, he grew anxious once more, settling his gaze on the black rock around him, as if trying to convince himself that he was really here, that this was really one and the same as the pictures in that beautiful textbook. Now, instead of looking and dreaming, in a childhood world, he was here, and it all seemed cold and lifeless. He had feared nothing, back in those days, as there was nothing to cause such a fear. It was later, when he became aware of his true Birth, and was newly overwhelmed by the Natural World around him, that he had first known the true fear, and that he was perhaps unequal to it.

And then he had asked to be alone, for he could not deal with the world of Humans. It was a world that did not understand him, and within its confines, he felt alienated, far from home. So he had turned to his mountain, his God, for mercy. He had received it. But never had it entered his mind to go, as he did now, and make the supreme journey, the true Pilgrimage. Why? He had said, long ago, that without Jerry, he would never climb *the* mountain. And just before Fran was killed, something went a step further. Something told him he might never again venture onto the icefield, that the memory would be unbearable. That voice, that intruder ... he couldn't make it go away, so he listened and obeyed.

These things he had said long before the Commission. And yet afterward, he would remain sworn to his word. Something about that fact now made his throat stiffen, and he was more fearful than ever before. It was fear itself that had driven him to his destiny, that which he now lived. He put his head in his hands; wondered why most of his life had been shaped by fear, as if fear could be made into a tool.

Perhaps it could.

He arose, and as he stood to full height, he looked beyond the so-called real world. A pale, holographic man-otter rose from behind a holographic stump. He smiled, and the scene vaporized. The fear was no longer a verb; it was only a noun. And he continued on.

At first, the ridge presented no difficulties; it spiraled above him at about a forty-degree angle, and it was wide enough for him to move comfortably, without the aid of his hands or his axe. Its texture was rapidly changing, however, as the strata was uplifted diagonally. Shale, composed mainly of biotite, made the footing hazardous, as the ridge was fast becoming a pile of loose material. He began to slip more and more often, his breath coming out of him in gasps. It was like walking on giant corn-flakes, and he dared not reach for a handhold, thinking that something would break loose and cause a loss of balance.

In his mind, he got a picture of himself, lying dead at the bottom of *the* mountain, with the red blood gushing from him and his limbs doubled under his torso. He would have this vision repeatedly, he knew, as the climb went on.

No one, that is to say, not a normal person, could have made it this far, to have stood where he stood ....

It was another flash from the past, and as he heard it sweep through him, he stopped, high on the rock ridge, and listened to the wind. It tore across the peaks, both above and to either side. He stuck out his hand, grabbed a piece of the loose shale, and brought it close. It was a part of this God. What was it telling him now?

He laid it carefully at his feet and continued to move upward. He had gone scarcely a hundred yards when he came to a solid mass of black granite, and there appeared to be not the slightest hold for his hands. He looked to the left, and the snow fell away into the basin below. Taking small steps, he started, hesitatingly, in that direction, testing the snow with the prong of his axe. It seemed firm enough, and so he kicked a hold for his right boot, then took a step out onto the snow face. It was so steep that the wall on his right was only twelve inches from his face, a face reddened and numbed by the mountain air. He kicked another hold for his left boot and continued on his traverse. After he had made about a dozen steps, he decided that it was time to slant his direction and start upward once more, so as to cross the lip that was ten feet above him, and thus regain the ridge. If all went well, his mouth told him silently.

His crampons became more of a hindrance than a help in this situation. He began to take upward steps, and he found it difficult to keep a hold on the wall of snow with his axe. Then he realized guiltily that it was in the wrong hand; with the slope to his right, he would have to shift the axe to that side.

Without reconsidering, he began to slip the axe strap from his wrist, right there where he stood. Below him was a drop of nearly one thousand feet to the basin and the crevasses. Just as the axe found its way to his other hand, he looked down and noticed the great space. And the view startled him; he pushed against the wall of snow, and his feet flew out from under him.

He opened his mouth to yell, and then he was hurtling down the slope, feet first, on his back. As his speed increased, he had a crazy thought. It was the idea that he was on his way to the center of the planet, and that it was drawing him in on a spring.

Then he reacted, and rolled over onto his stomach. He dug the prong of his axe into the snow as it flew past him. A rooster tail of white shot into the air, and then he was slowing down, more and more, until finally he came to a halt. He lifted himself up, on his toes and his hands, and went stiff.

He had done exactly as Fran had taught him. Without even having to think about it. It was unbelievable.

But now he was far from the black buttress he had been attempting to circle. Looking up slowly, he saw that he'd dropped nearly a hundred feet. Yet as he looked, he felt the iron will coming back to him, and he kicked the first in a long line of steps, back up the slope, to where he had lost his balance.

It took a full twenty minutes. And when he arrived, the job was not completed; he had to continue upward from where he had slipped. It was not far, but much more steep, and he stood panting, the axe pick deeply embedded. Finally, his breath returned to normal as he pondered how to attack the nearly vertical wall of snow.

He dug himself a handhold and balanced himself while chopping a small hole for his boot. He repeated this over and over, and slowly made his way up the cold white wall. His front prongs were of little help, as he climbed not on solid ice but rather a hard, granular snow. When at last he broke the plane of the lip, he let out a sigh of relief as he saw the ridge take up again as before, curling toward the shoulder. And out in the distance, he saw the Valley.

Struggling, he got his leg over the precipice, and was soon laying atop the buttress. He rolled onto his side and looked out into the lowlands. He saw the canal, and he saw the western side of the great U-shaped Valley, while the bulk of Thunder Mountain hid the area around his own neighborhood, its double peaks in full sunlit brilliance. He remembered that time, in his childhood, when he'd hiked to the top of the sagging ridge, with Dad and Stephen, and had obtained that wonderful head-on view of the snowy mammoth.

Could he have possibly thought, on that day so long ago, that he would, years later, be high up on that intriguing northwest ridge, the one that curled mysteriously out of sight, indeed at this very spot where he lay curled? On that day so long ago, in his childhood that wasn't so innocent, the memory of which seemed as real as his present situation. Of course he could think it. It wasn't a possibility, it was a certainty, perhaps the only kind of certainty in this otherwise probable world. He knew the truth. Today *was* yesterday, and vice versa.

In that great distance, the sky remained blue, and he knew there would be no rain today. He silently thanked the rock on which he lay, and then got to his feet. The crampons scraped over the shale as he began to ascend the upper ridge, which swerved off to the north in a serpentine manner, finally disappearing into the lofty shoulder, a thousand feet above.

Again the sun hit him. It broke over the shoulder, above and in front of him, and once again he was hot. He struggled along, and if anything, the route was becoming much more frustrating than it was difficult or dangerous. The ridge began to lay back and become more level than it appeared from down below. Once it split into three smaller ridges, each topped by a line of snow, and he took the middle one, feeling safe for the time being. At the point where they rejoined, he stopped to apply the sun cream and take another long drink from his water bottle. He stuffed in balls of snow before closing it tight, and again he started upward.

He tried not to look too far ahead, for he knew that soon the rock would come to an end, and he would hit the upper snows, which could be powdery and windswept, with frightening overhangs. He traveled at a constant pace, seemingly fast, but actually much slower than he would have thought. He was breathing hard, not from lack of oxygen, for he was only a mile above the saltwater, but from the steady motion, the upward journey, the slipping and scraping of his crampons on the cold rock.

The view was spectacular, but he cared no longer for the view. He felt only a sense of anxiety to keep moving. He knew that he was further up on the great peak than any Human had gone before, and all he wanted now was to struggle on.

His mind, though, would not let him do that.

As a young boy, I was different. Not a social deviant, but influenced by You. And that was fine. I fought my way along, learning, loving, appreciating. I felt myself ascending along a line which others did not follow. It did not concern me, not even when, at one point, I recessed.

But Mankind held me not forever, and soon I was gone, over the brink and beyond. The road became clear; it was open and full of new possibilities. I lived, learned, and … appreciated.

The drop-off to his right sharpened, and to the left, the angle became more slight. He saw things that had been undetectable from below. There was a small basin below the shoulder, and it contained a tiny lake, its borders lost in a rim of ice. It looked dreadfully cold, and the snowy peak was reflected in its still surface. *The pond and boulder.*

The peak itself, the westernmost and higher of the two summits, was closer than ever. It shrugged off to his left and above him, with the shoulder blocking most of it from view.

He started toward it, along the ridge that was now rapidly self-dispersing as it melted into the main thrust of the granite. But the rock too was disappearing and soon, he could tell, all would be snow. The sun had, for the past hour, alternately shown itself and hid, appearing from behind the ridge and disappearing behind it, but now it rode high in the south, above him, above the summit, above everything. The other peaks seemed to be falling away, collapsing into oblivion as he went, and all that remained was *the* mountain.

He tasted the sunscreen in his mouth, and his head began to pound. His eyes hurt, and he wondered why he hadn't as yet put on his sunglasses. He did so now, then took off the balaclava and parka, balancing himself carefully as he stuffed them into the daypack. The cool air worked on his damp, salty hair, and he combed it straight backward with his fingers to keep it from hanging in his face. The sun was becoming truly unbearable now, and he could feel the moisture on the skin of his back. The little yellow daypack seemed triple the weight it had been when he left the tent.

He struggled through the first set of snow hills, and came at last to where a much thinner white ridge led to the base of the towering shoulder. He started out onto it, and then was aware, almost too late, of the cornice. Silently, and so quickly that it was over almost before he knew it, a huge section of the snow dropped away and was gone. He leapt backward, unable to believe what he had seen.

From far below came a slight rumbling sound, and he knew that the loosened snow was now coming to rest, at least two thousand feet below on the south side, likely near the spot where he had seen the mountain goat, on his day of Commission. He trembled as he looked at what was left of the ridge, and he knew that the incident had been of his own causing; he had vibrated it enough to set it in motion.

And the cornice! It lifted into space, and it stuck a full three feet into thin air. He knew he would have to stay on the left side of the ridge, to its very end. He also knew that if he hadn't dislodged that section, it would have happened anyway, just a moment later, and he would be at or near the bottom, a participant in the small avalanche he'd created. He saw the picture again, the red blood gushing ....

At the upper end of the ridge, the snow rose in humps and hummocks, while the rock peeped out from beneath. The main thrust of the shoulder was away to the left, above the little basin that contained the lake. He began an ascent that took him along the border of the rock and the snow, feeling that he would be hemmed in and better protected. After but a short rise, however, the rock was gone, and the steepness of the shoulder was contradicted by its total covering of ice, and on top of that, a thin covering of granular snow.

He sensed a great danger in the conditions around him. Still, there was nothing to do but go on, and he began to front-prong up the steep wall. It was like nothing he had ever done before, and with each step he knew there was an element of risk that surpassed anything he'd experienced in his life.

Fortunately, the wall was not very high, and soon he reached a point where he could take hold with his axe and pull himself over the top. But no sooner had he stood up than he saw another rise, directly in front of him, and it was mixed rock and snow, something he'd not been able to see from far below.

Exhausted, he started toward it. As he did so, he became conscious of the narrowing skyline. He breathed deeply, and then told himself, out loud, that he was nearly there.

The exposed rock glinted in the bright sun, and even with the aid of his glasses, he blinked his eyes against the glare. And then he started up the second rise of the shoulder. Near the top, the snow became dominant, and he knew that there would be no more rock at all, except perhaps at the windswept summit. The wind itself had died away, with only a faint whisper now and then.

He was getting ever hotter in his wool clothing. But he couldn't pause to shed the heavy sweater; he had to concentrate on every step. The rise became steeper, and as he struggled toward the blue sky above, he noticed the overhang.

It was much larger than he had thought, and it hovered directly in front of him. But there was no other possible route, and he looked at it in astonishment. Soon he was in its shadow, and he realized that if he was to go higher, he would have to find a way around or over it.

It looked solid enough, he thought, as he came to the top of the rise. He reached up and touched it; decided that it wouldn't fall down on him. And then he hacked out a place to kneel, to think about his situation.

It seemed hopeless. He felt a growing mass in his stomach, as though a lead ball had been placed there. He was alone, without a rope and without a partner ....

Yes, without that Jerry boy! That was wrong. I have made it—alone—because I am indeed alone! There is no one else that could have done what I have done today. No, no, no! You have seen me safely this far, and now I ask

You, is this the final obstacle, where I will either be with You, or be a failure?

Remember me! I was Born and I worshiped You. Is that not all You asked of me? What more do You want? I have struggled up Your slopes, where no one has gone before!

He blinked.

No gradual steepening; his physical birth.

The snow ramp; his soaring childhood.

The twisting ridge; his departure from the norm.

The fall; his recession.

The upper ridge, and the view of the Valley; the Commission.

And now this, the overhang that kept him from triumph. And yet there was no turning back. Is this truly how he was? Is this what he was? Who he was?

My God, it cannot be true. What have You done to me?

He looked up, and he saw that there was no possible way over the cornice. He was not going to make it.

Mark sat there, on his knees, twenty-five hundred feet above the little blue tent, and wept. It was a sight never to be seen by the eyes of his species.

He was not going to make it. His God had spoken. Told him something. Exactly what it was, he did not understand, but now, he supposed, it didn't matter. He had failed. He would never stand on that virgin summit, and never come face to face with North, which he was certain was there.

"No!" he cried aloud, and his larynx throbbed with the pain of the spoken word. He put his hands to his ears and shook his head. "Don't talk to me!" It was too late.

For eighteen years I have been alive, according to the clock of homo sapiens, but I have always been alive. I am in possession of a power that I seldom acknowledge, and I always have been. I am today, though I do not know its name, or its source. It has been given to me by Earth and the stars, for I am composed of them. Everyone has this power, but most cannot use it because they do not hear what I hear, those faint voices from just after the beginning ....

Mark Nilsson stopped breathing.

For an instant, everything went blank. Then everything was back the way it was. But not exactly the way it was, for something had cleared its throat.

Mark Nilsson began to breathe again.

He watched himself get to his feet, and saw his left hand grab the ice axe. He watched his position shift, and he saw the bright metal of the axe fly through the air and strike the wall of snow. It rose and fell, over and over, and began to dig a tunnel through the overhang.

It was tedious work, and after a few minutes, he felt his arm growing weary. But the axe never stopped. He dug with the adze, then the pick, scraping and scooping out the hole to an even greater width, so that a person might crawl into it. And then the axe pick sank deep into the lower wall of the tunnel, and Mark felt himself climb in after it.

He was in control again, and he clawed his way upward, his feet sticking out into the thin air behind him. He reached out with the axe and began once more to dig away at the snow. Soon he was using not only the axe, but his bare hands as well, as he held his mittens in his teeth. Inside the tunnel there was no echo, and the faint sounds of the world around him were gone.

Soon he had made another foot, and then another. He kicked his way up the rising tunnel, and with a strong jab, pushed his axe through, into the open. He punched at the remaining wall with his fist, and then broke through with his head.

The world, and his World, was there, as they had been. And in front of him was a steep hump of snow, about ten feet high, all that remained of the peak's shoulder.

Clawing forward, he fought his way clear of the little tunnel. And he stood on the snow, breathing hard, nearly unable to accept the fact that he had made it. He put on his mittens and surveyed the tiny knoll in front of him, and after brushing the snow from his clothes, he started up the rise, aching with every step.

The hill seemed vertical as he began the short ascent. He struggled to keep from falling back, and angrily, he stuck the axe into the snow directly in front of him. It did not hold properly, and he yanked it out, too hard, and the curved adze struck the side of his nose. He felt a flash of pain and saw the blood, a red blur beneath his left eye. But he only wiped it away, then dug in the axe a second time, securing it properly to haul himself up the rising wall. With what seemed like the very last of his strength, he threw an arm over the top, then slung the axe in a wide arc, securing the pick. He scrambled up and rested on his side, with his head on his folded arms. For a moment he held his breath.

Then he looked ahead, exhaling slowly through his mouth.

There was a small, sharpened ridge of snow, curling away from him and rising less than twenty feet, and beyond it there was nothing but blue sky.

Never taking his eyes from the summit, he pulled himself into a sitting position, his breath returning to normal. He felt the pain in his gums, and ran his tongue over the blackened surface. He felt the tingle on the side of his face, and wiped the blood away a second time. He was aware of the lightness in his head, and he noted the sudden absence of the wind. The sun was bright. And he was there.

He edged forward, lacking the strength to stand just yet. He crawled for a distance, then as the summit approached, he began to rise, magically it seemed, until he was at full height and his eyes were on a level with the uppermost point of snow. The skylines rushed to meet him, and the suddenness of the peculiar sensation, as the world fell away below, made him stagger. He felt the blue sky engulfing him; felt himself lifting right off the ground and into heaven.

He walked slowly, deliberately, and then he crouched in front of a very small uplift, with a surface of bare rock on the far side. He knelt, removed his left mitten—the one with the blood stains—and reached out. With his bare hand, he touched the crown, grasped the snow with his fingers, and brought it to his eyes. And he kissed it, for it was the very top.

He had made it.

He was on the summit, and he knew it was meant to be, even though a small part of him could hardly accept it. He lowered himself down onto his side and wrapped his arms around the small pile of rock and snow. His body shook as he cried with triumph and wonder.

I am here! I have found North at last, and perhaps now the Gods will take me with them! I have struggled through this life, on the Human earth, and I have my reward! The place is mine, and mine alone, for I alone have come here! I pray my thanks to You!

And where shall I go now?

He leaned back, against the summit, and opened his eyes from thankful prayer. He looked around him, and he could see tens of miles in almost every direction. The Valley was beautiful. The icefield glinted, wonderfully black and white. Far to the west, the mighty Fairweather Range stood out bold on the horizon. He felt power within him, a power of being, and a power of having done the impossible, the unprecedented. He sat there and looked at what—until now—only his God had seen.

When all others had left him, had fallen away to his right, to his left, and behind, his God alone had remained. The dream he'd had, long ago, with the confusing artificial constructs, the train station, and the figures of men, women, and children struggling toward this very summit, but the dream flickering out before anyone could make it, himself falling further and further behind. That was it, that was the signal to become strong and determined, to persevere, for he was indeed on the right path, the path that led to the ancient voices. This was what he felt, as again he hugged the point of snow and rock, the very summit of *the* mountain. His eyes were wide open, and he let them travel over the surface of the snow, which was bright white, shining with its own Inner Light.

And as he sat, marveling at the World, and reveling in the indescribable warmth of belonging ….

There was the *groak* of a raven.

It soared directly over him, its wings acting only to give it stable lift. It zoomed away, then dropped quickly and became a tiny speck that mysteriously disappeared.

The ravens had never soared higher.

And Mark felt something. He didn't know what it was, but now the past, all the past, was with him. Not just the smiles, the anger, the adventure, the feeling of belonging to the Natural World, but also the messages. The subtle warnings, which he had tried to ignore. Kathy at the pond. The boom of the thunder. Finding his rocket parachute. The silent drop of the snow cornice. The raven. It was all happening right now, at this very moment. He rolled over onto his side, asking himself if there was anything more.

The thick slice of rock he saw, black and cold, for it too had its rightful place on the summit. He saw the glinting biotite, the faint streaks of the quartz. And tucked into a small crevice, between two slabs of dark shale, he saw the polished metal can.

His grip on the snow lessened.

His eyes widened.

He felt himself shaking, lightly at first, then with gathering force as he stared at the gleaming container. With a cry of sheer astonishment, he reached out with his bare hand and touched it, as he had done with the uppermost point of his mountain.

He tightened his fingers around it, working it loose from the rocks. He brought it to him and rested it on his chest, which was rising and falling uncontrollably. Something awful was going on, he thought; this could not be real.

It was not possible. It was not happening, he told himself. It was a dream, a night dream, from which he would soon awaken, to find himself in the tent, with the true ascent yet to begin. He felt his throat muscles working uselessly, then had a fleeting vision of a snagged salmon on a creek bank, gills undulating, and its eyes pleading for help.

He sat up straight and began to unscrew the top of the cold metal container.

And then he knew it was not a dream, and it was not a trick that his Gods were playing. Inside the container was a folded piece of notebook paper. He reached for it, took it from the can, and slowly spread it open. And he read it.

> Date: 8/14   Time: 1:40PM   Weather: Beautiful
>
> And I have made it! SE Ridge was a killer. After many years of dreaming, I have finally done it. I only regret that I am alone, and not with another I once knew. Must begin the descent.
> Congratulations to the reader!
> JF

The paper rattled as he held it in his hands. He read the message a second time, and then a third. And then he raised his head and looked out, into the distance, where he could see part of the Valley, the double peaks of Thunder Mountain, and the canal. He looked down and to his left, where the great southeastern ridge dropped away from him.

The vision he'd had, the morning after his Commission.

That basin, far below him today, where on two occasions he had stood, wondering who was actually gazing at the white slopes above.

His hands stopped shaking. He refolded the paper, stuck it back into its container, and screwed on the lid. Reaching over, he wedged the can between the rocks. Then he leaned back against the knoll of snow and closed his eyes. The warm sun burned his upper lids.

He had made it, and this was his reward. This was the ultimate destination, he told himself, the climax of his life. He had come, and now he had seen. This mountain was indeed a symbol for North, and North was a pathway, full of messages and gentle warnings.

He opened his eyes and looked again at the magnificent world of black, white, and blue. The peaks flared up around him, their lovely white cones stabbing at the edge of space itself. He felt the wholeness of the world around him, even the density of the air above and below. This air was fresh, cool and clean.

Down there in the Valley were the people. His mother and father and sister were there, and the ones he had called his friends. He stared at the Valley for a long time, as if able to see them. And he felt something that was new to him, so new that it frightened him into a near panic, though soon he was calm.

He felt as though they all stood and waited for him to return to them.

Mark looked around once more, at the mountains, at the great blue sky above him, and at the shiny metal can. And then he was laughing loudly, not with joy or happiness, but with a feeling he could not describe, in words or otherwise. He laughed and listened to the absurdity of the noise. He looked at the ridges that sloped down in all directions from where he sat, and the laughing increased. He laughed until his aching throat begged for mercy, and still he did not stop.

And then finally, the laughing began to wind down to a close. It stopped, and after a few spasms wracked his body, he felt the tears in his eyes and he was crying loudly, as he had never heard himself cry before.

He cried as he reached out, for the last time, and touched the summit of the mountain. And he cried as he slung the little pack onto his back and picked up Fran's ice axe. He began the descent, his vision blurred, his throat screaming in pain.

He turned to look at the summit, before dropping over the first hill of snow, and he nearly fell from crying.

Then he was going down. Later, he would remember only small fragments of it. His mind was gone, and his body was alone on the mountain. There was a dim recollection of the tunnel, and of a struggle at the bottom. There were the hills of snow, and the appearance of the rock. Somewhere, he couldn't remember exactly, there was a loss of control, and a downward slide that ended on its own.

He had a faint remembrance of a wall of snow, down which he climbed, with his back to the air. And there was the small, curving ridge with the frightening cornice, where the wide section had fallen away. Below that, a long, downhill toil on the loose shale, and here, he remembered, the wind picking up, wailing across the spiny ridge and carrying the stinging snow.

The blue sky pressing down on him. The rock, black and sharp, and the snow, white and blinding.

The base of the upper ridge; the wall below which he had fallen. He remembered his descent of the steep patch of snow, and then his climb down the lower section of the twisting cleaver. There was another fall, apparently from sheer exhaustion. He had cut his mouth on a piece of shale.

Then he was off the rock and onto the huge fan of snow. And here he remembered the rest of his mind coming back to him, and at the same time, his little blue tent was there, a blue speck, still far away.

Mark stumbled down the ramp, tripping often as the crampon spikes bit and held too tightly. He ate snow a number of times as he fell onto his stomach. But now the slope was lessening, and the basin was rushing forward, instead of coming up to meet him. He felt the peaks *above* him, and he began to breathe faster as he came near the campsite. He was back in the other world again. The mountain was gone. The parachute was nearby.

He staggered over to the tent. It lay secured, just as he had left it. Groaning, he reached out, pulled the line taut once more, and stuck his axe in the snow to help keep the rope in place. And he pushed his way into the tent, where he fell onto his warm sleeping bag. His feet stuck out the door, but he was not aware; he was fast asleep.

The dream that came to him was not confusing, nor was the reasoning behind its subject matter. He was at his desk, in school, and he was a small child. He was painting a picture with watercolors, and it was the most beautiful picture he had ever imagined. It was only in the rough stages when the dream began, but as his hand moved and the brush spread across the paper, the image of color grew in both size and complexity. It was a mosaic, and at first glance was only a maze of different hues, but the longer he gazed down upon it, the more he began to see patterns, which developed into material objects, objects that existed in his past, in the present moment, and in the future.

There was a tree swaying in the cool breeze. There was a dog, a malamute, and she was running through a meadow. And there were faces that he recognized. He felt excitement, and he called for the teacher to come and see his work. He was crying with pleasure and pointing to the watercolor painting. He was saying proudly that he had painted a past and a future, and that he could indeed paint as good as he wished; that all he had to do was move the brush, and the wonderful creations would come to life, as if by magic.

Then the other children crowded around him, and there were cheers and congratulations. He felt their arms around him as they hugged him tight and proclaimed him the best of them all, and expressed their joy in being his friend. And then ….

All was nylon blue, as he awoke and stared at the ceiling of his tent. He rolled over and pressed his face into the goose down, wishing that the dream had lasted forever and ever.

What was he saying? Did he want the ability to dream like everyone else? He balled his fists, and his tired muscles went rigid, as he lay there with tired eyes. He could not deny that in the dream he'd experienced a feeling that was missing in his real life, and he wanted it back. He became anxious, as he thought about where he was, in his tent, up on the great lonely icefield. Miles from the world of living beings. There was reason for being here, but the code, now deciphered, made his head spin.

He had been with the mountain, and the mountain had yielded its secret. Now it was time to go home.

He packed his supplies, and then he collapsed the tent, folded it into a flat blue rectangle, and placed it in the lower compartment of his backpack. He tightened the straps on the pack and took a long drink from his water bottle. The fruit punch was diluted, and the taste was thin, but he did not stop until the bottle was drained and the final drops had passed his tongue.

And he took a last look at the magnificent scenery around his campsite. It was truly an overpowering sight, and yet he felt an urge to leave it. He started through the high basin, and then began the downhill trudge to the eastern fork of the glacier.

Soon he came to the small pass, where he had gone the evening before and had obtained his unobstructed view into the lowlands. He wanted to go there, to that overlook again, but resisted; it was already far past noon, and he must make it home by tonight.

What?

He reached the lower end of the basin and made his way around the crevasses. He dropped down to the level of ice that would take him all the way to the main junction. Out of the corner of his eye, he saw a spot of red, and beside it, a gaping hole. He shivered, and for the first time, saw the place as anyone else would. He tried to imagine himself in such a predicament ... he could not. That was someone else, it must have been. He quickly moved past.

The sun was relentless, and he felt himself burning. The sunscreen was useless, and the salt got in his eyes and was blinding him. He felt the glacier becoming sloppy beneath his feet, and realized too that he was starting to drag along, too weak to hike properly. The weight on his shoulders was forcing him into a tucked position, and he looked like an old man as he struggled across the mile-wide fork of the glacier.

Passing the gray-streaked rocks, he quickened his pace yet again. He wanted out of this place, and he wanted to get back to the lowlands, to the Valley. The idea branded itself in his brain, and his head pounded as he wondered why he must hurry and leave the beautiful desolation of the great icefield. He saw his home, in his mind, and he saw those who waited for him. Why were they waiting for him? The snow became looser still, and he tripped and went down hard, the pack driving him into the slop, which sprayed to all sides.

One hour later, he reached the junction, and the Towers were behind him. He rounded the low ridge to his left, and the Valley was in front and below him. He stopped, reached out hungrily for it, and then bent over and continued.

It seemed a never-ending journey. He told this to himself, that his strength would give out long before he reached the rocks, and the safety of the woods. The woods! He had forgotten about them, had forgotten them for the mountain instead.

The black dot of Lunch Rock appeared, far in the distance. He straightened his course and headed directly toward it, watching as it slowly became larger. His feet were like raw stumps and were full of blisters. He could feel them pop, one after another, as he fought his way down the gentle grade. Without turning his burned and aching neck, he watched the peaks of the lower icefield drift across his periphery. He was dragging the ice axe along, and it carved a thin line through the slush as he went. Although he was sure he was traveling a straight path, he would have known the truth had he the strength to turn around and look at the crampon tracks behind him.

He approched the large, black granite, and then surprised himself by continuing on past. It slid from his view, and then he was heading downhill once more, as the angle steepened. Soon, he reached the level plateau above the second icefall.

He came to the huge crevasse, and without thinking, he started across the snow bridge. He was twenty feet onto it before he knew what he was doing, but he was too tired to consider fright. He made it to the other side, and then the sound of the running water, far in the glacial depths, was gone, and he dropped off the plateau, where the rocks and the glacier met in slip-strike fashion.

Never would he be able to remember how he forced himself down through the edge of the great icefall, with the pinnacles stabbing the sky like needles, and the yawning holes gaping at him from all sides. He did remember hitting the lower glacial plain, and sighing with relief as the last mile of ice came into view.

He found himself staring at the Valley again. Thunder Mountain loomed above, like an old friend, and for a moment he fixed his eyes on it. A jet roared down the runway for takeoff, the thrust from its engines compacting the molecules of air, and that compaction traveled over the marsh flats, across the Valley, and up to where he stood and marveled. It was an artificial sound, his lips told him. And then he smiled thinly, for he had missed that sound as well. As much as he missed the sight of Thunder Mountain and the smell of the alder trees.

He started across the lower section of the glacier, and soon the pressure of the sun, and the heavy pack, began to build toward a new climax. Again the axe dragged across the ice, and his thoughts became a blur. He approached the region of parallel crevasses, most of them open fissures, but some of them hidden under a film of wet snow. He stepped over a number of them, trailing his axe and stumbling on his crampons. And then he dropped suddenly, and the surface of the ice was level with his stomach.

He yelled, and then his cry was cut off as he sucked in his breath and his head cleared. Behind him, his pack frame had dug into the glacier and prevented him from dropping further into the crevasse. He put out his arms, sighed deeply, and pulled himself out.

The memory of the one who had perished occupied his mind, and with it, the hurt he had felt when it happened. He fought to maintain control and alert himself to his surroundings. He began to hike across the glacier again, and he felt, for the second time in his life—and the second time that day—a novel determination.

He felt his Birth coming back to him. He was passing through the holographic bear, he was being transported through a keyhole in the world, and he was staring at a red bell. His palm was also red, and he was tasting the watery goodness of the universe.

I will make it home. I am tired, but damn it, I will make it home! Don't give up, please don't give up. I am coming. Wait for me!

Almost crying in his anxiety, but not quite, he headed toward the rocks in front of him, to the wooded trail that led now to his home.

CHAPTER NINETEEN

Mark Nilsson awoke at noon. He lay in his bed and stared at the ceiling for just a little while, planning his day. His body was aching still, but the pains were slowly becoming little more than a tired soreness, and his facial injuries were mending fast.

He rose to his feet and walked to the bathroom, where he showered and then spent a moment in front of the mirror, parting his hair. He shaved, and after dressing, went to the kitchen. His stomach took notice of this action and growled accordingly.

He was alone in the house. Dad was at work, and Mom had left a note on the kitchen counter, saying that she had taken Amy shopping for school supplies. He nodded to himself and began to hunt up something to eat.

There was a bit of the lemon-orange mixture left over, so he decided to make crêpes Suzette. He worked slowly, carefully following Henri Carpenter's alleged original recipe, until he had made a small stack of crepes, and then he dipped them into boiling sauce, pouring the liquors over them as he did so. Lighting the contents with a match, he ceremoniously toasted himself, then sat down to an extremely enjoyable meal.

He read last night's paper as he ate, saving the weather for last and taking his time as he scanned the various high and low temperatures.

When the last crepe was gone, he got up and took his dishes to the sink, where he washed them thoroughly and stacked them to dry.

The early afternoon sun was streaming through the windows, and he knew that it was yet another clear day. He took neither a jacket nor sweater as he stepped out of the house and locked the door.

Sheka came to meet him in the center of the rock path. He knelt and hugged her tight, and then told her to look after things while everyone was gone. He strode through the gate and into the street, where he turned and headed toward the loop road.

He'd said *everyone*. He wondered about that as he walked along, avoiding the potholes in the narrow dirt lane.

The air was fresh, and a breeze worked on the tops of the evergreens. He breathed deeply as he went, and smelled the smells of the earth. A neighbor called to him as he went, and he waved a return greeting. When he came to the loop road, he crossed to the other side, checked his watch, and waited for the bus that would take him downtown.

After but a moment, a car pulled out from the intersection and slowed, coming to a stop on the shoulder. The driver leaned over, lowered the passenger window, and hailed him.

"Need a ride? I got plenty of room!"

Mark hesitated, then walked over and opened the car door. As he did so, he saw that it was the same driver who had given him a ride home from the beach, the winter before last. He bent down and sat himself in the passenger seat of the Volkswagen.

"Remember me?" the driver grinned at him. "I gave you a ride once, when you were way out there, all alone."

"Yes" Mark answered. "I never forget a ride. But you have some catching up to do. The number to beat is five, and you're a long way from that."

The young man whistled. "Five! You mean you really keep track of such things?"

"Of course. I wouldn't dare let my brain go lazy on me."

The driver laughed as he turned the car onto the loop road. "I think a good conversation is in order. I could certainly use some intellectual back-and-forth today!"

Mark wasn't sure, but unlike so many rides past, he felt the need for confession.

"You are right. About last time."

"What's that?"

Mark stared out through the windshield. "I … well, you're right."
I was way out there, all alone.

§

He walked the streets of town, looking at the buildings and the sudden rise of the mountains behind them. Such harmony, people would say, such a wonderful blend of two worlds. However, given what he knew, this could never be his description. He passed by many others as he traveled the sidewalks, feeling like an absolute foreigner.

He saw Richard, and he inquired about the future of his former classmate.

"Well," Richard began slowly, "It's getting to the point where I have to make some decisions, and make them soon. I want to stay here and work, and at the same time, I want to travel, and on top of everything, I need to further my education—sound boring to you? And hey, look at you! All scarred up. You been in a fight or something? And your face looks like you stuck it in an oven!"

"Had a little adventure," Mark answered. "I'd rather not get into it right now, if that's okay. Someday, I'll tell you all about it. And no, I don't think you sounded boring." He paused a moment.

"But you're willing to ask me for advice? I'm surprised, Richard."

"Why? After all these years, I can't think of anyone that I'd rather talk to. I mean, in a serious manner. Hell, I can joke with anyone, but … well, you know."

Mark did know, and it was more than a bit scary. He felt a dual wave of understanding and misunderstanding, but with it came also a new level of satisfaction.

"Thank you. Then I suggest you continue your education, if you can afford it. If not, then stay here if it's where you want to be, until you *can* afford it. How was that?"

They talked for a moment longer, then parted and went their separate ways. Mark continued to hike about the town, and thinking of Richard's attitude began giving him the shakes.

Next he saw his ex-manager, coming up the sidewalk in his direction. He stiffened, expecting the worst. But there was only a look of pleasant surprise on the older man's face as he approached. He waved a greeting at Mark.

"Hello, there! I must say, when you took off last Friday, I was mighty scared. Well, your mother called and told me what happened last weekend. Listen, don't look at me like that. I'm not going to give you a swat."

Mark tried to smile. "I truly believed that you would rake me over the coals. Aren't you in the mood for it?"

"Not at all. Sometimes things happen. Don't you think that maybe I can understand that? Now, I know you're about to leave town for a while, but before you do let's get together for some lunch, say on Thursday?"

And then Mark was down at the waterfront, sitting on an old, sawed-off piling, gazing at the boats moving about the channel. He watched as the seagulls fought over debris that floated on the surface, and looked at the peaks that rose in the distance, above the greenish waters.

He had come to town, if nothing else, to receive his social punishment. But it was not being dealt him. He was still Mark Nilsson, and the world was the same. He was a friend to his friends, after all the things that had been said, and after so much more had become undone.

He got up and walked to Dad's office. As he entered the room, he again felt small and uncomfortable, as he was sure that the story had spread to all who worked there. Dad saw him come in and slid the drafting machine aside.

"Well, it's about time you got up! And why is it that you always did have the knack of wandering in here right after your mom has called? Explain!"

Mark felt his cheeks crack, and the chapped skin was drawn tight. "What did she want?"

"She said Amy got sick while they were out shopping," Dad motioned to the nearest window. "So they went home, expecting to find you there. Looks like you've got more stamina than even I would have believed."

"Of course I do."

Dad chuckled. "So you drifted in here, just looking for a ride home, is that correct?"

Mark shook his head. "No. I guess I wanted to let you know that I was downtown. Nothing else." He shrugged and then said, slowly, "Um, by the way, is Frank around somewhere?"

"Oh, sure! You know him, never leaves. Across the hall, as usual." A pause. "And likely not too busy."

"Right. Well, I'll see you later." Mark walked through the dim hallway to the other drafting room.

Frank was there, bending over a set of blueprints. Mark, not yet wanting to vocalize his presence, shuffled forward, just a bit loudly, as a means
to attract the man's attention,

Frank Simmons looked at him. After only a brief hesitation, he offered
his seat and said, "Well, Mark, good to see you're up and about."

Mark gestured. "You can sit back down. Never mind me." He thought
quickly, desperately, for the right words. They did not come, so he said,
as he looked into the man's eyes, "I'm sorry, Frank. For what I did to Ree,
and all that."

"Noooo! Why should you be? Your dad told me all about it, and yes,
I know you upset the wife, but she understands, believe me. And I understand as well."

"How can you? There was something I had to do, and you could never
understand." Mark was ready to cry.

"Look, Mark. There's nothing to be angry about. I know what you
did. I don't know why, but I respect your reasoning."

Frank waited until Mark looked at him once more, and then he
extended his hand. "I know what you did," he repeated. "And I want to
thank you. It would have made Fran proud."

Mark shook the big, gnarled hand. "Okay, Frank." And with that, he
turned and left. He walked back out, into the sunshine, and headed for
the nearest bus stop. He couldn't take any more of this. It was too strange.

He decided the best thing to do was to go home, and after eating
something, get to bed early. He was still tired, and he needed extra rest.
And so he stood at the corner, fiddled with the coins in his pocket, and
tried to clear his thoughts, tried to focus his attention away from the
downtown activity.

But it didn't work. He found himself looking nervously at those
around him. He felt a sort of chilled excitement as he searched the faces
for ones he recognized. He wanted to believe what everyone was saying
to him, and although it was embarrassing, he was starting to think that he
could actually enjoy their comments.

A few minutes before his bus was due to arrive, he saw a young lady
moving along the far sidewalk. She was petite and had dark brown hair.
She didn't appear to be in a hurry, and as he watched her moving past, in
her late-summer clothing, he began to drift away from the crowd that was
forming at the bus stop. He tagged after her for a few steps, and then he
stopped.

They'd gone to classes together, graduated together, and lived through the rain, snow, and sunshine together. After the years in elementary school, however, they had barely spoken to each other. Mark watched as she turned and entered a boutique.

And he had a conversation with her.

"Wendy! How are you!"

"Fine. Hey, what's the matter with you? You look like you've been through a desert!"

(He laughs) "You're closer to the truth than you think. So, ready for college? You never told me where you were going."

(She tells him) "Really? Same as me! Guess we won't have to say good-bye."

"Yeah, that's great, Mark! When are you heading down there?"

"Soon. Uh, you know what ...." (Should he tell her, after all this time?)

"What?"

"Well, you remember, Wendy, when we were in the first grade?" (She blushes) "Yeah, I thought you did. Now, don't look like that! I have a confession that will even things up."

"You do?" (Her voice is light)

"Uh, huh. Later on, when we got a little older, there were rumors going round ... and on the surface, I hated them. But I won't keep it a secret any longer. When we were in fourth grade, I wouldn't have minded returning your hug."

(She grins) "Are you serious?" (He nods, and she looks at the ground for a moment) "Would you still?"

(A sly shrug) "Well, I suppose I'd have to go home and think about it. You know, all these years I've had you tucked away like an old photograph. You mind if I go and consider the question you have posed? (Bursts out laughing) "You know, I sound like a perfect fool! I'm glad I ran into you today. You be sure to look me up at school, and I mean that!"

"Of course I will, Mark!"

And he eyed the door through which she had passed. Cute Wendy Shelton from so long ago, when he played with the other children at recess and ate lunch with them in the cafeteria. When he was discovering the pond, and the meadow, and having his first daydreams of climbing what was once known as *the* mountain. When his best friend ....

That was where Wendy belonged, in the real reality. Not here, in the flimsiness of mere existence. Again the tears formed, tears that signaled failure at the ground-level end of the safety rope, thrown down by the ancient voices. He turned and walked back to the crowded bus stop, and a moment later, the diesel coach arrived. Mark deposited his fare and sat in the first empty seat he could find.

§

He had gotten off the bus at the familiar intersection, near the line of power poles. He had looked at the soaring peaks, at the tall spruce, at the speckled granites that lay on the ground all around him.

Of course he didn't know the phone number. He stood in the den for a moment, contemplating. And then he reached for the receiver; brought it to his ear. And he dialed.

He heard the ring, and then the voice of the directory assistant. He told her who he wanted, in what city.

§

He spent part of the next morning at a shopping center, near the foot of the Valley. He browsed through the mall and made a few minor purchases. Everywhere he went, it seemed as though the faces he knew were there, jumping out at him. It also seemed that no one could detect the slightest amount of social inferiority in him. He talked and laughed with the faces, and there were also a number of somber goodbyes.

He couldn't figure it out. He couldn't think of how to begin figuring it out. There was no ridicule, no wary eyes that followed him as he passed. He was being accepted.

Outside, he stuffed the merchandise into the little yellow pack and climbed aboard his ten-speed. He pedaled away from the stores, down toward the loop road intersection where, three years ago, the Tina/lupine had brushed his cheek.

His forward motion slowed as he neared the small bridge that crossed Jordan Creek. He stopped the bike and looked, through the willow shrubs, at the lazily moving stream. He rested on one leg, supporting both himself and his bike, and just stared at the muddy waterway. He knew that the liquid passing underneath the bridge had only a short time ago poured over and around the giant beaver dam, or what was left of it, up in the Valley.

Here in the middle of this strange time, where all seemed to be friends and laughter, was the creek, and it caused impatience to rise in the young man who now looked at the water sliding below.

And then he was on his bike and riding as fast as he could, to the loop road. He turned through the short cut, rode along the shoulder for a some distance, then followed the narrow lane that cut through the woods, to the beginning of the old logging road. Here, he stopped, dismounted, and hid his bike and daypack in the shrubs.

He was running, and his mind was whirling around in an uncontrollable way. He ran up the weeded road to where it crossed the creek on the old, worm-eaten bridge. He ran past and continued, toward the lower, forested end of Thunder Mountain. He came to the beginning of the old, flagged trail that led to the rock dam and the reservoir. Breathlessly, he whispered a greeting and hurried on past.

Now he was racing into the trees, and soon had come to the base of the mountain. He scrambled up a ravine, straight through the devil's club. He passed over the side of the gully and followed a small brook up through the evergreens. He came to the log where, at seven years of age, he had fallen. With a shout, he raced over to it, leapt from the bank of orange rot, and scampered across the log in three quick strides. He turned, told himself what he had done, and then he was off again, racing downhill to the logging road, and his bike.

He was pedaling up the dirt road, which led to the back side of his neighborhood. Before he arrived, he hid his bike for a second time and ran through the dense forest until he came to the meadow. He crossed a newly plowed road and wove between a couple of unattended bulldozers. He kept on to the creek, passing the bank where the fishing hole had been, and noticed that the contour of the stream had changed recently. Still, the memory of the bear, and of his first Dolly Varden, came to him as if it were only yesterday. Because it was.

He continued down the path that he himself had created, to the huge beaver pond and the enormous dam. He ran across to the far side, then on to the very base of the mountain, where it swooped directly out of the earth. He knelt, as he had always done, and put his finger on the point where the angle steepened. Then he bent forward and rested his cheek there instead.

Running back to the dam, he leapt out, and he slipped. His legs dropped into the pool, and he alternately laughed and sobbed as he pulled himself out. He slogged across the alder dam, and when he reached the other side, he sat down and wrung himself out as best he could.

He felt the earth below him. After a moment, his breathing slowed, becoming heavy and deliberate. He looked back at the dam, and then at himself, wet and thoroughly exhausted.

Why was he doing this? And why had he slipped?

He knew why. He'd figured it out. As his breath slowed and he calmed, the truth was spreading through him. He was no longer frightened. He knew what he had done, and what he was.

And why he was.

He had been born when the universe was born, like everyone else. And when he was very young, he had been infected with time, space, and mass, like everyone else. He had felt his stomach growl, felt his feet press against the ground, and felt his eyes water when he was sad. He had moved with his family to this great northland. And as he grew, one world grew with him, expanding, and another one shrank and became condensed. There was the world of Nature, and there was the world of Humans. At the time, they were inseparable, and seemingly, they benefited each other. He had lived with the illusion that his worlds were in balance.

But that was as a child. Later, when the pressure of living had increased, so had his need for escape. He had not taken an easy way out. He had done what was meant to be done, and he was not ashamed. Not then, and not now. He had taken the obvious course, the only road open to him.

He had nurtured his universe of pure consciousness, his own universe, and it was as much within him as it was before his eyes. He had protected it, and in return, it had protected him.

There was a time perhaps, when all people were able to live in harmony with Earth and with themselves. That time was no more, and at best, the people of this planet now appreciated Nature objectively, in a fashion necessary for personal or social gain. And that was fine. It was all right, for they knew no other way; it was not their fault. They had done only what the script demanded, and they were not ashamed.

People had created the artificial objects that Mark found useful. The spotting scope, the nylon tent, the hiking boots, and the sunscreen. They had mapped the stars, developed the laws of physics, and found cures for diseases. They had also taken the credit, but Mark was aware of the truly undeniable author of these advances. It was consciousness itself, much of which had been condensed and deformed into a physical universe—aka existence—in which all were trapped. Egos formed. The devil had been created.

When he made his break and said to himself that the world of his species was left behind, he knew, deep down, that it had never left him, and would never leave him. He had claimed the label of Nature Boy, with his Earth around him as his family, and there was absolutely nothing wrong with that. The clothes on his back and the change in his pocket stabbed back, denying this, for they were from the other world, and the ensuing argument was truly unwinnable.

From the moment he'd been created, then thrust into "reality", there was no way out. He was destined to be here in the physical world, and although it was a most unfortunate fact, he would have to live with it.

He never really had the choice to leave it; he knew this to be true. He had always known it to be true. At the time of his Commission, he had said that, for better or for worse, he must remain tied to society because he was already contaminated with it. There were a number of old verses mentioning the idea of all having fallen short; the teachings of various religions, and there was good reason for these messages. Unfortunately, the vast majority of people did not understand the incredible power of this idea, although they thought they did.

Again, he had not been wrong. He had merely gone as far as he could go, to the top of a mountain peak, only to find that it had been seen through the eyes of another as well.

His voiced frustrations, his anger, his categorizing of others, all had occurred not because he was right and everyone else was wrong. It had happened because he could not keep his worlds in balance. As he'd once said to himself, this wasn't anyone's fault. This wasn't about fault. It was about complete misunderstanding.

He had gone the full route, and he had seen the extreme of the Natural World. He had seen and felt what it could do to him, and now he could accept the ultimate truth. He would have to remain in this world, the one where people had, for whatever reason, created physical birth and death.

Would the world of Humans upset the balance and forge ahead? He knew that he carried, deep within him, something wonderful, something that was fast disappearing from the face of the planet; from the faces on the planet. It was the simple feeling of being one with Nature, and Nature being his guide. Of that, there was absolutely no doubt. It had helped in showing the way of true thinking, and to balance that thinking with feeling, sensation, and intuition. He had seen idealism's ultimate horizon. He *was* Nature forever, and forever Nature was him.

He had grown up loving the outdoors, loving the cool summer breeze, and loving the great peaks that dazzled in the sunlight. He had worshiped the Northern Lights and had felt the magic, the power they displayed. And he had been determined to display that power himself, to prove that he was equal to the world of which he was a part.

The mountain he had climbed was indeed a symbol for North. It was also part of the conduit for the messages he had been given by the ancient voices. The warnings he'd received were now all too obvious. What he'd found at the summit, in that artificial container, was indeed the final test.

He would forever understand that the determination that had led him to the top of the mountain had not come merely as a last-moment signal from the Natural World, not at all. It had been with him always. Nature had allowed it to come to the surface, complete with the subtle hints, nudges, and warnings.

He wondered about the future of his species. He knew that somewhere, deep within each individual, was this same wonderful power, this determination, and he prayed that it could be realized by all. And in the meantime, he knew he must struggle with them, to help them, as they did their best to help each other. However much he wanted to map the ultimate route back to the cosmic womb, he knew this was not his destiny.

The people appeared, and they moved past his eyes. There was his family, his parents and sister here in Juneau, and his brother, somewhere out in the Pacific. There was Jerry. There was Wendy, and there was Scott, who never tired of wearing corduroy. There was Robert and his huge eyeglasses. There was Richard. There was Tina with the dazzling blue eyes. Debbie and her fashion flair. Lia the socialite. Alluring Stefany, whose parents belonged in a treatment center. And there was Kathy, who still wore the black ear pins.

He saw Terry and Jeff, he saw Frank and Ree Simmons, and he saw Fran. He saw the Mitchells next door; Randy waving to him, and also Emily, the erstwhile bratty pipsqueak, now a lovely seventh-grader.

And he saw all the others, all those who made up the population of the place where he lived. He felt his eyes water, and slowly he got up off the bank and started for home.

He felt comfortable with his thoughts for the most part, but as he hiked along the path to where his bike lay among the shrubs, the moss, and the runners of trailing raspberry, he knew there was a final piece to the puzzle ... and he had diagnosed the problem, in his head, in his heart, and throughout him.

He cut across the shadowed woods, retrieved his bicycle, and rode down the bumpy graveled lane, past the pair of small lakes and the peninsula where, long ago—or perhaps just yesterday—the squirrel hunt had taken place. He wondered if he should go and visit the little wooded thicket, but after a moment's deliberation, he decided against it. He was seeing things clearly, and another memory recall was unnecessary. But the unfinished business ... it was upon him.

He came to his neighborhood and approached the house. The drive was empty, and he quietly opened the gate. After putting his bike in the storage van, he stepped up to the back porch. He sat for a moment, and then he closed his eyes. He knew what he had to do about that unfinished business. He was going to let it happen, one last time ....

I had always thought that I was a baby, and then I was one year old, then two, and so on ... and then something very strange happened. I was not a child, I was not an adult, I was not a human. I was just a soul, a mind, inserted into a piece of stuff in the galaxy, and I didn't know why. No concerns about society, no concerns about fame or fortune, no concerns about family. I just wanted to know why I was asking questions about solid and liquid and fire and the pressure of my feet against the ground, but I was getting no reply from anyone at all; instead, whispers were coming from the trees, and the wind, and the stars.

The voices spoke to me without words. My responses were also nonverbal, and my tone was sometimes angry and frustrated. I believed the tree, wind, and star voices were trying their best to get through to me, and that I was failing them.

I did not do it then, not in that year when the voices were strongest yet, after I had fallen through the bear and into the cold water ... my Birth. No, the Commission was three years later. But that earlier time was the balance point, the year I remembered most of any year of my life. The year that was truly every year, every day, every single moment.

Message sent.

I know You hear me. I tried, I really tried, but I have failed. I must have failed because I thought I was the only one to reach You, that it could be only me. I must have been wrong. You can forget me now, wasting no

more energy on this one. I am too weak. Another will hear Your voices, I
am sure, and perhaps this person can truly answer them. Perhaps today,
perhaps tomorrow, perhaps a thousand years ago, for that moment is also
this moment. If nothing else, You have shown me that simple truth.

He came back, from reality to mere existence, and opened his eyes.
Standing up, he grabbed the daypack and went inside the house.

Sheka was there to meet him, and she followed him to the living room.
He sat down on the couch and let the dog lick his fingers. He looked into
her eyes and spoke to her with his own. He didn't want to break the silence
that hung throughout, and after giving the malamute a slow rubdown,
he rose and went to his own room, set the daypack on the bedspread,
changed his clothes, lowered himself on the edge of the mattress, and let
his head drop, putting himself into a semi-trance that may have lasted for
perhaps three or four minutes ....

His door creaked; startled, he snapped to attention and turned his
head.

Amy was there, dressed in her nightgown. She stood looking at him,
and he fidgeted, trying to come up with something to say.

"Uh, where's Mom?"

"At a meeting, over at the school. The staff is having a planning session
today."

He felt his mouth turn downward. "She left you here by yourself?
How are you feeling? Still sick, huh?"

The girl looked down at her feet and slowly shook her head. "I'm not
sick at all."

Mark felt himself growing increasingly concerned. Amy was twelve,
but he thought she looked very small and very frightened, as if she had
recessed backward in time and was only just learning to read a little book,
and write something ....

"I don't understand. You're telling me that you're just playing?" He
narrowed his gaze.

"No," she answered, and her voice lowered to almost a whisper. "I'm
not playing. But I wasn't sick, like being ill. I just felt bad."

"Uhh. I suppose you're scared about next week. 'Junior High Initia-
tion'. You've heard all the stories about what might happen to you in the
bathrooms." He nodded in the affirmative.

Amy drew in a quavering breath. "No, no, not that. I don't care about
that." She raised her head and stared at him, and Mark thought he had

never seen her look so small and lonely. Her eyes searched through him, and she said, slowly, "You're leaving soon. You're leaving to go to college."

He nodded again. "That's right, I am. But not just yet," he quickly added.

"Oh."

Mark was confused. "What's the matter?" he asked, looking at her questioningly. "What has you so frightened?"

"Mark," she said slowly. "I was afraid that you were never coming back, when you went to climb the mountain. And after you had gone, Mom was acting funny, and I was trying to tell her that everything was okay, and that I understood. Even though I was scared myself."

He couldn't believe what he was hearing.

"And I was telling her that it was all right. Just like you told me to do." There were tears in her dark eyes.

"Now you're going off to college, and I'm going to be here all alone. There won't be anyone to be on … my side. I thought about it, and I got even more scared. I still—"

"Amy." He motioned to her. "Come here," he said, patting the bed next to him.

She ran forward, dropped down beside him, and put her head on his shoulder. She started to cry, and Mark kissed the top of her head. "I never left you Amy, you know that."

She nodded against him, and Mark continued. "And when I'm away this fall, part of me will remain here. In this room, and in this neighborhood, and all around the Valley. If you look and listen, you will know that."

"Yes," she whimpered. "But I needed to hear you say it."

Mark reached over and stuck his hand inside the little yellow daypack. He touched a flat box and withdrew it, setting it on his lap. "Look what I've got here," he whispered.

The girl turned her head, wiping away her tears. "Wow."

Mark removed the lid, folded back the thin wax papers, and selected a piece of chocolate. "These are the best," he told her. She giggled and took the brown square from his hand. "I think this one's mint," she answered, and popped the chocolate into her mouth. "Yewp," she said, chewing.

Mark laughed himself, even as his eyes began to sting. He reached for his own piece, and within minutes, the box was nearly empty.

They were there, sitting together on the bed, and around them was the room where Mark had slept for the past eleven years and eight months.

And on the shelf in that room was a display of rockets, and on the desk in that room was a wonderfully illustrated text, and down the hall was a sleeping malemute named Sheka, and outside was a dirt road, and a playground, and a school, and a line of trees, and beyond that was a mighty river of ice and the peaks of the Coast Range. There was a partly cloudy sky, and beyond that were billions of stars and billions of galaxies, but this enormous space truly had no size at all.

§

The setting was one of incomparable beauty. The black and white peaks rose to meet the limitless blue sky, and the air was fresh with the scent of late-season heather. The great glacier poured down from the upper snow-fields, and it glistened in the sunlight, its crevasses as blue as the sky itself. The sun was warm, and the soft breeze that drifted up the Valley tickled the dry, sticky leaves of the alders that rimmed the pond.

There was sound, and it was the sound of rushing water. Nearby, the misty rock canyon roared, in an unsteady rhythm, as the water from yesterday's rain washed from the mountainside and made its way back to the ocean. And from afar, there was the unbroken, low-keyed sigh from a distant waterfall, as the remaining snow patches of the upper basins melted and dropped through a gorge, in small yet raging torrents.

There were the sounds of earthly life as well. The birds chattered endlessly, and among the alders, a red squirrel scooted about, looking for a hide-and-seek partner. Seagulls had gathered on the lakeshore, and their strange, whistling cries pierced the air.

From below, there came a new sound, the sound of an approaching car. It grew in strength, then quieted and finally stopped. The Observer contracted, became the boulder that rose beside the pond, and waited for what was to come. A scurrying of tennis shoes, and the pattering and scratching of dog's paws, sounds from the nearby, quartz-veined gully. Earthly sounds from an earthly source.

And these sounds did come. From over the lip of the stoss-and-lee granite hill, Mark Nilsson and his dog, a malamute named Sheka, came into view and began to walk around to the far side of the pond, to where the boulder lay still and waited.

Immediately, it sensed something definite in the young man's eyes. There was no mistaking it, and the boulder was incapable of trying to fool itself. It could not sit there and pretend; it would accept what was to come, in a quiet and stoic manner.

It watched, as Mark climbed up, and it felt the weight of the human being that settled down into a sitting position. He was talking to his dog, who nosed about the pond, and he was staring off into space, which was wide and endless, even with the great mountains that encircled and hemmed in the scene.

The boulder listened as Mark told the dog about his dreams, his ambitions, and of all the things he had done in his life that would help him in the future. It felt the grip of Mark's hand, as his voice began to struggle and become forced. It heard the anxiety in Mark's words, as the young man announced that he was going to be leaving, and that he would not return for a long time. There was a whole new world to explore, a new start to be made.

And then Mark Nilsson slid off the boulder and hugged his pet for a long time, and as the boulder watched, it saw the tears, and the unusual rippling of the pond, as the reflections of the two living beings were marred.

There was a moment of silence, where all motion came to a halt, as did the thoughts of the young man and his dog. Only the boulder was stirring, and that was unknown to the pair of mammals.

They were departing now, beginning the descent of the gully. The boulder strained after them, and it watched as they dropped lower, finally disappearing below the rim of the hill. The young man was gone, to the path and to the road, gone away to the World of Humans, and his companion, fully domesticated, had no choice but to accompany him.

The sound of the car once again; it droned off into the distance. The Observer now saw the young man and his dog as nothing more than a probability wave tangle, their earthly existence being of no further importance. And then there were only the sounds of the earth itself. The water, the birds, and the squirrels. The rustling of the leaves. The boulder sighed. Not far away, a certain peak of ice and rock was seemingly hidden, but the boulder knew well that it knew.

The Observer saw, in a fashion unknown to Humans, all of the world. It saw the people become individuals, trying their best to categorize and define. It saw them organize and pollute their religions, dangerously so, resulting in wars, inequality, and so much pain and suffering, while all the time, reality was everywhere the people chose not to look.

It saw their fruitless attempts to objectify themselves rather than let go and become part of the mystery. It saw them discard childhood for adulthood, in a manner that blocked out so much truth about who they really were. The probability of success, when physical existence was factored in, dropped sharply; by the time individuals claimed themselves as matured, when they reached the faulty conclusion that their brains were the creator of their minds—individual minds, moreover—probability of connecting with the ancient voices neared zero.

The Observer wept. It was a sight unseen, and it was a sound that could not be heard. If all of the sadness discharged from the weepings of every Human on the earth could be wrapped up and tabulated, it would still not equal the sadness of the Observer. This was cosmic sadness, the weeping of the voices from a distant past and from non-Euclidean coordinates, where A was also B, and Here was also There. It came from a place so far North it could not be located or mapped by an earthly brain. Its presence was detectable only in the distorted manner known as tears, compassion, joy, guilt, regret, and remorse. It was a presence that was perhaps no longer to be recognized for what it was.

The Observer expanded, and the boulder, the pond, and the alders relaxed completely, then reformed. Reality cleared its throat.

Stratus clouds were moving inland. They covered the sky above the marsh flats and raced northward over the Valley. The day was darkening. As the clouds advanced, they began to descend toward the earth, bumping against the mountains at the head of the Valley.

Most would turn back long before the final gate, although the setting was perfect … it could not be better.

It was not for the Observer to worry, but to observe.

The Observer, having seen the birth of aspiration, now saw Humans aspire. And too many would fail.

The clouds continued to pour across the sky, racing north to the glacier and the icefield. They bumped the mountains on either side of the Valley, then mutated, becoming nimbostratus, grayish and without form. The air was dense, nearly saturated with vapor. The thunder did not come.

Stuck in time and space, mortals being what they were … having created their own mortality ….

And this one had failed as well. The Observer could do nothing about it, for the Observer was not the beginning and the end of all things, nor had it the ability to choose from a myriad of pasts and futures to solidify a favored present. It was but a living conduit formed by the ancient voices, a lightning stroke path for all of earthly life to follow, *back they way it had come*, to its Creator.

The Observer listened, and it heard a distant sound, the horn of an arriving ferry. Unable to say what would be, it did the only thing it could. It wanted the Creator's children to come home, but now it would watch. And it would wait.

ABOUT THE AUTHOR

ERIC C TRENT has worked as a tour agent, grocery manager, summer camp program director, underwriter, private investigator, restaurant chef, shelving and window blinds installer, plastic recycling manager, freelance writer, and "The list goes on and on. Not a chemical engineer, cartographer, or astronaut, but in a dreamy sort of way, I'd like to think those were possible as well". He wrote the original NORTHWAY manuscript in the early 1980s, sitting cross-legged in front of an IBM Selectric typewriter, often with a bag of cheese-flavored tortilla chips and a 2-liter bottle of cola within reach, and André Previn's treatment of Ralph Vaughan Williams' "Sinfonia Antartica" playing softly on his tape deck.

Eric enjoys reading historical fiction, watching classic movies, and studying theoretical physics. To keep his mind sharp, he spends 30-40 minutes each day solving math problems involving geometry, trigonometry, and differential calculus. Eric loves perfecting his homemade food recipes. "Pizza, sourdough bread, veggie omelettes, sauerbraten, and too many more to mention." When finding it difficult to fall asleep at night, he imagines that his bed is on board a small, interstellar-travel spaceship, set to autopilot. "It works everytime."

www.ingramcontent.com/pod-product-compliance
Lightning Source LLC
Chambersburg PA
CBHW050511110726
47899CB00005B/1413